Song Castle

Song Castle

LUKE WATERSON

Urbane
PUBLICATIONS

urbanepublications.com

First published in Great Britain in 2018
by Urbane Publications Ltd
Suite 3, Brown Europe House, 33/34 Gleaming Wood Drive,
Chatham, Kent ME5 8RZ
Copyright © Luke Waterson, 2018

A CIP catalogue record for this book is available
from the British Library.

ISBN 978-1-911129-88-2
MOBI 978-1-911129-90-5

Design and Typeset by Michelle Morgan

Cover by Michelle Morgan
Cover photography by Kerry Christiani

Printed and bound by 4edge Limited, UK

URBANE

urbanepublications.com

FOR KERRY, WHO LIKES SINGING

A List of Characters

(IN ORDER OF APPEARANCE)

RHYS AND HIS HOUSEHOLD
Rhys ap Gruffyd, Lord of Deheubarth and host of the festival
Maelgwyn, Rhys' eldest legitimate son and a headache
Gerald of Wales, Rhys' cousin and an ambitious cleric
Anarawd, the captain of Rhys' bodyguard and strong
The other festival judges, who like mead
Gwenllian, Rhys' long-suffering wife
Angharad, Rhys' daughter and a handful
Cibon, Rhys' chief fiddler
Gruffyd, Rhys' second-eldest legitimate son
Cadwaladr, Rhys' eldest illegitimate son

THE BARDS AND THE MINOR CHARACTERS
Avery, an earnest bard from York, with a haunting voice
Dog, a gruff musician, and Avery's travelling companion
The Healer, a pedlar of potions, and a giantess
Mistress Bell, proprietor of the last tavern before the border
Bernart de Ventadorn, a scheming bard from France,
with writer's block
Bernart's Bard, who tries hard to sing

Marie de France, a beautiful bard from Brittany, who many men fall in love with

Pierrot, Marie's gallant attendant

Hamid, a perfumer and bard from Persia, who has written the most beautiful words ever written

The Sultan, the Supreme Ruler of the World

De Braose, Marcher lord of Abergavenny

Cynddelw Bryddyd Mawr, a hearty bard from Powys, and teacher of bards-to-be

Millie, proprietor of the wine house on the track up into the hills

Gwalchmai ap Meilyr, a sullen bard from Gwynedd, and obsessed with winning

Meilyr ap Gwalchmai, a slightly-less sullen bard from Gwynedd, and Gwalchmai's son

The Priest of Llanddewi Brefi, who likes to enjoy himself

The Whore, to whom clients come from across the Holy Roman Empire

Chrétien de Troyes, a famous writer from the court of Champagne, on the search for inspiration for his latest epic

Sulien of Berwyn, a hermit

Olwen, Sulien's daughter

Iola, Sulien's wife

Owain Cyfeiliog, poet-prince of Powys

The Young Marcher Lord, who nobody can remember the name of

Niall Ó Maolconaire, a hard-drinking bard from Ireland, with a temper

Pirin the Fisherman's son, who cannot sing

Bran the Bard, who sings well enough

The Odds-maker, who takes bets

Olaf of Bergen, a lusty bard from Scandinavia

Azelais, a beautiful trobairitz from Occitania
The Jew, who Hamid meets upon his travels
Luciano, the song singer from the Kingdom of Sicily
Navarro, the wandering cantor of Castile
Meurig Full-Voice, who has something to say
The Monk of Blank Habit, who sings to celebrate God
Wace of Northumbria, who sings with hatred
Prydydd Y Moch, who sings about animals
Unwin Honey-Tongue, who sings with accomplishment
Marie, Countess of Champagne
Henry Plantagenet, King of England

EUROPE IN 1190

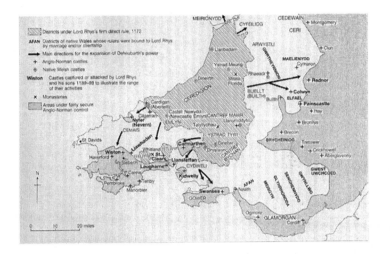

The Welsh Principality of Deheubarth under Lord Rhys in 1172

Map taken from the reference book 'Conquest, Coexistence and Change: Wales 1063-1415' by RR Davies, published by Clarendon Press/University of Wales Press (1987).

Preface

THE LAND that for simplicity's sake is referred to in this book as Wales was, in the 12th century, a very fragmented place.

To the Welsh their native land was perhaps already called *Cymru*, although what that really meant was liable to interpretation. They perhaps also knew it still as *Britannia*, even though that referred to the lands of the Brythonic-speaking peoples generally, including areas of northern England and southern Scotland. To the Anglo-Normans *Wallia* might have been the term used, but this in turn could refer to *Marchia Wallie* or the Welsh Marches, the part of Wales they believed they had brought under their control and *Pura Wallia* or native Wales, the part they had not.

More meaningful points of reference for most were the warring factions into which Wales had split. It was divided into dynasties: principalities and lordships that often vied against each other for increasing amounts of power and the territory that would augment it, rather than unite. Conflict between different domains was more or less constant, and invariably violent. Loyalties were localised: most likely to one's family, quite possibly to the nearest village, perhaps to the *cantref* (district) and at a stretch to the region or realm. But when boundaries between these zones were changing almost as often as the famously fickle weather, and with dangerous consequences for those caught on the wrong side of the line, conceiving of an amalgamated country was not at the forefront of people's minds. There were more pressing concerns.

In fact, there were but a few things capable of bringing this fractious collection of territories together. One of these things was language. And the mouthpieces for this were the bards: through the tales that they told and the songs that they sung.

And in the 12th century, the bards changed their tunes.

In their performances, the bards of the land that would become Wales had always drawn on a rich history of spectacular people, spectacular deeds, spectacular places; they had probably instilled in their audiences a certain shared nostalgia for when Britons still ruled Britain. But now they stepped up their act. Menaces to all of Wales-to-be—the Anglo-Normans—were encroaching from the east, pushing into its territory with unprecedented ferocity. And the bards, the *gogynfeirdd* as they became known, responded in kind. Performing in courts and halls from Gwynedd to Gwent, they used ever stronger, more evocative, more elegiac verses to call on the leading men of the land to rise up as one and repel these invaders. In the words of these bards, Wales became geographically and spiritually united. A disparate people were given cultural cohesion. Wales got its Welshness.

WITH CLATTER OF MEADHORNS, GREAT LIBERALITY!

FROM **THE HIRLAS OF OWAIN** BY OWAIN CYFEILIOG

Written by various monks in various abbeys over several hundred years, *the Brut Y Tywysogion* chronicles Welsh history from the 7th century to the 14th. In this, one of the principal historic sources for Wales during this tumultuous period in its past, is a somewhat scant paragraph for the year 1176 beginning as follows:

'And the lord Rhys held a grand festival at the castle of Aberteivi [Cardigan], wherein he appointed two sorts of contention; one between the bards and poets, and the other between the harpers, fiddlers, pipers and various performers of instrumental music; and he assigned two chairs for the victors in these contentions; and these he enriched with vast gifts.'

Those monks left out the juiciest bits.

Part One:

A SLAP OF STRONG WIND IN THE FACE

Rhys

(MARCH, 1194)

"MY SON..."

The trapdoor opened. He struggled to prop himself on his elbows and better see the figure framed in the torchlight above, but his eyes were too long accustomed to the gloom of the cell and the glare blinded him. He could discern no features. Yet he was certain, now.

"I know it is you. A father knows his first-born..."

The figure started on the descent, taking the rungs of the ladder hesitantly: bare feet, and bad-smelling ones.

"Why, son? Why are you doing this?"

A pause. It was a moment of consideration, perhaps. Even when the figure stood still, the toes twitched. Then, still saying nothing, they rapidly clambered back up. The trapdoor banged shut; the bolts shot across. He was alone again.

"Why?" When he had voiced the word, it had seemed an admission of age. He was an old man alone on a bed in the darkness.

Those first few days of his imprisonment he had felt too despondent to do much besides tend his wounds as best he could. They had been none too serious, but he was none too good at tending wounds. The back of his head had caused him most pain.

Whoever dealt that blow must have come at him from behind, the coward. He preferred dealings with brave men. There was brute's honesty in the duel or the raid or the battle. You charged, and your weapons clashed, and you lived or died. But the coward was a cat backed into a corner, could spring at you in a way you did not anticipate.

He dreamed a lot those first few days. Such dreams. The early times came back most vividly. Attacking some fortress or other with his brothers. A band of desperate gaunt men in threadbare tunics, they had been. Mostly up against Englishmen or Frenchmen or Flemish men with superior arsenal and greater numbers but often battling other Welshmen, too; often up against themselves. The fight against one's own: the hardest fight of all.

Once the pain had dulled he had begun to focus on where he was. The basement of a tower. Gaps in the stonework through which the wind shrilled. An odour of damp earth. No light save for a grill about head height, which emitted a pale grey chink of the morning but lapsed back into shadow again by mid-afternoon. This was March, after all, and a particularly foul one. Somewhere else, spring was coming.

He had not been captive long before the visits commenced. At first the figure had seemed contented with a head through the hatchway, but that had not been enough. Soon they were venturing several steps down the ladder. Soon the scrutiny was lasting longer. The watcher had uttered no words as yet. But he sensed that was about to change.

The figure tried to conceal things from him. The fact they suffered from a diabolical cold, for instance: after the bolts thrust home their racking cough would start up, although there was no coughing during the visits. They kept the left side of their face turned away from him, too. But whilst most of the country had their health afflicted on account of this damnable weather, and whilst a fair few of those might choose to hide any disfigurement upon their countenance, something else put the matter of the figure's identity beyond doubt. Madness. Once the trapdoor had closed, his gaoler's footfalls receded only so far then broke into a horrible, erratic little dance. Whoever was holding him prisoner was plainly deranged, and in the entire realm it was known such madness coursed through the veins of one man alone: his son.

His first-born had always embarrassed him. At the zenith of his power—the victory banquets, the meets with the King—there had always been that anxious glance over his shoulder partway through proceedings at what his eldest might be doing.

The visit of the Archbishop, for example: it should have been his proudest moment. The kind of moment chroniclers should chronicle.

His castle had been the equal of any Norman: sheer walls of stone, dominating the horizon. The whole town had turned out to the river bridge for the welcome. The Archbishop had been impressed, quite possibly awed; he had endeavoured to put the reverent fellow at ease; the procession had filed up towards the castle gates where, as he recalled, he had arranged for musicians to serenade them all.

Then—he would never forget it—came the squeal from the Archbishop's attendant as, whilst passing the assembled townsfolk, the poor man had been pinched hard enough on the buttocks to startle him right out of formation and trip over his cassock. His suspicions as to the cause were confirmed a moment later when he and that company of upstanding churchmen had observed several of his younger sons fleeing shrieking from the scene and his eldest, a brawny man in body by then, but still with the mind of a wilful child, smirking with the glee only the orchestrator of an event can muster. Of the entire mortifying occasion, what lodged most firmly in his memory were the words, murmured disapprovingly as an aside later that same evening between two of his guests but overheard by him: *'if only he could control his children.'*

He slumped back on the bed, exhausted through inertia. That was some clobber about the head he had received. A column of ants swarmed over the dirt floor. He wondered briefly whether it was the same few hundred, disappearing through that crevice then circling around the tower wall in order to repeat the procedure, or whether there were thousands more out there, lining up to march across the mud in front of him. Wales was going to the dogs, he thought.

When he opened his eyes, it was to the torchlight again. His captor stood at the foot of the bed, the scar gouging out the left cheek hideous in the flame.

"My father," the figure sneered, "the greatest of all the great men in Wales."

And this was true: he had been. There had not been a realm to rival his. Others had asked him how he achieved it and he happily told them: revelry. No hall in Christendom had witnessed the like. The best men had come to pay their respects. And the best women, he allowed himself a smile at this, thinking now of *that* time; that feast to end all feasts; those weeks that changed everything. It had been spectacular; despite the atrocities, spectacular. He had surpassed himself. Only great men could do that.

"What is it you want?" he asked, but on sighting the knife his son brandished, the question stuck in his throat. "So you have come to end it," he said quietly.

"End!" his first-born repeated mockingly. "My dear father, I have not even begun!"

He had imagined death. One did not rise to where he had risen without having imagined it. But he had imagined a cathedral, and his coffin being borne with much ceremony down the aisle, not murder in the darkness at the hands of a snivelling, scarred wretch, his own flesh and blood.

"At least tell me why," he said again. "Why, when I gave you everything?"

"Because of that," his son advanced to the bedside, stroking the knife blade with absurd tenderness. "Because you were always so damnably perfect."

$\mathscr{A}$very

(December, 1176)

A harp.

Avery lay, head on the tree roots, looking up the trunk as it rose, straight and smooth, to subdivide into the lowest of the branches some fifteen feet above. There, wedged into a cleft, was the harp.

Quite unlike any harp he had ever beheld, but a well-made instrument. Marvellous.

And the harp started to play.

A twang of jangling sound exploded from it so at odds with what his body, languishing in that fragile state between stupor and lucidity, then needed, that he felt compelled to fully open his eyes in order to understand.

It was a squirrel. It pranced back and forth along the strings, presumably as baffled by the harp's presence, halfway up a tree, as he was. And having so abruptly awoken him with its discordant playing, the impudent animal cavorted off.

He was becoming aware of other sensations. Being in a state of considerable undress. Being unable to move his arms, which were—he was right to have feared the worst—tied to the tree. Being somewhere he should not be.

In trepidation, he took in his surroundings. An open space he was not familiar with. On the nearside a palisade; behind it a church tower, the puckered chimneys of burghers' houses, the background clamour of hawkers touting wares. So he was outside town. And outside town, in this cursed frontier between England and Wales, was never a wise choice of locations to linger in, not without some form of weapon one felt confident about wielding effectively.

He cast an eye over what remained of his clothing. Undergarments: mercifully intact, and most mercifully of all because his remaining stash of coinage was secured within them. But the wool-lined cloak the choirmaster at York had donated from his own wardrobe, having weathered the gruelling 150-mile tramp to get here, was nowhere to be seen. One shoe was missing, too, and what kind of thief stole just one shoe?

He turned, wincing at the rush of nausea, to his left. Overgrown grass, brittle in the morning frost. Things in the grass: a broken cartwheel, a heap of mouldering vegetables and a calf, so starved each bump of its skeleton showed, picking through them disdainfully. A vague whiff of excrement, and only vague, he guessed, because the sun was not up yet. Several hundred yards off, opening direct onto the stinking meadow, he descried some squalid dwellings, more malnourished calves and a decrepit, hunchbacked woman tending them.

He tried his arms again, more opportunistically than in genuine expectation of freeing himself. Bound by someone competent in the tying of knots. There was no wriggling out of those ropes and there was no breaking them. And he was lying part-frozen in the middle of a vast dumping ground, in a district where the chances of the next passer-by being rather more unsavoury than that crone of a cow herder were high.

"Lady!" Avery hailed the old woman. "Help!"

But although one of her emaciated cattle managed an annoyed

glance in his direction, the woman shuffled off into the nearest of the shacks without any indication she had heard him.

His one hope of salvation, and she was deaf. He sighed; slumped back on the roots observing the harp. A fanciful tale his mother once told him about a harp that needed no musician but only the wind to play it came to mind. No such magic here. Just the steadily increasing smell of shit as the winter sun cranked a few notches higher in the heavens which, he thought, were hardly deserving of the name, since God was evidently not resident in them or not, at least, in the portion of the skies hanging above this no-man's land. The Lord's divine intervention, which he could have used a little of, had likely got used up in York or Rome. Worthy places. Faraway places.

He refocused. The old woman was leaning over him with a peasant's gawp. One of her eyes was gouged out and she stank of onions.

Avery furnished her with his most engaging smile.

"Your assistance is most appreciated, lady," he spoke, casually as he could. "Would you unfasten these knots and direct me to, ah…"

To where, exactly? He had no address in town that he could recollect.

Ghosts of thoughts, then, about how he might have landed in this predicament.

He did dimly recall certain events. A tavern. Off-duty soldiers, who had seemed particularly generous in the purchasing of mead. There had been someone he had fallen in with on the road into town, too: a morose character, who had irked him with his curt answers and could, potentially, have provoked a bunch of intoxicated fighting men considerably more. Why, then, was it him abandoned here alone? Was it possible it had been *he* townsfolk had taken exception to? He who shied away from conflict to the extent that he had once wept when another chorister back in York had plucked the legs off spiders he unearthed during practice?

Regrettably, nothing was yet piecing itself together into any sort of narrative.

"*Dw i ddim yn deall*"[1] the woman said. The words sounded ominously like Welsh and his heart beat a little quicker, for being trussed up on the Welsh side of town was a punishment most hardened criminals would quail at.

"Os-west-ry…Toooown…Gaaaate" he tried again. "Do you know where that is?"

"*Dw i ddim yn deall,*" she squawked, and prodded him hard with her crook.

The jab took him in the midriff, futilely forcing the plea for help from his lips a second time. Winded, his voice expelled like an old man's feeble, unnoticed sigh, and it occurred to Avery and the woman around the same moment that there was nothing he could do to prevent her onslaught. If the first hit could have been construed as a well-meaning nudge, the second was undoubtedly calculated: a slash across the jaw that drew blood. How to reason with her, Avery wondered, sucking at the smarting half of his lips whilst attempting a protest with the other half. He needed his mouth. Other body parts he could endure the loss of, but lips, teeth, tongue: these were imperative for what was to come. Once, with little more than gesticulation, he had explained a reasonably detailed history of York's principal churches to some foreign pilgrims, but hand signals were currently denied him and his words, presuming his mouth were not swollen shut, would clearly have been lost on the crone whether uttered in English, French

---

1 "I do not understand." There is significant evidence to suggest that by the 12th century, the English, along with the French and the Flemish, were approaching native Welsh speakers on Welsh soil, uncivilly shouting at them in foreign tongues, and deeming them stupid when they failed to comprehend.

or his best Latin. Words. He had always had recourse to them. It panicked him now that he did not even have those.

Another crack of the crook; the witch was finding her range. A stinging, wet pain. Droplets of his blood and flesh flying through the air, and through them the harp holding fast in the fork of the tree, staring down in disapproval: yes, its frame and strings forming a judgmental face. His head was thrust back now. The strokes had prostrated him. In the thickening mist of his vision the instrument became the only thing he could see with clarity. Those pilgrims had journeyed across myriad lands without incurring a scratch and here he was, pummelled to pulp before he had made it across the Welsh border. He envisaged a tribunal in an anteroom before the gates of Heaven, God and the angels and all that ethereal light just around the corner; a steady stream of souls passing on by to the joyous hereafter and him in the midst of an awkward interrogation by a row of cloaked skeletons with scythes. *Would you remind us how you perished, Avery? Indeed, at the hands of a frail, hunchbacked old woman.* And the skeletons opened their grimacing jawbones and they kept opening, ever wider, shrieking in mockery and interlocking their scythes to bar his passage. Avery shivered, eking out what began as an involuntary reaction to dispel the unsavoury image, and trained his gaze on the harp instead. Whilst he could continue to see it suspended there above him, and imagine seizing it and playing it, everything would work itself out favourably.

The crone paused in her attack. In the lull the pain from the wounds she had inflicted seared through him. Agony, but he could still feel each of his salient parts. With a rush of hope he thought of walking again. Just the pleasing act of placing one foot in front of the other, in a direction away from this stinking field, seemed then the ultimate luxury to him, and a suddenly attainable one too, step by step towards a warm hearth and a bowl of bubbling stew. He had been right to believe, too, that in a God-fearing country an elderly woman did not beat a young man to death for no reason; that knowledge comforted him.

The crone's arm was caught on something.

A fleshy hand gripped her wrist; another relieved her of the crook.

Avery recognised his saviour immediately: it was the sullen wayfarer he had entered town with yesterday. The man's mood did not seem overly improved after last night's festivities, either; Avery would have gone so far as to say his scowl seemed permanently embedded in his face.

"Here," the newcomer crouched to sever the outermost of the bonds with a crossguard, then thrust the dagger's handle into Avery's hands, which, being numb, could barely keep hold. "Finish untying yourself. And be sure to leave length enough for me to loop around that branch up there."

"Might I ask…?" Avery began.

"You may not," the man said sharply. "This isn't the place for it."

The stranger was still fending off the crone with one of his ox-like arms, and now turned to her, to Avery's surprise conversing with the old gorgon in her own tongue. Welsh a-plenty adopted the English language, but what sort of Englishman got to be proficient in Welsh speak? The woman's jabbering was subsiding, though, Avery fancied as he massaged some life into his wrists. More than that, a jerked thumb by his liberator in Avery's direction and she was unmistakably cackling, as if her beating him had been an amusing morning's diversion. Yes, laughing at his expense! His cheeks burned, with shame now as well as with his injuries; shame at needing assistance in preventing the onslaught of a hunchbacked crone but also envy, perhaps, at how this terse, burly man with a face like a red cabbage and the manners of a swine, could find favour with someone he had clearly incited hatred in.

"I thank you, friend!" Avery shouted to the newcomer, vowing at that moment to start learning the language of this strange western extremity of Britain so that no one could talk about him so in future. *Estron[1]*, he had overheard them say, *Angau[2]*. He had a fine capacity for remembering; he would remember all of this alien tongue in time and one day soon he would astonish people with it. "I do not know why she set upon me so…" he added lamely.

"To curb your prattling, I'll wager," the burly man growled. "You have the rope?" The crone was returning to her hovel, somehow pacified.

Avery handed it over. The man secured it around a branch, shinned up the tree with remarkable agility given his girth, and was back down with the harp before Avery had raised himself unsteadily to his feet.

"This instrument was all I'd a care to save," the burly man said, although in such a low voice that Avery did not know if he was providing an explanation or having a discourse out loud with himself. "It's all I have in this world and I take great exception to anyone who tries to separate us."

"In material possessions you are faring better than I," Avery trembled, feeling the cold of the morning now the shock of the attack had worn off. "I can hardly hope to survive long in this weather with no cloak and only one shoe, and several days journey ahead of me."

"You're heading west?" the burly man looked at him disparagingly, then turned his attention to the harp. He was examining it for damage; retuning the strings. A few twists and

---

1 Foreign.
2 Death.

plucks and the harmony was flowing from it. Beefy as his fingers were, they glided over the instrument. He can play, thought Avery; he really can play.

"I was. But perhaps this is a sign God has other plans for me."

The burly man snorted. He seemed, in fact, to have more of the traits of one who would harm a person than one who would help them. Avery could picture him sitting there as the town burned and women and children screamed, intent on nothing but striking his harp strings in a pleasing manner.

"Go with God's word a lot, do you?"

"Once I did," Avery said. "Lately we have been having our differences."

The other produced a richly brocaded leather carrying case contrasting sharply with the dull grey-green of his tunic, and placed the harp carefully inside.

"I'm heading west," he announced.

Avery was not certain if this was an offer of companionship; if it were, he was equally unsure that he would choose to accept.

"I doubt, friend, whether our journeys would share the same destination. I am bound for the coast; for Cardigan. There is to be a great festival there, I understand, of song and merrymaking, in a castle newly built in stone..."

"And it is announced a year in advance, throughout Wales and England and all Britain to the tip of Scotia, and beyond to Ireland and France and other countries. And it is to be held at Christmastime in the place where the greatest river in Wales meets the sea, in the castle of its greatest prince, and it will be the greatest festival—of music and of song and other diverse entertainments—that this land or any land has ever beheld. I'm well aware of the proclamation. There isn't a troubadour on the King's Highway that'll stop blathering about it. Why do you wish to go there?"

"I…" Avery was taken aback by the bluntness of the question. "It seems to me it would be a very fine thing to participate in."

"Fine!" the other echoed. "Fine like fine pottery before it falls and smashes in a thousand pieces, that's how fine the court of Lord Rhys is!"

"And you speak, friend, as if you possess a most extraordinary knowledge of his court. Were I inclined to inquisitiveness, I might ask how a man who owns nothing in this world but a harp could obtain such insights."

"You might," the burly man shouldered his harp. "But as you say we're bound in different directions, which I'll not lament for you strike me as a luckless fellow."

"You are going there too, friend?" Avery knew from the man's reaction he had guessed correct. One did not spend years in the company of churchmen without learning a thing or two about body language. "You are also going to this stone castle where the river meets the sea?"

"I might be," said the burly man, suddenly looking around guardedly as if he expected another assailant to appear any moment. "You're the dithering sort, I'll wager. And if there's dithering to be done, inside the walls is better that out. Ha, Oswestry here could be Constantinople were dithering a trade! But I'll vouch for one thing. Whether you go on, or go back, or dally drinking your nights away in this cesspit of a settlement forevermore, up there," he indicated the mountains of Wales rearing up to the west "the going is a deal more treacherous. And I'm not referring to the topography."

And off he strode across the stinking meadow.

A couple of carrion crows gave a low circle of the tree. Avery sighed. It was not as if he had been blessed by a huge choice of travelling companions, and he had been warned that when he reached Wales he would be well advised to find a few if he valued his safety.

"Avery," shouted Avery, after the departing figure.

The figure turned.

"Dog," he said.

Avery deliberated a moment, then hurried in pursuit, endeavouring to avoid the worst of the filth with his shoeless foot.

Tricks

(DECEMBER, 1176)

THE WHOLE OF OSWESTRY seemed to be suffering from the excesses of the night before. Carousals for the final night of the festival had claimed their casualties. At the makeshift market gathered around the western gate, drunks still lay sprawled senseless across the stalls. A group of Welsh farmers were keeping festivities alive, singing loudly in their own tongue and heckling the sentries in theirs, and one or two of the night's less successful whores were angling for a last bit of business. The pedlars, for their part, were frantically trying to set up their merchandise around the mayhem, eager to catch those leaving after the three-day debauch with black market produce for far lower prices than the licensed sellers in the centre could offer. The brewers and victuallers were notable by their absence this morning; what was on offer had a more rejuvenative theme. There were peafowl and ham hock and pork and hedgehog and lamb vendors, bakers and honey hawkers, saddle sellers and sword makers and smiths selling horseshoes and spurs and shields for those undertaking the long journey back to the provinces. The quality of the enterprise nevertheless deteriorated the further from the walls one went, through the mercenaries, and maids, and scullions on hire, through rag-and-bone men and beggars to those who stood at the trackside seemingly sizing you up to see if you were worth robbing once you had passed out of sight of the town and into the mud of borderland.

Avery adored markets. Compared to the cloistered life of the cathedral, with its silences and sepulchres and echoing corridors, markets had always seemed so full of life. As soon as he accepted it could well be a sin to derive such pleasure in something that so simmered with iniquity he had, it was true, considered whether dedicating himself to the church—in many ways a withdrawal from life—was for him. But propriety had kept him in York. Propriety had held him back in York, and what had he to show for his sacrifice? Where was God when he had been unjustly cast out? For the first time since his hasty departure from the cathedral a week previously, it hit him. He had nothing to go back to.

"What can I do you for, my two young ruffians?"

She was a giantess, six and a half foot at a guess despite her slovenly posture, slouched against her stall as though she could not care less whether she sold what was on it or not. Dog was already picking through her wares, mostly herbs and spices but also less savoury things, insects and amphibians and birds dissected in readiness for sale. The nausea washed over Avery again in an instant.

"Less of the young," Dog growled. "I'm after milk thistle, and a deal of it."

"How unlike most men who come to me, to know what it is you want," the giantess cocked her head on one side, regarding him thoughtfully. "And might I ask, my rogue, whether it is your own bowels you wish to ease or those of this entire town? For as I think you know milk thistle, when mixed with a little blood from a virgin, is just about the most powerful laxative there is."

Dog looked momentarily sheepish.

"Then by my faith woman make me a batch of it, and with a fraction of the noise," he stole a concerned glance at the sentries, but they seemed preoccupied with the Welsh farmers who were becoming increasingly confrontational the more their stash of mead dwindled. "Confidentiality," he muttered to Avery "is supposed to be a thing with these healers."

"I do not mean to be rude, friend," Avery said. "But my own needs are for footwear, and clothing, and to sit down somewhere warm to revive my circulation. I already feel ill, and much longer in the presence of these remedies will bring up everything I drunk last night."

"Hold on," Dog whispered. "I've business in a tavern in town, and I'll buy you a bowl of their best broth. But as you heard blood is needed for the brew this woman is making me, and there's plenty of it dribbling fresh down your face from the pummelling that crone gave you. I'd open my own vein," he added "but I cannot claim to be chaste, and she did specify chaste blood."

"You bring me to a healer in order to extract my blood?" Avery exclaimed. "Anyone with a trace of Christian charity in their hearts would be helping patch my wounds up, not adding to them! Besides, how can you be so certain I am a virgin?"

Dog raised an eyebrow.

"Come. You'd be far worse off were it not for me."

"And might I ask, friend, for what purpose you wish to acquire such a large quantity of potion, and why you are so keen to do so without those sentries noticing?"

"Revenge," Dog looked at Avery penetratingly, handing him a receptacle from in amongst the stall's piled-up animal parts. "Now do as I say and I'll wager it'll play out well for us both."

"Just a few drops, my plucky adventurers," the giantess said. There was amusement in her voice, of that Avery was certain.

He gingerly felt the side of his face that had borne the brunt of the crone's crook and squeezed; too hard, for the congealing blood opened to a trickle again.

"Easy my little knight, or this will be one mighty potent potion!" The giantess emptied the receptacle into the mixture she had prepared, and with a wink that had Avery flushing scarlet, handed him a cloth to apply to his wound. "Oh my! That will be a half a shilling," she addressed Dog.

"Half a shilling! I could drink myself twice under the table on the best spiced wine in Oswestry for that!"

"Three pence for the potion," smiled the Healer, raising herself to her full height and her voice enough to emphasise her words. "The rest, my swarthy scoundrel, buys my silence as regards whatever you plan to do with it."

Dog mumbled a few things about the guile of women. One of the Welsh farmers had become inebriated enough to expose himself and this had proven to be a taunt too many for the sentries, who were arresting the lot of them without much nicety.

"I beg you," said Avery faintly. This cold was cutting him to the core. "Be done with your negotiations, friend, for I refuse to freeze out here on your account much longer."

Dog slammed down six silver pennies.

"I'd debate this longer," he muttered. "But this fellow has an English constitution, and I can do without a healer's curse on my shoulders."

"Then, my stocky rascal, you are less stupid than you look, for you would want to be on my side were it to come to a debate... That the best you can do for a friend, my gallant gentleman?" she shouted at Avery as they made for the gate. "For if so I do fear for your wellbeing."

She had a point, Avery thought. He had no reason to trust his newfound companion except that at that moment there was no one else he could place his trust in.

Mistress Bell's was the most salubrious tavern in town; the clientele were sentries spending their latest pay and well-established merchants and members of the regional Lord's retinue. Mistress Bell herself was a true professional, brewing decent ale and keeping fine French wines in reserve for her connoisseuring guests. She never participated in banter; she preferred that it did not occur whatsoever under her roof. She held that a hostelry was for drinking first and eating second and that anything else should take place outside and well out of sight of her front door. There were not many who knew anything about her other than what they saw behind the bar: a straight, ageless face and an even temperament. She played fair with you if you played fair with her. Busy as her place could get, she kept a hawk's vigil on everything anyone was consuming. If you nursed a drink too long without buying another you would be ousted and if you drunk so many as to show high spirits you would be ousted too. Hers was the last tavern before the border and she was determined that it would be a respectable example of one.

So Avery could not blame her for the scrutiny she gave them both as they entered.

"No minstrels here, gentlemen."

"Depend upon it," said Dog. "We are not them. Two ales and two bowls of broth. The affront of it," he grumbled. "And I a harpist, and a crwth[1] and a pibgorn player, and a fiddler of fifteen years' experience!"

And he clanked down the required coins before Mistress Bell could insult him by asking for payment in advance.

---

1 A rectangular, six-stringed instrument played with a curved bow. The crwth was one of the defining instruments of Welsh music at this time, along with the harp and the pibgorn, a type of pipe.

They took pews in an alcove commanding a good view of the room, Dog keenly observing the other customers, Avery warming his hands at the fire and creating shapes in the flames.

"Now," said Dog through clenched teeth. "We wait."

"For what?"

"My business associates," Dog gave a tight-lipped smile, although it did not sit naturally on his face. "Broth's ready in a while. Takes some time, but the meat's fresh. Time, I'll wager, for you to pay a visit to the cobbler four doors down to get that shoe fixed, and the clothier's opposite for a cloak. Be speedy about it."

"And what am I supposed to pay with?" Avery was fighting a battle just to stay functioning after the morning's events, and was annoyed at the presumptuousness of this ill-mannered musician, using him as an apparently dispensable playing piece and without even telling him what the game was. Why did he always acquiesce? His family had so badly wanted him to try for a career in the church. *For your own good, Avery*, they had said. So he had left them and gone to the church. Despite his wan looks he had stout lungs, bellows of lungs, and the choir's fire had needed stoking. Ah, how he had stoked; he had been told his voice was the most singular amongst all York's distinguished singers, but it had counted for nothing. For the dean and his intimates, and even the choirmaster who he had regarded as his friend, decided in the end that he must leave there, too: for his own good. Obeying orders was always for his own good and now here he was doing it again.

"Tell them you'll pay on collection, they'll not turn down the trade."

"Very well."

The aftereffects of yesterday's mead were making Avery paranoid; he had inadvertently caught the glance of Mistress Bell and felt like a conspirator under it. She looked like one who could pick apart treason before the treachery had been committed. The other drinkers, now he allowed his eyes to drift around the tables, were keeping vigil on the pair of them, and Dog was staring back confrontationally. No, Avery was not enjoying the atmosphere one bit. Stepping outside awhile was perhaps the wisest move. He would let Dog complete his business. The man might be argumentative, but he had arguably saved Avery's life and was buying him a meal and new clothes.

"Take care, friend, for the enmity in this place is close to boiling."

He got as far as the clothier before the commotion began.

Dog was in the midst of a crowd of animated soldiers with surcoats adorned with the local lord's coat of arms. These barons of the borderland daubed their symbols everywhere, like dogs pissing out territory. Their garb might seem fancy, and they might appear merry enough, but one simply did not mess with a Marcher lord's[1] personal bodyguard: the King's writ did not run on Marcher land; they were a law unto themselves. And there was his companion, getting in what was at least a second round for them all.

"Well timed," Dog said. "Broth's about done. These fellows I believe you know," he referenced the soldiers.

Avery did. He realised too late. These were the men-at-arms that had played the tricks on them last night. These were the ones his crazy companion wanted vengeance upon; these, some of the foremost fighting men in the entire district! Avery opened his mouth to ask Dog what in God's name he was thinking but the musician shot him a look that shut him up; the giantess's concoction was in the drinks and the drinks were already in the soldiers' hands.

---

1 Along the south coast of Wales, and along its border with England, the Normans established the March: a series of lordships that acted as a buffer zone against the lawlessness and barbarity of native Wales. The Marcher lordships soon developed a reputation for lawlessness and barbarity themselves.

"What have we here boys? It's that sodomite from last night!" the soldier nearest Avery chimed up. "Come back for a kiss, buttercup?"

Avery coloured. The door was ten paces off but might as well have been ten miles, because the latest speaker was a real crowd-pleaser, curse him, and had won the attention of his whole brigade. No other recourse, now, than to go through with it.

"Not a kiss, friend, just this bowl of broth."

"Friend! As in bedfellow, eh cream-cake? I could use some company for those long nights in the tower…"

Snickers reverberated around the room.

"I doubt, friend, that we would be each other's type," Avery sipped his broth, heart hammering. He had said the words good-humouredly enough, but the blockhead was on the warpath.

"Not your type!" the soldier stood up, his big sagging face full of fury. "Are you calling me ugly, elf?"

"Steady," Dog intervened. "He's just foul-tempered because some fellows set upon him after we were drinking last night. Tied him to a tree; took his clothes." And, in a whisper no one but Avery could hear, but that spat with anger: "They took my harp, too."

"I'll say we did!" the soldier snatched up his tankard, clumsily guzzling the contents. "Should have given him a buggering into the bargain, eh my boys?"

The 'boys' responded with sufficient laughs to goad him on.

"Except," shouted the soldier, "that I'm not his type! Who is your type, dandelion, a bishop on an altar?" He was lumbering towards Avery but his breath was coming in rasps which caused him confusion because he had been well enough before. "A chimneysweep in a cranny? A peacock… a pea…" he tried again. And then he tumbled to the floor, clawing at furniture that could not support his bulk, making a mess of upturned chairs and nearby drinkers' ales, and finally lying still.

Avery watched on, horrified but fascinated as foam welled on his aggressor's lips. Before the crone had laid into him that morning he had never once had a beating, not even from his parents, but they seemed to be much more common in Oswestry than in York, and he had been bracing himself for another. As it so often did the scene as he had anticipated it played on in his head, the soldier lunged for him and he dodged, tried to hit him and hit the wall, his escape moves were so exquisite total strangers applauded and the bouts became theatre with Avery enthralling his audience and the soldier blundering about like the dumb villain in a mummers' play.

"Dead drunk!" Dog at least had the presence of mind to make a show of getting down and attending to the soldier. But at Avery, he shook his head, frowning. And instinctively Avery knew: the soldier was dead.

Mistress Bell's might have been a tavern of repute, but the regulars looked on as if a man lifelessly collapsing in front of them was nothing new, and resumed their repartee with nothing beyond a grumble at their good-for-nothing garrison.

Nor did the other soldiers react so hotly as might have been expected. They could not. Two or three were out cold. Another gripped the bar, the colour seeping from him, like he was gripping on to a ship in a storm. There was groaning, whimpering, belching and then the inevitable sharper stink of defecation. One made it as far as the privy doorway before his disintegration; one hauled himself to an unoccupied corner, clutching his stomach as if holding on to it tightly enough might contain his exploding insides.

It was utter devastation, Avery thought, entranced, the bodyguards of one of the preeminent Marcher lordships writhing on the floor like vile blabbering babes. Shit. What if it all ended not in sweet, swift passage to Paradise but in shit?

"I would call the law," Mistress Bell proclaimed to the room at large. "But they are the law, God help us!"

As she called for her hirelings to get the bodies off her floor because she was a goose if they thought it would be her cleaning up for a second time that morning, Dog shook Avery roughly.

"We need to get out of here."

"They are all dead, are they not?" Avery murmured.

"That wasn't my aim. Some half shilling's worth that meddlesome healer sold us. She'll answer for this, I'll vouch for the fact."

"But it is the result!" Avery said, voice quivering. He grabbed Dog's tunic. "Your thirst for vengeance is the doing of this!"

Dog grabbed his undershirt right back and there was no contest as to who possessed the most effective grip.

"We have moments," he urged. "Only moments. Then our secret is out, and your neck doesn't seem like it would swing long before snapping. Now help me drag meat-chops outside like the good mistress ordered."

Avery took the felled soldier's feet in a daze, Dog the shoulders; the weight and the smell made carrying the corpse difficult but it was true, they did not have much time to get out of the tavern or, for that matter, the town. For one soldier remained upright: he who had been clinging grimly onto the bar. He must have had solid iron for innards, too, for he was finding the strength to argue with the irate landlady. *We weren't drunk, the ale must have been bad; there is nothing amiss with my beer, you will try no better between here and London,* that sort of exchange. It would not be long before poison was mentioned and the blame for the chaos fell firmly on the heads of the oddball minstrels seen at the scene.

"*Our secret!*" Avery retorted. He was incensed; the more so because his companion did not seem ruffled in the least. They lugged the body over the tavern threshold into the comparative freshness of the main street. Passers-by were already stopping. A guard would be in evidence before long. You could go about eliminating guards all day in a town like this and there would still be more to crawl like spiders out of the walls. "I am your accomplice now, am I friend? Or should I say fiend, for you have now most definitely dragged us both to the gates of Hell!"

"I'll wager you are," Dog detached something from the corpse's waist and thrust it at Avery. A pouch jangling with silver pennies; Avery instinctively concealed it under his tunic. "You've goods to pay for, and meat-chops here has no need of them."

"Murder," Avery hissed. "And now robbery?"

"They left you for dead, didn't they?"

Mistress Bell's regulars had got the other five bodies outside. Incredibly, no one seemed to have realised yet that they were not drunk but very much deceased. But the group of spectators was growing, passive and slack-jawed for the most part—and in fairness, the key members of the Lordship's bodyguard lying slumped outside the town's most well-to-do tavern immersed in their own shit probably did constitute an unusual sight—but now a couple of apothecary's apprentices pushed through. Cutting, condescending Mid England accents; they sounded like trouble and sure enough they were.

"What is this, minstrels?"

Dog flashed Avery a look: *go*. "I am," Avery heard as he hurried away the defiant rumble of the musician's voice "by no means a minstrel."

Quite often on a busy town thoroughfare in broad daylight, murders can occur and surprisingly few people will care or even notice. They will be concerned with pettier things: my wife spends too much on trinkets, the priest was looking directly at me during mass, was ogling the girl in the bakers like that a sin?

Thus it was that Avery paid the cobbler for the shoe, and the transaction was casual and matter-of-fact. The clothier was warier, but not as bothered by the din down the street as he was with pocketing what he knew full well was far too much for the cloak. And Avery was glad to jettison the pouch and leftover coins; if he departed town with what he had possessed upon his arrival in it, this would under the circumstances be a happy result and perhaps all could still be well between him and God. He had something of his stamina and all of his clothes back. Were it not for the nagging concern that he would soon be wanted for killing the majority of the Marcher lord's bodyguard and could not figure how he could possibly get past the sentries guarding the gate with that hanging over him, he might have taken it as a sign God was already smiling on him once more. Escape. It seemed to be the one piece of the plan Dog had not considered.

Outside Mistress Bell's, the apothecary had got involved and determined death, sure enough, in all six cases. The landlady was staunchly defending the standards of her ale and saying that besides, even the foulest brothel beer would not bring on the shits like that. The apothecary was arguing for taking the cadavers back to his quarters to open them up and determine the precise cause. The regulars were out there too, debating who could have poisoned the drinks and already pointing at Dog, probably not because they had seen him in the act but just because he was the sort that stood out as culpable for his bellicosity alone. Dog was shouting something back at them, of course. He pushed one of the apothecary's apprentices. They pushed him back. A jostling crowd soon obscured him from view.

And now the guards were coming. Avery heard their whistles. The game was up, he thought, the pair of them would soon be swinging from that gibbet above town and God would pay no heed to their cries. *Avery*, the scythe-wielding skeletons in his mind called. *Avery!*

Then he grinned. He could not help it. The guards were coming, but they had not been alerted by any breach of the peace. They were doing what was always done after a big festival. Clearing out the disreputables. Driven before them like cattle were all the vagrants who had been tolerated during the merrymaking: vagabonds, swindlers, itinerant preachers and all prostitutes apart from those known to service upstanding members of the community. And in greater numbers than any other group came the performers, the jackanapes and the jesters and the jongleurs, the tune-for-a-penny troubadours and the bawdy balladeers[1]. Some were bound or shackled but generally the guards' truncheons were enough to keep all moving in a general direction towards the town's western gate and most were resigned to leaving anyway, having milked festival-goers for every ha'penny they might. In any other setting, with one shoe missing and several days on from his last proper wash as he was, Avery would have been easy enough to hunt down. But in this rabble he fitted right in. Down they came towards where he stood, this shuffling band of banished reprobates. He paused on the edge of the throng only briefly, thinking, ludicrously, about whether he should put on his new shoe or not. Then he slipped into their midst. Down they came again, enveloping the commotion unfolding outside the tavern with their own greater chaos. Avery kept his eyes fixed on the ground in the spat-upon, pissed-upon way of the very poor, not daring to look up. Down through the gate, through the pedlar packing up, through the beggars giving up, out into Wales.

---

1 The bardic profession had exacting standards and entering it required extensive training; any true bard or aspiring bard would have considered themselves superior to such groups of performers. Society did not always see the difference.

Bernart

(December, 1176)

AS TO WHETHER the Queen was to blame—after all, she had incited her sons to overthrow her husband—or the King—he had, it was true, conducted an extra-marital liaison with England's leading beauty for at least a decade—Bernart preferred to remain, as it were, with a leg on either side of the fence. But their split had harmed the Court. It was no longer what it had been. Once, it had attracted Europe's best entertainers. That sword-swallower from the Low Countries: not a blade in Christendom had failed to fit down his gullet! The lady from Aquitaine who could sing about love in a thousand different ways, and each of them guaranteed to make you weep. Oh, and the blind boy from the East who played the lyre with his toes. And him. He had been there, and been so well loved by Their Royal Highnesses that rumours arose about his relationships with both. He had not discouraged the gossipmongers. Stories of his visits to one regal bedchamber or another circulated so successfully they did more than his quill ever could to keep his reputation as an unparalleled master in the art of love songs intact. There had come a point when it was not even necessary to compose new verses: his supposed deeds were enough to keep the name of Bernart de Ventadorn synonymous with the noblest sort of courtly romance.

But then the Queen and King became estranged. There had been a scrabble for loyalties. Performers went to one Monarch's quarters or the other's to do their thing, or left court entirely because of the difficulty of remaining neutral. The sword-swallower defected to the Court of Champagne, and it was soon being said the most illustrious entertainers were all going there. Bernart had not reacted as hot-headedly as some of the other songsters. Talent brought a poet some success, but with talent alone you were a rudderless vessel; you needed a patron to steer your course. To be forced to cut yourself off from a patron and make a choice between Queen and King was most disagreeable. So instead he had cited a need to return to his native France awhile and told them both they would be in his heart forever.

But he had not remained in theirs. Not once had he been asked back, although numerous lesser troubadours had received invitations. 'I am done with the Plantagenets,' he would soon be claiming out of injured pride. But he would have bounded back had word been sent that his presence was requested; that there was a hole in their halls no other could fill. Nor had Champagne made him an offer, although he had expected the messenger with the summons daily. He had begun to feel emptiness in his days. In the end the Court of Toulouse asked him to join them. He had vacillated theatrically in the last-gasp hope of attracting attention from other, grander households, insinuating the position was beneath him despite being in desperate need of it. Then he had accepted. And there he had stayed.

The provinciality of the place had appalled him, the more so since he felt snubbed and demeaned. Ramon of Toulouse could not compare to Henry Plantagenet of England however many ways you said their names. Toulouse was a second-rate stage. The courtiers gathered dust like old relics. There were no young ladies among them and without young ladies Bernart's inspiration was a dried-up well. The Plantagenet Court had brimmed with beauties and before that, at the court of his first patron, there may only have been one lady but he had only needed one. *Marguerite*, he murmured her name. Curls the colour of straw and a neck like a swan's; her chemise had a habit of falling away as if her shoulders were striving to reveal themselves, even at official functions. The stanzas had flowed from him then as he had feasted his gaze on her. *Marguerite…*

He sat up out of his reverie into the grey of the present, forcing his mounting desire back down. Their boat was still cutting through the channel between the silt banks, the nothing land between England and Wales. The sea was flat; the sky colourless. The chapel marking the far side of the estuary remained a dark pimple in the distance. They seemed no nearer their goal. The rest of the boat's passengers were sunk in their own thoughts, withdrawn into better and brighter internal worlds, perhaps.

"How much longer?" he asked the ferryman impatiently.

"Can't say, my lord. Less time if one of your men pulled oars with me."

Bernart slumped back in his seat, making a dismissive gesture. Have his men row? What impudence! He drummed his fingers on the damp boat planks, looking up at the heavens. *If only you would burst*, he thought, *then the verses I once wrought might again be unleashed from within me.*

But instead of rain came a sea fog, rolling in thick like a warning. Along with the silence aboard, it oppressed him. Bernart hated journeys. He loved the big arena: the banquet hall, the best French wine flowing. He would walk the paces required to get in amongst his onlookers and stun them with his performance and not a pace more. When he was obliged to travel, he made his mode of transport as similar to a hall as possible. He took with him his cook, who would at least make the food en route palatable and his bodyguard, who made him look important enough to assassinate and a bard, because all great troubadours had protégés. His cook was responsible for bringing enough quality alcohol to lessen the tedium of the trip and his bodyguard's duties were normally confined to arranging his Pérouges linen pillows so that his skin did not bruise. The other boat accompanying them was actually so overloaded with Bernart's travelling paraphernalia that all six members of his party had needed to squash into this one vessel. But his wine and linens could not lift his melancholy today. He wanted to be *there* already, across this savage land, performing at this festival purporting to be the greatest the world had ever beheld and showing his doubters how wrong they had been. And the wretched fog was thwarting him, smothering him. He felt the old darkness rush up again, the bitterness of Bernart the rebuffed.

"Let us have a song!" he cried.

The cook and bodyguard looked at the floor. From the other end of the boat, Marie, the guide for the journey, and her attendant stared impassively at him. But his bard, just in time to avoid a reprimand, started up something. The boy had a pleasing voice. It was a few lines before Bernart recognised the song was one of his. One he had not performed in a while, and with good reason. In this fog, and with this adolescent's warble, it seemed more piteous than ever. "*Her from whom I may have nothing...*" the boy sang. "*...All my heart and all herself, and all myself and all I have she has taken from me...[1]*"

It had rained the day he and Marguerite parted. It was in the wood below the bluff; the place they always met. Married,

---

1 From *Can vei la lauzeta mover* by Bernart de Ventadorn

married Marguerite, and married to his patron too. She had entreated him to write to her. She had said that they could perchance still see each other, from time to time once things had calmed down. Calmed! His love for her, and hers for him, were like tempests inside of them. They could be channelled if they remained together, and quelled if they remained apart, but what could sporadic unions do but whip up those tempests and batter their hearts to breaking point? Their love could have no middle ground, he had been adamant. His patron cast him out from the castle on the bluff in the middle of the wood and had locked Marguerite up in its turret. He had torn, grief-stricken, off through the trees that had secreted their love. They had once frolicked on the roots and carved their lust on the trunks but that day each tree was loathsome to him. He had badly wanted to put distance between him and that wood. But he had got lost in his torment; stayed stumbling about in there so long he thought he might die of thirst or cold. Then he remembered collecting himself. He had sat down on a mound and replayed his last moments with his beloved, over and over again until the cansos[1] were honed inside his head. Then the path had appeared to him, where before he swore there had only been undergrowth, and he had found his way out of the wood. *I am going wretched not knowing where, I renounce and deny my songs and flee from joy and from love*[2].

As the boy bashfully concluded, the others on the boat burst into applause. Bernart seized his young protégé, passionately kissing each of the bard's lilywhite cheeks.

"He sung my words perfectly," he said, hardly able to contain the sobs surging in his bosom.

---

1 In Occitania, they were *cansos*, not cantos.

2 From *Can vei la lauzeta mover* by Bernart de Ventadorn.

"Encore!" Marie clapped softly. "Your bard is gifted, my lord."

He looked at her in irritation. It was the way she said 'gifted', as if by insinuation *he* was not. This was the fifth day of their travelling together. She always looked so composed—in a boat, on horseback, at whatever hostelry they had been accommodated—never ill at ease even when surrounded by somewhat motley menfolk. The way Bernart normally networked with nobility was to descry chinks in their armour, highlighting little holes then offering his services in the filling or fixing of them. His first patron's castle had been as silent as a tomb; he had enlivened the rooms with his singing and gained recognition that way. His subsequent patron had been the Queen herself. Knowing her weakness for tales of romance, he had drawn upon every last detail of his trysts during that trial by storytelling she had held in her halls; she too had been won over by his heart-quickening depictions of what love was. This Marie did not appear to have any such holes. Bernart only really knew how to talk to women by wooing them and this did not seem to be an option with Marie because of how her quiet confidence knocked one off one's perch. So far, therefore, he had not said much to her at all. Other than that she was familiar with his intended destination and had volunteered to guide him there, he knew very little about her. Bernart was going through trying times—his comeback to the pinnacle of his profession, no less— and he needed to feel on top of things. With Marie he did not feel on top of things.

"My *bard*, lady, receives his training from the best," his delight at hearing his old song recited once more was fast diminishing.

"One of your earlier compositions, was it not my Lord?"

She sat there, indigo cloak over violet tunic, hands folded in lap. Her demeanour was assured where Marguerite's had been anything but sure, her hair straight where Marguerite's had curled, but something in Marie reminded him of his long-gone love. She could not be far off the age of his beloved the day they bid farewell, but it was not that. No. Marie was of the Otherworld, just as Marguerite had been, with eyes that bored right through you and beyond, as if they could see mortal souls hovering there behind your back. Bernart shuddered. He had developed a cold on this blasted crossing. Since those lines composed in the wood, he knew, greatness had eluded him. He had sealed up his heart that day and his ability to craft new verse got sealed up with it. Ever since then he had been treading water, managing just shallow flatteries and mixing these with reworked versions of old material to pass himself off as a poet. But he had never again plumbed the depths. That was about to change. Marie would see that. Everyone would see that.

"You know this region well, lady?" he asked.

"I ought to, my lord. I live here."

"Then perhaps you can say with more conviction than our ferryman when we will arrive at our lodgings."

"You desire to press on towards Cardigan whilst we can, my lord?"

"On and through. I do not care for wilderness, and the festival commences not many days hence."

Marie conferred with her attendant and pointed.

"Look closely through the mist, my lord."

Bernart saw nothing but heard the bells of the chapel tolling nearby. Three hours after dawn, although in a slack backwater like this, by the time the bell ringer had exchanged pleasantries with every peasant he passed on his way to work, that could mean late morning. Then an outcrop of land loomed into view. Behind that, Bernart espied rank upon rank of dank trees, fading into the murk.

"The great forest of Striguil," Marie announced. "We are in Wales."

"It looks a decidedly gloomy place."

"Fear not, my lord. We common country folk find ways to occupy ourselves. We will lodge with the De Braoses, half a day's ride from here. I believe you will find their castle in keeping with your tastes."

What a delicious little mouth she has, Bernart thought.

They turned into a much narrower river, the forest closing around them. Their vessel put in at a hovel just upstream and a foul-smelling villein boarded, to help the ferryman 'bear the burdensome load' as he pointedly phrased it.

"You call *this* civilisation?" Bernart scorned.

"Wait," said Marie.

A wind and a couple of winds more, and a grand many-arced stone bridge appeared. On the left bank the forest receded a way and standing out of a patch of extraordinarily green farmland was a town Bernart was forced to admit looked rather attractive. Well-fed children splashed at the water's edge. He saw a hunting party just returned with two fine-looking stags slung across their horses. He spied a group of maidens—at least, to his eyes, they seemed virtuous—talking and laughing outside a church. His creativity, he thought, could soon flourish in such a place as this.

Several yards short of the edge of this paradise, their vessel ground to a halt. The ferryman expelled an oath or three.

"Boat's overloaded, my lord. Stuck fast. We'll need to wade in."

"Wade?" Bernart was not certain he had heard correctly. In front of these genteel townsfolk?

Marie's attendant was the first to leap out, as if it were no bigger a thing than accepting seconds at dinner. The water came up above his waist, but he was significantly taller than Bernart. Exceedingly slimy water it looked too, and chilly enough to exacerbate a cold.

"Off with you," Bernart addressed his men, trusting that with their combined weight gone the vessel might dislodge from the silt. Yet even after the cook, the wine, the bodyguard and the travelling linens had made it ashore the keel remained embedded.

Marie sighed, rolled her eyes and jumped in after the others. A few moments later she too was on the riverbank, shivering but laughing.

What delight Bernart might have gleaned watching that nymph emerge from the water under different circumstances! As it was his eyes flitted dubiously between boat, river, bank and the small audience that had gathered there, the maidens from the church—to his chagrin—included. They were seemingly waiting for him to humiliate himself. He would not do it. He would make an entrance chivalrously, up the wall of a tower if needs must, but not like this.

"You!" he called to his bodyguard. "Come, stand a step or so into the current there!" He turned to his bard. "You, lad, plant yourself half way between him and the boat." His men moved unenthusiastically into position. He turned to the ferryman. "The fee we agreed was to shore, and as I am delivering myself there I assume you are content to waive payment." Bernart hitched up cloak and tunic around his thighs, took a running jump and, using his men's shoulders as stepping-stones, launched himself for the riverbank with hope and with dread. Someone caught his hand and hauled him onto dry land.

"Welcome to Wales, my lord!" Marie gave him a wry half-smile. "A fire awaits you, I promise!"

Bernart sneezed.

"That was some spectacle, lord," one of the maidens said. "I have offered my hearth, should it please you and your company to warm yourselves there."

He was momentarily thrown until he remembered that with the exception of himself his company had just been immersed in an icy river in December. Gracing the maidens with his most ardently serious look—and perhaps in his forties he still had it, for their eyes certainly widened—he gave a protracted bow that brought his lips to within touching distance of their demurely folded hands.

"I am Bernart de Ventadorn, beauteous ladies, and I am a performer of spectacles. And I accept your offer with the profoundest of pleasure."

Deep down though, he realised his histrionics were not put on for any of these maidens, but for Marie. It bothered him that he did not know exactly why.

The maiden who had offered her hearth was, as it turned out, the wife of a highly successful timber merchant, one of those men who had been returning from hunting as Bernart's party had arrived. Knowledge of her marital status dulled his revived spirits slightly, the more so since her husband was young and vigorous-looking.

"I wonder how one who takes such delight in the forest for a hunt can chop it down for his business," Bernart, eager to discomfort the man, challenged him as he was carving up venison for their breakfast.

"It's like this, my lord. Keep the forest trim and she'll flourish. Let her grow unchecked and she'll choke. The King likes the light coming in when he comes here for a hunt and he likes the tax he gets from the timber trade."

That was the end of their conversation. Bernart was bored before the man opened his mouth. Poor ladies, being marooned in the middle of nowhere with such country-dwelling clods for entertainment; they deserved a portion of his wit. He made some remarks about the arduous journey contrasted with the delightful prospects the town offered. They laughed like they had waited weeks for the opportunity. One maiden fed him a choice cut of venison, and the other fetched him a fleece, fondly placing it round his shoulders and insisting he need not return it to her until the next time he should pass this way. And lines formed in his mind. *She waited for me on the shore as I sailed in on my barque; she warmed my hands by her embers and sparked a light in my heart*[1]. Not bad; he would have to improve before the festival, but it would certainly titillate. Perhaps, Bernart hoped, he was finding his range again. And all the while he looked at Marie out of the corner of his eye. As her hair dried curly in the firelight did she not look more and more like Marguerite?

He glanced at her and experienced again that plummeting in his stomach. Marie had not been paying his wordplay the slightest heed. He imagined his own voice as the babble it must sound like to her. They were but a fire's width apart. But that half-smile of hers put the world between them. She was absolutely detached from him, and listening instead to his servants.

"I went hunting once," said the cook in a low tone to the bodyguard and the bard. "Didn't much care for it."

"Hind?"

"Boar."

"Boar! Tough."

"Tough it was. I felled it. Pa-ping. One arrow. Didn't get to try a piece of it though. I had to prepare it for all the lords and ladies, see."

"They did not save you any?"

"Not a bone. Even heard some boasting it was them that killed the beast. I might as well have stayed by the fire and not bothered."

---

1   No record of Bernart de Ventadorn using these lines professionally exists.

"But in life one has to hunt," said the bard. "One has to strive."

"I couldn't care less," said the cook. He gestured at Bernart and Marie. "I don't get them. I don't get their ways."

"And *they*," the bodyguard spat out his gristle, "almost never understand ours."

And across the fire Bernart saw, in a flicker of Marie's eyes quickly concealed but not quickly enough, a thing only a poet can observe and the thing a poet most fears: the moment a rival conceives of a great idea.

Bernart knew then that Marie was not on this journey by chance. She was a composer of words like he was. She was going with him to the festival to compete. And in the contest of song, she would be fighting him every pace of the hall.

Hamid

(APRIL, 1176)

THIS TIME, the eunuch entered the antechamber with a rather large flagon of wine and a goblet encrusted in jewels.

"From the finest vineyard of Shiraz, *karīm*. The Sovereign of Mankind bids you drink your fill."

Yes, yes, like he bid me gorge on those pomegranates just now, thought Hamid. He wondered what to read into being addressed thus. *Karīm*: generous. Could the Sultan have given orders for him to be complimented so because he had a favour to ask? He was but a perfumer from a declining city, and he doubted the Sultan suffered from a paucity of fragrances. So what could he be wanted for?

"Tell the, er, Sovereign of Mankind that I am," he placed his hands on his heart, "abundantly grateful, but that I am as full as a stuffed duck."

He was, too. His waistline did expand upon his visits to the Capital. Being at the crossroads of the trade routes as Herat was, there was always some new delicacy to try. Food was his one indulgence and he justified gluttony every time because it facilitated thought. His most monumental ruminations had arrived whilst eating. Hamid thought about an awful lot of things, sometimes the everyday kind such as the ingredients that would make his latest scent, but increasingly life's deeper dilemmas. His treatise on the betterment of the human soul, for instance: a respectable work, and one he had been able to transcribe in an evening only because of the platter of stuffed prunes—divine little building blocks of the brain—at his disposal. Wine, however, led to foggy-headedness and floundering cognition, and he would not touch it.

The eunuch departed and a moment later returned. This time, he was not alone. A girl, an attractive young thing, accompanied him.

"The Sovereign of Mankind," squeaked the eunuch "bids you have your fill."

The girl came and stood before Hamid, quite disconsolately. She held a rattle limply at her side.

"I can dance," she said. "Or we can do other things."

Yes, yes, he observed how her robe needed but a short tug to bring it to her ankles, he knew what 'other things' meant. He supposed he was unlike other men. He had never enthused about conquests over the opposite sex. Conquests! In Nishapur, his city, even low-grade merchants these days had a lady of pleasure available for each of their dinner guests. Women were begging to be admitted to the harems of the wealthy; at the slave markets he had seen one girl mutilate another so as to gain the greater attention from the recruiters doing the rounds. And when families starved behind the walls of their once-grand houses, when the city was rotting from the inside out, then the career of a concubine offered a gold-paved road to greatness if you played your hand well. You could get to turn the eye of a King, and there were not so many ways of doing that. But the plethora of women on offer was abominable. Taking one to bed no longer required grace: they were everywhere, like spoiling grapes overloading a vine. He felt no need anymore for intercourse with anyone other than his wife: in fact, the more he dedicated himself to thought, the less he required intimacy even from her. It was a distraction and, in the case of this limp girl before him, a repulsively scented one.

"My dear," Hamid tried to give himself airspace from her; she smelled cheap, sweat and roses, like she had only recently made it back from entertaining a second-level court official. "Tell the Sovereign of Mankind that my soul is stirred to its depths by his offering me such a specimen as yourself, really it is, but my desire to converse with him outshines all others."

The eunuch ushered him down corridors of magnificent ornamentation, where peacocks fashioned from turquoise paid homage to the Sultan on the walls and the ceilings erupted into stars and moons and formations of dazzling complexity. They went so far Hamid thought they must be moving in elaborate circles, because surely not even a palace could be this immense. At the top of a flight of steps with candles higher than the height of a man burning either side, the eunuch finally paused.

"Undress, *karīm*."

Hamid did so.

"Go down the steps *karīm*—through the doors. And once you are inside, do not look, whatever else you do, beyond the central partition."

Hamid descended the steps.

The doors were emblazoned in a rising sun with the frame studded by golden lions, the kings of beasts. The Sultan's ancestors might have been kings for centuries but the Sultan's lands stretched from the Caspian Sea to the Bay of Bengal; he was the King of kings.

Hamid pushed at the doors, expecting them to be heavy, but they yielded easily and he almost fell, off-balance, into the room.

The steam made it hard to discern anything at first. When it thinned Hamid saw he was in a bathhouse. As with the corridors he had passed through, there was no one anywhere in evidence. Seven columns with fanciful mosaics depicting the ancient arts soared up into the fug. These surrounded a seven-sided pool almost as wide as the room, with a screen obscuring the half furthest away. The screen was surprisingly plain and cheap looking, like a hastily erected tent. There were gaps at the corners his eyes were drawn to, despite the eunuch's warning. For he knew who must be on the other side.

"Enter, Hamid."

The voice came from behind the screen. The Sultan. Allah's right hand—well, at least his forefinger—on Earth, so close Hamid could have splashed him. He had, occasionally, speculated on what the man might be like. Some said that since vanquishing the last of his main rivals he had grown a beard as thick as a beaver's pelt. Others held that he remained fresh-faced as a youth. His sense of humour and his wrath had been talked about in equal measure. But he certainly sounded like someone who wanted to converse. Hamid advanced until the water was up to his knees and the screen was mere steps away.

"Or should I call you by your trader's name, perfumer? Or by your poet's name, Farid Un-Din Attar?"

Could the Sultan know about his writing? True, he had sent copies of all his manuscripts to the Capital, but not in genuine expectation of one ever reaching the upper reaches of court. His work would have needed to get past thieves and plagiarists and those who would sooner destroy it than see its author win favour over them.

"By whatever name that pleases you, Supreme Ruler of the World. I am known across your lands as the former, and as the latter by very few. But I do find there is something transcendent in the act of scent mixing that inclines me towards concepts... er... nobler than myself and it is these I try to capture on parchment. The rantings of a dreamer, no more."

"It is in both capacities that I asked you here today," said the Sultan.

There was the sound of bubbles being blown on the other side of the screen. Hamid waited. He knew everything about waiting and he believed in waiting, because only waiting brought enlightenment.

"The matter, perfumer, is a delicate one. I could not impart it to any other courtier. My most trusted advisors say that I have achieved what no forefather of mine could: a far greater realm, and relative peace within it. They tell me now is the time to enjoy this empire of mine. Yet I feel no contentment from their words. Why, do you suppose, should I not feel content?"

"It is natural to have a hunger for furthering oneself," Hamid chose his words with care. "It is one I share."

"Let us call it that," said the Sultan, with more life in his voice. "For want of a better phrase: furthering oneself. And do you suppose, perfumer, that I should do this by conquering more territories?"

"I am no soldier, Sovereign of Mankind. But all rulers deserve peace in which to enjoy the wars they have won."

"Do you suppose, then, that I should make improvements to the city that lies beyond these walls? That I should raise mosques, or build pleasure gardens, or a library that preserves every word of beauty uttered in my court in texts so that visitors one hundred years from now will be able to see the excellence I attained during my reign?"

The Sultan was getting excitable but Hamid saw that he was some way shy of reaching his point, because Herat shone with mosques and pleasure gardens, and had just such a library in the final stages of construction. Yes, yes, Hamid had travelled to many cities and the Sultan's Capital was already superior to most.

"No, perfumer. Furthering oneself can take other forms. I realised this the other day, when I read your latest poem."

Hamid was glad then for the partition between them. As much as he longed to behold the Sultan, he was quite beside himself, and did not want the Supreme Ruler of the World to witness such a loss of control. Having the principal personage on Earth praising his couplets: it was worth more than all the frankincense in Salalah. He recalled the conclusions of his treatise: '*It is impossible in this life for a soul to improve itself sufficiently to share a room, or even a realm, with Allah. But one might and one must tread firmly upon a path towards perfection, keeping this lofty goal in sight.*' Yes, yes, one pace at a time. What more could a plump man from the provinces do?

"I realised when I read your words," said the Sultan, "that even those courtiers I had previously deemed talented were chattering apes."

Hamid heard himself faintly protesting that the Sovereign of Mankind was too kind.

"It could be that I spent too long on battlefields, and not enough time cultivating talent," continued the Sultan wistfully. "And if so now is the time to make amends. I do not offer you a position at court, perfumer. I offer you a greater opportunity.

A messenger arrived yesterday. He had come from the west: from so far west five horses died under him on the road. Once revived, he said he brought news from beyond the sultanate of Saladin, from the furthest edge of Christendom. You might know these lands for war, he said, but come the close of this year, on the day infidels call Christ's Mass, they shall be renowned for their revelry. There will be a festival. The known world may never have witnessed such a festival. At this festival will be two tournaments: one in vocal song, one in instrumental song.

Here you shall perform your verses, perfumer. You shall represent my empire on this exalted stage. And you shall not fail me. You shall emerge victorious."

Hamid dabbed water on his forehead and cheeks, and looked up at the mosaics on the columns: at a line of astronomers observing the night sky with dreamy glazed expressions. Once, in Damascus, a beautiful woman had approached him. *'You, scent-maker! Make me a scent for my husband the vizier that will make his stink less repugnant to me.'* He had stopped what he had been doing, as one does when words like 'vizier' are shouted about. *'I recommend the fragrance I am wearing,'* he had craned his head to one side to let his aroma assail her nostrils. *'There can be no other,'* she had agreed, purchasing a vial. She was back the next day, and agitated. *'Scent-maker, your fragrance worked. Now my husband visits my bed and there is no sickening stink. But when I smell him I think only of you.'* He had not taken her to his bed, because her husband was the vizier, and he had wished to extend his stay in Damascus. But he could have taken her—and from one of that city's most eminent men—with no more than a toss of his head to discharge the accord of his fragrance into the air.

"If you had asked me to represent you as a perfumer, Supreme Ruler of the World, I believe I would stand a chance of triumphing. Alas with my words…"

"Other words," the Sultan interrupted "are trifles. When I read your lines about the birds[1] and their quest to find a king to lead them I was overcome, do you hear me? What a difficult journey

---

1 *Mantiq-ut-Tayr* (Conference of the Birds), Farid Un-Din Attar. It would become, in time, one of the best-regarded works of Persian literature.

those feathered creatures undergo! But how worthwhile it is! What exemplary subjects they are! If one in one hundred men in my Empire would show one hundredth of the endeavour! Then I would have a court of Omar Khayyám's, a golden place in the chronicles…"

To write about a Herculean voyage was one thing, Hamid thought, but to actually undertake one was, for a fat man in middle age, quite another. He pottered about the Empire selling his scents, true, but Christendom was many months away, and if manners over there were as vile as he had heard, what in Allah's name must the food be like? His wife would nag him like she nagged him about everything; yes, yes, she would not miss him but would miss his income were he to go off wandering for the year. She was as cold as alabaster, that woman. Sometimes that coldness sharpened his appetite and he would come to her, late at night after finally emerging on top in a battle with his thoughts; he would see her sleeping there, unsmiling as a corpse, and see what he could do to elicit a response. It was his little challenge to himself.

"…I thought to myself that only one with your knowledge of scent could with no more than his quill so arouse the senses. Your words had a touch, a taste, a smell! Each one was a living thing, a breathing thing! There can be no other than you, perfumer, to go forth with your verses and win us glory. Go and win Islam glory and make these damned infidels in Christendom believe in us."

The Supreme Ruler of the World seemed resolved. And to object would mean a rather nasty death, which Hamid was not ready to experience until he had explored the limits of just how far souls might advance in this life.

"How could I refuse you, Sovereign of Mankind?"

"You could not," the Sultan stretched leisurely. Hamid heard him flexing every joint until it cracked.

"But it is not a matter of acceptance alone. It is essential you believe, as I do, that from this moment onwards your words are the most beautiful that have ever been or ever will be written. Can you do that, perfumer?"

Yes, yes, Hamid could do that. With his fragrances clients told him all the time: '*you did for me with labdanum oil more than all the money in the empire could,*' '*it must have been your musk that made her notice me.*' With his poetic compositions, he had always been conscious of creating something pleasing, but formerly felt his seed had fallen on barren ground—such as his wife, for example. But if a man like this was asking him to have faith in his own words then he would, surely as the Haji led to Mecca.

"From now on your perfume-selling will be your cover. Traders travel without arousing suspicion; writers of any kind tend to get suspected of deviances. But chiefly you will be a wordsmith, your brain the forge, your quill the anvil and the result gold Solomon himself would covet, do you hear me?"

"I hear you, Supreme Ruler of the World. And I will do my best to, er, deliver you the glory of victory."

The Sultan slipped under the water again; blew more bubbles. He stayed under so long Hamid was unsure whether he might already have been dismissed.

"There is one more thing, perfumer. Come closer to the partition."

Hamid was perspiring, despite the cool of the pool and a generous application of almond oil and anise prior to his arrival at the palace. He approached. A shadow pressed against the partition from the other side, indicating the Sovereign of Mankind had done likewise. If Hamid had been hoping for insights into the man at such close quarters—the style of his beard, or whether his shoulders were stooped—he was to be disappointed. The image projecting onto the screen was of a monstrously proportioned foetus.

The Sultan whispered some words to Hamid. Hamid managed to convey both his vow to obey them and, immediately afterwards, the regrettable development that a queasiness he blamed on the quails at breakfast necessitated his getting some air. Hamid was excused. In the sun outside he felt wretched. The facial tick he thought he had mastered was back, and more pronounced than ever. He turned this way and that in anguish. He tottered down the street to a wine house, ordered a carafe of their dirtiest wine, drank it swiftly and by all accounts began to look a few shades better only after some time had elapsed.

He would do it, of course; he had to. But the idea of doing it was abhorrent to him.

He ignored all overtures of conversation from the other customers and, mumbling about the heat even though it was not that hot, went to see a man about a camel.

Marie

DECEMBER, 1176)

MARIE WAITED until the last strains of the vulgar ditty had faded into drunken applause, then hastened outside. She inhaled the cold silent night like a tonic, glad to be gone from that insufferable hall.

Oh, De Braose, the most influential lord in all the March, had thrown them a lavish banquet. He never failed to do that. His Abergavenny residence was the preferred stop of dignitaries with business in the native Welsh territory rearing up no more than a bowshot from its western ramparts, but more legendary than the fine food and wine he provided for his guests was the entertainment during his feasts. De Braose delighted in pushing the boundaries of what was decent—he once patronised a tragicomedy about the King's sons scheming for the throne —but tonight's performance had been an abomination even by his standards. Almost a year ago to the day, the De Braoses had invited the Welsh chieftains with territory adjacent to theirs to a banquet within these very walls. December: the traditional time for resolving differences. And Seisyll ap Dyfnwal, most notable of De Braose's Welsh neighbours, came in good faith, had out of a desire for peace come and parted with his weapons and inside the hall been slaughtered along with his son and retinue. His ancestors had ruled Gwent for centuries and in an evening De Braose had eradicated their bloodline. And one year on he got some two-penny troubadour[1] to re-enact the occasion. In theatre, Marie fumed, Welsh princes could be fools and De Braose a noble knight: and in theatre alone. And how those Norman lackeys watching had laughed. Maybe some were unaware of their host's dark deeds under the roof they had belched and letched beneath this evening. But many had certainly known. And they had laughed regardless.

"Are you quite well, my lady?"

It was Pierrot, sweet ever-attendant Pierrot. There was no more faithful a servant, which was why she had needed him on this journey. Because there were eyes on her; here, particularly, but ever since their party had embarked from London too. Pierrot would defend her with his life, although she would never ask him to, and that made him more of a gentleman than any of the well-dressed ruffians seated on De Braose's dais.

"I shall survive, Pierrot. I am disinclined for company this evening. You should go back in and make merry. We still have several days' hard ride ahead."

"I should stay with you, my lady. The calm in a castle like this makes me think a storm cannot be far off."

"I need solitude after being cooped up with that ass of a troubadour and his brigade of drudges the whole day. I will take a turn about the bailey awhile. I can take care of myself."

She walked to the eastern side of the palisade where the lights of the small settlement huddled below the castle walls smouldered still. She climbed up to the ledge where the sentries were positioned, poised for action even at this late hour, and

---

1 The troubadour in question, Cecil, went on to make a name for himself in the enactment of light, trite parodies: bringing smiles to such famously miserable countenances as Baldwin of Forde, Archbishop of Canterbury, and John, King of England. He led a full and happy life. Other bards possibly exaggerated his lack of talent, jealous of the success he achieved without the slightest bit of formal bardic training.

proceeded around the defences slowly, keen to delay her return to the revelry.

It was a bitter night. Her breath smoked. When she reached the western perimeter she paused. Beyond the furthest flames from the torches she could make out the gleam of the river that separated Norman Wales from native Wales. She stared into the darkness. With a thrill, she imagined auburn moors at the start of a new day. She imagined men wearing leeks on their helmets running fleet-footed, fearless, swarming the castle walls, putting the Normans to the sword and taking the fortress back for Rhodri and Dafydd, rulers of Gwynedd; for Owain Cyfeiliog, Poet-Prince of Powys; for Rhys ap Gruffyd, Lord of Deheubarth and ruler of the southern Welsh; for today's true leaders of true Wales, for *Pura Wallia* and for banished Britons everywhere.

That river could be an allegory for her life until this point, she thought. It tumbled off these moors down to gentle Caerleon, her makeshift home, where you could board a ship bound for her beloved Brittany, her birthplace.

She knew what it was to be outcast. She had been a month shy of sixteen when she had left Brittany for these shores. What was the word people had used to describe her marriage? Prudent, that was it. Prudent particularly in light of the Bretons siding with Henry Plantagenet's sons during their failed rebellion against their father: grievous repercussions were anticipated in Brittany and a husband with lands in Buckinghamshire and connections to Queen Eleanor was deemed a lucky escape. But escape is never forced upon you. Buckinghamshire was just another sort of prison. And her husband was the unwitting gaoler. He was known at court, but as a figure of fun; there were those that would mock his affable simplicity and even do impressions of his slight limp, incurred falling off a stationary horse, behind his back. She did her best to defend him in public, but the only men she gave any thought to growing up were knights, or the troubadours who would stop by her family's house to sing of chivalry, and her husband was neither gallant nor gifted in storytelling or any of the other arts. Indeed, her spouse fell far short of any ideal, unless one's ideal was wealth. In wealth he was blessed. He gave her everything materially. But she had no great love of 'things'; her love was for what lay beyond—the tale to be told, the next horizon, anywhere that was not Buckinghamshire. She increasingly spent time at court, and soon enough without her husband. The stories she related about the Brittany of her childhood fascinated her listeners and allowed her to transport herself back to a land of bashing sea and striking light, far from the stuffy confines of her husband's estate. At home she retreated with her books to her chamber, feigning ill health so as to be let alone, or prowled the neat hedges rimming her new demesne like a captured beast prowls a cage. It was by chance she found out about her husband's other property far to the west. He held land in the March, in the valleys close to where King Arthur himself was said to have had his court, fronted by sea and backed by high hills. If she was to live out a life in these isles, would it not be more bearable in such a place as Caerleon? When she broached the subject her husband had protested in his whiny manner; he preferred the familiar and was wary of his estate in Wales because of the numbers of Welsh in the vicinity. But Marie persisted and to Caerleon they had moved. Her husband spent much time travelling back to Buckinghamshire for business as she had predicted he would, and his stays away were lengthy which suited them both, she believed, well enough. Now she discovered a strange sort of peace. Now she could be alone with a clear head. She could look south and watch the boats embarking for Waterford or St Malo. Or she could look north towards the mountains and think of the people there no Saxon or Norman ever conquered, King Arthur's people, a people pushed into a corner but holding their own and just maybe against the odds fighting back.

She supposed it must be by matrimony alone that she was Norman, for a Norman would be nervous of the route their party would take tomorrow: up into the mountains and amidst just such a people. She had no reason to fear the Welsh. Normans put about that they were bloodthirsty warriors, but at least they would not stab you in the back. Normans derided their lack of sophistication but they could sing like nightingales. And oh, how they could dance! Come evening in English households you sat coldly and watched the entertainment, getting gradually drunker. In Wales you got up and joined in. Maybe she was a Briton in her soul.

She drew her cloak tighter about her. It was chillier now. The sounds of carousal from the hall had waned. She must have been out here for much longer than she thought. Sleep, then. As a guest of honour she had a place up in the keep along with De Braose and his family and—heaven, how could she forget—the incomparable Bernart de Ventadorn. An honour it was definitely deemed, particularly in the March, as two secure walls between you and the enemy were better than one: unless of course your enemies were already on the inside.

The sentries at the gatehouse to the inner ward glanced away, suppressing laughter as she passed by which erupted again immediately afterwards. She ascended the first few steps quickly, relaxing only when shadow hid her again. In the keep above the candles already glimmered. She heard shouts: a man's, a lady's, a man's and a door banged shut in anger; a lull and then more voices this time from a lower floor. She slowed her pace. She would linger outside, maybe, until things had quietened; she was reluctant to re-engage in pleasantries now.

"…the chronicles record how it was just the bard singing that day," it was a dry, measured voice speaking. "But my father dispelled the myth to me as his grandfather had to him from first-hand account. We *all* sang. We sang the *Chanson de Roland* as we cut down those fleeing Saxons. Sweet Christ, the words were never sung with more spirit and it was the words that did it. It broke them when they heeded our togetherness. People sometimes ask me if I genuinely believe in the supremacy of our Norman race. Then I tell them that story. And then they see the stupidity of the question."

It could only be De Braose. Who else could speak so tonelessly about something so terrible? In the lee of the inner ward walls Marie shivered.

"Your business is the sword, my lord. Mine is merely the quill."

De Ventadorn. And just the two of them, it seemed, in this snug late-night *tête-à-tête*.

"In this matter, the principle remains the same. Battles are fought on many fronts. And not always on a battlefield."

"I am privileged to have your support, my lord."

"You will have use of three of my best men all the way to the castle in Cardigan. And within it, should the occasion demand."

"I have faith, of course, in my abilities alone being sufficient."

"Do not underestimate the Lord Rhys. He thinks like a Norman, and better than some of us. There is a reason he is the foremost leader the Welsh have. He will look to upstage us all at this festival. He will ensure the best bards are competing. And you are sorely out of practice."

"In the glory days of the Plantagenet Court, my lord, I humbly remind you that I was their most prestigious entertainer."

"That was two decades ago," De Braose bluntly interrupted. "Let us now look to future glories. Let us deal those Welsh a wound on their own turf. The quill works in the well-lit hall. The sword can find its mark in the dark. Goodnight."

Bernart remained alone in the gathering gloom. He took the knife he had pilfered during dinner and pressed the blade into his left wrist until the blood surged. *Unleash.* He cut deeper. Not so deep as to endanger himself but enough to feel the wet rush of release. Somewhere within him was his way with words. *Unleash. If there was a time for you to come, that time is now.* He held his arm, trembling, endured the blood flow until he could sense himself weakening then applied the tourniquet with the last of his energy. Spent, he fell to his knees, then slumped into a position not dissimilar to a woman's when giving birth. He sat despondently on the floor, watching the candle dim. His mind was still blank.

The inner ward seemed disproportionally dark as the last lights went out. Most, but not all; in an upper window a flame burned yet. One of De Braose's children was poking her head through the narrow gap, contorting her face and making a croaking, gurgling sound at Marie that was presumably an imitation of a small not-so-frightening monster. Marie stuck out her tongue in response and the girl, after brief consideration, started to shriek. Another face appeared at the window: Maud, De Braose's wife. Marie waved, but it failed to mask the fact that she had significantly distressed the daughter of the lady of the castle. She hurried to the doorway of the keep, snatched a taper from a recess, and found her way up through the shadows to her bed.

Marie's thoughts raced. Even now the keep seemed alive with the creaks one imagines in that strange stage before sleep are intruder's footfalls or conspirator's mutterings. One creak surpassed the others. It was the creak of a bedframe. It was close. And then came Maud's whinnying—*oh, William, do not stop, never stop, oh William*—as De Braose did something of apparent pleasure to his wife in their conjugal bed. Marie pressed the pillow over her head but her ears had become unavoidably attuned. She heard each of Maud's moans, but from De Braose came not a single sound. The lord of the March thrust home in silence.

And night sank over this outpost of Norman control with its habitual unease: with sentries peering tensely out over the ramparts, and with almost everyone inside praying for morning.

The Great One

(DECEMBER, 1176)

"**THIS, DEAR CHILDREN,** is a *wine house*. You will spend a significant amount of your life in such a place. Under no other roof will every sort of person the Good Lord created congregate. There are old men, like me, and young men, like yourselves, and an exceptional selection of women to serve the lot of us. There are warriors—be nice to them—and travellers—be cautious of them. There are rich men—befriend them—and poor men—make friends with the rich men before they do. Nor is it by chance this establishment is near an abbey, for monks are the biggest drunks of all and only us poets can come close to rivalling the rogues—although we at least can justifiably claim we are here to glean inspiration. Now gather closer and do not restrain yourselves, you at the back, from procuring me a pitcher, restraint is a verse-maker's worst enemy! Else I fear my voice may fail me and we know, dear children, where we would be if that happened. We would be nowhere," Cynddelw said to himself. "We would be nowhere."

The apprentices shuffled in towards their teacher, wary of his volatile hand gestures. They were *cerrdorion*, students learning the fine art of bardism, and did not care to be called 'children' by the big man in their midst for they were well towards the end of their training and could already construct verse in all twenty[1] of the established metres. But the big man could do as he pleased; he was Cynddelw Bryddyd Mawr, the Great One. And whilst the *cerrdorion* could likely have located another bard qualified to instruct them, as they were a talented bunch, they wanted to be able to boast that they had been schooled under the Great One. '*The Great One who served as bard to mighty Owain, the strongest prince Gwynedd has ever known?*' '*Yes,*' they wanted to brag, '*the same.*' '*Is it not true he is great only by way of his immense size?*' '*He is big, but his grasp of the craft of poetry is unequalled. He could converse all day in song if need be.*'

Several *cerrdorion* pooled the coinage from their share of the takings at the last performance the group had given, at the residence of a former bishop who had snored right through and dispirited everyone. As usual they were buying the Great One his drinks. It was always 'drinks' with him, never 'drink'. In all candour, some of them suspected their teacher of unnecessarily protracting their tuition because he enjoyed the constant supply of complimentary wine.

"We are fortunate today, dear children, to be tended by a *Goddess*. It is not often as mere mortals we get such an opportunity so we thank Millie here for her divine presence... could you give us a twirl, Millie, a nice slow one?"

"Go to Hell, Cynddelw, and I'll see you there. Some of us have work to do."

"Women, dear children! We need to commit them to verse because what would poetry be without plummeting us into the void of cruelty only to elevate us again to the giddy peaks of

---

1 Twenty-four Welsh poetic metres had been codified by the close of the 13th century; in the 12th, the four types of metre known as cywydd had still not appeared, making twenty metres available to bards. These included twelve varieties of awdl or ode (longer poems) and eight varieties of englyn (shorter and predominantly praise poems to patrons). A well-taught bard would know each and every sort of metre, but might regularly use only a handful in his verses...

rapture!" Cynddelw turned to better appreciate Millie. She moved between the bottles and barrels of her grubby enterprise with the grace of Calliope on her lyre. He did not pay any heed to the cockroaches when she was serving...

> *Crimson-cheeked as claret and sweet as a young mead,*
> *She pours wine never pausing for the drink she needs.*
> *Oh, I'd give her a draft for her fine affections*
> *All she gives a cup of is her sour rejection!*
> *It's a different tale come the end of her shift,*
> *She's parched for the vintage offered up to her lips!*
> *She takes her communion; takes long and takes it deep,*
> *And so Praise Be Dear Lord, for we'll get little sleep!"[1]*

Cynddelw surveyed his flock. "Who can tell me what manner of metre that was?"

"An awdl, Great One."

"What kind of awdl?"

The *cerrdorion* hesitated. There were twelve types of awdl, the ode form for addressing a person of note, and none of them wanted to get caught out.

"A rhupunt," one of the elder *cerrdor* said, using the hesitation of the others to full advantage and even managing to make it appear as if the question was pretty easy.

"A *rhupunt* is it?" Cynddelw cried. "And what Welsh ruler, known to even the tamest of troubadours, had a rhupunt composed for him on his deathbed which makes the case for him being granted a grand place in Heaven?"

"It was Madog, Prince of Powys, Great One. And I believe the poet was none other than yourself."

---

1 No record of Cynddelw Bryddyd Mawr using these lines professionally exists.

"Incorrect," sighed Cynddelw. "I did compose verses for that dear deceased prince. But I used an altogether different metre. You will buy the next pitcher, dear child, once we are quite done with this one."

"Perhaps we could also discuss my apprenticeship, Great One," the crestfallen student ventured. "I have been your *cerrdor* many months now and believe I am ready to qualify."

"Timing, dear child! Delivery is everything to a bard and yours is still most askew. In addition, I am in the midst of teaching, and how do you think your fellow pupils feel about you disrupting their study time with such requests?"

The *cerrdorion* did not get the chance to say what they felt about it. If they had, their feelings would probably have been mixed: relief at not being the ones hauled through the coals, and frustration because should the most experienced among them be denied that much-coveted qualification, their own chances became that much more remote. They were young men, and impatient. They knew they had a knack for stringing stanzas together, but any humming peasant might manage that. They wanted to be bards, licenced to perform and solicit for patronage at the best households in the land, and for that they needed the dub from their teacher. And this desolate wine house with the mountain wind blasting through its planks was far from the glamorous halls they had pictured performing in when the Great One accepted them under his tutelage.

"You're looking pleased with yourself Cynddelw," Millie said suspiciously, pouring out the next round of wine. "More so than usual."

"Should a man not be content when surrounded by poets and by his muse, fair Millicent, loveliest wine house owner in Wales?" he did not mean for his voice to be a bellow but it was, he could not help it.

"Your pretty speech might fool your students but it doesn't fool me. I know when the Great One is the Grumpy One and when he's the Good-Humoured One and I'd say you're dangerously close to the latter this afternoon."

What a woman she was. When age overtook him he would settle down with a woman like that. He especially liked her hands on the countertop, hams of hands, red-raw from scullery. A bard's hands were not like that. He was tall enough to dwarf most men and as broad as he was tall, but he still had a bard's hands, slender and smooth. Millie's hands excited him.

"Perception, dear children!" Cynddelw said with admiration. "As a poet one must *perceive* and this singular lady has just demonstrated more insight than the lot of you together in seven days of so-called creation! Yes, all-seeing Millie, I have today an added sparkle to my wit and a youthful skip to my step. Our winter's circuit through austere Snowdonia has been unforgiving—household upon household so lacking in appreciation for the brilliance of our band that we were pushed east towards the lands of the Normans—but those lean times will tonight be consigned to the chronicles!"

"You've found a sucker who'll pay you to sing songs for him, you mean?

"Yes, Millie, and a learned one with a love for the subtleties of our craft! We are come upon you today to polish our best words in readiness! These dear children are embellishing their compositions with *cymeriad*—that is the ornamentation of certain lines, a device of my own invention designed purely to thrill during recitation. And the gracious nobleman concerned has flagstone floors throughout his residence!"

"It will be an improvement on our billeting of two nights previous," the humiliated *cerrdor* spoke up. "A leaking outbuilding infested with rats."

"You will not complain, dear child, when you are stretching out by our new benefactor's hearth with a bellyful of the boar he loves to hunt," Cynddelw silenced his upstart pupil.

"Who is the lucky patron this time?" Millie asked. "We're not known for our nobles around these parts."

"Who else but Meirion de Manche, the knight who knows no overlord and has the only household close to being deemed civilised in this bog-entrenched cantref. Except for your own wine house of wonders, of course Millie."

Millie started to laugh, then stopped herself. When Cynddelw teased others it was accepted and even expected but somehow, when the time came to return the jest on him, you felt guilty. It was like mocking a child.

"Cynddelw... Meirion de Manche left for the Holy Land not two days back. He's closed up his house and left his vassal in charge."

"Millie, your laugh is like a soft summer breeze, but I implore you: this is no moment for mischief! These dear children and myself need this de Manche. His hall is to be the beacon of our bleak winter. Near all the would-be patrons we solicited this last long month preferred the cheap ditties of half-wit minstrels to cough life into their banquets; de Manche is alone in seeing that just a few pennies more buys our infinitely superior song-making."

"I'm sorry Cynddelw," Millie patted the big bard's shoulders. "He's gone."

The *cerrdorion* heard every word. They murmured amongst themselves.

The Great One had told them that soliciting—roaming the land free to perform the songs one felt in one's heart—was the only path for a truly gifted bard. The alternative was becoming a *bard teulu*, a poet permanently tied to the entertainment needs of a particular house and this, the Great One said, enmeshed one in the obligations of insipid praise poetry, even if one was blessed enough to gain a post at one of the predominant princes' courts. Soliciting got you attention from *all* the noblest households, the Great One declared; look at him, his verse had been beloved by leaders of all three Welsh kingdoms! He was erstwhile favourite of Prince Madog of Powys and Prince Owain of Gwynedd in the days before their realms dwindled—their epitaphs had been written in his hand, no less—and as for Rhys of Deheubarth, his realm might now be the mightiest in Wales but Rhys too should call on the services of Cynddelw Bryddyd Mawr if he wanted his reign remembered after his death. You do not come to be called the Great One for your size alone, the Great One said.

All those recent nights their band had spent together in unseemly barns across Powys with nothing but straw to abate the chill, their teacher had talked of the haven of Meirion de Manche's hall and how his hospitality would compensate for everything. And now that course was closed to them. How, then, would the Great One react?

Cynddelw ran a moistened finger around the rim of his empty tankard, creating a discordant sound that gave him inane satisfaction, a cadence almost to these times of woe. *Brightest star in the firmament, snuffed out; it laid us low and spent, then we wanderers wondered why we'd dreamed to look up to the sky*[1]. He had failed his flock. He could take care of himself, but how would his lambs survive the winter? They were still bleaters. They did not comprehend resonance or how to hold a raucous hall on a knife's edge with no more than a well-timed pause; they did not see that even though their lines were promising, they might as well be howling into a hole in the ground if they did not improve their delivery. Any audience but the most patient—and few audiences

---

1 No record of Cynddelw Bryddyd Mawr using these lines professionally exists.

in Wales were that—would roast those little lambs of his. They needed this winter to toughen up. And he needed this winter, he admitted to himself with sorrow welling within him, he needed this winter to prepare himself for letting them go.

"Couldn't you try the new abbey at Cwmhir?" Millie broke the uncomfortable silence. "They'll give you shelter for the night."

"We cannot," one of the *cerrdor* said icily. "The Great One has been ex-communicated."

"Filthy drunks, those Cistercians," Cynddelw muttered. "I would not stomach staying one night with those two-faced frock-wearers if they welcomed me back with open arms. They preach about purity one moment and guzzle wine by the gallon the next!"

He was not averse to reconciliation in principle; for the sake of these new bards he was nurturing he would do a lot, but he would never make peace with the church. The quip that put him in trouble had been innocuous: it was *true* those monks wore nothing under their habits. His business was entertainment and if the monasteries could not laugh along with it, why should he, or any one of the degenerates forced into those corrupt orders of theirs, accept what they had to say?

To create something worthwhile in this life, Cynddelw reflected, you generally started with very little or nothing at all. If you began with too much you lost it. He himself had come from nothing to grace the halls of the greats, and unless he acted soon not only would he be back with nothing again, but he would have dragged his pupils down with him without their ever having known magnificence. Coming under the tutelage of the Great One, it would soon be put about, was tantamount to suicide for a self-respecting songster.

It had seemed to him this last month that as they had travelled they had been working towards something, and this was what he had jovially assured his band in their moments of gloom. But news of De Manche's departure had demoralised even him. How he had looked forward to that knight's hall! Not for its warmth exactly, but because you could not be productive if you were forever out in the cold, not really; the desperation showed in your delivery and the purpose of a bard was to help people forget day-to-day wretchedness, not remind them of how closely it lurked to the door of the room they were revelling in.

Now it was just his dear children and him left in the wine house, and the wine house stood alone on the track up into the hills in the grey end-of-day light. Their prospects of finding respectable rooms for the night were once again diminished, and with their paltry takings used up on the wine, only Millie's kind heart stood between his band of bards-to-be and being out in the cold with nothing once more.

"You could stay here tonight," Millie was saying. "If you don't mind making way for my girls when they need the rooms."

Millie's girls were the only reason her wine house was standing. Locals would drink at home on the gut-rotting brews they had concocted rather than pay high prices for Millie's wine but for Millie's girls they would come. Accordingly, the upper level of the wine house was partitioned off into separate recesses under the eaves where peasants and pilgrims and no doubt the occasional monk sought satisfaction with whichever of the girls happened to have a vacancy. Demand exceeded supply, particularly during the months pilgrims were passing through on mass. Thus at times there were queues out of the door and even in a quiet season, such as advent generally was, it could get busy with men sick of the rigmarole of abstinence traipsing down out of the surrounding hills for a frolic. Scantly populated the district might be but the wine house was a community success. It had been known that husbands, seeking light relief, made the necessary excuses to slip off to Millie's only to encounter in their much-anticipated upstairs session their own wives disrobing before them.

No, a night's exposure to Millie's girls and their clients and all that commotion of carnal activity could do no good for his dear children. Nor could a band of bare-faced bards bedding down with their stocky old teacher in a recess usually reserved for strumpets bring much to wine house trade aside from ridicule. And who was he anyway, sunk so low that he could even consider accepting charity from a whorehouse?

"I was always praised for my quick wits, Millie," he said. "So if anyone can find another way out of our plight without us inconveniencing you, it is I."

"It's no trouble," Millie said kindly. She looked almost tenderly at Cynddelw. For years he had been coming here, always in this season, always on his scrounging songsters' circuit, always with apprentices in awed attendance. In the past when she herself had been younger and purse strings were tighter she had been envious of the big bard's laid-back way of life. No sooner had he opened his mouth than the crowds had thrown pennies at it. Even if to her his trade amounted to door-to-door begging only with songs thrown in to endear would-be benefactors, she saw how he was revered: in this valley and every other she had ever visited. She might have no time for fancy words, but Wales had always made all the time it could for them. Theirs was a land of song, after all. If there was no longer a place for Cynddelw at the halls hereabouts then she feared for the district: what other light did they have in dark times besides the certainty of a good bard stopping by to sing of better ones? Cynddelw's party had spent plenty at the wine house back then, and at a time she had sorely needed them to. He had worn that bear hide cloak a hunter from the north had given him ever since she could remember. He used to delight her girls by pulling down the beast's head over his and doing exotic animal impressions. But he was quite the gentleman beneath. He would stand up for her and for her girls and he had, on several occasions, when other customers had become threatening. Heavens, he had once challenged a Marcher lord to a duel—although admittedly a duel of balladry. She was not surprised his tongue had managed by now to offend even the Pope. He spoke his mind and spoke it loudly. '*I am not the best, Millie,*' he once confided in her, '*I am the best in any one given moment.*' People noticed Cynddelw. Eyes fixed on him when he came in. But Millie's reasons for helping out the bard were more to do with her than him. She was a woman running a business alone in a wild valley and at the end of the day when she looked out of her door at the moor rolling up and away and countenanced the manner of person that *might* be riding down towards her, having the bard and his band dawdle at her wine house seemed a comparatively light burden.

"Might I suggest one solution, Great One?"

It was that same plucky *cerrdor* speaking up as before; he seemed to have nominated himself as spokesperson for the group.

"What is it dear child?" Cynddelw smiled, but inside he was wincing. However soft he might have become in later life, he did not care to be upstaged by one of his own students.

"A solution, Great One, that will ensure we gain one of the most celebrated halls in Wales to rest within, and the chance to prove ourselves as the most accomplished of verse-makers."

Cynddelw could have predicted what came next; he had been pondering on how to prevent such a suggestion from being aired. But the truth was that there was no rational argument against it aside from the grudge he had nursed so long he was sometimes afraid it would bubble up above his good nature and consume him.

"The song contest of Lord Rhys ap Gruffyd of Deheubarth starts any day now in Cardigan: in a hall as big as a jousting field, and with bards from as far as the Kingdom of Sicily and the Norse lands competing. Even Meirion de Manche," the *cerrdor* added meaningfully, "could not provide such a prestigious platform on which to perform. For chairs will be assigned to the victors."

Chairs! Astonishment silenced the room; everyone's mind struggling to deduce how the *cerrdor* could know about the chairs. They had all been aware of the proclamation, gossip amongst minstrels spread fast, but the bit about the chairs had not been included in any version of the news. Where had the *cerrdor* been that they had not to hear that? Had he sneaked off to some tavern whilst they slept, teased a tale out of a traveller on the road without the rest of them noticing? Could he have resorted to rumour-mongering through desperation to be made a bard? A chair was not just a prize and it was not just a seat. It was a place at the table of a ruler's household. It was a share in that household's spoils from plunder and taxes. It was a position as that ruler's *pencerrd*: as his chief of song. And when that ruler was Lord Rhys ap Gruffyd, the most powerful prince in Wales, there was no greater honour at stake for a bard unless you were Cynddelw Bryddyd Mawr. If you were Cynddelw Bryddyd Mawr there was no greater displeasure.

The other *cerrdorion* debated in low voices; envy of their overly vocal fellow *cerrdor* ripening. How could one have the gall to mention Lord Rhys in the Great One's presence, let alone propose attending his court? The rift between them was legendary, and had become so embroidered with each subsequent telling no one knew the original cause any more. All anyone could say for certain was that Lord Rhys was the missing jewel in the Great One's crown, the one great Welsh prince he had not served as *pencerrd* during his lifetime. Then again, every living *pencerrd* of note had composed verses for Lord Rhys except for the Great One. It was a stand-off: the great schism of the bardic world. No one talked about it yet everybody *talked* about it. More to the point, the *cerrdorion* reproached themselves, why had they lacked the gall to voice any sort of suggestion? '*Where others hold back,*' the Great One had taught them, '*do not hold back. That is the way to gain notoriety.*' But look at them: they were little birds still stuck in the nest whilst the pluckiest of their number drew all the attention. He had even the Great One lost for words.

Cynddelw stroked his beard. It had become, in recent months, extraordinarily long and luscious, and now possessed the advantage of concealing his facial expression until you were looking directly at him. It gradually became apparent that, for the first time since the news of Meirion de Manche's abrupt departure, he was happy. In the face of adversity there was nothing else to be. Lord bloody Rhys. There were a few bones to pick clean there.

"Dear child," he said. "You are right. It gladdens me at least one of our band takes it upon himself to speak his mind. The festival starts, as you say, in a few days. There is not a moment to lose!"

The *cerrdor's* self-important smirk withered on his lips.

"I am honoured you approve my suggestion, Great One, but you surely do not mean to leave now, with dusk fallen?" He emitted a somewhat high-pitched laugh. No one without a death wish set out over the moors of Mid Wales at night.

"Approve?" boomed Cynddelw. "The idea is excellent!" He planted a firm kiss on each of Millie's cheeks. "Next time I pass this way, lovely Millicent, it will be to ask for your hand!" Millie laughed sarcastically, but little did she know he was in absolute earnest. He drew himself up to his not inconsiderable height, fastening his bear's cloak around him so that the head flopped over the top of his own. "Drink up, dear children! We leave this instant—bound for great things! Unless…" here, he looked hard at the pupil who had been rash enough to challenge him, eyes dancing. "Unless of course you are scared?"

Gwalchmai

(December, 1176)

GWALCHMAI AP MEILYR and Meilyr ap Gwalchmai came down out of the north onto the fertile plains of Deheubarth, sober and straight in their saddles. They were father and son, both bards just as Gwalchmai's father Meilyr had been and just as Meilyr's infant son Gwalchmai would no doubt become. Neither saw the need to introduce another name into their bloodline; 'Gwalchmai' and 'Meilyr' were to verse what Saint David was to the church. They did not flinch as they rode their horses onto the raft that carried them across the Dyfi, and they stayed mounted for the duration of the crossing. They resembled statues of men more than men. Once they had gained the far bank, paid their dues and become distant dots on the dunes, the ferryman involuntarily crossed himself. The driving rain affected father and son no more than it affected the gneiss hills of Gwynedd from whence they had come. Their pace remained constant. Their faces betrayed no emotion. They did not pause to converse or survey the way ahead or take shelter until they reached the church in Llanbadarn Fawr, where they knelt for a time to pray. Here, as they gave thanks to God, a difference could be observed between them. The older bard clasped his hands together fiercely, bending his head so far forward his forehead almost brushed the floor; the younger had his hands touching just lightly and looked more often at his father than he did at the altar.

What did they pray for? For the restoration of power to Gwynedd, back to how it had been in Prince Owain's heyday. Gwalchmai had served the prince as *pencerrd* up until the day Cynddelw Bryddyd Mawr wandered in surrounded by his usual band of ungodly sycophants and put on some prattling performance at a banquet that won Cynddelw chief of song and got Gwalchmai relegated to the role of *bard teulu*. It was Gwalchmai's belief the realm of Gwynedd had gone wrong right around then, and it was Meilyr's belief too because his father hammered in his views on all subjects in a manner that left no room for doubt.

Yes, the 1160s, they began so well and ended so woefully. Prince Owain had died as the decade closed. And his progeny proceeded to torment him from beyond the grave; his sons—products of unions universally condemned by the church—started killing or kidnapping each other in the succession squabbles that had raged now for each of the six years following his death. And the realm had crumbled as a result.

Cynddelw went skipping off to fresh pastures at the first sign of disharmony but not Gwalchmai ap Meilyr: he had stood by Gwynedd. No flighty itinerant he. He served each of Owain's successors even though they were illegitimates. Their failings as rulers were at least mitigated by the moral instruction he loaded into his poems until the things resembled sermons rather than songs. When he performed, it was less the after-dinner diversion and more the act of a priest eliciting Confession. The darker the times became for Gwynedd and the more words like 'incest' and 'inept' were associated with its princes, the more he knew his verse was the compass the realm needed to rectify its errant ways. Gwalchmai was reared in the snowy cwms of North Wales, and as he saw it he was defending them, not Gwynedd's current princes Rhodri and Dafydd; those two were no more than custodian rulers until the realm got a great leader once more[1]. *Dear God, restore Gwynedd to its supremacy of old, let this next new year be a new beginning, and let it begin with the men of Gwynedd returning home victorious from Rhys ap Gruffyd's festival of song.* Gwalchmai's hands were never clenched more fervently in orison than when he was having naughty thoughts. And this was the naughty thought he was having in the stumpy stone church of Llanbadarn Fawr that rain-swept December morning, just as the few paupers there were wondering whether he was worth begging from or not. *He deserved to win the song contest. It was his right. And it would be righteous of Rhys ap Gruffyd to proclaim him the winner.* He recognised the thought was wrong, but nevertheless it was such a neat and convenient phrase— *Gwalchmai deserves to win*—that he could not banish it either.

The immediate consequence of Gwalchmai having this thought was for him to spring from the altar in an eruption of remorse, dragging Meilyr to his feet at the same time. He strode back down the aisle, beating the beggars out of his path with the flat of his scabbard. His son hurried in his wake, giving the beaten men looks of apology. When they were on their horses and riding south again, Gwalchmai uttered his first word of the day.

"Heathens."

"Yes father," Meilyr said, although privately he thought that if begging in a house of God was what made one a heathen then the rich were always going to be devout, no matter what. *The rules of our world are defined by those afforded the luxury to sit down and make them*, he thought. "How long until we reach Llanddewi Brefi?"

---

1 Gwynedd was to gain just such a prince. As Gwalchmai knelt in the church that gloomy winter's day, in the hills of Snowdonia a child was growing up who would unite not only Gwynedd but all Wales under his rule. The chroniclers would—with some justification—come to call this infant Llywelyn Fawr (Llywelyn the Great).

"Dusk."

Gwalchmai ap Meilyr spoke sparingly, as always. Meilyr ap Gwalchmai sometimes thought that this was a very good thing.

Gwalchmai was convinced of the worth of competing in the song contest at Rhys ap Gruffyd's festival, but he had also planned the route there with the devotion of a pilgrim, and no pilgrim spurned the chance to stay at Llanddewi Brefi. Saint David had performed multitudinous miracles, but none as spectacular as making the ground around Llanddewi Brefi's church rise at the sides like an amphitheatre so that the crowds could see him preach. The Saint's staff was kept there to this day, and you could touch it for a penny or hold it for two. Gwalchmai had also heard of a cushion the holy man had reportedly sat upon whilst fatigued and was determined to sit upon it too, whatever the cost.

For the bard this visiting of the sites associated with Saint David—the most venerable man this land had known since the coming of Christianity—was certainly the closest to pleasure he would ever get, and he meant to maximise his time with each of the relics.

In his mind, these acts would serve one further purpose too.

If he stroked Saint David's staff and sat upon Saint David's cushion in the right way, without any omens occurring, then his triumph in the song contest was assured. The game Gwalchmai had been playing on the long ride from the north was what precisely would constitute an omen. Omens needed to be plausible occurrences: otherwise doing something omen-free was not remotely impressive. Equally, omens should not stand too high a likelihood of actually happening: otherwise the very venture you sought to straightforwardly legitimise risked becoming cursed. He eventually opted to compile two lists, one of good omens that, should they come to pass, would foretell his return from

Deheubarth as the song contest's victorious bard, and one of bad omens portentous of his defeat:

I win

Good omens:

1: As I pick up the staff, a bat swoops down from the rafters (Likely. There are always bats in these places.)
2: As I sit down on the cushion the priest sneezes. (Likely. Almost everyone in this infernal season has a cold.)
3: My son faints as we enter the church. (I could easily make that happen. He can faint like a girl. He might as well be of use to his father, and useful he has not yet been.)

I lose

Bad omens:

1: A flash of lightening as I touch the staff. (Not that likely. Although we live in stormy times.)
2: A beggar accosts me at the church door. (No beggar would dare.)
3: I trip over as I go to sit down on the cushion. (Unequivocally a bad sign. But my step will be steady.)

And so the journey passed, with Gwalchmai dividing up eventualities into white and black with rigour. By the time they reached Llanddewi Brefi, the only one he remained in any doubt about was the rain. In Gwynedd they had endured near enough forty days of it now. Should the Great Flood come, was that a good omen or a bad? Everything being wiped out, and all that dirt being washed off the face of the Earth, had always been a pleasing idea to Gwalchmai. He would have liked to be Noah, overseeing the rebirth of the human race. He could have taught it a thing or two.

Llanddewi Brefi was a small, tidy village, rather unlike its priest, an unkempt chub who had neither shaved nor washed in days and smelt of rancid fat from several paces off. Gwalchmai remained glowering in his saddle as the man ambled out to meet them and after one of the unspoken exchanges commonplace between father and son—in this case, a jab of Gwalchmai's gaze from Meilyr to the priest waddling in their direction—the junior bard alone dismounted to convey the demands of the senior.

"Will you not come in out of this wet to the lodging house?" the priest cried. "My boy will tend to your horses."

"My father desires to commence his devotions immediately," said Meilyr.

"All in good time! The light is failing us and I have had hot soup prepared. Today's rabbit, mind you," the priest ran his tongue along his lips as if this confirmed the meal would be a flavoursome one. "The others are already eating."

"What others?"

"The other guests. We are on the main road between north and south Wales, you know."

Gwalchmai cleared his throat, pointing to himself and Meilyr, and then drawing a circle in the air.

"We understood we were to be given private accommodation," Meilyr translated.

"Yes, well you see…"

"See to it. My father and I are in no need of soup."

The priest pulled his cassock up so that the collar became a hood against the driving rain, exposing a portion of his fleshy legs. Who did these pilgrims think they were? Royalty? And how could they stand there in this deluge after a day on the road, as if it were of no ado? Good God, there was no fun to one's Faith unless it could benefit from a bellyful of the body of Christ and a draft of the blood of Christ to quaff it with!

"Let me fetch you lamps," he muttered. "Seeing as it is dinner, you will have the church to yourselves."

Now Gwalchmai got down from his horse.

He swept back his mane of iron-grey hair, holding his cupped hands out to the rain then dabbing his head in various places almost as if he were anointing himself. Meilyr followed his example but made the ritual—if ritual it was—seem far less grand. They shook the droplets from their cloaks and made the sign of the cross against their chests. Without a word of thanks, they took the lamps from the priest, who in turn presented them with a large, burnished key.

"The staff is in a locked case in the apse. There is a hole in the case if you just want a touch. But you two do not seem like touchers. You seem like holders."

He took six silver pennies from them, two each for a hold of the staff, one for lighting their lamps and another because he would suffer no qualms of conscience over squeezing such grim travellers out of additional coinage.

Meilyr spared the priest a nod. Gwalchmai ignored him, but not any longer out of disdain. No. He was already transported. Saint David's spirit was close. In the tangled churchyard yews he sensed the man's presence. With trembling hand he felt the damp stonework around the church door; gripped the latch; thought about the Saint trailing his fingers over those same surfaces. Inside, he held the guttering light to the walls and saw ancient crosses propped there inscribed in Ogham, the language of the early saints. Now his pulse raced. His eyes swept up the nave and there behind the altar was the case. He approached penitently, knelt a respectful distance before and continued to the case on hands and knees. He did not notice how poorly maintained the church interior was, given the number of visiting pilgrims and the fee they had to part with to see the staff, nor how the keyhole and door hinges on the case were rather rusty. His only thought was for what was within. And out it fell anticlimactically into his grasp: a knobbly stick. Quite a small one, too, given Saint David had performed miracles with it. Gwalchmai was undeterred. He grasped the staff in both hands and held it aloft and as he did so there was a squeak and a bat swooped down from the rafters. The first and foremost of his good omens! He wanted to laugh and throw his arms around his son, but realised doing either would appear absurdly unnatural. Instead he solemnly passed the staff to Meilyr who held it waveringly, like an inexperienced serving wench might proffer a platter of food to a visitor of renown.

"Father?"

"Yes my son?" Gwalchmai struggled to keep the quaver of emotion from his voice.

"Might I go and get some soup now?"

"Yes my son," the elder bard said magnanimously. "We have come far this day."

And that naughty thought stole back into Gwalchmai's mind, not as a whisper in the dark anymore, more as a blazing torch to wield high above his head. *Gwalchmai deserves to win.*

Across in the lodging house, the priest phlegmatically cleared the remnants of dinner. Happily, guests were beginning to bed down for the night. It was a full house, mainly pilgrims, but also three mercenaries en route to England because of the better rates and a group of spice traders whose mealtime jest was that they had never enjoyed such flourishing business as in this land of bland food. The jest was slightly drawn out, the priest thought, given that he had seasoned the rabbit soup liberally, but one developed a tolerance of passers-by when they bolstered church coffers so amply. Coffers, he giggled, which one could justifiably appropriate for one's wine cellar and claim it was in the name of hospitality if challenged. But challenges seldom came. Archbishops, bishops, bah! They preferred fancier churches and better relics. To have a staff as a draw was not bad, but it could hardly compare to the saintly body parts some places of pilgrimage could boast and long let it be so: he was content with his slice of the pie as it was. Tonight's lot had been decent enough at table: none of the breaking of crockery, spilling of drink or other improper acts that it had fallen upon him to clean up in the past. He was soon done with the tidying and, pouring out a generous cup of wine, he went to join in the dice game the mercenaries were playing. Truth be told, he felt more comfortable down here with the commoners rather than in the upstairs quarters saved for special guests. He got lucky with his first few throws. The wine induced a warm, comfortable feeling. His duties as host slipped from the forefront of his thoughts.

Gwalchmai remained in the church after Meilyr had gone to get soup, thinking of Saint David. Now he had the Saint's blessing, he permitted himself to visualise the man: had he ever, instead of preaching to his congregation, sometimes wished to run to the closest cliff and scream into the crashing emptiness? The old bard swivelled round in irritation as the church door reopened; he already regarded this church as his personal sanctum, and any disturbance therefore was an affront.

"Father," said Meilyr. "There is a man in our bed."

Gwalchmai's natural expression was a deeply furrowed one and it was difficult to gauge the effect of this latest news upon him at first. He sighed, leaving his communion with Saint David reluctantly for the considerations of the now. He had organised the particulars of their journey south weeks in advance, courtesy of

Gwynedd's best messenger and at great expense. The stipulations had been plainly set down and sent and agreement to these terms had been sent back:

'Recipients of this notice are adjured by the highest authorities in Gwynedd, Princes Rhodri and Dafydd, and by God's grace, to accommodate Gwalchmai their court's pencerrd and Meilyr his son in a style befitting their elevated status as craftsmen of song, on their travels south during the third week of Advent to perform at the much anticipated festival of the Lord Rhys, Prince of Deheubarth.'

Gwalchmai despaired of his son. Meilyr brought the most foolproof arrangements into disarray. They were to be given lodgings separate from other wayfarers just as nobles might expect: so had it been written in no uncertain words. How *could* there be someone else in their bed? He got to his feet in order to demonstrate to Meilyr exactly how to remedy the situation, pointing at his scabbard then clasping both hands together and swiping them through the air in clear representation of a weapon making contact.

"It is best you come father. He will not be moved."

Gwalchmai inclined his head: so be it. But woe betide he or she that should force the bard into an interaction not of his choosing.

He followed his son across to the lodging house, absorbed the scene—the guests haphazardly strewn around the room like so many pieces of ship's cast-offs upon a beach, snoring off their supper, and the priest and mercenaries in indecently high spirits—and snorted his disapproval. Despite rising fury at the unwelcome intruder in his chamber, he had time to wonder, thunderstruck, how many of the Ten Commandments were being broken before his eyes. He ascended the steps to the floor saved for guests of nobler stock, squeezing the hilt of his dagger and seething. The atmosphere was as if the night's storm had blustered in with him. Bard he might be, but afraid to defend himself with arms he was not; he had fought with the princes of Gwynedd on a number of campaigns and had written a poem ensuring each was engrained upon collective memory. He thrust open the door to the upper quarters and saw an angular, gangling man in clerical garb, rummaging through a bulky traveller's trunk and humming to himself.

"Merciful Heaven!" the man turned with an amused look that could not quite be described as a smile. "So there *are* two of you, how snug tonight will be now! Would you kindly shut the door? My books dislike the draft."

Even the most stirred of souls, as Gwalchmai near enough was at that moment, would have felt obliged to slacken grip on his weapon upon such an encounter. It was hardly that the man taking up all four of the available beds with his luggage exuded a feeling of calm; it was more that the old bard felt shame at having made so violent an entrance, as if this had exposed a failing of his to negotiate with words.

Gwalchmai stood just inside the threshold, speechless and inwardly raging. Meilyr slipped into the room behind, closing the door delicately after him. The other man effected another mild upturning of his lips, as if at something humorous no one else could possibly fathom, and resumed his previous task. This, the two bards now saw, was the painstaking arrangement into piles of the books and manuscripts jumbled across the quarters they had believed to be theirs and theirs only for the night. This he did absorbedly and absolutely without hurry, producing a dainty handkerchief with which to dust each volume like a librarian alone with his library rather than a traveller preventing others from getting to their beds. Several moments—although they felt an eternity—passed like this. Meilyr helped himself to a ladleful of soup from the pot the priest had left, acutely aware of his father's anger and hoping for everyone's sake the tension might lift soon. And the man did presently seem to comprehend the obstruction he was causing. He swung his legs from the far side of his bed to the near, and faced the bards properly. His feet were bare and his toes were very long and delicate and white.

"How remiss of me," the man stood, so tall his head and especially the wiry hair sprouting out around his tonsure, brushed the beams. "We might as well be introduced if we are to spend the night together. I am Giraldus—forgive me, you doubtless do not speak Latin—call me Gerald," he held out his hand.

Gwalchmai's arms stayed rigid at his sides but Meilyr was quick, for the sake of a quiet night, to return the greeting.

"We speak Welsh," the younger bard said gravely, "which is the language of the land you now find yourself in. And when called for, the tongue of your land England too."

Gerald laughed.

"Lord above us, my good man, I only wish I was an Englishman! My life's endeavours would have been so much the easier! No, I am Gerald of Wales," he said these last words with an air of mystery, as if he were introducing a much-anticipated act at a provincial fair. "The accent suggests otherwise I grant you—time spent overseas, you see—but the lilt never *quite* leaves one's voice. And you are both minstrels I presume?"

This provoked two reactions in Meilyr. He was intrigued, for how could anyone have guessed so near to the mark? His father and he carried no instruments, and the little conversation between them this evening that could have been overheard had been devout in nature, without an inkling of gaiety. But he was also his father's son ,and he took further offence at the attitude of this Gerald of Wales where he had already taken a significant amount, this time at the crass reference to 'minstrels'.

"We are bards," he said, vexed at needing to explain the difference. Would a bishop suffer being called a priest? "My father here, Gwalchmai ap Meilyr, has served Prince Owain of Gwynedd as *pencerrd* and now serves his heir Prince Rhodri and I, Meilyr ap Gwalchmai, will one day continue in his stead."

"Oh," Gerald humoured him. "Bards."

"Bards who have been on the road since daybreak and wish to sleep in their beds."

"Why did you not say before?" Gerald, with a sigh at this disruption to the order he had imposed, fussily removed his books from the two furthest beds so that all his belongings now lay teetering in a heap on the third. "If you would not mind taking the two at the end? It is not that I object to sleeping alongside bards, certainly not *men of Gwynedd*. But books are one's friends and so much more interesting than most people one meets. One must keep one's knowledge close," he added confidentially. And again he commenced his humming, a toneless rendition of a Gregorian chant which did little to lift the mood.

The bards moved frostily to their allotted beds. Gwalchmai still said nothing, yet was saying everything by the way in which he gave Gerald the widest berth possible. Even Rhys ap Gruffyd, Gwalchmai thought, would not refer to himself as 'of Wales' and he was the mightiest prince within it. But something this brazen churchman had said caused the older bard's broodings to take a certain tangent. Gerald. The name was familiar. A staunchly Norman name: he would not have heard it in Gwynedd. A southern Welsh name, from Dyfed or Gower or one of those petty principalities Deheubarth long since conquered. The farce surrounding the St David's bishopric a few months back, that was it. The see had become free and it was a Gerald unanimously nominated as the successor only for the King to deem the choice unacceptable. A less popular and experienced candidate had been given the Royal seal of approval, but Gerald had controversially protested and the thing had become very awkward. There were few enough amongst the living who would dare defy Henry Plantagenet; could the long-shanked cleric before him be one and the same Gerald? In the only language he was certain the churchman would not comprehend—sign language—he instructed his son to find out.

Meilyr, who had reluctantly taken the bed between his father and Gerald and was already drifting into a doze, sat snap upright.

"My father wishes to know whether you are the Gerald recently rejected as Bishop of St David's."

If Gerald was irritated, he did not show it.

"Benevolent Lord, news does reach the provinces speedily these days! 'Rejected' my good man is one means of looking at it. No bishop has yet been definitively appointed and every man with a meaningful say on the subject speaks in my favour except for the King... in any case, I am already charged with overseeing one of this country's finest cathedrals," he hesitated for full effect. "Brecon."

"Oh," Meilyr did not normally attempt witty rejoinders and could only put this one down to being caught in the pace of the moment. "Brecon. Where is that exactly?"

Without preamble, Gwalchmai began to laugh. It was a splutter of a sound at first, a cartwheel straining out of a rut, but soon became a steady cackle. And it was infectious. Gerald's face also creased up, although whether this was in mirth or in connivance to engineer the situation to his advantage was hard to ascertain.

Meilyr, looking from one to the other of them like a child, laughed too.

"Blessed Mary and the Saints, could I tell you some stories about Brecon!" Gerald exclaimed. "It must be the most hard-working place in Wales! Anywhere else peasants would be glad of the Sabbath to take repose and thank God for the rest. In Brecon, these sorry churls station themselves around the grounds of the cathedral and *mime* the labours they are engaged in during the week! Imagine it! There is the farmhand, doing a dance as if in the motion of scything corn, there is the milkmaid, crouching and moving her hands in mimicry of the squeezing of udders and pouring of pails she has to do every other day anyway! You, my good man, with your ingenious use of gesticulation, would fit into the scene admirably," the churchman paused to smile innocently at Gwalchmai.

"The point I am making is that we all have something branded on us that says who we are and what we are. Take at random ten men freshly enlisted to an army and one can tell which was the smith, which the jester, which the blathering idiot. Take a room of guests relaxing at an inn and I can discern which are bards just as you could no doubt perceive I am a man of God whether I wear this lovely lambs wool cassock or nothing whatsoever. Lord of our skies, some even say I have the *nose* of a bishop! I think it more aquiline myself but I digress: the church is in me, and if a profession is in one, you see, one cannot help but rise to the top of it sooner or later.

And if you are bards, you are certainly bound for my cousin's castle at Cardigan? For that little gathering he is having over Christmas?"

"Yes..." Meilyr began, but his father was starting to say something at the same moment, so he fell silent.

"You are the cousin of Rhys ap Gruffyd?" Gwalchmai asked tightly. He was quite recovered from his laughing fit now.

"The younger better-looking version," Gerald grinned. "As a point of mild interest, I am on my way to Cardigan tomorrow to have a word with him on the very subject of hastening along my appointment as Bishop. Endure and persist, as Ovid says! Rhys has the King's ear for some strange reason, you know. My cousin strives to be good at a specific number of things and I grant you he excels at each. Battles: good. Diplomacy: good. Entertaining: very very good. But I cannot help but feel he is going to get thwacked over the back of the head by his insistence on adhering to Welsh law: just like your Prince Owain. Look at the shambles your Gwynedd is in because of the number of children *he* sired! *Of course* they all started infighting once he was gone! And Deheubarth will go the same way eventually. My cousin's offspring are in the double figures already: they will all feel they have a claim to a piece of his realm and legally they very well might. The moral, my good men, is relish the now! We live in a time of peace but history— and the chronicles back me in this—is vastly outweighed by bloodshed and barbarity. If there is a festival of song on and one is able to sing tolerably, one should go along and sing at it, because a Welshman or a Norman or even one of those Flemish folk one sees everywhere these days might arrive at any moment, raze the walls and roof above us to the ground and spark the next war."

Meilyr, out of demand, was falling asleep but Gwalchmai was fixing Gerald with his eagle's stare and soaking in the cleric's every word.

Often, at court in Gwynedd, people would be seeking Gwalchmai and he could not be found. Prince Rhodri might be bawling for a bard, but if Gwalchmai was off on one of his walks, Royal demand for a verse or snippet of wisdom would be put on hold until he returned from whatever wild tract of countryside he had decided to traverse that day. Where did he walk? Valleys, mountains, it did not matter. Where paths petered out he forged his own. In the countryside was simplicity; he strode through it with the speed and resolve of a young man and no thing was an obstacle to him. It was the talk back in civilisation that could confound him. He was one to mull each thought over, like a cow chewing cud, before voicing it and he was no match for Gerald's deft conversation. He did not know if he was a source of comedy or of intrigue to the cleric but those four words—*Gwalchmai deserves to win*—were bounding about inside his brain again, more intensely now than before. And Gerald could help him to victory: he knew.

"It appears we both desire Rhys ap Gruffyd to grant us something," Gwalchmai said. And as he did so one hand instinctively slipped under his cloak to the parchment inscribed with the notice from Prince Rhodri, hung around his neck in a leather holdall. It made him feel that he had princely sanction for the deceitful proposal he was about to make. "We could assist each other."

Gerald waggled a finger as if to say: wait. The cleric lit another couple of candles, so that the balance of light shifted to his side of the room, sat cross-legged on the top end of his bed and beckoned to Gwalchmai, patting the mattress invitingly.

Gwalchmai frowned. He peered at Meilyr. Asleep. *Dear God, thank you for keeping my son in ignorance of this.* The dozen or so paces to Gerald's bed already felt a betrayal. He sat down stiffly on a corner of the mattress. *I am only hearing what this churchman has to say,* he told himself. *We are just two people talking late on a winter's night.*

"Much better," Gerald said softly. "Now my good man. Before we go any further with this, I think you should come clean with me."

"What do you mean?" Gwalchmai's voice was hoarse.

"Why are you really going to Cardigan?"

"As you guessed. To attend Rhys ap Gruffyd's festival."

"My good man, I do not doubt that you intend to *go*. The proclamation does state, after all, that it will be the greatest festival this land or any other has ever known. Saints preserve us, what words! My cousin must have had his bard's assistance in the writing of them! And doubtless you mean to enter that contest between all the songsters too… why not indeed?" Gerald leaned forward. "But I know when someone is concealing something under their tunic."

Reticently, Gwalchmai produced the parchment from his holdall.

"Here. There it is in ink. The hand of Prince Rhodri of Gwynedd confirms what I say is true."

Gerald's eyes skimmed the lines. '*Adjure,*' '*by God's grace.*' These princes of Wales certainly loved grand language.

"Interesting," he returned the document. "But I was referring more to the other parchment you have in your pouch. The one with the seal that appears to have been amateurishly broken."

Who did the cleric think he was, prying into other people's papers? Gwalchmai choked back his fury, for he was furious mainly with himself at so carelessly revealing his secret. This man observed every little thing.

But he no longer had a choice. Trembling, he pulled out the second parchment. The churchman was examining the bard from beneath his eyebrows, which met in the middle of his forehead in a dark, unbroken line. Gwalchmai felt he was being judged. *Strive to enter at the strait gate, for many, I say unto you, will seek to enter in and shall not be able*[1]. His breath came in snatches, like he was

---

1 Luke 13:24. Gwalchmai ap Meilyr was familiar with the Bible—particularly its passages concerned with securing entry into Heaven—and with no other book whatsoever. Nevertheless, this was one book more than most people of his time would have been acquainted with.

being slowly asphyxiated. Such was the power guilt had. He must unload his burden. That was the only way, his only hope of making it through that gate.

In the end, it was difficult to say whether it was Gwalchmai that surrendered the document, or the churchman that eased it out of his hand.

Gerald unrolled the second parchment, the one that Prince Rhodri of Gwynedd had intended to be delivered directly into the hand of Lord Rhys of Deheubarth without its contents being read by anyone else.

"Oh!" his eyebrows arched. "Oh dear."

No-Man's-Land

(DECEMBER, 1176)

BARELY A DIP and a twist out of sight of town and the guards' self-important strut became almost a tiptoe, as if they were scared of waking whatever it was they imagined lurked in the quickly thickening woods at the wayside. Normans had laid crushed stone over the first few miles of road but soon enough the going became much muddier. Here the guards decided their work was done: they threw a few departing jibes and turned back, leaving the exiled entertainers to carry on alone.

Although the group, now un-chaperoned, could have splintered into its ones or twos along the differing routes such types take in the Christmas season in Wales—to castles, to churches, to great halls or grim hovels— they did not do so immediately. As if bound together through being outcasts they continued together to the border. In a motley ensemble that rose raucously through the cold and swiftly clouding-over afternoon, many chose to practise the skills of their trade along the way. They swallowed fire, they juggled, they sung songs, they jousted with wooden lances. Some swapped tales of patrons worth approaching or avoiding. Some, like Avery, said nothing, although because this was a throng of performers and professional tricksters they mostly loved to speak and those among their company who chose to remain silent soon stuck out. But Avery could not speak. He was at least partly responsible for the deaths of several guards in the employ of one of the leading Marcher lordships, and needed little imagination as to what kind of repercussions he would face if caught. And even though Dog had got them into this mess, Avery did wonder what had happened to him. The musician was not such a bad sort. He glanced along the line of entertainers trudging through the mud; most of them looked like they would sell their own mothers for a free meal and betray a wanted criminal for far less. Dog, however gruff he might be, was trustworthy.

Wales announced itself with a moss-covered milestone leaning drunkenly against a tree stump. It was tradition amongst those on the road to tend such markers when possible, to remove any undergrowth and to re-etch the destinations written on them if need be. But by the condition of this stone, either travellers on this route were few or they passed by with other things weighting their minds. Avery knelt, scraping back the moss and brambles with his knife.

"Are you mad?" another entertainer asked sharply. "This is no place to stop. These woods brim with brigands!"

"We would want it done for us, friend," Avery replied. And then he gave a start. The cleared stone did have a word carved near the base, but it was no destination. 'Death,' it said.

He got up and hurried on. He had achieved his ulterior aim anyway, which was to drop towards the back of the group inconspicuously. That Marcher lord's men would be along after them soon enough, and would be looking for revenge. However unsafe the woods and moors away from the highway might be, staying with this horde of performers was far more so. He furtively scanned the wayside, waiting for his chance. Ahead the road bent hard left and to the right beforehand was a break in the birch woods, a gully that ascended steeply onto the moorland visible in patches above. This was his opportunity. Heart thumping so loud a prayer it would not be heard by the others passed his lips, he dawdled to the very rear. Then as unnoticeably as he had joined this band of outcasts he stole away from them. Not one of them so much as turned around.

But unbeknownst to Avery, his actions had not gone unobserved. Concealed within the trees was another figure who had been watching him for some time and who now, as he scampered uphill, began to follow him.

Avery climbed, lost in contemplation, thinking of his family. He had stout men for brothers; plain-speaking men with colour in their cheeks and cracks on their hands. His sisters married similar types too. He, the youngest of the family, had turned out so fair, like a sickle moon. The professions his siblings or their partners had entered—the blacksmiths, the carpenter's—he had no talent for. The heat of the forge made him feel faint. His chairs collapsed the moment they were sat upon. So he underwent the lot of younger sons for whom other careers are out of the question, and turned to the church. His parents sighed in relief as they delivered him there, for their last-born had caused them considerable consternation and at long last was entering respectable employment, angelic but feckless Avery, it was so kind of the cathedral to take him in. Kind! The canons had enquired of his mother and father what exactly he might bring to the house of God. His father, after a hesitation: '*I am known for my honesty, and Avery has that in his blood if nothing else.*' His mother: '*Our son has few practical skills but a spiritual nature and we thought Your Reverences might put him to better use in here than we ever could out there.* The canons conferred, unconvinced; his parents had hardly extolled his virtues. They asked Avery if he wished to add anything in his favour. He had only been thirteen, and shy. He had opened his mouth and all that came out was what he had heard drifting from behind the cathedral walls he had paused outside whilst supposedly engaged on other errands: the chants of the canons. He had no knowledge of Latin back then, but a strong memory for the things that interested him, and there was something enthralling in the otherworldly songs of the church. He sung with the deepness of a man yet with the whimsy of a boy, with a cadence that transported the canons from despair to delight to frenzy and gave no pause in-between for them to collect themselves. *Credo in unum Deum, Patrem omnipotentem*, he had no idea what the words of Mass meant but to him they were entities in their own right, the syllables were mountains or valleys, and he was running up and down them unrestrained. He sung the devotional words of the canons back at them like an echo returns a voice many times richer than when it left the speaker's lips. And when he was done, the men of York cathedral could only murmur that they would of course be pleased to accept him into their custody. As for his mother and father, they were dumbfounded. They had looked upon him before as a dreamer and a good-for-nothing respectively. Not any longer. It had come to farewells. His father: a pat on the shoulder and a smile that had seemed more like a frown. His mother had taken his cheeks in her hands. '*Do you remember the story I used to tell you about the harp, son, the instrument tuned so fine it needed no human but only the wind as its player? Your voice then made me think of it. I always knew...*' then she had turned away, as people do when they hide their sadness, and Avery never found out what it was she had always known. Not a month later his parents were burned alive in a fire some children started as a prank. But he often tacked on imagined words to complete that long-ago sentence: '... how special you were,' '...you would make us both proud.'

He reflected on what they might think of him now, a man alone in a land fraught with danger as he was, fending for himself. He was not quite the whey-faced thing he had been.

"And He shall come again with glory to judge the living and the dead," he sang again the Credo he had sung to the canons all those years before. Now he had learned the meaning of the words he saw just how meaningless they were. "Of His Kingdom there will be no end... and I believe in the Holy Spirit, the Lord, and Giver of Life..." The lines of the liturgy could be the happiest in the world or they could be the saddest. He sang louder, the sound someone makes when they wish to drown out other sounds, for he was becoming aware of the distance he had come up into the thick of the woods and how the cloud had come down to meet him. Each creak the trees gave was more ominous now. He had become distracted. And he had become lost. "I await the resurrection of the dead... and the life of the world to come..." he tailed off. He could have sworn he had heard derisive laughter, coming from close by.

"Gloomy words. And by my faith this is a solemn enough spot without them."

Avery turned. Melancholy as he had been feeling, he could not resist a slight grin. Dog. His tunic was more in tatters than on their last encounter and one of his eyes was blackening into an ugly bruise but otherwise the musician appeared in remarkably fine fettle.

"I had given you up for dead, friend."

"You wouldn't be the first," Dog laid down his harp and stood, arms folded, scrutinising Avery. "Not a bad cloak. And your shoes almost match."

"I wish I could say the same for your eyes."

"Apothecary's apprentices are too busy to spend much time

practising how to throw a proper punch. The apothecary, on the other hand, found his target... but not before I'd dealt them all some knuckle marks they'll remember."

"But how did you evade the guards?"

"Cheap cloth," Dog replied, pointing to the tears in his tunic. "Rips when you grab it. I left the fellow who tried apprehending me a fistful as a keepsake, which I thought mighty generous given I've but the one change of clothes. Then led them all a merry dance through the back streets," he paused, wistfulness in his voice. "Always pays, acquainting yourself with back streets."

Avery coloured, not liking to dwell on what obscene reasons Dog might have had for loitering in back streets and yet wanting to dwell on it just a little.

"In any case, friend, I am glad you made it out. These are no woods to be alone in. And I am but recently arrived at the conclusion I am lost."

Dog leaned his hands on his knees, as if in part-concession to a need to rest.

"Bard in the making, you are: taking twenty words to get out what most say in two. The trick in Wales is to keep eyes on your goal whilst the cloud lets you," he pointed up, in a significantly different direction from that Avery had been heading in. "That way lies the moor and that's the best route for two men fallen foul of the law. I take it you're still set on attending this festival?"

Avery thought a moment. Visions of the choirmaster and canons and cathedral spiralled in his mind's eye, the stone and beams and glass of the building caving in on each other until the image became rubble from under which his mother, trapped in the wreckage, repeated the words '*I always knew*' and a harp that needed no player played the antiphons, the canticles, the hymns and the songs of scripture and every melody the church ever did inspire more exquisitely than any choir could hope to have sung them. And so beautiful was the song that it became a new form of song, never beheld before, a whirlpool into which you gladly plunged and allowed yourself to be carried away.

"Still set."

Dog nodded, shouldered his harp and led the way, on up through the mud.

The trees, last leaves of autumn still just clinging to them, gradually thinned. A freezing fog gathered. The russet moor that struck right through the heart of Wales reared up, sopping as a sponge and barren as Hell.

"The moor of Berwyn," Dog said, stopping to let Avery catch up. "So dire a place even King Henry gave up as he set foot upon it and turned around for England."

"I heard of that time. When Wales rose up as one and repelled the English[1]."

"Wales and the weather together. King Henry thought if he attacked with a great enough army he would surely conquer us. But Gwynedd and Powys and Deheubarth united, and we cut the King's forces down on these very moors again and again however many times they came at us. But it was the weather that crushed them. It rained more that summer than it had ever rained. Most men can't fight in weather like that. Not for long. But we Welsh can, and we did. After that was when the great peace began," Dog looked at Avery with a gleam of mockery. "Peace seems to be your King's policy… whilst he stands no chance of winning the war."

"You said 'we'," Avery observed. "So you are Welsh?"

"My father is Lord Rhys' favourite fiddler. You don't get any more Welsh than that."

---

1   The Battle of Crogen, 1165. It was the first time in history the rival realms of Wales could be said to have put aside their differences and united to defeat a foreign invader, in this case Henry II (Henry Plantagenet) himself.

"You embarrass me, friend," Avery hung his head. "There I was, rhapsodising about this castle of stone and its festival of marvels and it seems all along it has been your place of residence. You must think me foolish indeed."

"On the contrary," Dog stared into the mist. "I've not been back there in years. My father and I are not on speaking terms."

An awkward silence descended. It was colder now, and darker.

"We should carry on," said Dog abruptly. "These moors are much less treacherous to spend the night within than woods. Even brigands stay away from Berwyn."

Avery regarded his companion dubiously.

"Stepping out into the middle of the moor in this mist, friend, recalls to my mind the last bold plan you had, and that, as I recollect, resulted in six rather gruesome deaths."

Dog made a sound like he was syphoning spittle around inside his mouth, puffing out and sucking in his cheeks. Avery had heard it before, just prior to him slipping the potion into those guards' drinks. It was a sound signifying Dog was set upon a particular course of action.

"We can part company if you want. Then you can bed down in the woods with all the brigands you wish."

"No… we should stay together. Only…"

"Yes?"

"You have travelled across this moor before, you say?"

"Once or twice."

"In such conditions?"

"And worse," Dog tore up a clump of ferns, using the stems to delicately wipe in-between and along each string of his harp. The instrument looked spotless even though Dog, like Avery, was plastered in the filth of the road from his shoes to the tops of his shins.

"So tell me this, friend. What is it about you that whilst robbers and murderers shrink away from crossing this moor, you stride out across it so fearlessly?"

"Brigands have their superstitions, like lots of us," Dog said. "When they see a land where not much grows, where few men live or so much as go without very good reason, tales take root. Tales about fairies. Tales about mysterious types who appear to travellers worn half way to death by the wilderness and invite them to a hidden hall where they might rest, and warm themselves, and feast, but from where no living soul returns…" he broke off, noting Avery's perturbed expression. "How I differ from them is that I think it's all horseshit."

Avery laughed uneasily.

"Very well, friend. You lead. I will be close behind."

Dog grunted his assent and started off over the open land, over the blasted scrub and bog of Berwyn, moor of the damned.

Immediately, other shapes emerged from the fog: a tall figure, a long stick. The stick made sharp, sickening contact with the side of Dog's head. Avery saw his companion kneel then slump facedown into the sludge, lifeless. Then, with a movement the mist seemed to slow, the same stick sailed towards him. Just as he lost consciousness he heard something else too; a shriek:

"Got the Devils!"

The Whore

(NOVEMBER, 1176)

ON HER SCARLET SILK PILLOWS she was a queen; *the* Queen of the Holy Roman Empire; the merchants and the garrison and the churchmen and the lawmakers and most male members of the Royal Family itself were at her mercy. The bed was her throne. With her touch—and sometimes less than that— she made or broke a man. Her greatest love was the power of inversion: twisting her client's hopes and fears and playing them out. She whipped cavalryman until they whinnied like their horses; she forced priests to kneel before her and confess. But what should she make of the man before her now? Normally she gauged within moments exactly *what* a man was. Soldiers had a certain gait, traders were invariably brisk and brought their money out early, the most powerful men that visited her were also those with most to lose and they showed it, trembling even weeping during the act. And through knowing a man she could work out how to satisfy him. But the rotund foreigner in her chamber this evening was an enigma. She had entertained men with darker skin and stranger dress. Yet all of them—locals and travellers from distant lands alike—had come to her with one thing in common. They had wanted to get on with it. More time meant more money and this was never truer than in a brothel.

This bald man, his gaudy robes fastened by a sash that, her magpie's eye noticed, was interwoven with cloth of gold, seemed to have an abundance of time.

"Wondrous interior decoration, my dear," he glanced appreciatively around, taking in the damasks and the ermine furs, the carafe of wine on the bedside table carved in crystal from the lands of Saladin, the candles made with the wax of Bavarian bees, the shows of finery she surrounded herself with to make her surreptitious visitors believe they were in the presence of a fine lady. "Did you choose the designs yourself?"

It seemed he might be trying to break down her guard. She had never allowed any man to do that. Her work was an act and she was the most adept of actresses.

"They are but mementos, sir. Of men who have come to me, and got what they wished for, and who have in the happiness I helped them feel for a while decided to buy me a gift to remember them by."

"And do you?" asked the man, curiously. "Do you remember them?"

"Many are not memorable. The very wealthy or handsome have no need of me whilst the poor and ugly could never hope to have me. It is average men, sir, which I receive here. There are exceptions of course," she turned deliberately to the side so that her yellow hair fell over her shoulder. Foreign men liked fair hair. "There are those that lodge more firmly in my memory."

"Yes, yes," the man nodded. "There must be, my dear." There was a chair facing the bed, a heavy old thing that she used mainly for restraining those clients she believed would benefit from it. The man sat down. He was not, she thought, someone who could or should be restrained. But she opened up all her customers in the end, one way or another. The pleasure could only begin then, when they had surrendered themselves and lay defeated on the sheets. Every one of them possessed a dark little fantasy: something she could enslave them with. With this one there was just more work required to coax out whatever that was.

"This room," the man said, "reminds me of my homeland. It is the exotic fruit perhaps. However do you procure such fruit in these cold northern climes?"

"Ours is a prosperous city. We find the means to get what we want. And what of you, sir? What is it that you want so badly you venture this far from your home in search of it?" She was sliding down the bed towards him, inch by inch, a serpent closing in on its prey. "I am quite sure there are those like me in the place from whence you came," she whispered.

The man picked through a platter of fruit, selecting one with which he was evidently not familiar.

"I have beheld orange trees shooting from rooftops, and lines of rose-pink figs longer and wider than the ranks of all the legions Rome could have assembled at the apex of its might," he marvelled. He held the apple up in admiration, as if it was the world itself he was turning around on its axis with his portly fingers, then swallowed the fruit, all of it, in a few gulps. "But never have I feasted on such a sweet green sphere as this, not in all the manifold lands I journeyed through! My compliments," he wiped the juice from his jowls, "On your array of fruits. Even a man from the luscious lands of the far Southeast can appreciate their quality. The truth of the matter, my dear, is that 'wants' are the one luxury I cannot at any cost afford. He who so amply pays my way has set a course for me in stone and I am compelled to traipse it to the very end..." A familiar spasm shot up the side of his face and the tick asserted control. It plagued him most when as now he was under duress and he could not say if this latest bout was because of the unhappy task he had been charged with or because of the girl with the striking yellow hair sidling alluringly towards him. "Even if I should balk at the task," he finished.

"You know," she said softly, "that some call me a seer? I see such things! And not because of any gift of second sight," her dress followed the fashion of highborn Frenchwomen, hugging tight to the contours of her body and yet fastened just partially so that no more than a practised flick made it fall away entirely. And she wore no chemise beneath. Her breasts, long and full, hung close to her client's fat face. "I see your torment," she said.

The man looked at her glazedly. This was the point at which the feelings of remorse about the wife came, in her experience.

"It is the barbarity," he whispered. "That is what grinds me down, realm upon realm of senseless, relentless barbarity. So has it been upon the road from whence I have come. Yes, yes, there are rare pockets in-between where the people appear to aspire to more sublime things. But they are pockets. No sooner do I repose myself in such pockets—and to be sure, my dear, I include your city as one of these—and forget the sufferings of this world, than I am back out of the next city gate and into the suffering again. It seems to be kill or be killed, my dear, in my homeland and across the Byzantine Empire and here too, which inclines me to believe that whether we are Muslims or Christians it makes precious little difference…"

He stretched forward out of the chair towards her but she pulled back, teasing, triumphant.

"It is becoming clearer what you are, sir. You are a philosopher."

"I was, my dear, once upon a time. Now I am a scourge."

"Sir! Should I be alarmed?" she asked in mock fright, keeping him near yet still not letting him too close.

He smiled, possibly in acknowledgement of what he had got himself into, at what outstanding manner of woman the Sultan's money could buy in a sophisticated city like this.

"I am passing through, my dear. You need not fear. But there is a land not far to the northwest of here that should. I did not choose to go through with this, but go through with it I must," he added quietly, and his eyes, sad as a cow's, did seem to her to yearn to be understood. "I would like you to know that."

"Go through with what, sir?"

"Why, with the killings," the man said.

She had a look that she wore when she did not want anyone to guess what she was thinking and she wore it now as she regarded him, carefully. He could not be a murderer, surely not, for she had entertained enough murderers and they had been nothing like this. No. Wearied by the road he could be and addled as a result he might be but that, she thought, was probably the extent of it.

"I see no killer before me, sir," she said. She poured two large glasses of wine, sensational Tuscan wine from the south of the Empire, draining hers at a single draught. What a vast empire this was, and she was Queen of it, the most sought-after lady in its most magnificent city. "I see a philosopher who should change the way he thinks. Look around you. There are things from myriad provinces, all in this room. In mere steps you can behold so much. There is no suffering here, sir," and finally she let her nipples slide into his mouth, which closed about them as eagerly as he had devoured the apple. "There is only you and I and possibility."

She moved her body over his, running her hand along the gold in his sash, inhaling his scent, which was unmistakably the scent of a wealthy man. She pulled harder at the sash, but even her expert fingers could not loosen it. She grew flushed; frustrated. The circles she normally spun with such ease above the laps of her clients were putting her head in a spin. Confused, she dragged herself from the man, slumping back on her bed.

"The wine," she tried to explain, but her words were coming out slurred.

Still, the man seemed to understand. His smile was almost sympathetic.

"Why do you think I did not drink any?" he readjusted his robes and stood up as she struggled for breath that would no longer come. They said poison was a woman's weapon, but it worked well enough for a man who had spent years mixing substances for a living. It had taken its toll, carrying the odious purpose of his journey with him these many months but it was out now, and he felt the lighter for it. Yet some things when uncovered should swiftly be covered again.

"It was a pleasure forgetting myself with you for a while, my dear. I would go so far as to say I needed to do it. But the Sultan sees all. His agents are everywhere. And I could not face his wrath should I fail him now. No thing on this Earth is worse than the wrath of the Supreme Ruler of the World. So you see how this business really must remain just between the two of us."

And at last she lay still, dethroned, pale as plain cotton against the silk.

The Judge

(DECEMBER, 1176)

THEY WERE ALL THERE: grandfather, identifiable by that beard so bristling it threatened to interfere with his crown; father, seeming somehow submissive even when seated on his throne and in a depiction that had aimed to portray him flatteringly; the lion that had been the family symbol for generations in various places and postures. But despite the intricate carvings on the sceptre, he did not like it. The lions looked more like cocky rodents than kings of beasts, but it was not so much that he found the workmanship unappealing. Overall the effect was just too much; too ostentatious. He did not need emblems to announce who he was anymore. Everyone knew. The King himself sent him personal messages these days. And although the court smith, a sensitive sort who had put weeks of work into forging and ornamenting the staff, was before him awaiting his approval, he could not bring himself to say he was pleased with the thing.

"Every great ruler needs a sceptre, my lord."

Did they? Not like they needed to be able to pluck out the right word to avert a dispute, or raise a sword and a shield in their defence even when half-asleep or half-dead as he had been forced to, not like they needed a well-honed instinct of self-preservation and a composure more impregnable than the walls of Windsor

Castle. He held the sceptre at arm's length. He struck it upon the flags of the otherwise empty hall and it made an authoritative thud; a stone floor was so much better than a floor of packed earth when one was trying to strike it authoritatively.

"It becomes you, my lord."

"But I do not become *it*," he tossed the sceptre as others might a javelin for the smith to catch awkwardly.

"Would you like some alterations my lord?"

He shook his head. He did not want to see the thing again. His father and his grandfather had loved pomp for the sake of pomp and both had ended up with nothing. He had fought beside his men in the days when he had needed to fight just to stay alive. And he would make merry alongside them now the time had come for merrymaking, not sit aloof with some sceptre marking him apart.

"Will you turn your attentions to the drinking horns and the platters? For many are coming, many more than we thought, and without adequate means to serve mead or meat to our guests, the place will speedily descend into a shambles. It is imperative," he shouted after the sulkily withdrawing smith, "that everyone who attends these festivities—be they barefoot songsters from a hovel in Snowdonia or a highborn Norman with his own houseful of minstrels—is impressed by every last aspect of it!" The double doors closed behind the smith, pitching the hall back into shadow. It was a grey hall; made with Preseli stone by the best masons, but grey and cold, with just one man slouching in a rather average chair at the end of it. The greatest prince of Wales… the greatest festival this land or any other had known… was this not what the proclamation he sent out all those months ago had said? Yet it was still like a damned mortuary in here. "Never let it be said that Rhys ap Gruffyd was found wanting in his hospitality," he said to the shadows. Therein of course lay the crux of the matter. No one had ever said anything about his hospitality whatsoever, no one who mattered. He recalled something that bear of a bard from the north had said about his erstwhile adversary, Prince Owain Cyfeiliog of Powys: '*in his halls there is drinking without want, without refusal*.' The words that smarted most were those that sung the praise of others. He wanted the singers of the great songs to record such words about his halls because life was fleeting and one's achievements lay precariously in the hands of one's sons, but if one died and continued being sung about in halls that had not yet even been built, then one had a legacy. One entered the realm of legend and a legend could not be burnt down or overthrown.

There was work to be done. Sitting idly by was not his way; it had not been before when he had wars to win against the odds and it would not be now he had a fortnight of festivities to arrange. He leapt up, eyes aflame with an energy that had never really left him since that day forty years before when he had taken it upon himself to take back Wales, when over the just-murdered body of his brother he had vowed to get vengeance not just for his family but for every Welshman unjustly slain because their land was coveted by others. The vow had seemed too ridiculous for a six-year-old to utter out loud and he had not. But they would hear him now. He thrust his hall doors wide open, letting in the light.

"Is everything well?" the captain of the bodyguard, standing outside, was surprised at the sudden movement.

"Never better, Anarawd," Rhys replied, clapping his trusted kinsman on the shoulders. "How is Cardigan this fine morning?"

"Pissing it down," Anarawd glanced at his lord shrewdly. He appreciated that they could still speak informally like this after all these years, and he knew Rhys did too. Ruling embroiled you in etiquette and any respite you could get from it was sweet relief. "You *sure* everything's well?"

Rhys sat down on the stone steps. After a careful look around and a barked order to bolster the guard on the castle gates, Anarawd squatted alongside.

"Here, try this," the captain handed Rhys a pungent-smelling ceramic vial. "Got it off a travelling Scot the other day."

Rhys smiled. As the head of his *teulu*, a retinue formed from the bravest most loyal men in Deheubarth, and sworn to protect their prince to the death, his *penteulu* was supposed to stay sober. It was written thus in Welsh law: the logic being that a *penteulu's* reaction to danger would be dulled by drink. But he knew Anarawd was more than a match for most other men in Britain even after a few jugs of ale. And his captain had taken an arrow in the haunches for him on one occasion and poison that caused disfigurement on another; he would sooner have Anarawd dead drunk in his defence than the next-best warrior were they half the age and abstinent from alcohol altogether.

"The first two draughts are protection in weather like this," Anarawd seemingly read his thoughts. "It's only on the third that it counts as drinking on duty."

"Santé," Rhys took a swill. "We should be practising our French, Anarawd, for when our foreign friends arrive."

"Let's have it then. What's bothering you?"

"I like matters to be in my own hands, Anarawd. Do you remember when we trounced the King at Crogen? Or that time we subdued Owain Cyfeiliog and deprived him of a couple of his castles?" Anarawd chuckled and they exchanged a few grisly stories that might have interested those who had participated in Rhys' military struggles and seen how his realm came together slowly battle by bloody battle, but that would horrify most other listeners. It was only when Anarawd, by now spluttering with laughter, mentioned how the eyeball continued to stare straight at him accusingly for some time after it had come to rest right on top of the horseshit, that Rhys shouted: "Exactly! There was shit and blood everywhere in those days but at least our fate was in our own hands! We knew if we fought well we had a chance. With this festival it feels beyond my control. I am reliant on the townsfolk to give everyone a fitting welcome without coming across as peasants, more men-at-arms to increase the security, my fiddler to arrange for some seemly music as the nobles arrive, the bishop to relax and refrain from ranting about the dangers of debauchery, carpenters to craft the banquet tables, cooks to see the food and drink is fine enough for those with taste buds accustomed to the things they serve for dinner in Aquitaine and at least a dozen decent bards and musicians to turn up and give the song contests a semblance of excellence..."

"Hark at you, clucking like a broody hen, the same man who started eliminating his family's enemies when he was scarce out of swaddling clothes!" Anarawd let the fire of the Scot's drink sear his mouth until the burn became uncomfortable, then swallowed. "Fear not. I gave your grumbling smith the promise of a box round the ears if he didn't hasten on and forge more tableware and prospects of further pummelling if there was a paucity of gilt drinking horns when feasting begins. There's enough livestock inside the castle walls to fill the Ark and the banquet tables are so big they've been dismantled so as to fit through the gates. So quit your fretting and get that second draught down you."

"You are right," Rhys laughed. He downed the remaining contents of the proffered vial. He saw why the Normans got supercilious about their southern wines when the only other options Britain could offer were mead, bad beer or foul spirits like this. "I am being a broody damned hen. I will go and harry them somewhat: chase along the servants; offer to help that slothful baker bake his fancy loaves if he finds loaf-making so difficult. But we are too involved now not to go forward with it. Not unless we want to be the laughing stock of every man and woman from the March to the Tower of London. It would be tantamount to retreat from the field of battle," he used language he thought Anarawd would relate to.

"A good carousal is one thing. Even inviting that bastard Rhodri from Gwynedd or the princes of all the pieces Powys is divided into these days, I can see the merit of that. But why ask the Normans? Why try to make it all so grand?"

Rhys' mind strayed momentarily to the last time he had met the King at Gloucester. A remarkable city, Gloucester: a city of unrestrained learning. It had been his task on that occasion to smooth over the grudges the lesser chieftains of Wales had with England. Afterwards, he had been summoned with some of the English barons present to an antechamber, where the King with characteristic enthusiasm was poring over a device so large the six or seven of them in the room could stand around it with ease and so elaborate everyone gazed a long while at it, taking in the complexity and trying to work out what it could be. It was a water clock; a gift to the Crown from a crusader knight, transported in countless components from the Holy Land and requiring several weeks to reassemble. *'It may be the most intricate thing any of us ever see.'* So the King had said, and it had been. Now, when some rankling thing clogged Rhys' thoughts, he remembered those intertwining tubes channelling through water at precisely the speed with which the hours of the day also elapsed, and he was soothed.

"The truth of it, Anarawd, is that one can keep fighting one's neighbour: abduct his wife, annihilate his bloodline, annexe his lands, and do the same with the next neighbour and the next.

And some of it does give one a thrill. Sometimes one pauses in the bloody chess game; one compares it to an earlier point and sees the position is advanced with pawns a-plenty sacrificed but at least with castles won. But you never sleep easy," Rhys switched to a more personal tense, because it was a well-known fact he never had, not in his fighting days and not really now he had achieved peace. *Don't cross Rhys, he'll get you in your sleep:* so went the saying. And it was true he had planned entire campaigns during wakeful nights, and been content to let stories about his sleeplessness metamorphose into talk of his invincibility. "You start to worry whether that next neighbour might get you before you get them. And you are forever destroying things. I remember one of my best men in the early days—Iorwerth the fair we called him, on account of his womanly looks, but in battle he had the strength of two men—could cut down soldiers like cornstalks, but wept when we trampled down a daffodil wood whilst in pursuit of the enemy. He asked leave to return there when we were done with the fight and replant the damned flowers!" Rhys recalled fondly. He liked to look back and recollect what a ruinous state Deheubarth had been in. Now he had melded his realm into a force to be treated with respect it seemed all that blood shed along the long road to peace had not been lost fruitlessly. "Destruction abrades men: those who bring it and those who receive it alike. Sooner or later, like Iorwerth there, an urge comes upon you to replant."

"Drink's all I need after a fight," Anarawd said. "Numbs the pain; fires the belly. And I'll say this freely: I'd rather be readying for war on the morrow than I would be playing host to a horde of foreigners. I never liked bards much. The revelry that goes on around them is fine enough. But bards make me uneasy. They take one thing and make it one hundred different things. I'm telling you now. A roomful of bards is trouble."

But sometimes, thought Rhys, trouble must be suffered. For if great men did arrive as he anticipated, if great sayers of words and players of instruments came, then great things would get composed under his roof and his hall would become a pantheon of greatness; like the Plantagenet Court or the Court of Champagne, it would live on long after he Rhys had rotted into the leaf mulch.

"Yet you *will* suffer it, Anarawd, for me," Rhys stood up. "You will suffer our guests and be cordial towards them…" he broke off. There was a disturbance at the gates: a heated one, for several guards had abandoned their posts to deal with it.

"One of your guests, I daresay," Anarawd rejoined.

A cart had pulled up outside at an angle that both blocked the castle entrance and obstructed most of Cardigan's single thoroughfare; a four-horse team Rhys discerned straight away had been flogged too much and fed too little. Neither carter could control their beasts, that much was plain as day, and in the quagmire the street had become during the rain, the cartwheels could get no traction under their load and had stuck fast. Then he saw why the load required four horses. The cart was full of criminals, petty ones Rhys guessed, because he was always notified of major crimes committed in his domain: these were likely poultry pinchers and pickpockets, no great danger to townsfolk. But nevertheless this was a higher-than-average number of miscreants for one round-up. And because the same sets of shackles were worn by this lot as they were by the mass murderers, and the iron on the restraints weighed almost as much as a man, it was easy to see how an ineptly driven load like this could get bogged down.

Yet none of these things were creating the real panic. It was the prisoner who had attempted to escape as the cart was turning into the castle gates that had raised the alarm amongst the guards, caused the carters to lose control, blocked several wagonloads of fleeces from meeting the Christmas shipment to the Low Countries and drawn the usual contingent of gawpers.

Rhys was concerned at how men he was stationing at his gates to protect those within could have become so straightforwardly sidetracked as to get down unbidden from their defences into the mud to start shifting the blockage. A cart driven by idiots was one of the oldest decoys around, employed by invaders to illicitly gain entry into strongholds for centuries. And his guards, kind-hearted fools, would have fallen for the trick and doubtless for other tricks too. But he knew Anarawd would get his *teulu* in order. Rhys turned his attentions to the prisoner that had tried to abscond, struggling futilely to free himself from the guards' grasp.

"The wretch has only been in town a moment and is on five charges of *sarhaed*[1] and counting, on top of the lewd remarks I myself overheard him make towards my nephew as he was passing the gates just now," said the guard.

"How *dare* you oafs manhandle me so!" The prisoner squirmed, but with no more effectiveness than a mouse in hawk's talons. "Accusing me of crimes I do not understand! As for complimenting a boy in the bloom of his youth on his comeliness, if that constitutes a crime then this world is a sorrier place than I hitherto believed!"

"*Six* counts!" the guard butted in, triumphant.

Rhys surveyed the offending young man. Tightly coiled white-blonde hair and a nose that hung too far down from his forehead but did not stand out enough from his face. He might have been deemed handsome but for that nose. But Rhys possessed sufficient knowledge of French to perceive the man was speaking English

---

1 An insult or injury payment, payable under Welsh law by the offender or offender's family to the victim at a rate predetermined by the victim's status and, where injuries were concerned, also by the importance of the body part damaged. As Chrétien deplores violence, we can assume it was his words that offended the guards: these he could hurl out just as effectively as a more violently inclined man could blows.

with the accent of the Norman aristocracy; he was unlikely to be a common criminal.

"The prisoner has no shackles, neither on his person nor in the cart that I can see," Rhys observed.

The young man spun round to Rhys with a glimmer of hope.

"That, seigneur, is what I was trying to communicate to this brute. I am shackle free because I am a free man, and more than that an honourable one!"

"Honourable? Travelling with a cartload of criminals carries no honour that I am aware of, in this land or any other."

The young man looked crestfallen.

"I… had resolved to complete my journey here as cheaply as possible, seigneur—it is not that I lack money you understand, I am tasked with the writing of enthralling adventures for my work, but never had a real life adventure myself and this was to have been it. And I almost managed it: all the way from Champagne with barely a penny spent! But you know what a desolate wilderness it is south of here—nothing but stony moors and sinister forest—and I hitched a lift with these felons out of unadulterated desperation…"

Under Anarawd's command the cart had been freed from the rut. The rest of the criminals were being borne out of sight to a dark little dungeon at the basement of the keep, the most notable feature of which was a window that let in the morning smell of freshly baked bread from the kitchens nearby and led to particularly high confession rates amongst prisoners driven mad by the aroma.

"Return to your posts," Rhys told the guards sternly. "And unhand this man with your sincerest apologies. This is no way to treat a guest of Rhys ap Gruffyd. Champagne you say?" he addressed the young man benignly. "I ask pardon for your treatment, and trust I might redress matters over a horn of wine?

I recently received a shipment of claret—we are in the throes of preparing for a festival—and I would welcome your opinion on the vintage."

The young man rubbed theatrically at a slight redness on his neck where the guards had restrained him. But his indignation was gone. His eyes shone.

"The greatest festival," he murmured, "that this land or any land has ever known. I read your proclamation with fervour in my bosom but that fervour is as nothing compared to the agitation I now feel stirring within me seeing the author of those words in the *flesh*! I would be enchanted to drink with you, seigneur. I must say you are every ounce the Celt I supposed you might be when I lay tossing in bed in my faraway homeland dreaming of our meeting!"

"So you are come here to participate in the festival?" Rhys was intrigued, and not a little complimented. "We are not expecting the first guests for a day or two. You find us unprepared I am afraid. We are only today getting the damned banquet tables together," he motioned the young man to one side as a group of carpenters staggered past weighed down by table parts.

"Alas whilst I am a writer, seigneur, my words do not lend themselves to oral performance. What we call in my land the troubadour and what you call the minstrel…"

"Bard," Rhys corrected. "Bards perform their own songs. Minstrels mouth other people's."

"I am sorry. I once attended the court of the King of England to improve my grasp of his nation's language, but the nobles there converse continually in French so I was obliged to enlist the services of a young serving boy to teach me my English and mercy, was his grammar appalling! Troubadours and *bards* must strike up a tune for their audience at a finger click, and maintain a merry rhythm if they are not to be jeered off—we writers take on projects only after grave consideration and build up but subtly to the points we wish to make. We are less prolific but in some ways we are more profound. I always equate it to the difference between feeling a short, fiery rush inside and a long, lingering warmth," his hand lightly brushed Rhys' shoulder. There was a time, Rhys reflected, when he would have cut a man's hand off for brushing his shoulder unsolicited. So why had he let this hand remain there for several moments longer than was appropriate? He strode hurriedly, awkwardly on out of the rain to show his visitor his hall and effect a change of subject. But the young man's words drifted after him, soft but oddly chosen: "Festivals are all very well. But I am come to see *you*, seigneur."

Thrown, Rhys deflected the conversation in favour of talk more familiar to him, the tour of his castle that he liked to give all guests.

"The best stone in Wales built these walls," he said. "Sourced from those same moors where you boarded the cart rounding up our realm's latest rogues. People of old sought out this stone to bury their dead..." he hesitated. He had been thinking of death a lot of late, but why, when he was in the prime of life, at the peak of his success? Could it be because he was becoming increasingly obsessed with being remembered? "Stone like that lasts. We Welsh regressed after that. We lost it; built basely out of mud and sticks. Most of us still do: even those among us who adjudge themselves princes. Not like you French. You French always aspired to something better. In Wales this constitutes a palace. Yet to a Frenchman this must seem like a backwater..." he searched for the correct words because he was keen to get the young man talking about Champagne, the land he claimed to have travelled from. "Particularly Frenchmen accustomed to the finery you must be in your homeland."

"Mercy, *no* seigneur!" The young man gushed, looking about him in awe. "I find the darkness... mysterious! And if it is cold, all the more reason to cosy together and quaff good wine! I can just imagine you brave Celts assembling here in your shimmering armour after a gambolling good tourney, you and your queen presiding, all merrily seated about a round table..."

Rhys burst out laughing.

"You have romantic notions about our people!"

"But you *surely* have tourneys?" The young man sounded disappointed.

"Normans have them," Rhys said, ushering his visitor into the *ystafell*, the chamber attached to the main hall that he used for hosting special guests. He had wanted to show the young man the seven towers around the battlements, for they were but recently completed, and what other castle in native Wales could boast seven towers? But the rain was battering down now, and at least in here there was a good fire and fully assembled furniture to convey an impression of proper hospitality. "Welshmen do not have the men to spare. If an urge seizes us to maim for entertainment we will launch an attack on our enemies, not go killing off our own kinsmen. As for armour, it just rusts in rain like this. And what tales, pray, do they tell about us in Champagne that have us dining from round tables?"

The young man gratefully took the horn of wine that was proffered and clasped it in both hands, crossing his legs and regarding Rhys mischievously.

"You know, I saw your stout townsfolk out there toiling with their fleeces through the mud and I thought of the grand cloth fairs that take place in my own town, Troyes. It got me musing on the concept of causality. Here you shear the sheep in the little green fields and in Troyes we weave the wool of Britain into beautiful cloth to be transported throughout Europe! Seigneur, are you a believer in destiny?"

Rhys was not.

"They are just bloody sheep."

"Oh yes," said the young man. "*They* are. But one day not so long ago my patron back in Troyes, or should I say patron*ess*, summoned me to her chambers. She is a benefactor of the arts you understand, like no other I have come across. She employs men to scour every corner of the continent for stories to be brought to her for turning into works of literature—I, seigneur, am the one who does the turning—and on the day to which I refer, her men had just delivered her their stories. There was one about some fox supposedly representing a king's conniving courtier, that wriggled into his master's confidence through various despicable deceits as I recall; there were the usual cycle of big, bold Norse heroes who defeat all types of nasty monsters *very* valiantly. And there was one of those tales that seem to captivate audiences more than any others these days: the tales of a kingdom within a grim, war-torn land that stands out for glory, for its chivalry, for right over wrong, light and laughter and love over darkness. Perhaps you are familiar with the tales too, seigneur: those of King Arthur and his court. Over in Champagne they have become *quite* the fashion… A sign of our times, that we escape for our recreation into a world where decency is still so important, where devotion does not merely mean love for God but *physical* love… for a woman… *or* a man… an all-encompassing love outlasting any barrier placed in its path even should that barrier be a king…" the young man leaned forward, head propped on hands, looking deeply at Rhys with an ardency that seemed too absolute to be real. "And my patroness said to me, '*Chrétien, ma petite cerise*'—she loves to call me by the names of fruits—'*Chrétien, another of the stories about Arthur* *has come in from Britain'* and I actually rolled my eyes because I have already composed two such works about the man, but she placated me, *'Chrétien, ma pêche, this one is different. It surpasses all others. It is more vivid, the court portrayed more colourfully, the adventures more entertaining, it is without question the best such tale yet, will you transpose it to parchment?'* And a writer cannot refuse his patroness, not one as wealthy or as beautiful as mine. So I agreed and we started to establish the details of the work, for the nobles of Champagne had been pressing my patroness to commission me for another epic endeavour after the raptures my previous writings had aroused, and time therefore was of the essence. We talked of what concepts the work might feature— tragedy and comedy and love, of course, and because the tales foretell of an impending doom that would destroy this mythical king's court from the inside out, an element of foreboding too. But we could not for all the crown jewels in Christendom concur on the setting. And then who should come knocking that instant at the chamber door of my patroness but a messenger bringing tidings of the proclamation written by your own fair hand, seigneur. And then we knew," Chrétien beamed. "The setting simply *had* to be Wales."

Anarawd stuck his head through the doorway, seeing his lord conversing with the mincing foreigner as if he had no other responsibilities in his realm. He eyed Rhys with a frown and Chrétien with suspicion.

"The judges have arrived. Are you done?"

"Have mead fetched for them," Rhys said. "I will not keep them waiting long."

Anarawd stared at Rhys like he had taken leave of his senses. The judges were easily the town's most important residents outside of Rhys' immediate family and principal court officers; they were nobles with significant influence. Keeping them waiting for a reason like this was not wise.

"As you wish," he muttered. "Enjoy the fine wine."

Rhys smiled diplomatically until his *penteulu* was gone, swigging from his drinking horn to mask his excitement. Greatness might be nearer than he had imagined.

"So," he asked neutrally, "your patroness is Marie of Champagne? I hear her court now eclipses the King of England's for splendour."

Chrétien nodded.

"They say," he murmured, "that even her lowliest servants dine off silver from the mines of Melle!"

"I meant its entertainers, its musicians, its writers such as yourself."

"Well it all began with the sword-swallower, seigneur."

"The sword-swallower?"

"Why *of course*. He was the English King's star performer. Then he came over to us. The Plantagenet Court has been in the shade ever since. And small wonder, I do declare I have seen the man thrust the better part of a lance down his gullet."

Rhys erupted again into laughter so hearty Chrétien could not help but join in. Rhys roaring and Chrétien tittering they laughed. Rhys liked Chrétien but business before pleasure. He seized his opportunity and when the laughter reached its peak stopped dead; his old tactic; more effective than any amount of buttery talk. When a man's guard was down one should make one's move.

"So what is it you want from me?"

Chrétien's titter died an excruciating death in the half-light.

"I... I want to stay with you, seigneur. I want to observe the particulars and the peculiarities of your court until such time as I feel stimulated enough to embark on my next work of literature," he smiled sweetly. "It promises to be a monumental one and I know you would win a place in the heart of my patroness for your kindness."

"The judges," Anarawd appeared again with more urgency, "are becoming restless."

"Do not let me detain you, seigneur."

"On the contrary," said Rhys. "It is I who am detaining you. We are one judge short. I trust you will do me the honour of making good the shortfall?"

"Mercy, seigneur! The honour quickens my pulse but alas in criminal matters I believe I would be a poor judge…"

"Why, it is the straightforward matter of sentencing those scoundrels you came into town with: some for hanging, a few for torture, a couple for no more than lifelong imprisonment. As you shared a cart with them, I thought you the ideal fellow for the task."

Chrétien paled.

"I simply could not bear the suffering, seigneur! To think that a man's agony in the noose or at the stocks would be on my conscience, I beg you…"

"I had him!" Rhys called to Anarawd, exuberant. "I had you," he said good-humouredly to Chrétien. "Fret not, as I told you we do not have enough men in this realm as it is. We can ill afford punishment by death. Pledging their victims and me a portion of their barley harvest will likely be the extent of their penance. We do well for barley cakes here after holding days of judgment, eh Anarawd?"

Anarawd gave his customary gallows smile.

Rhys could bludgeon his way towards getting what he wanted but Satan's sister, could he parley the best of them into surrender too! He didn't see life like Rhys. To him it was a course with a series of obstacles to scale and to help with the scaling the odd hearty carousal. Rhys followed no course; he seemed to take pains to avoid courses entirely. Anarawd was thankful Rhys was not his enemy. Were he defending a castle against the Lord of Deheubarth, he would have no idea what to expect: a bombardment, a siege, a trick, a trap or a tunnel into the very foundations. Rhys had a host of weapons at his disposal and most of them were not even weapons but words, schemes, stratagems. And although he didn't know how, Anarawd could tell Rhys was about to use one of those weapons against the foreign popinjay any moment now.

"The sentencing of that cartful of rogues is a formality," Rhys informed Chrétien amiably, relishing the Frenchman's unsettledness. "The judges here have dealt with more breaches of the law than they have downed decent mead—and free rein on my mead is all that motivates them into dispensing the necessary verdicts to keep criminality in my lands at a low. No, it is best we leave such pronouncements to the town's professionals."

"Then what, seigneur, do you wish for my help with the judging of?"

"Those villains will be the last of the season to be tried. In Wales a new year is a new start. Old wrongs are forgotten; drink flows. It is an easy season in which to be a judge..." Rhys paused, "...normally. This season is different. There is the matter of the festival and as you are aware the proclamation put word about of its brilliance in every province between here and Constantinople. A great song contest requires great judges. And the judges in that room," he indicated the rising sounds of coarse frivolity from the main hall as the most lawful citizens of Cardigan got onto their second horns of mead, "are not literary men. You, by your account, are acquainted with all the arts. You will join the judges on the bench for the song contests. The festival gains merit, for how many festivals can boast Marie of Champagne's foremost writer of words among the revellers? Meanwhile, you as my guest gain all the time you need for observing our court's… peculiarities. Agreed?" Rhys asked brightly, standing up in readiness to go and appease the other judges.

Quite frequently princes and kings and emperors forget this: that firm rule mainly entails going from one room to the next appeasing others. Pleasantries are overlooked, for they do not make such engrossing stories in the chronicles, even though restraining oneself from swiping the sword and smiling requires ten times the strength the sword-swipe does.

"I fear for the man that was *not* in agreement with you, seigneur," the wine had coaxed out little spots of red on Chrétien's cheeks. "And I should add that I would be delighted."

"Come then," said Rhys, "and meet your fellow judges."

He liked this end of his *ystafell*. The builders had put in a small aperture to let in the light. Pale grey light; Welsh light. One could never see far through it. Yet today he looked through it as though he really could see a long way, all the way north and east a day's journey, a week's journey, over the Preseli's to the Beacons, the Berwyn's, Snowdonia, the King's own castle at Windsor and beyond to Scotia, Scandinavia, the Low Countries and the Holy Roman Empire, he looked through the grey and he saw them in his mind's eye, all of them who would make him great coming with their songs to his castle.

"There is one more thing," Rhys said to Chrétien. "Afterwards, when the judging has been judged, when the last reveller has left and you return to your court that everyone speaks of with such awe, you will inform all those lords and ladies of how spectacular a festival Rhys ap Gruffyd held here at his seven-towered castle of stone, where the greatest river in Wales meets the sea."

"If the festival is half as fine as the proclamation promises, seigneur, I see no reason to restrain myself in what I impart to others of the frivolity."

"You misunderstand," Rhys turned to lay both hands on Chrétien's shoulders and look levelly at his guest. "You *will* tell them. Regardless of what may come to pass you will say it was the most spectacular thing you ever beheld. You will tell them all, and I will make certain that you do."

Pierrot

(December, 1176)

THERE WAS SOMETHING ODD about the beggar from the outset: his limp exaggerated, his clothes not quite soiled enough. Even his presence in such an unpeopled district was untoward. Vagrants tended to stay close to towns and villages and for a day's ride in either direction from here there was nothing but scattered farmsteads with tenants that withdrew behind closed doors in wariness more often than they showed signs of hospitality. The road had deteriorated after Brecon, and by the time the beggar shambled into their path there was little space to pass him, the woods from which he had emerged pressing on one side and slopes of scree dropping steeply into a valley on the other. The three men De Braose had sent with them for protection had not slackened their pace, their barked threats pushing the beggar back to the wayside, but Marie was not about to treat the poor unfortunate with such rudeness. As she slowed to offer the man money, though, she gasped.

"Pierrot, he is a leper!"

Her attendant reined in his horse and pulled back hers, so suddenly the beast reared up and almost threw her. Word resounded through the group with alarm, Bernart melodramatically grumbling that he had told everyone they should have gone on the coastal road and this was the price paid for paying him no heed. The beggar, sensing charity perhaps, advanced to the middle of the road. There was now no means of passing the man that did not involve uncomfortably close contact, and most believed even breathing the same air as a leper was enough to spread the contagion.

"Stay back, leper, and let us by!" Pierrot warned in his most ominous voice, which was still rather a reedy one.

"Spare some coins, my pretty lords and ladies! Does a man with a face like this not deserve some coins?" The man part-lifted his hat. It was a conical broad-brimmed hat common to travellers in cold, wet lands, a hat that overshadowed the face of the wearer almost entirely and in this case fortuitously. Pallid clumps and valleys of dead flesh pockmarked the beggar's forehead and cheeks. His leprosy had reached its vilest stage.

Tears pricked at Marie's eyes as she saw the man's disfigurement. Pierrot's hand shot hotly to his sword. Behind him, Bernart arranged his men into the formation he thought fitting when under threat, he furthest from the action with his bard and his cook and bodyguard shoved forward towards the fray.

"Coins you shall have, leper, should you stand back and let us pass. But I can hurl this sword as well as I can wield one if you do not do as I say," Pierrot spoke in the courageous language he had learned from his time serving in Norman courts, although he could not say if he had heard nobles actually speak like that, or if hearthside storytellers had planted such words in their mouths during animated retellings of exploits. Marie glanced at Pierrot in surprise for it was news to her that her attendant was a skilled swordsman, much less a spear thrower. He was loyal and for her that was enough.

The beggar raised his arms as if in surrender. Then with a flick he tossed his hat up into the air, a bright summer green hat contrasting sharply with the brown of the dead and dying trees. It caught on one of the spindly branches and hung there ridiculously. And then they came.

There were maybe ten of them, but because they were approaching from the woods above their numbers seemed greater. Pierrot instinctively made the quick calculation every traveller needed to when encountering strangers on strange territory. It was clear these newcomers did not mean well. They were bareheaded and on foot; Welshmen then, but armed only with swords like he was. So they were even for weapons. Bernart's bodyguard doubtless knew how to fight and with De Braose's men too that would be two to dispatch apiece. Not insurmountable odds. But De Braose's men were nowhere to be seen. Why had their protection melted away at the very moment it was most needed? Pierrot gripped his blade but did not draw it, not yet.

"What do you want from us?" he called, but only to play for time whilst he looked searchingly along the line of would-be attackers massing on the bank for the one who led them. These were well-to-do men to judge from their dress; likely acting at the behest of a more powerful overlord. Their leader might have something to gain through carrying out this ambush, but the others would just be following orders. Eliminate the leader and you cut the head off the monster.

One of the men standing just forward of the others leered, spitting a fat glob of spittle that landed on Marie's face and Pierrot tensed: so this was the head he must sever. The rest of the men sprang at them.

Pierrot was Anglo-Saxon by blood; his great grandfather fought to the death against the Normans at Hastings, but his grandfather and father had fared well serving under a Norman lord, and ever since he could remember he had aspired to nothing less than becoming Norman nobility himself. To his mind, there was a clear path. Squire, knight, bold knight, rewarded knight. He had even changed his name from Peter to Pierrot to further his cause. There was much to admire in Norman society: their efficiency in battle, the sophistication of their townships. But it was their culture that hooked Pierrot, their music and their song and how the two fused in the compositions of their trouvères and troubadours. What young man would not wish to be as the subjects of these chansons and cansos were, men who fought bravely and loved fiercely? And how he had pressed for his opportunity! Taking on any task, doing it well, doing it with good cheer, first for the Ashby's and then as squire for one of the De Lacy's who held greater influence. De Lacy loved to joust. He would have gone on a crusade had there been one, but in the absence of a decent war to participate in he jousted. As Pierrot was getting him ready—helping him mount, leading him out onto the lists—he would sing refrains of the *Chanson de Roland* so uproariously it aggravated his adversaries, provoking them into revealing their true selves. De Lacy was not the best fighter but he won his fights and he did so because he got the measure of his rival in a moment. An aristocrat jousted by the book so against them he fought dirtily. Poor men tilted with nothing-to-lose rashness like sheer force of will and force of thrust would enable them to prevail, and with the poor he sparred until their energy was spent before landing his lance on them just once with once being enough. An adversary in love was more cautious; against them De Lacy hit out early and hit out hard. '*You do not unhorse them with your weapon*', he would cheerfully tell Pierrot. '*You unhorse them with your mind.*'

The assailants targeted Bernart's bodyguard first, probably because he looked like he could put up the most resistance. Bernart's man impaled the first on reflex but two more leapt at him from the bank and tackled him to the ground; now he went down as tamely as a scuttled ship and did not get up again. The flat of a sword knocked out the cook before he could land a blow. Bernart whimpered and enjoined his bard to protect them both but neither the troubadour nor his charge could boast a weapon between them. De Braose's men had still not appeared. It was just Pierrot now. He quivered, not with fright, really not, but with anticipation. A knight must prove himself, and do so for a lady he loved if the chansons were to be believed. And there had never been any doubt which lady he would want to prove himself to.

"Stay close by me," he said tenderly to Marie.

"You cannot take on ten men Pierrot! I will talk to them." And to the man who had spat on her Marie held up her purse and said in Welsh: "Here is enough silver to buy you all the best food and wine you wish. I offer this to you. There is no need for bloodshed this day!"

The two that had grappled with Bernart's bodyguard were picking themselves up. The words of pacification had scarce left Marie's lips before one hurled his dagger at Pierrot. It sailed within a whisker of his ear, embedding in a trunk nearby. He seized it and threw the weapon back to greater effect, the blade burying several inches into the owner's neck. As the second struggled to stand up, Pierrot turned his steed and trampled the man into the ground, then pivoted again to charge at the men who were now surrounding Marie.

"This is not a time for words, my lady," he said. He was not certain if she heard him. One man held her bridle fast; a couple more tried to drag her from her saddle. Even though her horse kicked and reeled and she somehow stayed on and even managed to jab one assailant full in the face with her boot, it would not be long before she was unseated, and when she was she would be defenceless. Yet it was obvious to Pierrot the ambushers had no wish to kill Marie, and if such types did not wish to kill a woman there was but one thing they could want. The idea of these animals defiling his lady gave him a new rush of anger. And the anger spurred him on.

They did not understand me, Marie thought as the men tried to bring her down. *I spoke to them in Welsh and they did not understand, so who can they be?* As he charged at his lady's aggressors Pierrot looked up at the bank and saw, pale yellow amid the midwinter deadwood, the daffodils blooming. And he wondered: *how can they be here now, in this bitter weather?*

Then they were upon him, all around, hacking at him tugging at him assailing him any way they could, and he lashed out and wielded and parried as he had watched young nobles do at the jousts. For each time he raised his sword to strike them there were two or three blows to contend with, and each successive swipe took twice the effort of the last; through the tangle of arms and legs and blades he saw flashes of the indigo of Marie's travelling cloak, and it helped him to think of the men as weeds, not as mortals who prayed to God, as undergrowth as if he were hacking a path through undergrowth through bramble through bog and waiting on the far side was Marie, composed as an island.

De Lacy excelled at jousting and Pierrot knew every line of the *Chanson de Roland* before long; before much longer De Lacy's reputation was such that members of the Royal household came to watch him tilt and in return for his feats on the field he was welcomed at court. And with the knight came the squire. Pierrot still saw Marie as he glimpsed her that first time, arriving at Windsor with her bumbling husband. His initial reaction had been to wonder what crime she could have committed to be punished with a marriage like that, but Marie was stronger than she first seemed. Entrapment in the real world impelled her escape to a dream one. Her imagination nurtured hundreds of characters and plots at any one time, and some of these she wove into tales to impart to courtiers, but most she told to Pierrot or to no one at all. She blended history and myth and invention with such colour, her audiences could see before them nothing but the scenes she painted, and yet outside of her recitals she was so guarded it was as if a veil hid the real Marie from view. Pierrot knew her. He knew the Marie that had begun to appear at court without her husband in evidence, the Marie who on her journeys between London and Wales came to have need of someone who would watch her back, someone like him. She would put herself in such situations! But somehow they always both emerged to laugh about it afterwards. And this was but another situation.

Marie looked about wildly, calling on Bernart cowering beneath his bower to do something, anything, just one valiant action, but Bernart shrugged as if the request was preposterous and shrank back into the bankside vegetation, drawing his scarlet cloak around him like an out-of-season flower.

He shrank back but still he watched her, how her pale form twisted and turned in distress, how her honey-blonde hair fell over her shoulders, how fine those shoulders would be to seize, sweep back the hair and plant with kisses on up that long neck of hers to her mouth. He watched her limply as she was torn from her horse and dragged off and he watched her oh-so-gallant attendant galloping to try and save her with rather more pluck than could possibly have been predicted. And something in the scene struck a chord within him and words trickled into his head where before had been nothingness: *As hounds as boars as bears they appeared, snapping and snarling around her, malign, I cut down beasts to gain that love of mine, bore her up, held her, told her not to fear.* Marie was that something. He watched her only once she was looking the other way, once she was forced to look away as she was dragged away, as her arms were pinned behind her and her cloak fell to expose something of her throat and chest and that delicious little mouth of hers began to scream.

Time spent alone in dark quarters in Toulouse had filled his mind with dark notions. There had been no one to temper them and he became accustomed to embellishing his fantasies until they bore the detail of parallel realities. Oh, he had loved Marguerite long and deep but that was long ago; he had to unlock that ardent heart of his if he wanted his words to flow again, and flow they must by the time they reached the castle holding this contest of song, flow they must or he was finished. He needed new love: a love that expanded his knowledge of love, for love was what he wrote about best. He had been looking for the right lady to unlock him for some time and Marie was she; Marie was the key; she was young and alluring and elusive enough to whet his long-starved appetite and he had chosen her. He was not a man who could have gone off with any common wench. He was better than that and he was richer than that. He had amassed a fair amount of wealth during his stints at court, more than most troubadours could hope to have from a lifetime of performing and sufficient to get what he wanted. Once he had set his mind on Marie, the particulars were easy to arrange. The attack had to be seen as carried out by Welshmen, for the Welsh made good scapegoats, and thus it had to occur far from Norman territory. It had to be sudden. It had to take Marie unharmed, and this would mean it must guarantee the elimination of her attendant—who like all silly youths styling themselves on chevaliers would probably defend his lady to the last—and to put Bernart beyond suspicion, the elimination of one of his own men too. De Braose, like all Marcher lords and more than most, was forever on the lookout for funds to finance his campaigns against the Welsh and was amenable to supplying the necessary men for the right price. So Bernart watched Marie and he watched the mêlée with the concerned eye of one who has carefully planned a thing and waits for it to unfold accordingly. The only thing he had not planned for was what he would do afterwards when she was brought to him. Should he try his usual way of wooing? Would gaudy praise work on a woman of words? Or would he play the waiting game, commiserating with her loss and winning her slowly? There were more forceful methods, of course, but it was important to him that Marie gave herself willingly. She would give herself to him and as his mouth closed over hers he felt certain his inspiration would come.

But Marie was not going without a struggle. It was the ruffian who spat upon her who had seized her. She was sweating, despite the Welsh cold, sweating. Why did Bernart not try to help, how could Pierrot hope to help, where were the three men De Braose had assigned them for the journey he had gravely warned her would be dangerous without his protection? She struggled; knowing any extra moment she remained on the road and not dragged off to some dark corner out of sight of it could save her. She screamed and got the ruffian's paw clamped over her mouth for her trouble and then in the tumult was a new sound.

Hooves. Hundreds of pairs of hooves, vehement curses in Welsh and a great deal of mooing: drovers. Drovers drove Welsh meat to the burgeoning markets in England: cattle and sheep and turkeys and geese to Chester, Birmingham, Bristol and London. They forged their own routes from wherever the beasts had been assembled through the north and middle and south of Wales, carving trackways through the desolate tracts of *mynydd* and *coedwig*, moor and wood where before people feared to tread at all. They took the wild ways to avoid the tolls and the interrogative bands of Normans along the coast. They were rough men one would normally cross a mountain to steer clear of but as they thundered closer, fifteen weather-hewn Welshmen with as many brawls to their name as the land had alehouses driving five hundred bulky cows before them on a narrow road, Marie breathed a sigh of relief. The men who had carried out this ambush were not Welsh and they were in the drovers' way, two things drovers cared little for. And the ambushers knew this, the leering man who had spat on her dropped her and cursed and called off his men, scrabbling like a scared rabbit to get back up the bank into the cover of the woods. They were, it would seem, saved.

Pierrot was tiring, he might have studied the combatants' every move in the jousts but had never carried them out in practise, De Lacy had wanted to be led prettily onto the lists but saved little time for training his squire, little time for telling how one man might take on ten in a fight and cherish a hope of coming away from it in one piece. He looked up from the skirmish to see where his lady was and there she was, that leering oaf of a leader had her and then he threw her on the ground on the rocks at the roadside, where she lay unmoving.

She could not die. She had told him just yesterday of her idea, conceived in the timber merchant's house in the forest of Striguil, her idea of taking forward verse into new territory by making it appeal not only to aristocrats at banquets but to ordinary people also. She had told him modestly how she thought the telling of tales had become an art form for the few, how every famous storyteller she knew of tailored their work exclusively to the rich and how this was wrong, for poor women and men should be able to enjoy the best-told tales too. Every great composer of words wrote about such a narrow strata of society, she believed. Bernart de Ventadorn in his day or even Chrétien de Troyes today barely mentioned anyone in their work who was not a lord or a lady or someone with wealth and if the poor did feature they were monstrous, dwarves or giants, it was almost as if these writers were frightened of common people. Observe how our Lord de Ventadorn deals with the poor hopeless people we are seeing every day in huge numbers and how he acts like they do not exist, she had laughed bitterly, maybe because such men were accustomed to male privilege, and poking so much as a toe out of their privileged male world to note what other people walked this Earth was unthinkable to them. '*Well Pierrot,*' Marie had said, '*I am a woman and well used to being downtrodden, so now I take it upon myself to represent the downtrodden in my work. I will try out my new words at this festival where the commonalty will outnumber the nobles and we will see what is applauded the loudest, adornments of the same staid metres or a new form for all. We will see whether those men of privilege in attendance do not come to shamefacedly berate themselves that it was a woman who did with verse what they could not or would not.*'

Marie could not die, Pierrot panicked, and with his last reserves fought on. He could not leave her with any of them, not with the assailants and not with De Braose's escort and certainly not with that cold fish De Ventadorn: he had seen the lecherous looks the troubadour stole at his lady. '*Marvellous and weighty the combat,*' Pierrot murmured, recalling the words De Lacy sang as he started down the lists toward his adversary, trot canter charge, armour gleaming, singing all the way.

Marie's shock at the ambushers taking flight, at being able to feel relief when she had prepared for the worst as their leader dropped her and with his fellow ruffians scrambled out of the way of the oncoming drovers, it almost numbed her from eluding the new threat of being crushed by cattle. But as the first of the beasts was about to pass the place where she lay, she grasped a tree root protruding from the bank and hauled herself fast up against it, and they tramped by with the humbling disregard animals have for humans when intent on their own purer purpose. Soon enough behind appeared the first of the drovers, a wildly smiling man whose teeth stood out very white against a coiling black beard. She wondered momentarily if it had been premature to view these cattlemen as being her salvation. But the drover narrowed his smile to a thinner harder line and nodded to her and passed on, without giving her very much more consideration than his cows had.

Then twisting her head to the other side Marie saw Pierrot, scarred but still standing, calming his horse as the herd rumbled past them. And she saw Bernart and his bard and his cook squatting above on the bank, out of harm's way of course, and caught the look in Bernart's eyes with surprise. It was not the look of one who had been propitiously saved. It was the look of one who had been robbed. It was disappointment. And Bernart looked back at Marie with love and with hatred in equal measure; sometimes the two can be diabolically close. The love he could explain but the hatred he could not. Perhaps it was because it seemed she had second-guessed him all along; that she had always planned to make him believe he would have her only to snatch herself away at the last. And he did not have her nor, critically, did he have what she had which was inspiration. He had not one line in readiness, just blankness just blankness and an ache where he willed words to come and nothing came.

The herd surged by. Great beasts. Dinefwr whites, and the best examples of the breed, immaculately and mythically white, so fine creditors wanted debts to be paid with them rather than with gold. Yes, a sea of stamping jostling snorting white and in its wake the after-echoes, the sounds of a wood after things have passed through, branches bending back, insects and birds scuffling back to their places.

"Are you quite well, my lady?" Pierrot asked, his voice charged with emotion. "I feared…"

"Ovid is dead," Marie said dully.

She had given her horse a name, all poets give things names, they cannot help it and it is to their detriment because some of these things will die, and their death seems the sadder for their having been named. Pierrot glanced at his lady's steed, ran right through by a blade and he gave her his hand so that she could stand.

"Share my horse for now," he said.

Shakily she stood and got ready to carry on. Because that was what she did, Pierrot realised.

He was closer to her than almost anyone but he was not close to her at all.

"I thought…," she began as he helped her mount. "When I saw them all around you, you disappeared from my view, and I thought…"

"I am here, my lady. And we should make haste out of these woods and on to the next town before those men return," he turned to Bernart, asking tightly: "Are you and your men ready to continue, my lord?"

"Of course," Bernart said, perfunctorily. "I am relieved to see you and your attendant unscathed, lady. If he wrote as well as he can fight, we should have a favourite for the forthcoming contest of song amongst us." And because he thought some small further explanation might ease the tension he added: "Alas, such scuffles are best left to other men than me. I would have hindered more than I could have helped."

Marie recalled his stony indifference as those ruffians had torn her from her horse and dragged her off quite likely to violate her.

"I appreciate your concern, my lord."

"I too have suffered loss, lady. My best man, no less," Bernart felt her silent accusation.

"We have no time to bury the dead," said Pierrot softly. "But we can no more leave them in the middle of the road like this. The less people that know what took place here the better. Would you assist me, my lord?" He made the sign of the cross over the six human corpses and over Ovid too, then started to lift the first of the men he had slain up by the arms to drag him towards the valleyside plummeting away below them.

Bernart had never touched a dead man before, and a steady rain was now sluicing down that would make gruesome work all the dirtier, but he saw no way of refusing.

"It is strange, is it not my lord?" Pierrot observed as they threw the first body over the edge, "Our attackers were wearing Welsh outer garments but armour beneath. I have seldom known Welshmen wear armour, much less attempt to conceal it."

"This is a strange land," Bernart looked away.

"How about another of your songs, my lord?" his bard ventured. "I have recently committed to memory your marvellous cansos about the love that burned within you so through the iciest of midwinters that you needed no clothes to keep out the chill[1]. I confess I would welcome the opportunity to perform it to you, my lord, as I was thinking I might play it as we arrive in Cardigan to evidence your mastery of the love song and thereby strike fear into the opposition. Visualise it, my lord, the contest barely begun and the other entrants already trembling at the prospect of facing the veteran of versification, the sublime Lord de Ventadorn, in the field..."

1   *Tan tai mo cor ple de joya*, Bernart de Venadorn

"Not now, blast you!" snapped Bernart. Not now, when his scarlet travelling cloak was daubed in repulsive gore!

Then he froze. There was the escort De Braose had assigned their party, trotting back along the road as if they had been on nothing more than a minor divergence to gather herbs for the seasoning of supper or to take in the view. They had ridden on ahead then been obliged to let the drovers by, so went their excuse that satisfied nobody. Bernart seethed but could say nothing. For they had been privy to his scheme, instructed by him to lead the party into a suitably desolate spot where the ambush could occur undisturbed, and they could have unmasked him had they so chosen. He shot them a cautioning look that he hoped communicated the plan was spectacularly foiled, foiled by a load of lumbering cows, and that they must bide their time before making their next move. They must have been taken aback at the sight of other men-at-arms in De Braose's pay reduced to corpses and in the midst of being tossed into a gorge but happily they possessed the intelligence to remain silent.

Marie suppressed a sob as Ovid too was tipped onto the scree far below. He had been a gentle horse, and more a friend to her than most in this inconstant world. At least she still had Pierrot. Without her ever thinking about it very much, he had become a familiar part of her life and a welcome one, very welcome indeed.

Pierrot eyed the return of De Braose's men with misgiving. He needed to deliver his lady to the festival, and speedily, for time was trickling quickly away. Speed, he grimaced, hobbling to his steed, grinding his teeth against the pain so that Marie did not see, one needed it most when one could not muster it. In the drover's tavern in Llandovery he excused himself from eating with the others. By the time they reached Lampeter, a fulling settlement a day's ride upriver from Cardigan, he was whey-faced and mumbling things no one quite understood. It had been that moment in the charge when he glanced up briefly to see if he could see her, the lunge had come from outside of his field of vision and whilst he had reacted immediately, pulling up abruptly to strike the perpetrator senseless to the ground, it was then already too late. The wound was deep, deeper than he imagined; he had hardly felt it in the heat of the moment and afterwards it had hardly been his priority. Making certain Marie was safe was his only aim and once she was at Cardigan, where even if there were those there who would resent her there would be plenty who would love her and look after her, then he would tend to his own injuries. But he had lost much blood. On the last day, outside the village of Cilgerran, he slumped in his saddle and they had to hasten to a house there where he could receive treatment. Marie watched over him herself, mopping his forehead every now and again with a cold cloth and holding his hand tightly. At one point, in the late hours or the early hours, no one could really say but it was in the deadest part of the night, he woke and saw Marie beside him and beheld her with clearness in his eyes.

"There was but one place I could have been struck, and I was struck there," he said.

Marie roused herself out of a waking dream, a dream in which she and all she knew was engulfed by fire only she did not burn but walked or sleepwalked through the flames bemused at how everything else she held dear was breaking blackening crackling into ash around her, she heard the words of her attendant and clasped his hand and kissed it tearfully.

"Dear Pierrot, you defended me and protected me more than anyone else would have…"

Pierrot perceived that his lady assumed he was talking about the wound he had incurred during the fighting. Like Achilles, he thought faintly, remembering a tale Marie once told him. She knew all the Greek and Roman myths, like she had been acquainted with all the Gods, the Goddesses, the mortals and the immortals personally.

"No…" he started to protest. He did not mean that the sword had struck him. He meant that she had. All knights made declarations of love to their ladies at some point. Every tale of chivalry he had ever known said so.

But it mattered not, not now. There were other battles to fight. Out of the fetid bed he sprang. His armour was on, his visor down, he was astride his horse and galloping down the list field, it was a wonderful day. The crowd was cheering but the sun was bright. And then, though they shielded and strained their eyes, try as they might in that strangely bright light they could not see him anymore.

> *But Rollant feels that death had made a way*
> *Down from his head till on his heart it lay;*
> *Beneath a pine running in haste he came,*
> *On the green grass he lay there on his face;*
> *His olifant and sword beneath him placed,*
> *Turning his head towards the pagan race,*
> *Now this he did, in truth, that Charles[1] might say*
> *(As he desired) and all the Franks his race;*
> *'Ah, gentle count; conquering he was slain!'*
> *He owned his faults often and every way,*
> *And for his sins his glove to God upraised[2].*

---

1 Charlemagne, otherwise known as Charles the Great. He was crowned King of the Franks in 768, King of the Lombards from 774 and from 800 became the first Emperor Europe had known since the fall of the Roman Empire.
2 *Chanson de Roland*, verse CLXVIII.

Holiness

(DECEMBER, 1176)

A GIRL, NINE OR TEN AT MOST, but already with a wicked sting to her hit, was slapping him awake. For a moment he was back in his family home in York and it was his oldest sister rousing him: '*get up Avery, you sluggard, get up and do something useful!*' But his bed in York had been conducive to lying on until late in the morning. This ungodly spot was not; nor did it bear any similarity to the part of the moor he remembered being in before that ungentle thump to his temple knocked him into oblivion.

He was sprawled prone on a stony stretch of ground part-covered by a rock overhang. The overhang formed a recess that went back some way; deep enough that inside he could hear the voices of whosoever it was that had brought him here but not see them. A few feet from his head a mountain stream rushed by to tumble down a waterfall not far off. Remnants of a fire smoked beside him, but neither it nor the sight of Dog on the other side in a similar state of befuddlement were any comfort. His lip at the hands of the crone, his cheeks at the hands of this girl… it was all too much.

"You can stop that now, miss," he sat up stiffly.

The girl, a dark bony thing with impudent eyes, jumped back, staring at him like a wild animal.

"What'll you do if I don't?"

Dog laughed mirthlessly. He only ever seemed to laugh when the situation was distinctly unfunny.

"The little chit makes a point. I've seen you outmatched by the very old and by the very young within one day's ride of the English border. If she wants to keep on hitting you I'll wager she will."

"You use your girth to escape from your misadventures, friend; I prefer common sense," Avery glanced crossly at the musician. "As our current captors have taken pains to bring us here and neither killed us nor robbed us yet, I intuit they mean us no serious harm and are far more likely to want to converse with us."

He glared at Dog and Dog glared back.

Sodomy, torture, enslavement, nice juicy sacrifices to the Gods, Dog could think of plenty of reasons why they had thus far been kept alive, but privately conceded Avery was probably right.

Avery saw his companion was in as sorry a mess as he was, his face the ruddier for the grazes incurred in their capture, and in the process of spitting out dislodged teeth. They were both scratched and dirty enough to resemble convicts and indeed, Avery reminded himself, had between the two of them committed significant crimes. A small mercy it was that the desolation of their surroundings at least confirmed they were not on Norman territory, because then they would be being bound for execution and an unmarked grave far from consecrated ground for the things they had done.

"Are they in the land of the living, Olwen?" squawked a man's voice from within the rocky recess that Avery knew straightaway was that of he who had walloped them with the stick. "If not then with my blessing revive them with the foulest bog water you can find, just not with the fucking holy water, that would be wasted on the devils!"

"We're awake, no thanks to you," Dog shouted bad-temperedly into the recess. "Now show yourself rather than getting your chit to do your bidding and tell us why you've dragged us to this miserable cave."

There was a vexed sigh in the darkness, and a man with a bald head and a beard dangling down to his belly emerged. He tossed two clean-looking tunics on the stones.

"You are fucking filthy. Have the good grace to wash and then perhaps I will permit you into my miserable cave to converse with me. If not, feel free to fuck off, there is a rainstorm coming and no shelter for a great many miles, I would be intrigued to find out how many hours you would last."

So saying the man retreated into the gloom. There were sounds of female laughter as he said something else and the smell of roasting mutton, fine indeed to Avery and Dog who had tasted nothing so good in many, many days, diffused onto the moor.

"I don't like him," said Dog. "I'd rather brave the weather and whatever other dregs Berwyn can dredge up than tarry in this rat's hole."

"Are you not curious as to why he wants us here?"

"No. Neither did I survive crossing Berwyn before by being curious."

Avery arose, undressed awkwardly and made his way to the stream, cleaning himself carefully but rapidly, in case the girl Olwen or worse one of the other women in the cave might clap eyes on him. Soon his wounds smarted less and his skin regained its grime-free shade, Saxon pale, but he caught cold for his pains and started to sneeze loudly.

No tough Brythonic stock, thought Dog, that's what lets you get by out here, his travelling companion was like a sapling grown up but not out, with winter sneaked upon him before he had put down proper roots.

"Do as you wish, friend," Avery snivelled. "I have followed your advice several times to my detriment, and the prospect of roast meat and that old snow-beard's company is preferable to tackling the open moor assailed by a storm and your constant grumbling."

"Ha! I'll wager it's the prospect of his womenfolk that tickles your fancy." Dog was hurt at Avery's snub and hid this behind a cruel dig. "My faith! If you didn't succeed bedding a filly in York where there are plenty what makes you think you'll manage in the middle of this mud-caked heath?"

In the stream and then beside the fire Avery cleaned and dried and dressed himself as best he could. He shivered but it was not now the midwinter chill making him do so. It was the memory of that night in the cathedral just prior to him fleeing York. Perhaps because of all that had passed since his journey to Wales began he felt more able to confront it now, but found he could still only do so quaveringly. Just two weeks ago his future had been as bright as the cathedral's lavishly painted ceiling. York's most senior clergymen had been talking about him so glowingly: he had been the future of the church; part of the Archbishop's big plans. Now he huddled on the most Godforsaken expanse of moorland imaginable looking upon a dank cave as an improvement to his circumstances. Such a turn-around in fortunes alone he could have handled. It was not the first time his life had been abruptly upended, but the reason for this particular upending would make him retch for as long as he lived. He did not reply for so long even the thick-skinned musician began to think that perchance the dig had been too base.

"In the church many things are denied you, friend," Avery said finally. And into the dark of the recess he called out: "We are cleansed!" Then he stood and added pointedly: "At least, I am."

He walked into the cave without waiting to see if Dog came after him.

The cave roof pitched beyond the entrance. One needed to crouch then crawl along a low passage before the main chamber opened up, sufficiently so that seven or eight could have fitted in around a substantial blaze there and still had space to sleep behind. It was a strange thing meeting strangers on hands and knees. It made one appear somehow foolish. And for Avery, who had met so few members of the gentler sex, meeting women in this way was particularly awkward. He paused, conceding the farcicality of the situation that he should feel no unease towards the foul-mouthed old snow-beard and only towards the women gathered around his fire whose laughter was in fact one of the pleasanter things he had heard during his days on the road.

The cathedral and the town of York were of course not separate entities; duties had on many occasions taken him into the secular world. But there was always a need to return to church hanging over him, Lauds Prime Terce Sext None Vespers Compline Matins, there was no time for lingering over any one thing least of all a woman, it was easier to be afraid of one than lust after one. Yet like the sweet stench of rotting fruit or the brush of a foreign fabric as he wound through the maze of a market, like the ale smell spilling from a tavern, like the titter issuing from a house of ill repute as he hastened past, there was something fascinating about a woman too, something he could not put out of his mind even during fervent prayer. The older canons advised him: *'occupy yourself with God, son, the Almighty has devised many methods to save us from succumbing to pleasures of the flesh, best to concentrate yourself on song, on the path God has chosen you, draw on your Kyrie, your Gloria in Excelsis, your Alleluya and Credo and Agnus Dei as we know you can, until they sound divine or superior at least*

to the song that comes out of Canterbury.' But York cathedral for all the time and space it afforded for devoting oneself to the Lord was designed with one flaw fatal for a young churchman susceptible to hankerings for the life without: a view. Not the principal building, here the windows were painted with scenes of stern men and women with eyes forever upturned to God and these very much inspired piety, but the buildings in which Avery and the other young men of York aspiring to a life in the collegiate church were lodged did have a view. Avery had heard her one morning on the little street below. She was singing *In Rama sonat gemitus*, the lament they sung back then about the exile of Thomas à Becket, Archbishop of Canterbury, but that had gained greater popularity after his death—and with such a voice! Indeed her breathing really did impress him for she sung from dawn until dusk that day and those after it, not just the canonical hours but straight through, her bowl soon overflowing with coins. He invented every pretext he could to be in his lodgings then. This still did not buy him nearly enough time but it bought him some. *These are what they teach us to avoid*, he had marvelled, admiring how the girl's lips parted how the veins in her neck trembled, *heavenly creatures like this*. She had caught him spying the third morning. She had smiled and he had blushed and hid but resolved to smile back at her the following day, only the following day she was not there nor was she ever there again. No one could furnish him with an adequate explanation as to her sudden disappearance for she had sung well and been popular, but he suspected the senior canons of arranging it. Too much more singing about the Archbishop of Canterbury as if he were the most revered saint in Christendom could only make the Archbishop of York appear increasingly like the devil incarnate.

"At long last!" cried the old snow-beard. He sat on the far side of the fire, picking things out of his facial hair. "You have made yourself look pretty, I see." The two women laughed again and the snow-beard introduced them all. He was Sulien of Berwyn, a hermit whose reputation, he said, went well beyond this heath and extended to every corner of the land where there were people who sought truths and wisdoms. She with the softer laugh was Iola, the snow-beard's wife, she looked half his age and still quite beautiful. The girl Olwen was their daughter.

The other woman needed no introduction.

"A good morning to you, my little knight," winked the Healer, her red hair redder yet in the firelight and looking every inch the witch she was. "What news?"

It was possible this giantess might not know about the deaths of the Marcher lord's men following the ingestion of her so-called potion, Avery thought, but it was probable that she did. It would be wrong to blame her entirely for their being wanted on multiple counts of murder, he held Dog chiefly responsible, but her charlatan concoctions and the musician's thirst for revenge were between them the reason he would have to forever steer clear of lawmen regardless of having led an honest and well-intentioned life. He elected to say nothing at the present time on the off-chance none of them here knew a thing about the incident but Dog, worse luck, barged into the chamber behind him.

Dog let out a low growl.

"Did I not vow to you," he said in an ominous tone to Avery, pronouncing each syllable with deliberation, "that I would give that meddlesome potion pedlar something to be sorry for when I saw her next. And behold who I should take shelter from the very next storm with…"

"Is there something about my product you disliked, my dastard? Buyer beware, my burly rascal, for it was your choice how much you used of my medicine, and I can call on plenty who will testify to its effectiveness."

The Healer sat cross-legged and because of the length of her giantess's legs and the difficulty no doubt of getting a tunic cut to fit them, there was a gap between the hem and the place on her shanks to which her boots and stockings were pulled, a gap of grubby white flesh, knees and thighs which had Avery's full attention. He tried to restrain Dog, for he was more and more certain the Healer was unaware of what had taken place in Mistress Bell's, but his companion ploughed on.

"Effectiveness! My faith woman, no one disputes the power of your potion. Six bodyguards of a Marcher lord lie dead because of it! And we've a sure noose around our necks should the law discover us."

"People live and people die," Sulien spoke up sharply. "And the living are best advised to worry about their own lives than about deaths that cannot be undone."

The Healer grinned smugly as if to imply no truer words could be said and stuck out her tongue at Dog, who rose to the bait like a bear at a fair.

"So *these* are the pearls of wisdom poor fools risk all to come here and hear?" he retorted.

"Listen to me you fat fuck," squawked Sulien. "I will clout you about the jowls a second time and fucking dismember you if need be but you will show me the respect due to a man such as I and listen if I command it, you are my prisoner in my cave, *I* am Sulien of Berwyn, *you* do not have the word 'Berwyn' in your title whatsoever as far as I am aware whilst there is good reason why they add 'Berwyn' to mine, I know Berwyn like my own beard, every shit clod and sheep path upon it, whereas you would be exquisitely fucked were I to turn you away from my cave, you would blunder around in that wilderness until you dropped because you have not the slightest notion where you are, so you will cease thrashing your bulk about and you *will* hear me. Fuck!"

Dog muttered something about how they had hardly sought out this hole, that they would gladly have traded their time here for the wilderness and its wild storms combined and retracted their respective whacks on the head into the bargain. But he was sufficiently subdued. It was worth backing down to stop Sulien from yapping if nothing else.

"Now, you pair of fucks." The hermit's outburst had tired him. His wife moved to ease her hands under his armpits, guiding him back so that the rear wall of the cave supported him, and he evinced his gratitude with a canny spank of her bottom. "You interest me, which is a very good thing, as I dislike nothing more than being bored. You do not have that bland happy look pilgrims have, the story about your encounter with men-at-arms of the March and your fecklessness generally inclines me to think you cannot be fighting men and if you are merchants you are fucking hopeless ones as you have no wares. I would have hazarded you were entertainers but so far you have not exactly been entertaining. In any case most minstrels I have come across would have already dittied the patience out of me by now, I find such knaves to be mindful only of the money that jingles into their soliciting bowls rather than giving due care to the tunes they make, so as you have attempted no dittying, I can only assume you have some higher purpose here."

"You are right in thinking us entertainers, friend," Avery took the piece of roast mutton Sulien's silent but kindly smiling wife was proffering him. Out of the side of his eyes he had been watching the Healer eating hers, she ate without restraint with much licking of lips and grunts of appreciation, he had inadvertently become absorbed by her during the hermit's rant and, embarrassedly realising this, tore his gaze back to the old man. "But there are variations of quality within our business just as there must be within yours, and we aspire towards the utmost reaches of the ambit."

"I know about the good entertainers," Sulien said, "but they never make it out here."

"These are not your normal minstrels," quipped the Healer between mouthfuls of mutton. "They make a killing at performances, these ones!"

"We are not in any way average," Avery flushed. "I may not have attended the bardic schools of Wales, but I am schooled in the art of song and am told by elders of the church in York that my voice is exceptional. Not only that but I am familiarising myself with all twenty metres of poetry the gifted bards are supposed to know in this land and have experimented with writing both an awdl and an englyn, which few Englishmen and not that many of the Welsh can claim. My companion here is descended from an illustrious line of musicians, his father is chief fiddler to Lord Rhys of Deheubarth no less, and for fifteen years he has played the crwth and the harp and the pibgorn with masterful accomplishment."

"And Berwyn," Sulien surmised dryly, "stands between you and your destination?"

"Yes."

"Fucking bad luck."

"We are veritably assuaged by it."

Sulien tugged at his beard, regarding Avery shrewdly and Dog not at all, for the fat fuck deadened the hermit's delivery by virtue of his own barbed mannerisms whilst the thin fuck gazed about in such goggling wonder it served to make the words and actions of others seem weightier. And a dispenser of truths and wisdoms comes to love best the sound of their own sentences as they leave the lips, wise yes but most of all weighty, wondrous weighty and rich like the first drop of fine wine on the back of the palate after a time of going without.

"I will tell you something you young fuck, I am old and I mention this not to gripe about incontinence nor the occasional limpness of prick that encroaches with age, but to emphasise the fact that I have been upon this Earth some time, half a century or more, half a century on this fucking moor and my father Sulien for a similar length of time beforehand in the very same place. We hermits need space for our contemplations, yes a good fuck from time to time, but chiefly we need to think and the wider the expanse the wider ranging our meditations. Thus on Berwyn I am able to think more or less about All Things. This is why the people come to me to seek my wisdom. Now what do you suppose might occur if every misguided oaf or even every tenth oaf in Wales stumbled onto my moor with an *I am lost Sulien* or an *I want shelter Sulien and perhaps a portion of your lovely roast mutton too?* I will say unto you, fuck: I would be impinged; my thoughts would become impinged by the minute chirrups of the everyday. But in this matter Sulien my father had devised a countermeasure, he too had considered the unthinkability of being distracted from his thoughts, and so in his half-century and then in mine we invented deterrents, ways of keeping fucks like you away you might say. It could be a well-woven myth, stories of fairies always work well, although it did not matter so long as the people did not venture onto the moor anymore, not unless it was of the uttermost importance, not unless they were coming to see me. Some with lowlier motives still come of course, the especially desperate fucks mainly, and these I still have to decide what to do about…"

"And what, friend, have you decided to do about us?"

"Nothing," the hermit's eyes glittered within his bowling ball of a head. "Your business appears to be for the common good rather than for the bad, in this sense we are fighting on the same side, Sulien of Berwyn would not wish to impede anyone who fights for the furthering of a thing above and beyond the mud and the blood that are too frequently the standard in our land... I will send you on your way with my blessing: with a bellyful of mutton, with a cold compress for the injuries you regrettably suffered at the rough end of my stick and with my daughter as your guide back to civilization ... provided you are who you claim to be..."

Dog laughed hollowly.

"I knew it! Rats like this never make clean deals."

"A story for a story," said the hermit. "I gave you mine. You are entertainers, you say, you can sing twenty types of fine verse on the woes and wonders of our world, you can pluck fine melodies out of the air and hold them on your harp strings like netted birds until their beauty overwhelms and we laugh or weep. Entertain us!"

"We are honoured by the request, friend," Avery smiled wanly and answered before Dog could make another of his retorts, "but our art lends itself best to halls or buildings with lofty roofs for the projection of sound, not caves in which one cannot fully stand and with the winter wind whistling in."

"As you wish," the hermit's tone became immediately more hostile. "Then leave my fireside this instant and brave the rainstorm, fucks, finding your frozen corpses in a few days will perturb me precious little I promise you!"

Avery glanced at Dog, who was likewise keeping an eye on the Healer's legs as she fidgeted for a comfier position. Dog shrugged as if to convey neither of them had a huge deal of choice in this matter.

"Very well, friend," Avery sighed. "I will sing to you, and as I have but one song in readiness…" he broke off, surprised at the tremor creeping into his words, "on a subject right close to my heart." He drew back from the fire, finding himself for the first time the focus of everyone's attention and finding that this did not worry him. "Forgive me," he whispered, watching himself almost from outside himself, as the awkward voice of Avery the nobody cantered easily freely down the tones into the assured voice of Avery the singer of songs. And his song, even though he had never set it to music and would not in any case know how to do so, unconsciously assumed the melody the girl outside his lodgings in York had sung, *In Rama sonat gemitus,* the song one sung to conjure the sense of a good thing coming to an end and another thing, a far darker thing, looming up to take its place:

> *Autumn in the church, a great church – supreme!*
> *The bishops preen, like peacocks perch.*
> *They don their best gold, a sight to behold – then*
> *Incense to veil their souls and to uphold*
> *The grand pretence their piety – is real.*
> *For the Cardinal from Italy*
> *Is come with intent, with Godly words – and*
> *Like sycophant pawns, bishops converge.*
> *From Canterbury, York, from Bath – as well*
> *As Wells, Salisbury, Durham, Llandaff,*
> *Ants before their queen, teeming to take seats*
> *By His Holiness, to get the great*
> *Benefactions bound for their churches,*
> *In the surge to cry: "my church deserves!"*
> *Two foremost men of God then start – to brawl:*
> *"Who's fairest of all, whose fine hind parts*

Will sit alongside – His Holiness?"
And madness set in; they bicker, vie
Vicars and canons in on the tussle,
For lust of lucre their aggression.
I, come late, can see: this great – comedy
Clergy their cassocks disarrayed, irate,
Crucifixes and mantles muddled – as
The asses, all for His Holiness
Mercilessly smash to sad small pieces
Each other and their integrity
Like Jesus with the dealers in coarse trade
On the Sabbath day, on the temple courts,
I want to drive them, drive them out – in rage
But they're the pillars, they're our devout!
(The most devout men of God – existing)
Bringing these columns down brings all down.
Instead floundering, I say not one – thing
I who see this mess as the autumn.
Autumn in the church, through the church doors – blow
Dead old leaves though, in rage in remorse,
I let leaves pile up, I the seer – of mess,
Autumn holiness and winter near
I, seer of messes, of the oncoming
Of winter in church, I do no thing.

As Avery had sung Dog had seized his harp, and with the ferocious expression his face assumed when concentrating, accompanied his companion with a striking of strings that rendered the verses still richer, adding depth and dimension, giving the listeners a whole world, a world marvellous but momentary that as their mouths dropped in joy he snatched from them. Then gave them again then took from them, gave and took, gave and took, toyed with them and teased them. And finally singer and player were done, drained and spent, unable to so much as nod to the other in acknowledgment that together they had created an inexpressible extraordinary thing. And Sulien's cave lapsed into the shocked silence that has to follow a thing like that.

But not for long.

Out pealed the Healer's laugh alongside her boisterous clapping and Iola's more moderated applause.

Everyone turned to Sulien, who seemed satisfied at their waiting in this way for his opinion.

"You pair of fucks really can perform," he proclaimed. And to Iola: "where is the quintessence of herbs, woman, the one prepared for helping me attain states of trance?"

Iola, still sweetly smiling as if she were dishing out nothing worse than bread of the sacrament, distributed drinking receptacles of differing sizes. The receptacles were filled with a foul liquid, murkily tinctured by a number of unidentifiable moorland plants, and the largest were for Sulien, Avery and Dog.

"To Berwyn's best entertainers!" Sulien cried, and as the old man gulped the horn's contents they realised with rising nausea they were expected to do the same.

At least, thought Avery, as he reticently brought the quintessence to his lips, he would now have an excuse for why the tears were coming to his eyes.

It was not the girl that had sung outside his window in York. One cannot long lament the loss of someone one had not so much as summoned the courage to smile at. Toward the church he felt emotions in abundance, true, but these were mainly rage or revulsion of one form or another, they made him tremble but they did not make him sob. His tears were tears of happiness. He had entertained notions, in a byre or a tavern on the trip here, that he might be able to do it: master the patterns of the Welsh verse, the most intricate metres in existence, put words to them and perform them. But they had been in his head alone. He had turned lines around and about *inside* but never let them *out*, not like this. The old snow-beard was right. He could perform. And he would, too. When he reached the castle where the greatest river in Wales met the sea, he might not be close to the best of those who would stand up in Lord Rhys' mighty hall and sing, but stand with the best of them he would.

All that day the rainstorm did not let up, so they sat about the fire and drank. Come early afternoon, when the quintessence was having its effects and night already looked to be drawing near, Sulien instructed them to light a second fire, as near to the cave mouth as the deluge would allow and with as big a blaze as they could.

"It is the solstice, the day when the dark comes closest to taking over from the light. We must burn the brightest flame we might to ensure that after this day the shadows retreat in defeat."

"Pagan horseshit," Dog muttered, but it was he who was most active in getting the fire going, and he who stared off into the night once it did press in around them with the most apprehension.

"What if this rain should not stop, tomorrow or the next day or any day soon?" Avery wondered. "How then should we ever reach the festival of song?"

"It will stop," said Sulien, eyes glistening with intoxication. "On the morrow you will leave, and in three hard days' walk you will be at Cardigan for Christmas morning: in good time for the festival's commencement."

"Never fear, my gallant gentleman," the Healer nudged Avery who felt his cheeks begin to burn again at her touch. "I am not a woman to be thwarted as I think you now know and I too mean to be in Cardigan for Christmas, for I have an appointment with a certain highborn there I can ill afford not to honour."

"You too are going to sing?" Avery asked, the quintessence emboldening him.

"No, my lionheart. My gift is just for healing but the Lord gave it to me with a bad side as well as a good, I can curse as powerfully as I can cure and I will hold this highborn to his appointment or it will be the worse for him," she leant close to Avery. Her mouth smelt of meat and herbs and hotness. "He has got me with child," she murmured, in a voice that sounded slightly vulnerable.

"The swine!" the words fell out hoarsely. "Who is he?"

But the Healer's vulnerability was gone as suddenly as it had exposed itself.

"Oh my! You *are* a funny one, my gallant young knight!"

Sulien himself took the quintessence whenever one who had come seeking his sagacity asked a question even his immeasurable hermit's knowledge could not answer. In the trance, with access to the greater plain parallel to that normal humans inhabit, he located those last unknowns and made them known.

And who among that group could say to what extent the quintessence affected them as the fire to ward off perpetual darkness burned outside? But they all wondered things about each other that day that would otherwise have stayed locked well away. Avery wondered about Dog, who appeared changed from his usual irascible self and preoccupied less with picking a fight than with the Healer, looking at her legs and even the parts of her that were clothed with undisguised lasciviousness. Dog wondered about Avery. It was as if since the singing of the song a hitherto latent part of him was boiling to the fore. Dog had regarded him before as a mouse of a youth, but he did have fire in him. After all that time with choirboys and bishops, being suddenly amongst womenfolk, and two striking women at that, had seemingly turned him into some protector of the sex. Some Galahad, Dog thought scornfully and then, more warily: some rival. The Healer wondered about Sulien and his wife, he so old she so young and fair, he so vocal she so quiet. What did a man like this give a woman like that? Sulien was such a precise man, deriving great pride from wisdom-giving. Once, so the hermit had said, when a youth married early had come to Berwyn complaining of desire for another and how disappointed the family would be if anything happened and they found out, this wily old man of the moors had only gone unbeknownst to the youth and got them all to come to the cave to talk about it, the wife, the lady lusted after and members of all the respective kin. The youth, returning a week later according to Sulien's instructions and in expectation of a well-considered solution, had encountered every aspect of his predicament there in the flesh staring at him. The Healer wondered if the wise man's eye for detail extended to intercourse, could it be his tender and exact attentions to his wife in their lovemaking was what elevated the hermit into a category of his own? The Healer was born tough and she was born tall which enabled her to be tougher; her last encounter was the rough one that had got her with child, and tenderness was not a thing she missed, having always had other overriding concerns. But she had heard tell of the tender ones, the men who desired to please women, and she could not resist speculating whether Sulien was one of these. Perhaps he did it slowly to Iola in the darkness on the cold slabs of stone at the back of his cave, perhaps they ascended first into absolute trance and in autoscopy frolicked with more fervour than those poor people denied entry to the greater plain could even envisage doing. Sulien wondered about Avery and Dog. He was not second-sighted like his father Sulien, quite regularly in these most un-mythical of times seers get by just fine with nothing more than astuteness, but he did have the odd flash of future happenings. And since the two entertainers had arrived at his cave a flash *had* come, a flash as troubling as it was distinct. Sulien deliberated whether to tell them or not. Knowledge did not necessarily nurture. Sometimes it pulled the ground from under your feet and plunged you into the abyss. As to Iola, no one knew what she was wondering. But she seemed more at peace than any of them.

Olwen skipped off over the moor next morning with the sure-footedness of a goat. The Healer who had the least difficulty keeping pace came after and Avery or Dog alternated at the rear.

"Best place to be, behind her," Dog said wickedly to Avery. "Every aspect of that colossus of a bottom for our eyes alone."

"You would do well to treat her with more respect, friend."

"Would I now... *my gallant young knight?*" Dog spikily replied.

Avery said nothing more to Dog for a while after that. Nor did he say anything to the Healer although he would have liked to. The going was toilsome and merely maintaining the same speed as the others was hard enough; to catch up with her and say something of worth when he did so would have required much effort. If only he could speak as smoothly as he could sing. It was not her bottom as his companion crassly inferred that captivated him, although by the day's end he had looked upon it for far longer than any other in his life, it was that she had confided in him and he felt a need to reciprocate, to reach out as she had reached out, to show her a kindness.

The trail they trod was not much more than the faintest indentation in the bracken, and the route in the rain-swaddled murk almost featureless, but Olwen led them above blanket bogs around meres over inclines so inhospitable the vegetation withered away completely into stark scatterings of boulders, and with no pause to wait for the less fleet of foot. Late afternoon, and they pulled up by a ruin: a barton long abandoned by a farmer driven to despair by the barrenness. Now it was the domain of rowans that had shot through the stone in mockery of the very attempt to try carving out a life in such a spot.

Olwen informed them that over the rise was the village of Dinas Mawddwy, where there was a tavern and the road south to the coast and then to Cardigan.

"By my faith, if there is a tavern with a solid roof close by why do we not bed down in it?" Dog grumbled.

"Do as you please," said Olwen. "But that village has the worst reputation of any in Wales, and I would advise you rest in this ruin if you want to rise tomorrow with everything you went to bed with."

"I have no fear we will find a means to keep warm!" the Healer said spiritedly. "A little mountain goat like you as a guide and two hardy heroes to watch over me, a woman could want for no more."

It was cold roast sheep that they ate for dinner and it was the stink of dead sheep and the bleat of living ones that prevented them falling asleep that night. Avery drowsed, lines for a song circling in his mind but finding no form because of the distracting drumming of rain on rock. It was to be a love poem though, he was certain; he had no need to confine himself to churchly subjects any more. He imagined the ranks of the canons, the sombre black-and-white-clad men of York at evening prayer, and for his song he thought about the subjects that would scandalise them most of all. Then he realised he did not really know what they would be. He was roused it seemed for at least the tenth time that night, but this time it was not the wretched sheep bleating for once. It was, however, a bestial sound and it was coming from the adjoining room where in former times the farmer's animals might have slept.

Dog was supine in the hay and the Healer was on top, her great white bottom moving up and down in the shadows. The sound was a medley of his groans and her barely contained laughter, breathless, a cross between a squeal and a gasp and a cackle as if Dog had said something blackly funny only he had not, he was pinioned by the Healer's tremendous thighs, and she rode him ruthlessly like a racehorse at full gallop and the overall effect upon the ears Avery could only equate to a pig being butchered.

And she saw him. Dog did not but she did, before he could recoil and disappear into the darkness, she spun round or rather her head spun, although her body stayed facing forward her head twisted right back at an impossible angle and shook just once: '*no*,' it mouthed, '*no no.*'

He could not return to sleep. He thought he might as well keep watch for all the good that would do. He crouched in the entranceway until the paleness of approaching dawn was spilling across the sky and thus she found him, rocking on his heels as Olwen tossed and turned and Dog snored.

"I needed a brute," she said to him simply. "Not one such as you."

"One such as me? I sometimes wonder who I really am."

"You, my little gentleman? You are one of the tender ones," Avery glanced at her, presuming she was jesting, but she was not. "You could not have done this." And in the half-light she showed him the fresh, ugly bruising on her face and arms. "I asked him to do it. No, really, I did," she calmed him as he started up, he might be no match for Dog when they stood against each other in the light of day but by night as the musician dozed, why then some damage could be done! "For all the remedies I know of," she said, "there are none that are a certain cure for this," she patted her swollen belly ruefully. "None better than rough treatment at the hands of a man."

Avery was dumbfounded. He was about to spout something about how it was a sin to undo God's work and if the good Lord had intended for her to have a baby she should not go against His wish. But he stopped himself. Quite often people will shamble along with a set of beliefs because these have been banged into them since birth yet should they check themselves and even briefly examine the beliefs with stone-cold reason, they will see absurdity. Just absurdity.

"What about this, ah… highborn," he managed, "he who you were to meet in Cardigan? He could have been made to feel a responsibility! He could have offered you recompense, remuneration, a place to raise the infant…"

"He could clap me in irons or arrange for my murder too, my knight."

"So you choose to destroy a life?"

"It was a moment of weakness, my lionheart, have you never had one of those? Besides," she said, snatching his hand and placing it over her womb. "It did not work. Feel. Stout little minnow, this one."

He had never touched a woman like this and his hand shook as it came to rest over the warm curve of flesh. But to do so and then feel the kick of a new life —life!

"It is a sign!" suddenly the words were flooding out of him from all directions. "We must… let me help you… you will let me… you must!"

"There are no 'musts' in this world, my wayfarer. But you are right. I will go through with it now. After all, I can already picture the expression on that highborn's face. I would willingly wait with this little minnow to see that alone!"

"I walked to the rise at first light," he said tremulously. "It is as Olwen says. I saw the road to Cardigan. The way will be easier once we leave this moor behind us. Two days' walk more!" He did not dare touch her but his eyes shone full of the things he would have done had he been a different type of man, a type that had gone out early into this world instead of spending the majority of his adolescence shying away from it, and she understood this or so he believed. "Two days and you can confront this man and who knows, it may go better than you think, if he has an inkling of goodness in him I have no doubt it will!"

"I say the same right back at you, my lionheart," the Healer replied, grinning. "It might go better than you think; I heard you and that stocky scoundrel you travel with perform, remember. When they have the conversation about who fared best at this contest of song, they should be considering you if they have a spoonful of sense between them."

"We should carry on," Avery said bashfully. His cheeks were burning but not so much as they would once have done. "You had best wake him. If I do so I fear I may kick him much harder than necessary."

"That is what marks you out, my knight. Others would just go ahead and kick."

It was a grey old world, this Wales, Avery thought, huddling into his still-damp cloak then taking a gulp of December air as if to clear his throat and his larynx and his lungs, but it was a lighter shade of grey today. In the intense irrational joy that then stabbed through him he totally forgot about what the old snow-beard of a hermit had said to him just before they had left.

"Fuck," said Sulien in the depths of his cave. His wife placed the quintessence in his hands, and he drank, and by and by came to ascend again onto the greater plain. The flash this time was more vivid; it could have been intensified by the level of trance into which he had arisen but one of those fucks had given off a fucking awful aura, a stink of an aura to hound his visions like this, that was for fucking sure. "Fuck!"

(DECEMBER, 1176)

IN THE FRUITFUL lands of England and the Low Countries and the Holy Roman Empire and beyond, so they said, in the Byzantine Empire and even Persia, the crops flourished, honey-yellow corn, russet-red apples, oranges, olives, emblazoning the land in gaudy hues and dazzling the passersby or driving them to distraction. And the roads through these lands were wide, wide and level and well-paved and true, built by the Romans to get to places that mattered and maintained by the populace out of pride, out of duty, out of consideration for the travellers that travelled them. As one journeyed the sun shone with real heat on the nape of the neck and the air smelt of good things growing, rye and rosemary and the musty scent of grapes ripening on vines. So sensual could the experience be, that on occasion the wayfarer was tempted to idle a-while, pluck those good growing things and sit at the roadside gorging on them, with the sweet juices thick around one's lips, imbibing whatever was going on nearby, a farmhand sowing and reaping, some passing knights bound for Rome or the Holy Land, maidens pausing to pick berries having taken the longer more lingering path back from church. And the villages and towns along the way had taverns with stone walls and tiled roofs; sometimes they had a hearth with no fire burning in the evening because the sun had so pleasingly warmed the building and its occupants during the day.

Wales was not like that.

In Wales the mountains pressed in and the rivers cut in and left little room for cultivation of any kind; still less for roads fit for travel. Vegetation there was in abundance, the travellers that came commented and complained within moments of crossing the border on *that*, the woods and the forests, the moss and the mulch, the briars and bracken, but it was inhospitable greenery, impenetrable, yielding nothing. There was no fragrance of fruit, there was only earth, the damp loaminess of earth, just earth. The sun was seldom warm and when it was the wind and rain outdid it. It could be noon in high summer and one's feet would be wet, wet as one walked, wet as one ate, wet as one slept, and it was harder to think about things not directly related to the weather or to the onerous country one was traversing.

So the way in Wales became a head-bent, cloak-huddled, looking-ahead-not-around-or-about way, a tramp not a tarry. And Wales became about the way, more than anything else about the way, whatever way that was, and this was because there were fewer ways than elsewhere and those there were, worse.

There was the way by the coast. This seemed safe enough at first, for the Normans controlled much of it; common sense dictated that if there was to be devilry in the land then at least it should take place inland and let commerce pass by on the coastal route unchallenged. But 'safe' was a nuanced word, especially for those towards whom the Normans bore animosity, especially then for the Welsh. Welsh men had to watch out for the tolls on such roads, unreasonable tolls changing with the whim of the toll operator, and Welsh women had to watch out for their maidenhead. Then came the estuaries, the Clwyd and the Conwy, the Teifi the Tywi the Taff, boats there were for the crossings but also were there storms and quicksand and unprincipled pilots who, if a fee was not to their liking, would paddle passengers not over to the other side but out into the open ocean to the ships of the Norse marauders that prowled the deeper water.

There was the way by the valleys. There were enough of these ways for there were more than enough mountains, and mountains usually had passes between them; somehow somewhere passes; along these were rivers and settlement and ribbons of decent grazing ground, all of which warranted access of one sort or another. Once upon a time, the Romans had recognised the value of the ways by the valleys as a means of policing the interior and constructed fine highways accordingly, but Normans were not Romans, and now these routes were rubble as were the destinations they had served. Rubble was still better than mud, of course, and the routes Romans had never bothered with became quagmires in the not-infrequent rains. Enforcement was certainly more minimal on these ways than on the way by the coast, but sensing this outlaws often chanced attacking wayfarers. The valleys did do better for overnight shelter than most places because of the monasteries, notably the Cistercians, who let guests stay for free and fed them well. But this charitableness ensured every traveller good and bad for miles around would descend on monastery guesthouses; they were the most over-run lodgings in the land, and put other nearby lodgings out of business, meaning in many cases it was the monks or nothing. The old-fashioned way of hospitality, the knocking and asking for refuge from the relentless road, could still be called upon, in the valleys and on the coast both. But valley-dwellers particularly were a temperamental lot, friendly and ferocious by turns, and bedding down in this way was a risk for the journey-maker.

Then there was the way over the top. Each *coed* each *cwm* each *blaen bwlch bryn* of it, up in elegies of rock, up in odes of scrub, by cairns by standing stones by tumuli over the top of it all. And here was lawlessness. In these regions was such absence of law, no lawman would dare spend the time required even to keep vigil on what manner of villainy was being perpetrated. Some of the stories about what went on up here were so bad they arose straight into legend; became tales to tell around fires sufficiently far away and even then inducing involuntary shudders from teller and listener together. Pick a path over the boulder-littered bog-entrenched, bereft-of-hope *mynydd* and one might avoid the treacherous estuaries and tolls and if one struck lucky, gain the far side in better time than on the way by the coast or valleys. But the *mynydd* was not associated with luck. It was associated with people and with things of such abominableness they could surely not all be of human origin, some must be magicians, monsters, worse. Whatever lay in wait on the way over the top stopped most from going there. Yet there were trails nevertheless. Trails trod by the devout of former times. Tracks stamped out by cattle drovers. There were the ways made by animals too, and sometimes these were best of all because animals understand better than people how to survive in the wilds.

Still in spite of everything there were ways. Negligible neglected ways, mud-thick, marsh-ridden infernal ways but ways even so, and some over the top, more by the valleys and most by the coast they came, many giving up or perishing in the process but steadily coming, head-bent, cloak-huddled, looking-ahead-not-around-or-about but ever-coming.

Unforgiving was Wales. A stone around the neck, a swamp about the shins, a slap of strong wind in the face, this was Wales. But though one hastened through it the beauty was not lost on one, harsh as it was and hard as it was one stored the beauty, down below one's rain-buffeted skin in a special deep-down place, a heart some called it, a soul some called it. One committed the beauty, the turtleback hills the valley-arrowing skeins of geese the tide-out beaches bared to their rockpools and sparkling then like Viking plunder, one boxed this beauty and lidded this beauty and later, when one was out at last from the outside, in a cowshed or church porch or if one had done well for oneself a castle hall, then one removed the lid.

Now in the evening-time chatter in the elongated embellished recountings of day's doings, out it all bursts, this beauty, sudden as smoke off a hot coal. And these storytellers might not have so much to work with, they might have no sun-soaked sittings at roadsides gorging on grapes watching maidens to tell of, but oh the sights are scarcely the point any more, the sights assume majesty anyway in the teller's merry telling.

Now sound, sound, sound is what matters, a moor is brown but in the story about the moor there is red and green and beasts and brigands too. The most lustreless thing can thus be wrought into a support for the most ornate verses; can inspire the final frenzy on the strings that makes a melody memorable.

Songs on the air currents, like birds on the wing, swooping over the top and through the valleys and around the coast of Wales, vocal songs and instrumental songs, the means by which the Welsh outlast the weather and all the rest of it. In song they are unconquerable.

For those who walk and ride the ways of Wales now, *this* end-of-year day, *this* tired old old-year day that pines for the new year to relieve it like all old-year days, they are practitioners of song.

They are bards and want-to-be bards and never-will-be bards, they are the *pencerrd* professionally devoted to song in all its twenty forms and plentiful subtleties and they are the tavern loud-mouth who has bawled out a bawdy tune or two in inebriation and does not mind trying the same again; there is a shepherd who has faith in his formidable oration, for he calls to his neighbours on the valley's far side and they hear each word he utters; there is a monk who seeks to bring honour to his order by his singing but does not have his abbot's blessing to do so outside abbey walls, so must make his way in disguise.

They are practitioners of song and they are descending on a castle that has implored them to come. Some of them do not know what to make of this, for such a thing is without precedent, the halls of the pre-eminent prince of Wales opening to all and sundry, asking only that they come either to perform their verses or to play their instruments and, should they do so more pleasingly than any other guests, offering them the finest prize conceivable, a chair at the prince's table and a share in the prince's wealth. Some do not entertain the idea of triumphing in the contests the castle is hosting, as a plenitude of food and ale will be there, and such sustenance guaranteed for such a length of time, for all Christmastide and maybe beyond, this is a marvellous thing in itself. Some are more serious about winning. Some are deadly serious.

They are practitioners of song and they are converging from Gwynedd in the north, from Powys Cyfeiliog and Powys Maelor in the northeast, from the Marcher lordships immediately south and east and from who knows where beyond that. They are come to the centre of *Pura Wallia*, to a town taken back from the Normans and thriving like it never thrived before. They are come to a castle recently raised in sheer walls of stone just like the Norman fortresses only superior, in some respects, because here the greatest river in Wales meets the sea and Flemish traders ship the famous fleeces of Deheubarth across to the Low Countries and make this the great wool port of Wales, the capital of the commodity of the moment. And whether the Welsh like it or not, whether they resent this town's success because it emphasises the prince's success at their expense to some extent—or not, whether the Normans like it or not, whether they feel threatened by the rise in power of the prince in the west who is the friend of the King and a better friend than many of them—or not, staging a festival in a town like this sends out a message. The Welsh, the message intimates, can accede to grand things without raiding, without skirmishing, without thieving, without usurping, without violence, without war and without any help from England.

And it is an irrefutably grand thing, this festival. Because of it, the town resembles a war encampment, and this analogy is used because only war, until this moment, had ever been able to amass such a huge number of people in one place at one time. The town is an encampment, a colourful clamour of the newly-arrived, of tents and banners flying from them and fires smoking between them and the most disparate bunch of souls imaginable intermingling, in the castle bailey, around the grounds of the church and priory, in the fields and orchards, along both sides of the river bridge. And the reason why is not war, it is song.

A festival of song is an irrefutably grand thing, but it does not necessarily follow that the practitioners of song scheduled to perform at it are great or even good people. The thing is, there is one part of one's brain reserved for creative thought, and in the brains of songsters, call them minstrels, bards, tune-touters, musicians, call them performing poets call them pipe players call them ditty singers call them spoon drummers, that part of the brain is better used. But the direct consequence of this is that other areas of cognition are lacking in some way or absent entirely. It could be there is no sense of empathy, it could be there is no sense of restraint, it could be there is no ability to deal with the real world outside of their highly-active imaginations, but some cog does not turn as it is supposed to turn, something is snapped. This is all very well at an average gathering, for one entertainer or a few are present as a rule and they do their thing for the others gathered, some splendidly, and are applauded, and have their abnormalities humoured or overlooked. But Welsh law does possess a strange logic and it does specify a lot of points about a chief of song, a *pencerrd*, one of the supreme songsters of the land. And amongst the other points it makes is that there should be no more than one chief of song per district. And there was one stag per herd and there was one king per kingdom too; no one challenged rules like this because they made sense to everyone. But when one hundred, one thousand individuals, all of whom have some cog in their heads not turning quite right, most of whom consider themselves worthy of being a chief of song even if their song-singing is woeful and many of whom are just not meant to be together, come together for the purpose of competing, then the abnormalities overlooked in the modest gathering cannot any longer be overlooked.

Back-biting.

Big-mouthing.

Reputation-wrangling. Rumour-smearing.

Trickery, treachery.

The ruthless pursuit of esteem or self-esteem no matter the cost, because entertainers need esteem like nectar or they are ruined.

A coming-together of songsters is not necessarily a great or a good thing and it can be the worst thing thinkable, the very worst.

"Great One?" one of the *cerrdorion* shook him out of his daze. "We have arrived."

Part Two:

THE ONES THAT SET YOU SHIVERING
WITH THEIR SHRILLNESS

La Promenade

December, 1176)

"**THERE WAS TALIESIN** and there was Aneirin and then not a damned thing," said Rhys, to the group at large. They had just left the small chapel above the castle gatehouse, into which all had crammed for the *plygain* service to usher in Christmas morning, and were at Rhys' insistence accompanying him on one of the walks about his stronghold he loved to take on all days of the year and most especially today. Down Cardigan's main street they walked. It was the town's only street, but Rhys referred to it as 'main' as if the muddy thoroughfare had innumerable other alleys and side-roads and squares branching off from it. Down in the grudgingly emerging dawn they walked towards the dock, crowded not only with the usual fishermen's coracles but with myriad other vessels, cogs and knarrs and longships and a galley from the south that had arrived this past day or two, loaded with those desirous of attending the festival. When he saw the boats close up, many in styles or with colours he was not familiar with, it was underscored to Rhys how far afield his proclamation must have been spread. The last mooring had long since gone and later-coming craft had lashed port to starboard right out into the Teifi, the river marking his southern border with the Norman lordships. There was Gwynedd here and Gwent here but there were Scottish, Scandinavians, Mediterraneans present too. He cast a glance at Anarawd, who was observing yet another new boat rowing upstream towards them and wondering how many more hundreds a town normally populated by one hundred could sustain. This was beyond anything either of them had imagined. "Not a damned thing in the way of bards for over five hundred years until now, and now they are jostling to be heard at every hall between here and the Severn. They were too occupied with fighting each other, perhaps, or there was nothing worth singing of. Anyway, there is a gap. Blackness," he smiled. "I do not want for people in five hundred years to look back on today and say the same."

"My husband is something of a chronicler," Rhys' wife Gwenllian turned to the others, for the most part bleary-eyed at rising so much before the hour to which they were accustomed. She, like the rest of the group, was humouring him by coming on this dawn-time *la promenade*, as he had called it for the benefit of the French-speakers among them, this traipse-about in the damp to show off the castle's wretched seven towers again. The difference was that she had been required to do it at least once weekly, every week for the last twenty years. "I daresay he would have dedicated himself fully to history had it not been for his princely duties."

"A chronicler that has forgotten one crucial thing," spoke up the tall cassocked figure at Rhys' shoulder, the only other person wide-awake. "The secular world may have endured centuries of blackness but not so the sacred one. I could tell you of countless texts produced by the church during this period. Endeavours of literature, annotations of music… there have always been candles burning in the house of God, my good lady."

"History tells us who we are," Rhys said, companionably but briskly. "And we can thank the church for preserving parts of it for universal benefit. Parts I grant you that cast them in a spectacular glow of righteousness, but nonetheless unquestionably for everyone's benefit. I know your own history causes you some concern, cousin Gerald, being far more Norman than you are Welsh yet alas almost as Welsh as you are Norman."

"And as the Lord and you are aware my good cousin," replied Gerald easily, "unjustly shunned by both." Husband and wife might bicker, brothers may wrestle but this was the form of sparring that he and Rhys had fallen into, he grown up in the church, his cousin making a name for himself in the state, one-upmanship of sorts, a cordial enough combat of retort and counter-retort every now and again, their respective positions did not allow for it to be any more than that. Rhys was ahead at the present time, Gerald allowed, but his cousin had thirteen years on him. In thirteen years much could change. *Mousy*, he recalled the name he and some of the younger cousins had called Rhys growing up. *Mousy mouse.* You could never call Cousin Rhys that within earshot unless you wanted trouble, but being youngsters they sometimes had. Rhys caught Gerald once in the woods at Dinefwr, back in the days when there had not been much more to Deheubarth than that and Rhys had not even been first in line to inherit the little there was, pinned him down and boxed his ears then looked absolutely astounded when Gerald twisted an arm free and hit back.

"Yet you are here, and welcome," said Rhys. "And just back from Paris, I understand? Is that where you met your companion?"

This was the prompt many would have taken to introduce themselves to the most redoubtable ruler in Wales, but Gwalchmai ap Meilyr remained tight-lipped.

"Benevolent Lord no!" exclaimed Gerald. "I have been back in Wales a while, patrolling the parishes of the diocese as it were. And I must confess to you there were numerous outrages to address, despite my only having been absent a matter of months and Advent supposedly being a season of restraint! Inappropriate appropriation, indecent acts on church grounds in certain instances, *consanguineus*—that is incest in plain language, my good cousin, and we do need to set aside time for talking more about that, perhaps privately...? But I digress. *This* man I met in Llanddewi Brefi. He is from Gwynedd, *pencerrd* to Prince Rhodri would you believe and come like so many of us from so far to take part in your festival of song! His verses are *very* clean. None of these modern and frankly amoral themes like chivalry or love beyond the bounds of holy matrimony, just good old-fashioned godliness through and through. You two will doubtless have much to discuss."

Gwalchmai bowed his head, glowering in awkwardness.

Rhys waited for the customary greeting but none came.

"Any man of Gwynedd is welcome here," Rhys said at length. "Owain of Gwynedd and I put aside our differences a decade or more hence. I pray the peace between our lands holds. Who knows when again we shall need to stand together on the field of battle? If you want for anything during your stay with us, ask and it shall be yours."

Gwalchmai croaked out some words about the honour being his, but Rhys was already off among the others in the group, Chrétien and the six other judges, his former foe Prince Owain Cyfeiliog, who he could afford to now count as a friend because the man's power in Powys was greatly diminished and who so happened to be a talented poet, and finally the young Marcher Lord from the next territory to the south of his, whose name escaped him but whose favour he was anxious to court. "You fish? Why, this river has fatter salmon than any other in Wales! A new means of shoeing cattle? How fascinating. You were last in town whilst it was under Norman control? I like to think things have evolved since then. Yes, the seven towers are best appreciated from just down here." In any case, thought Gwalchmai, left alone with Gerald and Gwenllian, who were talking about some triviality over his head like he was not even present, there was only one thing Rhys ap Gruffyd could give him. And the prince would know what that was in due course.

"Greetings to you, brothers! A happy Christmas and all the bloody rest of it." The hail was from the boat just in, a currach from Ireland flying the colours of the Kingdom of Connacht.

Rhys had known of its arrival well in advance, because a messenger had galloped full tilt from the abbey of St Dogmael's downstream on the Norman side of the river the previous evening to tell him about the Gaels lodging there. Rhys always insisted on being informed when boats from Ireland were coming in. He had no quarrel with the Irish but they were a volatile race and all the more so since the Normans had invaded.

"We're looking for the castle of Rhys," the men shouted from the boat, and roughly enough now that Anarawd and the two members of the *teulu* with him tightened their hands around their weapons.

What Rhys feared was that the Irish could have a quarrel with him. After he liberated Cardigan from Norman tyranny in '65 he had kept the former constable, Fitz-Stephen, under lock and key. You never kill a valuable prisoner, this advice Rhys' father had given him and this Rhys would pass on to his sons, you can only kill a person once, so be sure you will not regret it before you do so. But Fitz-Stephen had become too valuable to keep. The exiled Irish King of Leinster, Mac Murchada, had been over in England and Wales in excess of a year, sniffing after soldiers to help him win back his throne. And Rhys had seen an opportunity.

He had released Fitz-Stephen on the condition that he would rally the Marcher lords owning lands bordering Deheubarth to sail for Ireland and help Mac Murchada get his kingdom back. The Normans liked acquisition, Rhys knew, and had bitten the bait, leaving their territories in Wales less well-defended and with bounds that were easier to push back. But the Normans had done well in Ireland, too well perhaps. Fitz-Stephen's vanguard had triumphed, more Marcher lord-led forces had followed in the wake and now even the High King of Ireland's lands were under threat. And Rhys felt responsible. He thought there could be reprisals too.

"You're Rhys!" A man with flowing jet hair and beard bounded over the sides of the other boats to jump onto the dock, squinting up at them. "I was told to watch for one with a moustache the colour of Connemara sand and there's no other here matching that description, brother. It's a nice colour, Connemara sand," he added, when no response was forthcoming. "Makes you want to take your clothes off and go for a swim in the Atlantic, or make mad love to your sweetheart on it, that kind of colour."

Arms folded Rhys contemplated the newcomer, on the brink of a smile. How he thrived on these moments. He had come down to the dock knowing the score: it would be trouble and he would deal with it or it would be an opportunity and he would seize it. Waves came and you rode them or sank. And this Irishman was an opportunity, Rhys could tell.

"I am Rhys ap Gruffyd, Lord of Deheubarth, the Prince and the King's Justiciar of South Wales," he said. He did not do this to brag, but he wished to lend a sense of theatre to the occasion for the benefit of those there he was seeking to impress. And he wished the newcomer to know exactly whom he was speaking to.

"An honour, Rhys brother. Niall Ó Maolconaire. In the employ of the High King of Ireland, as a poet when called upon but more often than not as a welcome diversion from the monotony of ruling an arse-end of a kingdom about to go to the dogs."

"In Wales we have not gone to the dogs quite yet," said Rhys. "As you see," he waved a hand in the direction of the riverbank and the fields behind, along which the tents of nigh-on one thousand of the land's greatest entertainers were pitched in a spread wider than a London fair.

"It's a pretty sight, brother. You'll have to pass on some counsel for the High King of Ireland, for I feel he could use some. Assailed by Normans at the moment, so he is."

Rhys sighed. Why did the Irish always have to make things political?

"We welcome you to Cardigan, Niall Ó Maolconaire, as we welcome men and women from many lands this Christmas season, Normans included. I assume you, like they, are come here to perform?"

Niall Ó Maolconaire gave Rhys ap Gruffyd a look.

'No brother, I am come to avenge my countrymen for the disgraceful bloody mess you put our nation in, so I am, and only taking your life will satisfy me,' Rhys imagined the reply.

"That's right, brother," the Irishman answered with a grin. "Only bloody thing I'm any good at, performing. Normans *and* womenfolk, you say? Some spectacle that will be; a feast to end all feasts, that will be."

"We Welsh have a proud history," Rhys said, to everyone except Niall Ó Maolconaire. "That is no secret. One of the reasons I sent forth the proclamation that brought many of you here is to celebrate that history. As my wife has said, I have a keen interest in the chronicles: let me say aloud that I would be happy if I heard one thousand songs celebrating history! And our history is as Britons and as Romans as much as our present is about the

Normans and the Flemish. But before any of that we were Celts like the Irish. My belief is it must have been around then that we started to sing, because if there is a nation that can out-sing us it is our friends from Ireland. It is a privilege, therefore, for us to have guests from this island accustomed to singing in the very finest of its halls. Our *brothers*." Rhys did an adequate impression of Niall Ó Maolconaire and everyone laughed including the Irishmen. Those on *la promenade* even began to relax, and to feel that this Christmas was turning out to be quite interesting.

"Your husband is a man of great wit," enthused the young Marcher lord from the next territory to the south of Deheubarth whose name escaped everyone.

"He can be," said Gwenllian.

But the arrival of Niall Ó Maolconaire had made Rhys uneasy. The point of this festival was to herald in a new chapter in the chronicles, not to aggravate old wounds.

"They keep on coming," he said to Anarawd. "We must curb the flow."

"I told you bards were trouble. Foreign ones especially. Speaking of which, that French popinjay you've appointed as a judge is keeping a record of all the new arrivals, so he told me. Marks them up on big slates in his fancy writing. You should talk to him."

Anarawd, whose quarters were nicer than most others in town, as befitted a *penteulu*, disliked Chrétien lodging with him. Anarawd could hardly stretch out and down ale of an evening without sensing the Frenchman's faint disgust at the mess his place was in. It was a worrisome task, taking the defence of prince and realm upon one's shoulders, and Anarawd was equal to it, but he reserved the right when off-duty by his own hearth in his own home to leave the odd drinking horn or mutton bone lying around. And he resented the role Chrétien was assuming in the festival preparations, undoing what Anarawd had already done then doing it again only more theatrically. And the Frenchman talked in his sleep, mouthing out loud lines from his would-be writings and tittering over those he thought especially good. Anarawd was no scholar. But he could see that to Chrétien this was all a delightful game: Rhys, the festival and Deheubarth too, and that none of them served any further purpose to the Frenchman beyond exaggerating for future use in his fictions. Anarawd would have liked to ask Chrétien what he would do if he needed to march through a bog all night to take a well-fortified castle with a scant force outmanned ten to one, and he would have liked the Frenchman to flounder for a reply, and for Rhys to smile. But the Frenchman would have responded with clever words. And then only then would Rhys have smiled. Rhys took some things for granted. Anarawd's unconditional support was one of those things.

"I have something else to show you, if you care to indulge me," Rhys called to the group.

Quite commonly amongst rulers, civil talk is absent; they perceive people will indulge their whims whether they care to or not. But civility as practised at the very highest level is not altogether superfluous, it masks things with other things, it puts people at ease even when chaos is close at hand.

Rhys shepherded them all onto the path that ran alongside the river connecting the dock to the priory on the far side of town. Cardigan when beheld like this appeared strikingly flanked, he did think, particularly when brightened by the sea of festival attendees encircling its perimeter, and it was important to him others thought so too.

"Some say we Welsh are barbarians; across the border in England they can talk of little else. In answer I point my finger at our church and priory here, pillars of our Christian Faith and not, I think, wholly uncivilised. I draw your attention to the stone: harder than granite and requiring more skill to carve, too. Masons from leading English towns have journeyed here to behold it," he added, not without satisfaction. Sometimes he could not resist a jibe at the English. "And one further surprise awaits us in the church; one that must be seen to be believed. Come."

And everyone came, Niall Ó Maolconaire included, although he had not been invited.

Further back in the group, Prince Owain Cyfeiliog of Powys Cyfeiliog, a shadow of the Powys that had existed until recently, but a strategic region nevertheless with England just east and Gwynedd to the north and Deheubarth to the southwest, turned to the young Marcher lord whose name no one could remember but who held the next territory south of the river they now perambulated along.

"The Lord Rhys is an apt ambassador for Wales, eh?" Owain Cyfeiliog asked. "The talk is he will have all us lesser lords united soon enough."

"I pay little heed to gossip," flushed the young Marcher lord. "But I cannot think that he would deprive his guests of honour of lands he knows to be ours."

"I stood by his side on Berwyn when we Welsh repelled the King's men from piercing the bosom of Wales. A year later he was annexing the lands my forefathers held for centuries, appropriating my castles and making my men-at-arms the generous offer of switching allegiance to him or being annihilated. Now he invites me to make merry. I do not know what to make of him, but placing faith in him? In the midwinter cold when the lakes freeze, do you place faith in the ice to hold when you step on it? The talk *is* that many would be in favour of a united Wales," Owain Cyfeiliog nudged the young Marcher lord good-naturedly. "But us lesser Lords might not be so thrilled, eh?"

Chrétien was easily spotted, his corn-yellow cloak and Phrygian cap topped by a parakeet feather markedly contrasting with the browns and greys the other judges were wearing today. The man from Champagne was taking his new role as judge seriously, questioning Cardigan's longer-serving lawmen on anything and everything and inducing a degree of liveliness from the old stalwarts Rhys had formerly found only mead could muster. "Indubitably, you are as brave as you are learned, seigneur! You and your lord here should be at the helm of some force of knights in the Holy Land, that would cool all the hot talk that Saladin is spouting out about an attack on Jerusalem!"

"A piece of advice from a judge, if I might intrude?" Rhys fell into pace with Chrétien, muting his tone so others did not overhear.

"Seigneur, I pray you know by now I will give you anything within my power—anything."

"When one has put out a proclamation inviting any entertainer with the inclination to attend a festival, and stated simply 'Christmastime' as the date of commencement, when does one commence?"

Chrétien stole Rhys an impish look. Then came the lightly placed hand on the shoulder that Rhys dreaded; the touch just long and firm enough to suggest the Frenchman might do it longer and firmer if given encouragement.

"Mercy, seigneur, look *around* you."

Chrétien was referring to the expanding encampment of entertainers.

In the strip of land between the river and the town walls, from the western gate near the dock along to the river bridge and castle and on to the furthest extent of the priory grounds a half mile east, the ground was no longer its usual mud-green. It was multi-coloured by vermillions and violets, silks and satins, lavish canopies and crude lean-tos, bards mumbling stanzas, musicians fumbling strings and songsters from alehouse bawlers to aspiring town criers, lute-players to pipers and versifiers to viol-strikers, bad to good and good right back to bad again, gorging themselves on meat and wheaten loaves, guzzling beers and meads and wines, gathering about fires. And waiting.

Rhys had been admiring the exoticness as it had grown up over recent days, and the colour outside the walls was of course in addition to the many colourful guests with the fortune to have found lodging within. He had been admiring too the way this city of tents had assumed its own order. Food hawkers had established themselves to augment the supplies he had his own kitchen wenches distribute twice daily. A pathway of sorts had been left free for people to get to the river to piss or shit. Those who had clearly been strangers were meeting and debating how an awdl should be aired or a crwth plucked rather than moving their hands mistrustfully towards their swords as was the tendency upon a chance encounter elsewhere. There were those too who seemed to be seasoned itinerants, performers who had travelled the halls of Deheubarth and beyond and who recognised each other from past merrymakings. And with a quiet pride Rhys had overheard even these veteran entertainers say that they had seen nothing like it, nothing on this scale, song was a background to a banquet but never before to their knowledge had it been the centre of attention as now.

So Rhys had, as Chrétien had put it, looked around him, but he did not want a man like Chrétien, accustomed to frequenting Europe's most cosmopolitan courts, to know that he had spent too much time doing so.

"Entertainers *take*, seigneur. And when they are done with taking, they take more again. They take without shame and without restraint. They will eat you out of food, drink you out of wine and burn your firewood until Deheubarth is denuded, and the majority will not be too downhearted if they do not sing one song or strike one string the entire time they do so. But you, seigneur, will be downhearted, I know. I who have been here since the beginning can see what you have invested in this. Show these songsters firmness and get them performing as soon as you can, or you will have a siege on your hands that will bleed you dry."

They were now approaching the river bridge that was the link between Welsh Wales and Norman Wales. Of course Rhys wished to say a few words about this as well he might. It had the same number of arches as his castle had towers for one thing: yes, seven. For another, his side of the Teifi was industry and cultured entertainment, and the opposite side was damp woods. These observations were all the better received for the horns of claret and honey cakes a serving wench was waiting to offer the group.

Also waiting here was Rhys' eldest un-betrothed daughter, Angharad, not quite twelve years old. Nor was she quite the innocent child any longer. She knew her looks already turned heads. With amber-brown hair, piercing grey-blue eyes and a scarcely concealable insolence she was her father's daughter and as unlike dark, dour Gwenllian as could be. She ran up to the six judges hugging each like they were pet dogs, and in a most inappropriate manner for a young lady, and neither of her parents possessed the energy to stop her. She kissed Gerald too, causing the churchman's eyebrows to knit in disapproval, then rushed up to Rhys.

"Father, Maelgwyn has gone. He left before first light and took Cadwaladr and Owain and Maredudd with him. One of the best boats is gone too. One of the Norsemen's longships; they are rather furious about it."

"And Gruffyd?"

"Gruffyd left just now to search for them."

Rhys groaned. Maelgwyn again. He would like to see his eldest son bearing some of the responsibility of the realm by now, but Maelgwyn was wild, wild as a bull set apart from his herd. Maelgwyn's absence alone from proceedings he could cope with; despite how odd that must seem to outsiders he would almost welcome it because his first-born unnerved him with his meanness and brooding ways. But disappearing with three of his other sons like this he could not accept. Maelgwyn would not drag anyone else down with him. Not today. Thank God for his second eldest, Gruffyd.

"This is not a good time," he spoke in a low tone to Angharad, but even this reined her in more than the raised voices of others could. "Can you not see I am entertaining? Did I not tell you this morning was important, important for me, important for all of us?"

"It is not my fault," protested Angharad.

"You might better choose your moments for bouncing around," he reprimanded her, and then felt bad, because he liked her liveliness. She would grow up lively; a handful; not a bit like his wife. His eyes ran with concern around the group to check no one had been unduly affected by his daughter's outburst.

The young Marcher lord holding the lands to the south of Deheubarth—the name escaped him—looked the most uncomfortable.

The fellow was immediately forgettable, the inheritor of a frontier territory he felt duty-bound to run for his father's sake when his heart was probably in a chateaux amidst pretty gardens in Cherbourg or Rouen. You had to have your heart in Wales and your feet stuck in like a limpet's or you would fall right off the face of it. But in this moment the young Marcher lord was Rhys' guest of honour because he controlled the land Rhys coveted most of all at this moment: the land as far south as St David's. St David's was the ecclesiastical and cultural capital of Wales, the resting place of the saint and the foremost place of pilgrimage and because of these things a fine producer and preserver of illuminated vellum manuscripts remembering the past lives of the people that first carved out civilisation in this wet green cranny of Europe; take St David's and you took the Welsh soul. Rhys was dreaming of late of a passageway connecting Deheubarth to St David's so that the soul of Wales was back in Welsh control again, in Deheubarth's control, in his control.

"Angharad," he said. "I would like you to meet the lord we have as our esteemed neighbour to the south."

Sometimes it was a blessing to have children.

"It is an honour to meet you, lord." Angharad pranced over and planted a kiss on his cheek, too. "My father has told me so much about you."

"Get your men to get my sons back here," Rhys said through his teeth to Anarawd. "I do not care how it is done but I want it done. The songsters begin competing this evening no matter what."

And, he swore, his family would all be there at the banquet table and—just for this one time—behaving.

Rhys turned his attentions back to the others, but need not have worried. His family discord had gone unnoticed. This seemed to be because of a warbling voice performing lines presumably in preparation for the festival, but it was a voice very much in the process of breaking, consequently comical, and funnier still because of the voice of another, enraged, interrupting every time an attempt at recital was made:

"*He is the great…*"

"Blast you, you are mewling like a cat then growling like a wolf with a hoarse throat! Again!"

"*He is the great De Ventadorn, the master…*"

"Stop mewling!"

"*He is the great De Ventadorn, the master of romance,
Ruler elect of rhymes of love across the vasts of France[1].*"

The group, incredulous or in Niall Ó Maolconaire's case in outright laughter, peered over the parapet for the voices were coming from directly below the bridge. There on the bridge base cowering from the drizzle, a man clad in a costly scarlet cloak and a squirrel fur mantle, and gathering both about him to keep the Welsh mud at bay as best he could, was just coming to terms with having been caught in the act of urging his servant to sing a song about him, and racking his brain for an adequate excuse. There was a profusion of protocols amongst bards, and whilst rules about metres to use or patrons to solicit varied, the universal rule was that one did not let others overhear one's rehearsals, least of all one's rival. It was akin to Achilles revealing the secret about his heel, like airing a dirty weakness. No man or woman was invincible, but good bards must appear so, as if God had given them the gift, not as if they needed to practise for it. Niall Ó Maolconaire in-between tinkles of laughter pointed this out and the face of the man beneath the bridge reddened to the hue of his cloak then whitened again.

"And what would an Irishman know…" he retaliated haughtily but checked himself when he realised he had other, evidently well-to-do observers. "There are so few places in this mudpit of a town to find peace in which to trial one's lines!" he said, unctuously, assuming amongst those in *la promenade* there was a shared disdain for the provinciality of this festival which was not shared whatsoever,

---

1 No record of Bernart de Ventadorn using these lines professionally exists.

not even by Chrétien who spent evenings a-plenty at Europe's best courts or by Gerald, accustomed to the grandeur of Paris; indeed sipping or in some cases gulping their clarets as they were, those standing on the bridge were in good spirits at that moment, and appalled most of all by the man beneath them. "I believe I found one of the few dry places!" The man clambered up, bowing gravely and, on seeing ladies present, exemplarily. "I regret I was not able to inform you of my presence directly. As you heard from my bard's little ditty, I *am* De Ventadorn. Bernart de Ventadorn, formerly of the Plantagenet Court, now of Toulouse and like many of you travelled far and through quite deplorable places to be here. But here I am," he smiled. "And still in hope of finding *some* touches of sophistication to warrant the pomposity of that proclamation that summoned us all. I mean, Toulouse is no Rome but at least…"

"*This* is Rhys ap Gruffyd." Anarawd had been waiting for this bard to shut his weaselish face, but like so many other songsters he had the verbal shits and had it bad. The *penteulu* resisted the temptation to knock this cockroach back whence he had crawled from.

"The bard who travels with his own bard to sing his praises," Rhys said evenly. The anger was just about ironed out of his tone, but Anarawd knew the reference to provinciality had pushed his prince to the verge of almighty wrath. Rhys was highly sensitive about his nation's provinciality. Anarawd didn't know why. He didn't see how France could be that much better. France had produced Normans, after all.

"Forgive me, lord!" Bernart inwardly cursed his remissness, and cursed his bard several times more. He was in pieces. Why? He knew why. Marie was why. He had to gather himself. Outwardly he kept his composure only by hiding beneath another sweeping bow. "I had not realised…"

"You are accommodated in my *ystafell*, are you not? With a remarkable amount of luggage as I recall? If this arrangement is not satisfactory I must ask you to leave. There are no finer quarters in Cardigan. Many who have come here must be content with far less as you can see. Many would willingly take your place."

"Indeed, it is more than satisfactory, my lord. Forgive a bard a figurative way of speaking. I merely meant…"

"It is of no consequence," Rhys said curtly, as though nothing Bernart said was or ever could be. Chrétien whispered something in Rhys' ear and he promptly added, and suddenly with much more pleasantness: "join us; we are bound for the church on the other side of town. I have a surprise in store. One you particularly could benefit from."

Bernart hesitated. He was insulted not to have been invited in the first instance. He was further insulted because he was used to his name being known and none there had seemed to know of him, none bar one. One out of what, fifteen? There had been a time when he had been the *beau* of the Plantagenet Court. Blast Toulouse. Toulouse had thrown him into the gloom of the no-longer-so-known and it was a dark, dark place to be. Admittedly, this was Wales, and in more cultured places he would not be so easily forgotten. But he was here. A pox on that proclamation of empty promises for enticing him here, but here he was. The greatest festival that this land has ever beheld, indeed! Compared to what? Compared to shivering around fireplaces slurping foul brews, as he had done on his journey here? The only decent food he had eaten in Wales was at the castle of a Norman!

"Is it our company you object to, my good man?" it was the long-shanked churchman at Rhys' side who asked. "Or do you decline a visit to church with us because you are a non-believer?"

Here was Bernart de Ventadorn. One's return from the brink, one's revival and one's resurgence: these must begin somewhere. Bernart de Ventadorn was here. And he had amends to make.

"I thank you for the honour," Bernart humbly replied. And he moved seamlessly to join the back of the group. But at his bard he shot a look like a rainstorm of arrows. This was more than enough for the master in the art of love songs to convey to his protégé that this time, he would be going alone.

"Do not fear," shouted Rhys from the front. "It is not *God* I want to show you."

The words were thrown over Rhys' shoulder at everyone but Bernart could not help thinking they were intended for him, and suppressed a shudder. He had dallied in more trysts than he could remember and seized on the most memorable of these to turn into commercially successful songs, had been guilty of a good many impure thoughts, and had lived in what might have been deemed flagrant disregard of the church. But he was a man of his times. And he lived in fear of the Day of Judgment.

Rhys led the way away from the town walls across the fields, through the throngs of entertainers readying for the festival, towards the church. He had words for everyone he passed: 'until tonight then,' 'there will be extra mutton and ale,' 'we eagerly await your songs.' He walked and small-talked with his wife and daughter but mainly he brooded over his sons and what he was going to do with them.

Behind him came Anarawd, looking around him as ever with the gaze of a bird of prey for anything that might be amiss.

Beside Rhys' daughter came the young Marcher lord that no one could recollect the name of except she; Angharad showered him with girlish attentiveness and he was happy indeed and thought the other lesser lords of Wales must just be jealous of the

Lord Rhys to badmouth him so, jealous they could not assemble such a mighty realm or finance a festival of song.

Just behind Rhys' wife came Gerald.

"Are you *certain* nothing is amiss with my cousin, my good lady?" he enquired. "It must take a toll, hosting a gathering like this. He does seem a trifle unsettled."

"He is the same as ever he was," said Gwenllian flatly. "Only normally no one else is here to see it."

After them came Niall Ó Maolconaire and Owain Cyfeiliog.

"This is a pretty place, so it is brother," Niall Ó Maolconaire remarked. "Not wild like Connemara, pretty in a peaceful way. There's much to be said for peace. You must be thanking the Lord for the peace in your land."

"We Welsh are so conditioned to war," replied Owain Cyfeiliog, "that we are never more tense than during a peace like this."

Behind them came Gwalchmai, moderating his pace to that of the judges because they, being old like him, knew that if a man does not choose to speak it is a bad idea to make conversation with him.

And fallen to the very back of this group came the seventh judge, the young man with the parakeet feather in his cap who had whispered in Rhys' ear just now, and in a few words changed the prince's attitude towards Bernart from anger to amenability.

"What did you say?" Bernart had to ask him.

"Why seigneur, I told him what I know. I told him who you are. And he was most impressed."

Bernart was satisfied. Then his hackles rose again.

"How did you know?"

"I am attached to the court of Champagne, seigneur."

Champagne! Bernart's heart began to beat as maniacally as a Moorish drum. With a heaving bosom he remembered how he had felt all those years before, compelled to quit the court of the Queen and King of England and forsaken, lost, patronless. For him one star had shone in that night and that star had been Champagne. How he had waited to hear from that capital of courtliness! He could not have gone begging for a position, after his time with the Plantagenets that would have been beneath him, but he had initially expected the invitation from them, then hoped with a hope that dwindled eventually into resentment. It was a pivotal point in his life as an entertainer. If the very best no longer wanted him, Bernart had thought then and for a very long time after, it was irrelevant who had him. So he had gone to blasted Toulouse, a court seemingly waiting for its own death with almost no ladies to fill it and aging courtiers that sat through performances with straight unreceptive faces. And his inspiration had wilted.

"They know of me in Champagne?" he asked, with tears in his eyes.

"Mercy, seigneur, when Marie of Champagne heard you were no longer with the Plantagenets, she could talk of very little else save how she would adorn her treasure trove of performers with the jewel of Bernart de Ventadorn!"

"Then why...?" Bernart began, bewildered. Then it dawned on him. "It was you."

"I was new at court," the young man stared ahead at the others, and did not look at Bernart with any of the wonderment with which he had looked at near enough everything else since his arrival at Cardigan. "I knew of your reputation, as any entertainer makes it his business to know of his rivals. You were a threat. I persuaded my patroness she did not need you. I know enough about you, seigneur, to know you would have done the same had our positions been reversed."

"But you reversed my entire career!" Bernart hissed.

"You know it does not work like that seigneur. I simply advanced my own."

The group walked along the edge of the well-tilled priory grounds. Several of the monks emerged to watch them. Their black habits rendered their faces pale as ghosts. Rhys called out a greeting but none replied, and once the last of them had passed the priory's far boundary, the monks filed wordlessly inside again. Their habits brushed the grass so that their feet were invisible. They did not walk. They hovered across the ground.

The church stood just apart from the priory, and was built of the same fine dark-grained stone, grey on green. But this was the people's church; the monks had their own separate place of worship. With Cardigan's population swollen like a river after rain, it was busy. Townsfolk—the good ones who attended service regularly, and the not-so-good coming along now compunctious having never attended all year long—and songsters—the few among them who were genuinely God-fearing, and the many among them who wanted to seem so, because they believed however progressive this festival of song claimed to be it would be a nice respectable religious type who would win—filed in and out. This was Christmas morning, and if any man, woman, child, beast or thing was to make peace with the Heavenly Father it would be this morning above any other morning.

Apart from the flow of the faithful, this was a church that looked better than a lot of churches but not as impressive as others. And precisely because of the averageness of the building, everyone except Rhys' wife and daughter and Anarawd and some of the elder judges who dwelt in the town and were all too familiar with the goings-on at this particular house of God was obliged to ask themselves why Rhys had brought them all out here, when they could have been resting for a few hours before the merrymaking began in earnest. Rhys paused as if to let this very thought have time to blossom within each of their minds. Then he opened the door.

Some aspects of the interior were familiar to some of the group; there was a cross at the far end and a number of today's churchgoers were indeed knelt around it murmuring this or that to God. But the rest were crouched by the walls. They jostled for any piece of wall space they could, their hands, their cheeks, their feet tight pressed to the stone, their bodies contorting in perverse positions in order to have as much flesh as possible flat against the stone, so much so their poses were more lizard-like than human. Their nails gouged the stone. Their tongues licked the stone. Some were even attempting to gnaw at it: to gnaw at a stone that was harder than granite.

"They come," said Rhys "to be cleansed."

"This…" Gerald spluttered, as everyone else stared in shocked silence, "is an abomination, my good cousin."

"It is history," Rhys turned to Chrétien. "We spoke before of the people of old that raised fine monuments to their Gods in this stone. The spirit of those times survives in every boulder of it, or so the penitents you see before you believe. Once, sacrifices on these rocks ensured the next year's crop came and staved off death or disease. It is something of interest for inclusion in your works of fiction perhaps."

"People can only be penitent at the feet of the one, true God," Gerald admonished. "Not in front of pagan spirits!"

"You approach the topic with your enlightened modern mind, cousin. We imposed our God upon this world. Before that there were other Gods and these possessed their own power too. As you see. These penitents are God-fearing. They believe in Christ, Our Father and the Holy Spirit. But they are ill and want to become well, and they have heard the stories of those who arrive here with ailments and depart renewed. They come to Cardigan as they would to shrines at Durham or St David's. To be healed."

Rhys' eyes, sharp as the sea that bashed the Welsh coast, scanned the group and came to rest on Bernart, who, not for the first time that morning, had the feeling that someone was digging his grave. Bernart had them often these days: leaps-forward in time to his own burial, where he was lying on his back, in a pit but not in a coffin, and he could behold clearly but helplessly the spade slinging the soil over him. And Rhys ap Gruffyd, his oh-so benevolent host, brought on these visions all the more vividly. The man should be grateful, Bernart thought coldly, to have a celebrated exponent of love songs attending his backwater banquet. But he was Bernart de Ventadorn, he could out-smile the best of them for now, and later once his gift was back and he had sung the other songsters into submission, just as he had in his days with the Plantagenets, then he could distance himself from these rustics.

There was a sound then. A sound such as a rusted cog makes when it is oiled and slowly slowly starts to crank around again. All eyes turned to the glowering old bard from Gwynedd.

"I was at Llanddewi Brefi the other night," Gwalchmai said. "I held the staff of St David in my hands. *That* is a shrine. To compare this with that is heresy."

The words hung heavy in the room because Gwalchmai had the capacity to make even Rhys feel like a scolded silly little child.

"I did warn you," Gerald said smoothly. "My companion leaves an archdeacon such as myself seeming a little dirty! But the lamp burns bright when the wick is clean, as Ovid says! The wick is the church, my good cousin, just to be clear. The lamp is what the world sees when they look at Wales, but I digress: we have already set aside some time to talk about that have we not?"

And to Chrétien he said, casually enough but not *that* casually, for he was not about to allow this brightly-plumed peacock to hamper his scheme: "I have spent time in France my good man, Paris *naturallement*, and I am all too aware of the French taste for flamboyance. If you choose to write *fictions* it is not my place to prevent you but I think now a ripe time to point out that I write *actualities*. And the rather critical document I am preparing at the moment—to be read by the archbishops and most probably the Pope—does concern Wales. Critical in the sense that upon reading Their Graces and Holiness must above all else comprehend this country has immense potential if only it could be polished a little. I would so hate for our purposes to clash! Wales must not be portrayed outlandishly," he gave Chrétien a business-like smile and patted him on the back. "Not at any cost."

Niall Ó Maolconaire became bored easily. His gaze had drifted by now from the penitents in their ridiculous poses to a veiled lady knelt by herself by the altar, her head bowed in such a way that certain tresses could not help but spill from under her wimple. Niall Ó Maolconaire's eyes followed a particular tress from the bowed head of the lady to the point where it brushed the floor. Like bloody nectar, so it was. He imagined himself with his head tipped back and his mouth wide open, and such a tress being lowered with exquisite slowness into it and the taste actually being nectar-sweet, and him gorging on this sustenance of the immortals until he attained immortal powers himself, then returning to Ireland with them, sorting out all that shit with the Normans, and repopulating the country with nectar-haired women so that all the problems went away for good. He sensed that the lady had no inclination for stone-licking like most of the churchgoers. In fact, he thought the more he looked at her, she was a lady apart; the fabrics of her cloak were foreign but not fancy; she was not common like some of the townswomen indecently splaying themselves about the church walls but neither was she as careful with her appearance as a highborn like the wife of Rhys, although she was far prettier. She was a mystery and this excited him greatly, and whilst he also sensed she was doing her utmost to distance herself from the rest of those in the church and concentrate on her prayers, this did not deter him in the slightest.

"Not nibbling the walls with the rest of them, lady?" he knelt alongside her with his disarming grin.

Black. She should have been wearing black. Pierrot would have worn it for her. But journeying to a festival of song as she had been, she had packed no black. She hoped that Pierrot would forgive her dark blue, and not properly mourning him until over two days after he had passed on. Two days she had spent in near numbness but today she had awoken and realised she had many things she wanted to say to her attendant: that she could have hoped for no better, that he had been braver than any of the knights she had told him stories about, that he could ride her old horse Ovid as much as he liked now. It warmed her heart somewhat to think of the two of them together up there. But a lady alone could not afford to wander forever in a daze, even in a church in one of the safest townships in Wales, there were people like this unshaven uncivil Irishman wanting a piece of her. She had perfected the pretence of staring straight ahead when really she was glancing to her side at an early age, it was the sure way for one who was naturally curious to still seem as demure as the times decreed, and this look she practised now, perceiving that the man beside her was not one who would be off-put easily.

"It is their custom. I do not judge them for it. As I am certain you will not judge me, my lord," Marie turned, raising her veil and looking at Niall Ó Maolconaire coolly, "for wishing to be left alone with my thoughts."

Sparkle-eyed, Niall Ó Maolconaire returned her look.

"It's a pretty place, this Wales," his voice tinkled. "And with creatures like you in it I daresay it's a land several steps closer to paradise than we are over in Ireland at the present. But where I'm from in Connemara, lady, the comely ones don't last long if they walk about alone, and I've seen a few happenings since I arrived this morning that'll raise questions about how safe it is for a fair thing such as yourself to be here unprotected," he leaned close to her, close as one could whilst ostensibly seeming like he was giving thanks to God. "Profanities," he whispered. His breath smelt strongly of spirits. "Indecent acts, and not all of them consensual. And that's just by the radiant light of this Christmas morning, lady. Think how much more wild things will be once feasting commences and the fine wine starts a-flowing."

"Are you offering to become my guardian angel, my lord?" Marie asked thinly.

"I'll keep an eye on you, lady," replied Niall Ó Maolconaire with a wink.

"Forgive the Irish for their sins," Rhys was suddenly behind them. "They do not necessarily know when it is appropriate to talk to a lady and when it is best to let her pray in peace. I ask your pardon for the disturbance; every one of us needs our time with God. May I welcome you as my guest given you do not appear to be one of my subjects?"

Marie hastened to stand in the knowledge it would be to face for the first time Rhys ap Gruffyd, Lord of Deheubarth, Prince of South Wales and host of the greatest festival of song any land had ever known. She had long awaited the moment. He was the man returning Wales to the Welsh. Everyone at home in Caerleon was talking of how he had achieved the near impossible and snatched the town from under Norman noses, all by arming a princeling to carry out the rout. Rhys had not raised a single weapon himself. He had no need to do so these days for he was a landslide already rumbling down from the mountaintops towards that thin strip of coast still held by the Normans with his own unstoppable force. If such a prize as Caerleon could be reclaimed by Rhys, Caerleon the glory of Roman Wales, Caerleon where King Arthur built his court, then why not St David's, why not Cardiff, why not all Wales? She was an admirer of Rhys' methods for at the core of what he was doing was the championing of the abbeys and the driving of the industries, because it was harder to vanquish a country with a big heart. And she knew what his motive was, filling his halls with the land's best bards and musicians as he had. She was not certain many knew, but she did.

"In fact I have recently become one of your subjects, my lord, under Prince Iorwerth of Caerleon."

"Caerleon," Rhys smiled broadly. "It is a beautiful place. You must certainly find it so, for there are those who would liken a Frenchwoman voluntarily residing on Welsh soil to Daniel lingering in the lion's den of his own choosing."

"My accent gives me away, my lord."

"You give away precious little beyond that, my lady."

"Forgive me. I am Marie. Marie de France."

Rhys laughed as if she had told a jest. Gwenllian dealt Marie a very narrow look as she detected an inflection in her husband's voice she was sadly familiar with, the tone he had used to all those women over the years that he had wished to take for mistresses. Behind them, Chrétien opened his eyes wider, for he was an entertainer who made it his duty to know of other entertainers, especially those he considered worthy opponents, and this was a lady he had heard of before. Bernart dragged his gaze up with dread at Marie's mentioning of her name, praying that this was a coincidence but knowing from the way the words were said, with an ever-evading coyness that would have one running up a tree after it only to throw one off from the top, that this was the lady who had been plaguing his every waking moment and a fair amount of his sleep as well. They had avoided each other since arriving in Cardigan, but to Bernart's mind only as gladiators paced around each other after entering the amphitheatre, each waiting for the other to make their move.

"Come, my lady," Rhys said. There must be thousands of Maries in France. You might as well inform me that you have no name at all!"

"With respect I do not quite wish to say that, my lord. After all you are Rhys of Deheubarth and there are many named Rhys in your domain."

"Then perhaps you choose 'Marie de France' to communicate that of those myriad Maries, you are evidently the best of them, and need no further introduction?"

"Less still that. It is merely my storytelling name; my *nom de plume.*"

Nom de guerre, madame, Bernart thought bitterly in the background. *Nom de guerre.*

"You are here to compete?" Rhys could hardly contain his surprise.

"My personal feeling is, my lord, that it is a very long way to travel to lick a wall."

Rhys was good at covering himself; he supposed it dated to a time when he really had feared there was someone who wanted to kill him at his back. Covering himself from a lady, especially one like this, he found harder than dodging any of the hosts of arrows that had hailed down on him in his fighting days. But cover oneself one must, wear one's propriety tight about one like a suit of armour one must. It would not do for anyone to see into the heart of the prince of South Wales.

"I meant that bards—storytellers if you prefer—of all lands usually wish to announce their presence in the hall in some extravagant way. Take this man here," he turned to Bernart. "He goes by the title 'Master of Romance' and even has his own songster to sing it out to everyone in a skull-splitting squeak. Yet you," he turned back to Marie "are implying that in this most ostentatious of professions you crave anonymity!"

No, she wanted recognition, but she wanted to walk into a hall and earn it with her words alone. She wanted to start from nothing like most contestants would, like the unfortunates entering the church this very moment, performers for certain because one carried a harp on his back, yet poor chancers to judge from their soiled clothing, who looked as if they had slept wild a good many nights. She did not care to use her reputation to gain unfair advantage over those for whom it was a novelty just to be in a dry place with their teeth not chattering.

"I suppose I am different, my lord. At the very least I would like to think I am different from the Lord De Ventadorn here. Our styles are as opposite as can be."

"I fear I am in danger of being misrepresented." Wearing a ghastly expression but eager to salvage his good name before he became laughed at or loathed, Bernart stepped forward. "This lady and I travelled here together from London my lord, a week's journey as you are aware, and ample time in which to vex the other. I am certain we could both relate some stories. But they are *trifles*," he emphasised this last word, "compared to being here with you as our host." His eyes briefly left Rhys to slide over Marie. "The lady and I hail from different regions of France. I am what we call in the south a troubadour. The lady comes from the north of the country, where they call their troubadours trouvères, composers and performers of songs like us and like us in a different league from the jongleurs who just blurt out the verses of others, but like us because they were originally inspired by us and came into being because of us. A slight difference to an outsider, I grant you, but a gulf of a difference nevertheless."

"I am astonished, my lord, that you take it upon yourself to interpret my words and do it so miserably. That was not at all what I meant by 'opposite.'

"The differences between us, lady, are not ones we would wish to detain the Lord Rhys and his guests over now, here in this church. We can agree on that point at least."

"Until the hall later then… *my lord*," Marie trembled as she replied.

Quite often wordsmiths, for all the glib and gilded phrases they hide behind, cannot find it within themselves to hold back when it comes to the matter of their true hatreds and true loves, which even the most modest among them have been known to vent to the world whilst the world stands by and winces.

Rhys intervened.

"I would hope for no less than healthy rivalry between contestants at a festival such as this promises to be," he said crisply. "Snow is in the air, my lords and ladies! Some added heat in my halls cannot do any of us much harm!"

Everyone broke into relieved but not altogether easy laughter.

"Your father should consider performing himself!" the young Marcher lord whose name escaped everyone gushed to Angharad.

"Merciful Heaven, my good man!" Gerald could not help but butt in exasperatedly. "My cousin *is* performing. He is conducting his greatest performance yet. Do you not see that?"

"Do not mind cousin Gerald!" Angharad linked arms with the young Marcher lord in what she considered a very grown-up gesture. "Sometimes he opens his mouth and all that comes out is what he thinks the church wants to hear. But he is not as perfect as he thinks he is."

Niall Ó Maolconaire had bowed out of the conversation the moment he saw he was not going to get the French lady with the long tresses to himself. He always went for the best women and that was his downfall because the best never did want to go off with an Irish bard. Once they heeded his accent, he might as well have admitted to being a pirate. Respectable womenfolk wanted nothing to do with an Irishman, it was hurling yourself off into a life of hard drinking and heavy fighting. And so most women and men too would carry on thinking whilst the troubles lasted. Pirates probably did fight less than the skirmishers in his country. Skirmishers he called them because there was no proper warring and there was no noble thing that anyone was hoping to gain, or if there was people had lost sight of it, it was land-hungry Normans against blood-hungry Irish Kings and it was horses stolen and houses burnt and women raped, no open honest battling as such. It was a bloody mess so it was and this was what he needed to chat to Rhys about. Rhys held sway with King Henry and would be seeing him at the King's Council in the spring, Rhys could put in a good word for Ireland and might just do that because Rhys had a fair bit of benevolence for a ruler and additionally perhaps felt remorse for the mighty storm of shit he had helped to unleash over Niall Ó Maolconaire's homeland. And a man knows when another man wants the same thing as him, especially when that thing is a woman, so in what could be termed an ambassadorial move Niall Ó Maolconaire had backed off from Marie when he saw Rhys had designs on her himself. Yes, in absence of anyone better he was ambassador for Ireland, other bards might get used as go-betweens and there were those he had seen around the town of Cardigan this Christmas morning who looked devious enough to be eavesdroppers or even spies but he was the bloody ambassador! He turned his attentions to the penitents along the far wall. One old woman, fast against the stone with her hands and left cheek pressed against it, had her face twisted towards him, so that he could observe her in detail. Like all of those seeking healing or cleansing or whatever it was, she seemed utterly detached from everything else going on around her, as if each fibre of her being was focused on absorbing the restorative powers out of the rock. And there was such relief in her expression, as if she really had at long last found tranquillity. The secret to real peace, thought Niall Ó Maolconaire, could well be minding your own bloody business. He might say something to Rhys to this effect when they had their little chat later: in the nicest possible way, of course.

"Come for a spot of stone-licking, brothers?" he asked the latest three arrivals, who stood in one of the few free spaces, ragged and rubbing their hands. "My apologies, lady," he added, when he saw that one of them, the tallest in fact, was a woman and a redhead too. "In Ireland…"

"Do we look like we've come here to lick stone?" one of the men snapped.

"Excuse us, friend," said the other, a callow youth with the lesions from a recent beating on his face, "we hear the Lord Rhys is here and desire to speak with him as a matter of utmost urgency."

"That's him over there, brother," Niall Ó Maolconaire smiled. "Him with the moustache. Although he's rather in demand as you can see and you have the definite disadvantage of not being nearly as pretty as she with whom he's engaged in conversation with at the present."

"This cannot wait," Avery drew back his hood and made his way to where Rhys was deep in discussion with a lady indeed as beautiful as the Irishman had implied.

A few paces shy and a man with arms as wide as Avery's thighs suddenly blocked his path, a portcullis or a battering ram of a man depending on whether he was being viewed from a defender's or an attacker's perspective, but now very much the portcullis.

"What do you want with the Lord Rhys?"

"We are entrants for the contests of song."

"Entry is closed."

"Closed?" Avery repeated the word but it made no sense. The festival was not starting until an hour after darkness fell this afternoon. Not one entertainer out there had even put on their performing garb. You could not issue an open invitation across the known world, calling upon whosoever wished to participate in the greatest festival of song ever held to come all the way to the castle of the greatest prince in Wales at Christmastime, and then when against all odds people do arrive, tell them that they are too late, despite the hall set aside for the merrymaking not yet having a single merrymaker within it!

"Has the number of bards and musicians and rhyme-wrights and tune-tinklers out there escaped your notice, lad? We're overwhelmed. And what were you doing when my men went around just now clanging big bells and shouting out to the sundry songsters in town that they needed to make their mark immediately to show their intention to compete or forfeit the right? We have to set limits somewhere."

He was a sturdy-looking man, Rhys' bodyguard, but the work was plainly enflaming his mood and if there was one thing the church had taught Avery it was that humbleness could make a good ointment.

"Please, friend. We have endured much to be here."

"This town is on the far side of a dangerous country, lad, who here has not had a trying time on the journey? This proclamation was put out a twelvemonth ago. If you'd been coming from Asia that would have been notice enough! Entry is closed. I'm not going to tell you again."

They had got as far as Aberporth late last night and collapsed on the sands with fishing nets and their threadbare cloaks for bedding and an upturned boat for a roof, and that had been by no means the least savoury of their resting places these past few days. That on top of a seven-mile tramp this morning that they begun before first light. Avery was into his last drops of energy, and a more impulsive man might have lost his temper at such a time after such treatment, but he could see the man before him was used to backing up words with actions and doing so to great effect. And so Avery nodded, feeling the fatigue of the fortnight since he had fled from York well up and whirl about him like a mist. It had all been for nothing then.

Avery, he heard the skeletons shrieking. *We cannot let you pass, Avery!* He could see Heaven, the happy faces and the harp-playing cherubs; it was so close. But the skeletons' scythes locked together in an impregnable wall around him then reformed into a tunnel that led off in a different direction, into a pit of suffering and sulphurous rock. *There is a place for you over here, Avery!*

He heaved himself back into the now and to Dog's deliberately loud and unpleasant laughter. Dog did not have a charming laugh. At the best of times, it was a sound like a hound nursing a bone. Now it sounded like a blatant provocation, and it had Rhys' chief bodyguard spinning round with his hand on his hilt again.

"Anarawd Angor!" said Dog, so that everyone in the church could not fail to hear. "Anchor in English but in Welsh it rolls off

230

Song Castle

the tongue better. That's what we used to call the fellow when I was a child. On account of the fact that, like an anchor, you can be sure that if he's on board with you, the worst tempest in Christendom can blow up and your ship would stay safe and sound. But anchor too because he's a stubborn, unyielding bastard. And that was back in his more freethinking days."

Something in the way Dog said these words and the way Anarawd reacted, striding with clear and fuming intent across the church floor to stand as close to Dog as a coffin lid comes to a dead man, caused the penitents to scuttle well out of the way.

"Only one person still living on this Earth would have the balls to address me so!"

"Don't speak to me about my balls," Dog lowered his hood. "They're mighty sore after what I've been through these past days."

"Madog the fiddler's son," Anarawd growled, but there was incredulity in his voice too. "You've grown fatter."

"Almost your size in tunics these days, Angor. And I've dispensed with the 'mad.' It's just 'Dog' these days: to my friends, at least."

"Well I suppose I shall have to call you 'Dog' then. You're with the English lad here?"

"You could say that. Him and the witch both."

Anarawd regarded Avery and the Healer.

"You never were much good at choosing your drinking companions," he said gruffly.

At first during this exchange, Avery had been thinking that Dog had met his match. Then he thought that Anarawd had. But actually, he realised, they were both simply very similar, physically a little but in their behaviour a lot.

"I hate to mention my balls again, Angor, but like I said they're sore. I could tell you why but none of us have the time. Let's just say that my companions and I have had a tough few days. And we all know it's within your considerable powers to let this fellow here enter the vocal song contest and me enter the one with all the musicians in. Do it for the sake of the good old times, Angor. I know you remember them."

Anarawd looked penetratingly and dubiously at Dog. He was considering, and the wait whilst he did so was made more painful by whatever he was chewing on, a piece of bark it sounded like, he chewed it around in his cheeks like a cow. The sound was more pronounced because the other sounds in the church had faded as everyone, Rhys and the beautiful lady he was in discussion with included, observed with interest these odd-looking new arrivals and waited to see what Anarawd would do.

"It might easily be altered on the slates, seigneur," Chrétien ventured. "It is the simple matter of having three rather than two in the early heats."

"If I bend the rules for you," Anarawd addressed Dog and steadfastly ignored Chrétien, "we must bend them for everybody. Limits must be set somewhere. Else we'll be here until New Year drumming our fingers on our drinking horns waiting for some late-coming minstrel or other. Entry is closed."

It was preposterous that this much-battered battle axe, with every experience of fighting, but so little of culture that he referred to making marks instead of writing names, should be the one to decide their fate, and even Dog now looked defeated.

"Might I intercede my lords?" Marie broke in. The most powerful prince of Wales had at that moment asked her if she wished to join him on the dais with his family for the feasting. She had no idea how best to reply because to encourage a man who was taking a liking to her could only lead to disaster, but she was mortified to be receiving preferential treatment whilst on the other side of the church those three poor unfortunates were being turned away after their arduous journey. If no one else would stand up for them, she would. "I travelled long and far to be at this festival because it announced itself as the greatest this land had ever known. I ask *you* my lord," she looked gravely at Rhys, "and not your *penteulu*, whether you can find it in your heart to deny these entertainers their right to perform and still when you are an old man looking back on this Christmas claim that your festival was truly the greatest? One of these three might become the best performer Wales ever witnessed! Would you want to look back, and would you want chroniclers to look back, and concede that you did not permit the very best to participate? And when these men have travelled long and far like me and certainly with the same aim, why should they be denied entry whilst I am accepted?"

"My lady!" Rhys said lightly. "I trust I have done nothing within our all-too-brief acquaintance to make you think me a cruel man! If it were my reputation for cruelty I wished to spread I would have declared war on you all, not invited you to make merry with me! Have these entertainers entered and be done with it! And now let us go to get our rest, before revelries commence!" He started towards the church door, then checked himself, and murmured in Marie's ear: "I take it that is a 'yes' for dinner."

Rhys and his guests of honour on *la promenade* began to make their way back towards the castle. Anarawd stiffly gave Dog and Avery confirmation of their participation.

"Which contest will the witch here be entering?" Anarawd asked resignedly. Satan's sister, if there were Frenchmen and Englishmen and many more foreigners besides singing their foreign songs here, there might as well be a witch too.

"Not a single one of them, my swarthy strongman. I have other business in town. Though I may sing a few songs over my cauldron later."

Anarawd eyed her from under heavy lids.

"Your *companion* should take heed," he said to Dog. "Witchcraft is punishable by death. As disrespecting the captain of the prince's bodyguard can be."

"You need betony, my champion!" the Healer shouted cheerfully after him. "For the toothache."

This time Anarawd did not even turn around.

"I'll keep on chewing bark if it's all the same to you."

Avery was about to go over and thank Marie, who had dropped again to her knees in front of the altar, but Dog put a hand on his arm.

"If we're to captivate a hall or even half a hall, I'll wager we need to wash and eat and get at least slightly drunk."

Avery agreed. He looked a moment longer at this lady with her hair like honey and her eyes that stared right through you, and this he knew because they had stared at him in this way. They had fleetingly broken away from the Lord Rhys to stare at him in their green and brown and gold, all the colours of woodland when the springtime sun slants at last through the branches. Why, he wondered, should she ever have wished to help them?

Marie beheld the wooden cross before her. She felt silly saying words out loud to an inanimate object, but if she did not say them at all they would stay like flies in a room on a hot day stay, buzzing irritatingly, so she half-said them, glancing around with her perfected sideways glance to be certain no one could overhear: *'There are eyes on me, Pierrot. I sensed it since the start of our journey here. I sensed it at De Braose's castle and then we were ambushed and I thought that was it, a feeling of foreboding about what was to happen in those woods. But it is still close by, whatever it is, even here in a place where I believed I would be safe, it is a darkness looming and yes maybe Lord De Ventadorn can account*

for an amount of it, but it is more than that and I wish you were here to face it with me. Your death will not go unsung, Pierrot, I promise. Your eulogy will be performed in its most fitting place, in the banquet hall where those who wish to hide from its revelations will have no stone left to scuttle under. And everyone shall hear the truth.'

Outside a yellow band of light had shot across the sky, hanging there for a while illuminating the murky morning. But it did not fool anyone into thinking better weather was coming. Halfway back to the castle gates, snow started falling. Rhys looked up with a wry smile at the heavens and gathered his cloak around him. And he locked eyes with someone who at that moment happened to be crossing his path. For that moment, the rest of the world froze many degrees below the actual temperature of the town that Christmas morning, froze away into immateriality and left just Rhys ap Gruffyd and Cynddelw Bryddyd Mawr the Great One, eyes locked like jousting stags lock antlers. Rhys nodded at Cynddelw. Cynddelw nodded at Rhys. They both passed on their way.

Gwalchmai At The Seaside

(DECEMBER, 1176)

OUT GWALCHMAI STRODE, following the river to the open sea. In the sea was something; only in the mountains and the sea was there something and the rest in-between was compromise. The snow fell steadily but it was inconsequential. It settled on him as it would on a rock; he was a shard of rock on the mudflats and marram grass and sand dunes of Cardigan. He utilised the daylight to spare himself from the others, because come tonight and every nightfall for the next fortnight or more he would be stuck with them. He disapproved of their pleasantries and he condemned their needless chatter; the fawning fool with the parrot-feathered cap; and the weasel under the bridge who employed a bard to brag of his accomplishments; and that temptress who attracted men to her like wasps. It was small surprise they were all French. But his countrymen were worse than the foreigners. Look at Rhys ap Gruffyd, marching around like he was the most magnificent host since Solomon welcomed the Queen of Sheba. Look at Cynddelw Bryddyd Mawr. Not many had seen, but Gwalchmai had, when the Great One, as the man blasphemously referred to himself, stumbled past them earlier drunk to the eyeballs on wine. He did not understand how a drunk like that was so loved. Budding bards worshipped the

Great One and sang his songs as they went about their errands, but no one sung Gwalchmai's songs. People sickened Gwalchmai. Yet he reserved a special strain of disgust for drunks. He himself drank only water, ice-cold from the brook, he had not touched alcohol or pleasured himself in any way since Prince Owain of Gwynedd died six winters ago, and in his mind he moralised over how much closer to God this had brought him in comparison to others. In his mind alone. No thought Gwalchmai had ever made it into the open as he intended, unless he had first rigorously hewn it into song form. But of course he did not *sing* his songs—singing required joy within—he thundered them like a preacher. His verses were urges to reconcile with God, they were purges against all that sinfulness into which mankind kept on lapsing. They might not be fancy like the words of those French songsters, but they did scour the soul and that was what one wanted before setting sail for the sweet life that began after death. And *he* did not require some colourful costume to ready for this evening. He simply needed time away from those other drivellers to clean off the dirty film he felt settling on his skin whenever he tarried too long in their company. Gerald was the only one of them he could tolerate. An institution needed a face like Gerald of Wales. A human face. Gwalchmai did not have one of those. Gwalchmai knew in his heart that, even though he was only trying to save souls when he delivered his lines, he probably made the threat of being baked in brimstone seem more acute and imminent. Gerald could say the same things in a different way and have the same audience that had started with fright at Gwalchmai's words pleading for help with purifying themselves for entry into Heaven. But Gerald was not a bard; Gerald had altogether different aspirations. And this was good for Gwalchmai, who was able to seize as his very own speciality the song style of hard-line sanctitude.

His fingers slipped inside his cloak to the hold-all and touched the parchment with the prematurely broken seal. Still safe. And still not delivered to Rhys ap Gruffyd, although Prince Rhodri had expressly said it was imperative it should be handed over at the earliest opportunity. One document, with the power to resolve or rip asunder so much, and he Gwalchmai ap Meilyr was in possession of it.

He was on a flat expanse of sand now, hard glue after the tide had gone back out. He did not check his step but carried on out after it. All was grey around. The land behind, the snow-burdened sky, the sea ahead: grey. This was like purgatory, he thought, a nothing state.

At a boulder he paused; undressed; laid his clothes precisely on the rock.

He carried on. The sea lapped over his toes, surged to his flaccid member, swept about his shoulders.

He carried on, deriving perverse pleasure in not flinching once, until the point when his toes still just touched the seabed and waves crested the top of his head. Utter immersion.

Then he returned to shore again, much in the way he had left it.

The only moment of panic came when, knee-deep, he spied a girl and a boy, cocklers or winklers probably, gaping at him from the sand. He supposed he must look quite absurd. But he was clean! He was a clean-living man! He raised both arms until they were perpendicular to his torso, until he resembled a human crucifix. Then with a roar that began as a gurgle, for his voice box was not accustomed to creating such sounds, he charged. The girl and boy fled before him. He chased them until he knew they would not come back.

The snow fluttered down in part-melted clusters, without real bite. It was nothing to a man habituated to the harshness of

Gwynedd. He put on his garments again; skin tingling from its briny baptism. He was ready now. He took the parchment the whole way out this time, just to be certain of every word of what Prince Rhodri had written. Very well. Let it be done.

And guiltily but giddily that thought furiously thrashed through his head again: *Gwalchmai deserves to win*.

Without further ado he began his walk back to Cardigan, leaning forward into the weather like the bow of a ship leans into a storm.

He was going to see the only other man with the knowledge this message, from one of Wales' foremost princes to the other, had been intercepted. Someone who, being a man of letters, possessed a lot of sealing wax; someone who, being family, knew how best to broach a subject with the Lord of Deheubarth; someone Gwalchmai did not really know the capabilities of at all.

Gerald

(DECEMBER, 1176)

"MAKE HASTE, LITTLE BISHOP! They are coming!"

His mother; beautiful; tall like he would become, but always so worried.

It was the Welsh, reportedly, who were coming.

But they were supposed to have been coming yesterday, and the day before, and they had not. Gerald in fact believed that they would not come at all; why would they? Cousin Rhys, or the Prince of Deheubarth as he was somewhat prematurely calling himself given he only ruled over a small band of bog and woodland around the basin of the Tywi, had more pressing things to do than attack his own family. At the end of the day it was unofficial stalemate. The Welsh knew they could not oust the southern seaboard from the Normans in their heart of hearts however bravely they battled, and the Normans knew that even if they held the whole string of pretty little coastal townships from Striguil in the east along to Pembroke in the west, the Welsh would always be lurking threateningly just north beyond the periphery of their vision.

"I will finish my prayers in church, mother. God will protect me."

"You had better pray he will! There is one wooden door between you and any pillaging Welshmen in the church; in the keep you can at least depend on several feet of stone and iron! I have known Rhys longer than you, little bishop. He might not be a madman, but there must be madness in his blood to make him think he has a hope of retaking Deheubarth like he says he will, when he has no more than a couple of tumbledown castles to his name. I see him mounting raids more than I do rebuilding kingdoms. I see him attacking and attacking to take what he can while he can and if there is trouble nearby as our messengers tell us there is then you can bet on it being him behind it. Now come on inside."

But Gerald thought that his cousin was much more than a marauder. How many fourth sons rose up to become the head of their family, the head of their dynasty? He was a contriver of circumstance and a force to be reckoned with, but that force would not come at you in the form of some brutal or botched raid. It would grind you down. It would lower you a groove as it raised a groove, until one day you would glance up and it would be dominant.

Gerald had not gone to the castle, but stayed in the church, his beloved little church in his beloved little village of Manorbier. He had never prayed harder than he did that day. The boyish way of praying: eyes screwed shut, hands clasped. But it worked. The Welsh had not come. Cousin Rhys had not come. When Rhys had next visited their family home, in fact, it was to invite them all to his court at the castle of Dinefwr. He had newly rebuilt the fortress, and no one could deny that it looked rather impressive.

Little bishop. Even though Gerald stood head and shoulders above most men, his mother would still be calling him that today were she alive, benevolent Lord above rest her soul. His parents had thought it would only be a matter of time before their youngest son wore the mitre. They had talked about it in the way they talked of next Candlemas or next Lammas Day: as a certainty that would come to pass like any other calendar date. But that mitre was still not his.

In the *ystafell* of Rhys' castle, the first stone-built seven-towered castle in *Pura Wallia* and the first in Wales or England or anywhere to hold a festival quite like the one that was about to commence, as the last wolf-grey light of Christmas Day drained away, Gerald slid his bishop across the board and put Rhys in check.

Rhys bent forward, pulling his moustache as he did in moments of intense concentration. His eyes flickered as if he was considering every combination of responses possible five, ten, twenty moves ahead and doing so in an instant, for he nodded as if he had expected the offensive and covered with a pawn, threatening Gerald's rook in the process. Gerald retreated again.

"It is so good to play," Rhys proclaimed heartily. He poured Gerald another horn of claret. "There are few at my court who do."

Gerald moved his rook back a square. But once more Rhys disguised an advance with defence, and Gerald hardly had time to sip his drink before it was his turn again.

"I am afraid you find me woefully out of practise my good cousin."

"Do they not play chess in Paris?"

Gerald upturned his lips.

"I suppose I had other things on my mind."

Rhys bit his lip, because his cousin was young and handsome, yet had sworn himself to celibacy. And Paris was famous for its temptations in the opposite direction.

"As you do now?"

By now Gerald had almost moved his rook back to its starting position. He sighed.

"I know we want the same thing, my good cousin. Now, I hear you have plans to reconstruct the Roman baths at Caerleon.

I even hear you are in the throes of raising a castle at Rhyader right within sight of the border with De Braose's lordship! Lord of our skies, as if the Normans needed any further evidence of your intent! I am all in favour of this advancement, really I am, there is Welsh blood a-plenty in my veins and I would jubilantly climb to your battlements this instant to champion our nation's betterment! Only…" Gerald was hemmed in; he could not move any main pieces forward. Desperately he tried a lone attack on the other side of the board with a pawn instead. "I want the progress to extend to the church, too."

"This is why I endow the monasteries, cousin. Whitland, Strata Florida…"

"With respect my good cousin I am not talking about the domains of the Cistercians. The white monks do quite well enough according to reports!" Gerald sifted the disapproval from his voice: the Cistercians were nothing but acquisitionists in habits in his enlightened opinion. "I am talking about the *people's* church. The monks shut themselves away for contemplation with Our Lord and that is all very lovely, but meanwhile the remainder of the populace suffer. Those in charge of the parishes, the benefices, the deaneries and archdeaconries: I have found them to be lacking in morals to the point of theft, of corruption, of dice-playing and deity-praising and betting and buggery, and as it is at the top so it becomes further down the pile!"

"As I recollect, cousin, this was how you attained your position as archdeacon was it not? By exposing the scandals perpetrated by the previous incumbent?" Rhys picked off Gerald's pawn with his knight.

"I am in the middle of preparing a document, my good cousin," Gerald smiled a smile as thin as an apple skin, and ignored the goad. "York and Canterbury will see it; the leading cardinals of Christendom will see it. The document concerns Wales. It advocates bringing the Welsh church in line with the church elsewhere."

"And you seek my support?"

"Not exactly." Gerald leaned towards Rhys confidentially. "I wish you to back me as the new Bishop of St David's. It will lend great weight to the findings I will present to the high clergy. The canons have already stated it is me they want to lead them, but you have Henry Plantagenet's ear, my good cousin, your backing will sway the King."

"But the King has deemed you an unacceptable choice. Advocating your abilities as bishop, cousin, is not far off treason. And treason precipitates war with England when I have only just begun appreciating the peace."

"No one is suggesting endangering the peace! But a few words subtly said could make a world of difference. Countenance the countless other advantages presented to you, my good cousin, with a friendly family member in charge at St David's! Were you, hypothetically speaking of course, to wish to advance Deheubarth to the south..." Gerald shrugged. "To have a helping hand at the finishing line would doubtless smooth the course. Think of it," he whispered. "Sacred and secular control of St David's in Welsh hands. The last time Wales could boast that was before the Normans came! Not since the days of your great, great, great, great, great grandfather, not since Hywel Dda himself founded Deheubarth will one of its leaders have had such power!"

Rhys thought again of the water clock he had seen at Gloucester. All those mechanisms, those levers and pulleys and wheels moving this way and that and water burbling along tubes of differing lengths and shapes but the thing had one pure purpose: to tell the time. How he had fought for his own reign to be like that water clock was! His cousin was a persuasive fellow. He had been able to twist his parents around his little finger: they had lavished more on his education than on all the weapons and armour and horses they bought his elder brothers. And these days it seemed he was able to influence archbishops and popes too. But he would not persuade Rhys to jeopardise the peace he had constructed in his realm from the bottom up.

Rhys castled, his own king well out of harm's way.

"Do you remember the first time we met?" he asked Gerald slowly.

"You ruffled my head and asked me if I was going to grow up and be a fighter like my father and brothers," Gerald nodded. "And I said 'no' quite adamantly as I remember."

"You did. And I said to you that cutting your own path was better than following the well-trodden road, even if it would be bloody overgrown at times. I am going to have to ask you to cut your own path in this matter, cousin," he watched Gerald's smile getting thinner and tighter. "I cannot risk piquing the Plantagenets. Privately, of course, I wish you every success."

Gerald stared at the board, stroking his scraped-clean jaw. Rhys' rook had a sight on his queen, and so did his knights. He was struggling to stay in the game. It annoyed him that his elder cousin had spent years molesting Normans whilst he had done his utmost to get along with them, and yet when it came to the one Norman who mattered more than all others, the King of England, Rhys jested and drank and hunted with the man whilst Gerald accrued increasing amounts of Royal rebuke.

At length he looked up at Rhys from under his thicket of eyebrows.

"You play a tough game, my good cousin."

"On this issue my hands are tied," Rhys said, in a manner that would have put the subject to bed had the person he was speaking with been anyone else. He craned his neck around the doorway of the *ystafell* to see how preparations were unfolding in the hall: favourably, it seemed. Cibon, his fiddler, was already rehearsing. The fire was a fine blaze. He could smell meat, good roasted meat. He had adapted to battle easily enough; he had been born into it after all. But he was developing a taste for revelry. "Now let us dispense with this bloody talk of kings and bishops, cousin, and make merry for Christmas has come!"

"If you mean the chess game then I concede. But with your permission…" Gerald paused, his eyes roaming around the *ystafell* and also turning to the doorway as if in expectation of someone or something appearing. When no one or nothing did, he rose with a roll of his eyes and went to look out across the hall, hectic as a hive of bees with the banquet being laid, across at the one unmoving figure on the far side. Gerald gestured and over he marched, the miserable old bard from Gwynedd, his cloak strewing clumps of snow on the floor and his face an atrocious scowl, quite the last person anyone would wish to see before during or after a festival. "I do respectfully insist a *little* on your backing me for bishop, my good cousin."

Rhys' mouth fell open.

Long before he read the parchment Gwalchmai thrust out to him, he perceived that for the first time in his life he was being blackmailed.

He pored the contents, his face unreadable.

The hand of Rhodri of Gwynedd. The unsteady scrawl of a desperate bastard. But the essence of the message was plain.

The lord of the most northerly Marcher lordship, Chester, having tumbled out of favour with the King was angling to redeem himself and regain his lands. And this man had made Rhodri—

who ruled western Gwynedd—and his brother Dafydd—who ruled the Gwynedd across the other side of the Conwy—a proposal. The proposal was a three-pincer attack on Deheubarth from the north and east, sudden and swift at New Year whilst it was well known Rhys would be making merry in the southwest. An attack devastating enough to take the affluent pilgrimage centres of Llanbadarn Fawr and Llanddewi Brefi, all the fulling mills in the pasturelands and the seat of power at Dinefwr too. Enough for Rhys to be forced to come to terms, with the Marcher lord of Chester let off his past misdemeanours, and Rhodri and Dafydd granted lands in Deheubarth for their pains.

It was patently not the best proposal Rhodri had ever received: Gwynedd might be floundering, but Rhodri's loathing of the Marcher lords was no secret and he hated his brother even more. It was desperate men who carried out desperate schemes, but Rhodri was not nearly so desperate as the Marcher lord of Chester currently was, and the proposal promised great risk for uncertain reward. What Rhodri wanted from Rhys was a better offer. The document did not specify what Rhodri deemed appropriate, but trade agreements and tributes of cattle were tentatively suggested.

Rhys bristled. Compromise his hide and fleece and fulling industries? Give his finest cows to that northern Welsh bastard? Compared to fighting a war on three fronts an amicable arrangement with Rhodri might seem harmless, but Rhys was the mightiest prince in Wales, he paid tribute to the King of England alone. Everyone else made tributes to him. It was the principle of the thing. Rejecting Rhodri outright was equally unthinkable. Then there was the chance the attack alluded to really would go ahead. Rhys could not disrupt his festival of song, and did not wish to endanger the lives of his subjects. And what of the option of ignoring the communication from Rhodri entirely? People who considered themselves important became more incensed through being ignored than by being rejected; ignoring Rhodri would lead to war most surely of all.

"I have had the luxury of time to dedicate a little more thought to your predicament, my good cousin," Gerald edged in.

"I was wondering how you fitted into it," Rhys said heavily. "Aside from answering to the charge of treason, which I will see no reason not to press once we are done with this."

"Merciful Heaven, we are all in this together! Now my good cousin, I have committed no crime against the King nor defied his council, so terming it treason is inaccurate. And although I understand a ruler *might* be down-mouthed by other parties —me, for example—being privy to the contents of his private parchments and *could* do the Lord only knows what to me in retaliation whilst I remain within his domain, I really think the sensible way forward is to examine how we can resolve things satisfactorily!" Gerald glanced brightly up at the unamused faces of Rhys and Gwalchmai. "War we can safely say is not in Deheubarth's interests. Gwynedd requires some... *offering* to convince it cordiality with Deheubarth is the right path but Deheubarth cannot demean itself by making tribute. A lesser region gives a greater region tribute, for the greater realm to give to the lesser would be horrible humiliation!" The churchman's hands, silk-smooth as if they spent each day every day opening his and other people's letters, spread palms down on the tabletop. Then he wagged a finger at Rhys. "But what if this was your offering, my good cousin?"

Gerald indicated Gwalchmai.

Rhys looked at the silent and grim-faced old man dripping snowmelt over his hall and then back to his cousin again as if some further explanation was required.

"He is a man of Gwynedd," Gerald said. "He is entering your

contest of song, and why not, when the prize is so grand? A place at Lord Rhys of Deheubarth's table and a share in Lord Rhys of Deheubarth's wealth: an honour beyond the dreams of most. Were a man of Gwynedd to return to his native land in possession of this prize, my good cousin, Prince Rhodri would surely be pleased. And if not…" he shrugged. "Then what with the length of time messages take to be delivered up to the far side of Snowdonia and back, you would have bought yourself the days you need to conclude the festival in peace. By which point you would be able to muster an army sufficient to subdue two bastard princes and a disinherited Marcher lord if the moment demands it. Your gathering tells the world that there is more to Wales than war, and so peace must reign during it, but afterwards? No one," said Gerald gently, "could blame you, my good cousin, for crushing a rebellion and laying waste to the lands of those that started it."

"And again I ask you, cousin," said Rhys. "How do you fit into all this?"

"A learned man by the name of Ovid once said that one should use the occasion, my good cousin, for it passes swiftly. Follow my advice and I do not come into *all this* whatsoever. This man here goes home to Gwynedd a worthy winner, the north is content— as much as it ever will be—and your realm glisters bright in the eyes of those who choose to look for having hosted a remarkable winter's merrymaking. Meanwhile my lips remain as sealed as the wax on a well-sealed piece of confidential correspondence."

Rhys poured another horn of claret and drained it steadily.

"What secret would you be keeping exactly?"

"There are several hundred entertainers out there. Some, it is true, are frail fellows, and a good many, having set aside the sword in favour of the quill, would probably not put up much of a fight should it come down to it but still, several hundred entertainers receiving the tidings that, unbeknownst to them and despite their most heroic efforts, the champion in the contest of song has been fixed before any of them had performed a single verse! Lord of our skies, my good cousin! I would not like to be in your halls when *that* news spreads about."

In his fighting days, Rhys had managed far worse than seizing the necks of two men like his cousin and his sour-faced friend simultaneously, and squeezing until the life spluttered out of them. But this was the great bloody peace. And in peacetime people like his cousin emerged from whatever library they had been hiding in and waged a different sort of war: a war of rhetoric. And it took as many prisoners, and was as impossible to oppose.

"You could worm your way through a stone wall, cousin," he said testily.

Gerald smiled sweetly.

"And I would need time."

For the first time that Gerald could recollect, there was a note of pleading in his cousin's voice. Only an attuned ear could have heard it.

"Oh, time!" Gerald spread his hands, like he had vast sums of it to loan out. "Take all you need. Provided that you are aware it is fast trickling away for you," he raised his drinking horn, brought his nose to the brim so that it was all but touching the little lapping circle of ruby red claret, and inhaled and exhaled exaggeratedly. His face smirked back at him out of the drink and he took an appreciative sip. It really was the equal of anything he had tried in France. "To your *vigorously* supporting my claim to the bishopric, my good cousin."

The little bishop was not a fighter. But this did not mean that he did not know how to fight.

The Song Contest

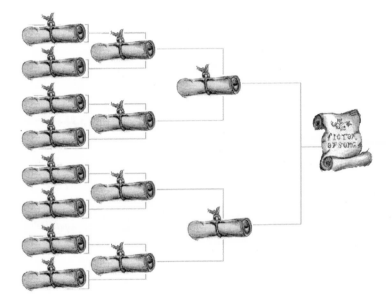

Round One

(December, 1176)

AS THE LAST PLAINTIVE NOTE faded from the seventh chant the seven monks from the abbey of Strata Florida had composed especially for this Christmas evening, appreciation rumbled across Rhys' hall. The richness of voice and syrup-smooth cadence of the monks struck even the poorest and most tone-deaf in that room; a little light was shone into the foulest recesses of the darkest soul there. Everyone felt a surge of his or her version of joy; felt better; felt their husbands or wives *did* care and that their children *would* look after them when they were old. The festival was opened, magnificently open.

"Wales…" stammered the lank-haired boy, striving to wipe away both the sweat and fringe from his face. He was first up. The first of hundreds. He had taken advantage of the reverberations of ovation from the monks' chants to hurry up to the stage unobserved, and like a night-time animal trapped in sudden torchlight, his large, fearful eyes now flitted around the room.

No refuge for him there.

The platform on which he tremulously perched was not high, a step higher than the dais on which Rhys, his family, his principal court officers and his guests of honour sat, and a step again above the rest of the revellers, but not high. Yet it must have seemed a cliff-edge to the youth, a cliff-edge with a rough ocean below.

The audience were only on their second or third drinks, ale for the masses, ale or mead or claret for those on the dais, and had not worked out at this point what reception it was best to give the performers in the contests of song. Should it be applause? What then if it outstripped the cheers *they* received when their turn came to step up? And if they should jeer? What if those they derided now exacted revenge by deriding *them* more deprecatingly? For the moment, then, these onlookers stayed silent, for an entertainer perhaps the most terrible damnation of all.

But however the hall dealt with this lank-haired boy, he was an undoubted embarrassment; a shame to the world of song, chalk squeaking on slate, cat fur combed backwards, salt in a sore.

"W… wales… a land of… h…happiness," he sputtered. "A land of hope…"

"My faith, if ever there was a time to call on God!" Dog muttered to Avery at the lower end of the hall, where the draught was coldest and the ale pitcher was taking the longest time to circulate. "It would be now, to save us from this rambling rabbit."

"Easy on him, friend," Avery's mind was far away, a fortnight's journey away to be precise. It had taken a two-week tramp to begin to forget York and a few moments of monkish chants to catapult him back there. The church might frown upon the monastic way of life, but the songs sung were similar. And the choir stalls of course were where it had happened.

"No good getting the shakes," Dog carried on. "You could be the best striker of harpstrings in Britain but if you get the shakes in front of a crowd you're finished. Same with bards, I'll wager. Writing verses is pointless unless you can sing them with a bit of spectacle. Like dressing for battle without knowing how to fight."

"Pirin the fisherman's son," Avery faintly repeated the name the poor boy performing had given. "Perhaps he sung to the fishes as he was hauling in his nets and imagined he could do the same in this hall. But fishes do not judge you as humans do."

"If their mouths weren't being prised open by big hooks I wager even his fish would have voiced their disappointment. They don't seem too pleased up on that dais either." Dog nodded in the direction of Rhys and the others on the top table who, it was plain to those who looked closely, were not quite themselves, then stared sharply back at Avery. "What's ailing you? You were all dew-eyed and gawk-mouthed about attending this festival and now when you're sitting at it you're half the world away," he expelled an oath when he saw the dewy-eyedness this time was due to weeping, and passed Avery a rag of dubious origin. "Get out. Don't let these vultures see you like this. They'll spot a weakness a mile off and they'll use it against you. Go and compose yourself. Go!" The musician pushed his companion towards the hall door.

But a minstrel from Carmarthen two places along who had already spoken out rather boldly about how Frenchmen made superior lovers to Welshmen did exactly as Dog had predicted anyway.

"What's that one's performing name, Snivelling Saxon?" she asked the room at large with a mean laugh.

"Cancer," the Healer, seated between Dog and the minstrel, whispered loudly in her ear.

"What did you say to me, witch?"

"They call me a witch because I identify illness so quickly, my tricky vixen. And I would guess from the size of that growth you have weeks left rather than months."

Dog nodded approvingly.

"I can see why your reputation for healing precedes itself," he said in the tone the Healer knew by now was as close as he came to good-naturedness. She smiled playfully.

"I am just warming up, my ruffian."

Chrétien got Pirin the lank-haired fisherman's son off the stage without too much ado and introduced the next contestant in this bout, a clerk from Anglesey by the name of Bran the Bard. This one *had* to be an improvement on the last, he thought.

Chrétien was always around people. And he had become sensitive to the undercurrents that flowed through large groups of them. At the Court of Champagne pulsed a palpable sense of endeavour. He loved this. The work was mainly devoted to entertainment in some form, be it literary composition, music, painting, pageantry or spectacle, and it was hard not to be happy with being a part of that, working towards the furthering of these ultimate cultural pleasures. His experience of the Plantagenet Court was different. There it was more energy-sapping, courtiers were running to stand still because of the great vigour of the King, on the verge of collapse, driven until their last dreg of drive. But in this court, the court of the foremost prince of Wales, the officers of the Royal household seemed unbothered by what was happening around them at all. They were weathering this festival, heads-down waiting for it to go away like cows in a rainstorm, there was no contriving or conniving or dashing around to make themselves appear better than they really were, and in this they were unlike any other courtiers he ever encountered. So Chrétien watched currents flowing around a roomful of people, watched their speed and direction, and perceived when and where they were going. And this room desperately needed a lift.

It would be unfair to blame poor Pirin the fisherman's son entirely for this. It was also the mood on the dais. It was strange and no one knew why. In a court of unforthcoming courtiers like this it was no surprise that the mood would be carried by Rhys and Rhys, up until the moment the banquet began, had bubbled with enough enthusiasm to buoy the whole hall. Mercy! When Rhys was enthusiastic Chrétien just wanted to give that Celt a big hug. But Rhys looked troubled. The reason could be his cabbage of a wife, no love lost there, or the beautiful young Breton lady he had seated opposite him, without question filling a fair percentage of his thoughts. Or it could be his sons. They did project the strong impression of being a bunch of brutes. Rhys' eldest had a fresh wound to the face like a common tavern tussler, and whether it was incurred on some escapade or received from a flash of Rhys' wrath, Chrétien had no doubt the man deserved it and was the sort to go out seeking trouble to saddle his family with. Whatever the case though, Rhys was being very cruel, cruel to Chrétien who was channelling every effort into ensuring this festival was a success and who with his brilliance and good cheer and theatrics in-between acts was right now the cream and most of the cherries on the cake.

What Chrétien did not admit was that he was not doing this for Rhys anymore. He was doing this for himself.

He would never marry, he did not think about women that way, and all that fuss a parent would have poured on their child, he put into other projects.

Normally, Chrétien lavished attentions on his literary work. His characters benefited, becoming vividly defined, coloured in and coloured up from their robes to their habits, until nobles soon began approaching him unbidden in the street to beg him to allow this or that protagonist to return in his very next story.

But normally when Chrétien undertook a new writing commission, he was up and above his subject matter in a matter of hours, viewing it as a flying bird views land with all things visible neatly below in their places.

With Chrétien's latest literary venture, with this Welsh court scene he needed to experience in order to transpose it into words that would move those nobles back home, it was more like he were stuck at the bottom of a steep and narrow valley in the mist. He had been stuck like this for days. His characters and the plot that should weave them together were up in that mist above him, elusive, indistinct.

Chrétien needed a King Arthur, but could that and should that be Rhys? He needed a court, but could that and should that be Cardigan? In his fiction-to-be, the court would represent safety for the King and Queen and knights that would inhabit it; it was outside of that, in the wilderness he would sketch in the form of forests and other dangerous places, that the misadventures would occur.

But this hall was the wrong way around: the misadventure was here, within these walls. For as performers masterful and performers mediocre performed, and ale or mead or wine or meat was quaffed or scoffed in quantities not seen even in the days of the cosmic Viking debauches, as stupid ballads and bland cantos and verses every so often of total beauty got sung in a cornucopia of song into existence for the first time, as the festival unfolded in multifarious ways, it was becoming more apparent to Chrétien that the appearance of merriment was only membrane-thick.

Many people, poor innocents, might be in this hall for the purity of performing, but some were using this festival as a cover for something altogether viler. If one of Chrétien's fellow judges had asked him where his proof for all this was, he could not have said. But he understood undercurrents. And on the dais he sensed it. On the lower banquet tables he sensed it too. Sizzling and spitting away like lava just below the surface. Murder.

So Chrétien might not at this point in time have been able to put quill to vellum and write of Rhys' festival in the way he wished, because he did not know exactly what was going on yet. But he would. For the time being he saw his role as keeping things together, he would keep the acts a-coming, keep his commentary with the quips interspersed a-coming. But Chrétien would find out what was afoot. And the stage bared the soul. All he had to do was sit here and wait, and one by one they would come up and perform, and eventually he would find out. He knew everything there was to know about undercurrents.

"I'm watching you, parrot-feather."

Chrétien blinked. Anarawd.

"I am... flattered seigneur."

"Don't be. Just know I'm watching you. Whether you're prattling your pretty words up on this dais, or sneaking out the back for a pretty little shit, I'm watching. You know how many decades of service I've given Rhys? Three. Three, and a foreign popinjay that came into Cardigan on a criminal's cart is chosen over my head to run things around here. Well you run them parrot-feather. I heard that heart-warming way you introduced yourself to everyone earlier," Anarawd put on a fey voice in mimicry of Chrétien but it sounded more menacing than amusing. "*I am a writer of fictions!* Well that doesn't save you. You run things until the moment the last song is sung. Then you leave. You fly on back to France, you hear me?*" Anarawd ground bark against his molars. His breath was thick as tar in Chrétien's ears. "You don't want to be around when I start asking questions, parrot-feather. I don't ask with words. I'm a very direct man. I ask with implements. And we both know what I'd ask first, don't we? Because we in Wales rise up in one of two ways. Because everyone else in line ahead of us is dead, or because we've *proved* that should everyone else in line ahead of us die, we could step up in their stead. Some of us prove ourselves crushing men's skulls. Some of us show we can breach defences or parley well, or lead a charge on horseback or swordfight or at least lance a lot. But where's your proof, parrot-feather? How do any of us know you are who you say you are?"

Chrétien gazed at Anarawd through his long, angelic lashes. That was it! Incredible that a brute with no knowledge of literature should come up with it, but there it was! Lance-a-lot. His new hero! Mercy, he could visualise him now, a fearsome fighter but a love-besotted fool too, and both his skill in combat and his skill as a lover would be tested to their limits in the depths of the forest of misadventure...

"You, seigneur, are an exceptional man!"

"Did you listen to a word of what I said, parrot-feather?"

"Avidly," Chrétien raised his hands high above his head and clapped as Bran the Bard—whose performance really had been decent, conducted with a clerk's clipped measuredness, but good enough to animate the hall somewhat—finished the final lines of his song. He clapped, the dais clapped, everyone clapped. "Would you prefer I take my leave now, seigneur? I am quite certain you could keep the *ambiance* a-bubbling. It is the little matter of reading this..." Chrétien indicated the several huge slates it had taken two servants two trips to carry from his quarters earlier, slates as tall as reasonably sized humans and covered top to bottom in his scrawled recordings of each of the many hundred entrants for the contests of vocal and instrumental song. He had simply adored the fact these quaint Celts wrote on slabs of stone—so *biblical*—and had insisted on preparing his lists of entrants on the stuff. But Chrétien could have held a knife to the neck of each of Anarawd's last known relatives and the *penteulu* would have experienced nothing like the cold dread that now seized him as he stared at the tiny scribblings, which to him no more resembled words than a swarm of insects did. "Read them, and do so with sufficient variation that it does not sound *too* like a dirge, seigneur, you can be brief with these lesser entrants but as you can see with the bigger names, which I have annotated with a star for convenience, a touch more pomp is fitting for their introduction."

"No," Anarawd said quickly. "You began it, parrot-feather. Best see it through."

A dark, dark forest, mused Chrétien, and his protagonist riding on through having all manner of misadventures, and this charming little castle at the far end of it, shining like a beacon…

Going outside to compose himself, Avery soon discovered, was not so easy. There were crowds out here in the bailey too: those who had not been fortunate enough to gain a space inside the hall, huddling around fires and continually opening the hall doors to see what was happening within. There were those for whom the food and drink had already proved too much, intoxicated or incontinent or insensible in some cranny or other. Guards muttered and told what sounded like very obscene jokes. The snow was settling, and Avery, inhaling great gasps of the icy air, walked as far from the hall as the battlements would take him. The perimeter wall burned bright with torchlight, but there were places in-between with shadow and he stood in one, looking out at the Teifi. Where the greatest river in Wales meets the sea, he managed a smile through his tears. But the dim silty curve did not seem all that great and it was an estuary, not open sea. The sea he had still never really seen. When he first found out about the proclamation, that mention of the sea had decided him. He had thought of it as a place to leave behind the old at long last, leave it behind and wash it away and begin the new. But this was not the sea. This was not the sea.

Someone else approached the ramparts and he instinctively hid his face, because people feel extreme shows of emotion are wrong, they feel other people care to know only that they are at least and at most doing passably.

"I beg your pardon, my lord."

If only he had been a lord. He would never have had to see what he had seen in York. But something in the voice made him turn towards it, for he had heard it before. Good English, better English than the English spoke, but not her native tongue. She hesitated very slightly over her words, not like she was struggling to think of them, but like she was selecting the finest fruit from a stall rather than grabbing any old bruised ones. The French lady from the church.

"You wish to be alone. I know what that is—to need to be alone. We are cooped here like chickens, after all."

"I would be an ingrate indeed, my lady, to insist on you taking your leave when I have not yet had a chance to thank you for what you did for my companion and me."

"I could not have borne the injustice of you being refused entry. You had clearly come from afar to be here."

"Far!" Avery echoed, as if temporarily forgetting he was no longer alone with his demons. "Far indeed, yet no distance at all and not distance enough."

They both looked away, awkwardly away and out over the walls to other places.

"Forgive me, my lady. It is perhaps better I am alone. I… forgive me."

"As you wish. I will stand elsewhere."

Avery nodded and as soon as she was gone wiped the tears from his eyes.

Asperges. Attende Domini. Jesu Dulcis Memoria. The processional chants.

The songs they had sung to purify, going around all the places in the cathedral and purifying them so that its sacredness did not diminish. The chants had not been precisely the same as those the seven monks from Strata Florida sung the festival open with, but chants do not have so many variations and hearing one can bring to mind others, can conjure up the abject sadness which they all have at their core.

Around they would go, the most senior canon down to the youngest almonry boy, singing the chants and blessing the altar, the font, the chapel, the cloisters, but they begun and ended at the choir stalls and *it* began and ended there too. The Archbishop and the dean and the elder canons standing at the back, the younger boys in front. Sing-singing away.

Coarse laughs from the guard tower told him where the French lady had gone. He guiltily hurried to find her. What kind of a man was he, exposing her to the derision of others like that? He contemplated saying a thing or two to the guards about behaving correctly in a lady's presence, but checked himself, for what did he know? He had only ever entered into conversation with one member of the fairer sex. What kind of a man was he? *One of the tender ones.* That was what the Healer had called him, but was that not just a kind way of saying that he was the spineless kind, the most purposeless kind of man there was? One so purposeless he could sing, only sing, sing better than he could earn a living, sing better than he could stand up to another man, certainly sing better than he could behave correctly towards a lady.

"I… I have memories that I wish to dispel," he said to her by way of explanation.

"I am sorry for that, my lord."

"I am no *lord*, my lady. If I were things might have been a lot better for me," he floundered as she regarded him questioningly. "I am Avery, of York."

"York. A beautiful city."

"It is a city."

"I suppose I was brought up on a wild coast a long way from settlement. When I visit anywhere more populous than a village I think it very grand indeed. Grand at first," she frowned and gave a funny little smile, as if she were analysing herself. "And then oppressive, like something were telling me I should have stayed well away all along. It was a pleasure to meet you, Avery of York. But I must take my leave in order to be rid of these animals," she said the last word distinctly enough that the ribaldry aimed at her from inside the guard tower ceased, as surely as if arrows had sailed back through those slit windows and pierced the gullets of the hecklers. She bowed and, hugging her cloak around her, started back across the bailey.

"Are you... headed back to the hall, my lady?" he called after her, heart clanging in his chest. "Only..."

"Only it is so dangerous out here in the snow?" she asked him with a trace of amusement. "Men here keep offering me their protection, Avery of York, you are not the first. But the greatest danger is seated in there on that dais. And there is no *protecting* against it."

He caught up with her, breathless. Her footprints were small but very deep. She sidestepped and drew a 'M' in the gathering whiteness.

"I wish it were within my power to offer you that, my lady, but I cannot even protect myself, let alone another. Yet I wonder..."

She finished the 'M' with a little flourish.

In the end, he blurted it out.

"Might I ask you to do me a kindness?"

Wrinkling his face in distaste, Bernart put one daintily shoed foot then the other out into the snow. Blasted weather. He did not mind weather when it was unnoticeable; when the temperature without was as pleasant as the temperature within; a mild summer day, say, provided the stench of blossom was none too strong. But extremes of hot and cold and precipitation of any kind he despised, particularly snow because it stayed for a long time and he did not have the requisite footwear for it. He picked his way like a wading bird, peering through the loathsome flakes, through the shivering songsters and hunched guards and the others who had for one reason or another left the light of the hall for the chilly December night. His eyes alighted on the worst of it. On a fight between two minstrels over a half-mauled leg of mutton. On one drunk pouring ale down the throat of his unconscious companion. On a guard with one hand clamped across the mouth of a serving wench whilst the other pawed her breasts, rubbing himself against her from behind. A cackle here a scream there. Such baseness. Yet this was the darkness he must dabble in. These lowlifes revolted him, but to do what he must do he needed their kind. They who did things by shadow. He had tried everything else. He had blood-let until he was as white as a phantom. He had stalked the walls of castle and town recalling past liaisons, not Marguerite because he had sung of her already until he was spent, but Leonora, lady-in-waiting to the Queen, yes, Blanche of Castille, oh yes, praying that dredging up memories of one of them would set off the strains of a new song in his head. But each pace made these beauties harder and harder to remember. Because the reality was that they had happened to him long long ago. Now, there were other bright young things. And Bernart was getting grey in his hair.

Grey crept over him these days. He knew he could survive the early heats. He had once reigned supreme in the realm of romantic song-singing and could shake up some verses about one of his long-gone loves to get past the mumblers and bumblers that would be pitted against him to begin with. But later on in the contest he would clash with talent, real talent. He would need new material. And so he needed new love, and he had it—almost at his fingertips!

There she was, the object of his ardour. No one else wore indigo like that. Not in Wales anyway. He gave a sharp intake of breath. She was with someone else. Some *man*, more a boy than a man by the look of things. Some nobody. She was in Bernart's sights then out of them again, gone around the far side of the hall to where the gardens were. Gone, with a boy-man, to the gardens!

He moistened his lips, resisting the urge to follow. After what had happened in the woods on the way here there could be no more bungles. He had devoted the full force of his thought to how he would possess her these last days. And there *was* consummation in all the best love songs. But he would wait awhile yet. The mightiest Marcher lord in Wales had, after all, given him three of his best men to use should the occasion demand. Well the occasion just might. And this time when it took place it would take place flawlessly. He would tame her. He would take her. Oh, what flow he would have then!

Now though, he felt the urge for flow of a different sort. He had drunk a fair quantity of fine claret. He picked his spot and ungirded.

"Tsss."

Bernart whirled around. He imagined it might be a whore hissing at him, but it was a decently attired middle-aged woman with a double chin. She squatted in a corner, counting a number of coins into a bulging sack.

"Tsss, veteran of versification!"

He sighed. He could not *go* with a woman watching.

"How do you know me by that name?" he asked coldly.

"Does it displease you?" she made no effort to address him by any other title, which suggested to him that she thought rather a lot of herself, or did not care what opinion people had of her. "That's what you're called on our books."

"Your *books*?"

"We've got the odds on every songster here. You're the favourite, you know. It's a close-run thing with a few others. Someone called the Great One? He's a way behind you at the minute though, mighty talent but a big mouth, so we figured even if he said all the right things on stage he'd say some of the wrong ones too and wouldn't win the judges. Someone called Gwalchmai? We're betting on him frightening the judges, he's known for his harsh words about who gets to go to Heaven and who to Hell and those old men are precious close to the grave in all honesty. Someone called Avery? Former choir singer, exquisite voice: we got an exclusive tip-off on him. Then, what have we here, a Marie? Unknown quantity, but there's not a soul she's told a story to that hasn't been stunned by her style. And another foreigner, can't pronounce his name because he wrote it back to front, peculiar dress, only just arrived? Funny fellow but his servant did say he had written the most beautiful words ever written and, well, it's Christmas and we're taking a chance on him. Want to place a bet?"

Bernart was speechless, thrilled to be still the favourite in spite of his creative blockage, but outraged that a mere novice in bardism like Marie should be considered as a contender not far behind him. *She is young enough to be my daughter* he huffed.

"I am not a betting man," he said at length. "I deal only in certainties." Yet he arranged his features to look more warmly at the woman, because instinct told him she was someone who it would be advantageous to have on his side. "But I am gladdened to hear of the faith placed in my abilities and, indeed, interested: upon what factors do you calculate the favourites?

"History," shrugged the woman. "Talent. Standing with Lord Rhys. It depends."

His time with the Plantagenets! That would be it. Who else competing here could boast so many years of service at the mightiest court on the continent? He took his leave of the woman, who was unperturbed at the preposterousness of his bow. Here was Bernart de Ventadorn. Bernart de Ventadorn, veteran of versification, favourite in the contest of song. Bernart de Ventadorn was here.

And he let it out at last, a golden arc of steaming piss, thawing a hole in the snow, which already came over the tops of his ridiculously inappropriate shoes. Then he jumped back, still in mid-flow, partially wetting his scarlet travelling cloak. Through the circle of piss-melt a lifeless human face gaped back. A drunk, frozen to death: the first of the festival's casualties.

"I had been having impure thoughts," Avery said. He glanced at the French lady. Marie. She had asked that he call her just that. He was not her servant. Nor was he a man of privilege to insist on titles for the sake of titles. He was commonalty. He was one of many and she was one of many and 'Marie' would suffice as 'Avery' sufficed. Now she was as silent as the muffling whiteness of the garden; silent as the skeletons of fruit trees and snow-bowed shoots of leek. She kept her eyes down on the ground, and the ground was not interesting, it was white, so he could only assume she was making the telling of what he had to tell easier for him. "In the church, we are urged to confess our sins at the earliest possible opportunity. They are not so bad then, you see," he laughed bitterly. "I woke up in a guilty sweat. It was the first really cold night of winter but I was sweating and still in a half-dream I rose and saw a light burning in the cathedral. To my mind this light was lighting my way to a swift confession, as if it were meant to be there and then that I came clean with God. I know what you are thinking: yet another tale of a miraculous vision! I only wish it was. But the light was burning, and at an hour when this was highly unusual, so I followed the light. I did not use the main door, if I had been in the habit of doing so I would have found it locked and perchance returned to bed bemused but none the wiser, but I always used the side door and those inside had neglected to lock that, so in I went. In to my undoing! At York we would often have these processions, everyone from the dean down through the ranks of canons to the almonry boys visiting together the principal places in the cathedral and purifying them—purifying them! And of course I thought it was something to do with that. How would I have known any different?" he appealed to Marie tearfully. But she was a storyteller herself, she knew when a listener should interrupt and when they should stay quiet and this was a moment to stay quiet. "But that dim candlelight was light enough to see that it was no ceremony taking place. For why the underhand hour, why should only a couple have been asked to attend? The Archbishop was there. He had returned from his business abroad unbeknownst to the rest of us. I heard his nasally voice first. He spoke as if his nostrils were clenched together, whiningly, and now he sounded as if he were entreating someone to do something in his nasally whining tone. Entreating someone to sing," Avery's voice shook. "Because then they did. It was one of the younger boys. Theo. In choir he could reach notes the older boys no longer could. The topmost notes, the profound ones, the ones that set you shivering with their shrillness, the ones that convince you there must be a point to singing songs for blessed with song like that we become like the birds, we become free... Theo sang, but not from the choir stalls where such songs were always sung. He was singing from the sacristy, the room across the aisle where the vestments for services were kept on a table; a private dim little room. The vestments were not on the table that night, but Theo was, bent over it with his tunic bunched up and Archbishop Roger right behind him panting and commanding that he carry on singing. And Theo duly did. He hit the notes high and true. Then his voice soared suddenly. No boy in any choir makes a sound like that." Avery could not contain the sobs any longer. "And I was a boy just like him. I was a boy just like him."

"Let the tears flow, Avery of York," Marie placed a hand on his shoulder. "Let the tears flow. It is behind you now."

"But it is not," Avery stared at her. "You must surely see. It is here too! Who is the happiest soul seated in there on that dais, smiling and chattering away whilst everyone else, even Lord Rhys, looks troubled? There is one soul for sure on that dais that means devilry, and it is the churchman."

"You speak as if you know him."

"I know of him," Avery said quietly. "But not nearly so much as I fear he knows about me."

Gerald pontificated in his penetrating voice about cathedral architecture with Meilyr ap Gwalchmai on his right, and about the imperativeness of church tithes to Owain Cyfeiliog on his left. He asked Gwenllian if she was aware what substances went into dye and if she would like him to enlighten her, which he proceeded to do at some length, whilst simultaneously expressing great surprise that the Marcher lord no one remembered the name of could be in ignorance over the habits of the beavers prevalent on the rivers making up his borders. His manners were polished and he was good enough to tell some of the revellers seated nearest him how they might improve theirs. He only mentioned his education in Paris once. He stopped speaking when he sensed someone else wished to air an opinion because he relished the debate he would do his utmost to bring about as a result. His criticism of each of the performances taking place behind him was largely constructive and no one could say he drank or belched too much. And he was witty.

Those on the dais had to smile at Gerald's jests in spite of themselves. But they were light, polite smiles, absence-of-anything-better smiles, because, in truth, they felt more than a little lethargic and subdued. For their host Rhys ap Gruffyd was lost in a great gloom, like a comet fizzled out, and none of them quite understood why. The Lord of Deheubarth did host a hearty carousal, so some of the pre-eminent poets gathered had begun to scribble in the first drafts of the songs they hoped to immortalise this occasion with; Rhodri Mawr the father of modern Wales had hosted no better, and who was to say that the Romans had? But this great gloom their host had wrapped about him was ruining the merrymaking, and no one could sing about the festival that almost was, but was not quite. Rhys must rise above his gloom, and soon, or this whole thing would be undone.

Gerald sounded out about a Cistercian monk who stole from a blind woman, and about a prince whose realm was known to have collapsed because he indulged in periodic bestiality, but all the while he was looking out from under his eyebrows at Cousin Rhys: was he going to go along with his dear cousin's wishes and support his claim for the bishopric, or was he going to do something silly?

And there it was. Finally. A slight nod from Rhys unobserved by the others, and yet as final to Gerald and to Rhys too as a king knocked over in a chess game.

Gerald had of course been acting bishop some time, cleaning up after Arthur of Bangor, Adam of St Asaph and Nicholas of

Llandaff[1], the knuckleheads, and after the Archbishop of York on a couple of occasions. But now, with Rhys' backing, he felt as good as bound for the St David's bishopric, and that would be but a stepping-stone. It was not expedient for the likes of Cousin Rhys to know the details of the document he was preparing on the state of the church in Wales, but one key recommendation was that St David's became an archbishopric, on a par with York and Canterbury. It just made sound sense. Anyway, Gerald was pleased. His cousin—in this regard—had acted rationally. This way everyone was a winner: everyone that mattered. The Prince of Deheubarth had peace. The Prince of Gwynedd had prestige. And the contest of song had a *very* clean and churchly victor. Wales was a land of such immense potential. It simply needed a little scrub and a polish, and Gerald was happy to oblige.

Now thought Chrétien.

Chrétien knew some things about currents in crowds.

He knew when crowds were nervous, and needed to laugh.

He knew when crowds were angry, and needed pacifying.

He knew when crowds were whimsical, and needed whimsy.

And crowds knew some things about Chrétien. He was the sort whose appearance and mannerisms people who had never clapped eyes on him could nevertheless describe in detail. It was as if a coin bearing his likeness had been circulated at some point, or as if a travelling theatre had put on a show about him in every town from Berwick to Trieste; that was how much of a household name he was. Courtiers *will* spread stories about themselves, for to be talked of even for the wrong reasons was far, far better than befalling the fate of not be talked about at all. But in Chrétien's case he genuinely did seem to have a lot going on, both in reality—

---

1 Bangor, St Asaph and Llandaff were the three other dioceses of Wales in 1176 besides the diocese of St David's, the latter being one which Gerald had a very special interest in taking charge of: an interest which bordered on obsession.

whispers about his flirtations with several young men at the court to which he was attached appeared to have more than a grain of truth—and in his fictions—his literary endeavours were well-received by nobles in a number of lands. *Goings-on.* Chrétien's *goings-on* were the reason people were captivated by him. He was the act-between-acts, and they would listen to what he had to say.

Now, thought Chrétien, for he knew about currents in crowds, and he knew how rapidly they spread, and he knew that if the great gloom that had gripped Rhys spread then to the lower tables, it was venom in the bloodstream, it was the end.

Now it was time to feed the hall with something.

The audience had wolfed down flatbread and curd cheese and mutton in multifarious forms, and beef hearts cut from the white cattle of Dinefwr and mussels from the mouth of the Dyfi. They had drunk ale and braggot and in some cases Rhys' own mead and claret. They had heard Olaf of Bergen sing of an ancient battle between Vikings and Welshmen. They had heard Azelais the beautiful trobairitz sing of what happens when love dies, and been stirred. They were mellow. They were malleable. They were ready to be truly moved.

Now Chrétien motioned to Cibon the fiddler, who gazed off at an unreal point above everyone's heads in the woodsmoked half-light as musicians do when they leave the world of the living and enter the world of their instruments and the sounds they create. Cibon's fingers found his strings as ecstatic lovers throw themselves at each other, but he could sing too, and a few lines in, as was the custom, the hall joined in.

Armes Prydein. The anthem of Wales. The song about the Welsh uniting with the Scots and with the Irish, and rising up to drive the Saxons from British shores forever, about retaking Britain for the Britons. The Welsh knew the words, of course, and if the foreigners there did not they had Cibon as their guide and learned them with good heart, for this was not a time of war anymore and this was a song, just a wonderful song.

The hall sang as one.

Chrétien surveyed his slates. He conferred with the judges and wiped out the names of those performers who had been appalling or average, starting with Pirin the fisherman's son. A new list of reduced names, the best from each bout thus far, began to take shape.

The hall doors burst open abruptly just after halfway through *Armes Prydein*.

Snow and a cold wind blustered in.

The revellers spun around in surprise and irritation: who would have the gall? A guard, mortified at becoming the centre of attention like this but still making no move to close the door, started jabbering at them all, and jabbered such extraordinary things that people assumed he must have become addled by the cold. Anarawd sprang up. He shouted at the room to shut up so loudly that they did instantly, and invited the guard to say what he had just said again, with no jabbering this time.

"A man with robes brighter than a king… on a beast twice as high as a horse with fur thicker than a sheep, and…"

"Spit it out, damn it."

"With two humps!"

Anarawd shoved the guard to one side and strode out into the snow to ascertain what the madman could be blathering about. Two-humped furry beasts twice as big as horses, indeed! He did not get very many more paces.

"Satan's bloody sister!"

In the hall doorway appeared a beast twice the height of a horse with fur thicker than a sheep and two huge humps sprouting from its back. The beast was being led on a rope by a grey-beard Jew with a pointed hat and a fed-up expression. On top of the beast, his substantial hindquarters nestled in the valley between the two humps, sat a man with robes brighter than a king's. The man on the beast waved a corpulent hand from side to side in front of his face, in the way one shoos away a fly, and this seemed to be a signal for the Jew to speak.

The Jew cleared his throat, but it was already so silent in the hall one could have heard a maggot squirm.

"Farid Un-Din Attar," the Jew announced, "has travelled long and far these last eight months; across Wales, across England, across the Low Countries, across the Holy Roman and Byzantine Empires, across Persia, from no less a place than the exalted Empire of the Supreme Ruler of the World. He has come to be here with you this Christ's Mass for the tournament of vocal song, in which he requests the right to participate. He requests this right because he has written the most beautiful words ever written by a mortal man and is eager to adorn your festival with them so that you can become enriched. He understands that 'Farid Un-Din Attar' must be difficult for you to pronounce with your western mouths. So he permits you to call him Hamid."

Rhys Looked

(December, 1176)

RHYS LOOKED at his brood. It was fifteen strong if only those dining on the dais with him tonight were counted, and over twenty including the sons and daughters already married off and the infants still being wet-nursed. A greater number than Prince Madog of Powys or Prince Owain of Gwynedd ever produced, and he was not an old man quite yet. But their realms had gone from as great as could be to nothing lands after their deaths, dashed to pieces in weeks by quarrelling offspring. They said that one sired children for security in one's old age, but where was his security? His men had discovered his sons, moored in a cove on the Norman side of the river with two tavern wenches, filthily drunk and with the boat they had stolen so damaged, he had needed to make the Norsemen who owned it a grovelingly generous offer to redress matters. Maelgwyn ought to have known better. Maelgwyn was supposed to be his heir. Rhys had punished him with a good cuffing and by letting the next-eldest, Gruffyd, take the place of honour on his right-hand side for the revelry. But Maelgwyn was clever. Maelgwyn would not strike back straightaway if struck; he would sulk and plot his revenge exactingly. Perhaps he had already drawn some of his brothers and sisters in to whatever scheme he was hatching: that would not be unlike him, and would account for the glowers Rhys was getting from around the table. Gruffyd and Angharad were rare rays of light. But was the procreation worth the hassle? Had it brought him anything apart from havoc to fray away at the peace he had achieved at immense cost across the land? Rhys looked at his brood.

Rhys looked at his wife. The mysterious raven-haired daughter of Prince Madog of Powys had seemed the best match for Rhys twenty years ago, but whilst the raven locks were still there, she wore them scraped back severely like a nun now. And if Gwenllian hid her true feelings inside a sturdily locked and guarded chest to this day, Rhys no longer had a desire to see what was in her chest. Dust, he suspected, and trinkets. She had never given any indication it was otherwise. And their union had not got him a single clod of earth in Powys. She never complained or opposed him, and let him lie with her when he wished, but it was all done under sufferance. His wife was suffering him; suffering life. Dark, dour Gwenllian. There was not a single light burning within her that he could see. Rhys looked at his wife.

Rhys looked at the officers of his household. He had chosen them well enough, he believed, but chosen them from the best that had been available, and the best available in Wales was not so very exceptional a selection. Most were warriors, and although some were wise, even these ones did not see the wisdom of hosting a festival and throwing his gates open to all. They did not comprehend that if one shone a light on the poetry and the music, and the monasteries and the industries and the townships, and the way waves broke on the shores of his realm in orange and blue and green and white and brown and grey depending on where you were standing and what time of the day you stood there, if one illuminated those things then Wales was no longer a land that could so easily be dismissed or destroyed. The officers of Rhys'

household bore what he was doing but they did not buoy it, not like courtiers in Paris or London or probably even De Braose's retinue across the border in the March could. They prevented things from getting any worse. But they did not help things get better. He was trying to lift Deheubarth up more or less by himself and they were lead weights and dead weights adding to the load. Rhys looked at the officers of his household.

Rhys looked at his guests. They were supposed to be beacons blazing brilliantly in this long, long midwinter darkness. He had imagined splitting his sides with laughter at their performances, being elated and anguished by turns at the songs that were sung. And there had been glimmers. But the visitors to the castle of the greatest prince in Wales this Christmas had thus far brought with them more problems than they had sweet relief from them. Rhys looked at Marie. Beautiful. The most beautiful thing in his hall but too complicated, too much effort. He saw ahead into a version of the future, and her challenging what he had said or chastising him for some policy or other he had implemented after or even during their lovemaking. He saw Gwenllian's unspoken accusations hanging in the air. He saw dissipation. Rhys looked at Gwalchmai. What a grim certainty it was to have that sermonising sour-chops assured of top prize in the song contest before the contest had played out. Rhys liked a contest. He liked sport. He liked for the small man to have his chance against the big man; for the peasant to be able to battle for his right to beat the prince. This was Christmastide, after all, a time when a fool really could become a king: for a time. But he had been deprived of his sport, and given Gwalchmai instead, and this was a miserable exchange. Rhys looked at Gerald. His cousin, the cause of his woes, who had him in a thumbscrew and a noose and a rack all at once, who would have no clue how to use any of these devices in practise, but who had achieved the equivalent discomfort for Rhys with stratagem alone, which smarted more than the actual wounds would have done. Rhys remembered the time he chased the little bishop through the woods at Dinefwr for calling him names, pinned him down and boxed his ears and then felt the slap as if from nowhere as Gerald hit back. Not a hard slap. And Rhys might there and then have hit Gerald hard enough to knock his head right off. But he had not, because grown men should not kill children, he had let Gerald alone and ran off, fuming. So Gerald's slap had been the winning slap because it had been done not with strength but with calculation, the calculation Rhys would not could not respond to it. And now his cousin had come to his festival and ruined it, just like that over a game of chess. Rhys had never had terms forced upon him since the early days, when the King had forced him into a fair few, the days before he became too important to molest. Yet there was the bloody little bishop, thumb-screwing him hanging him drawing him quartering him, without so much as getting out of his seat or breaking off from the jest he was telling. Rhys looked at his guests.

And Rhys could not hear the other voices in his hall anymore, not Gerald's resonant tones at one end of the table or Chrétien's shrill ones at the other, he could not hear the clink of drinking horns, or the verses of *Armes Prydein* being sung, although he would normally have been singing them the most vigorously of anyone.

He heard only a dull crackling roar, like a desert wind. He recognised it as a desert wind although he had been no further south in his life than Southampton. He was struggling through a crackling desert wind and somewhere ahead, he could not see it yet but he knew it must be there, the water clock the King had once showed him was waiting, lying there by itself in the desert in its baffling beautiful intricacy.

Roar, crackle. Crackle, roar.

Rhys looked at the doorway of his hall. It was open. The cold hit him in the face. He saw a beast twice as big as a Powys steed, covered with fur thicker than a sheep from Deheubarth's finest flock and with two humps on its back like the dreaded duel peaks of Gwynedd when glimpsed from afar. A Jew led the beast, and on top was a fat man clad in robes that would render a king's lustreless. The Jew announced that the fat man with the gaudy robes had written the most beautiful words ever written and had spent eight months travelling to be here, here in Rhys' hall.

"Stable the beast!" Rhys cried. "Shut the doors!" To the Jew and the gaudily robed fat man, he smiled. "Come."

Waves came and you rode them or sank.

The Sultan's Man

(DECEMBER, 1176)

ON THE WAY IN to Nishapur from the southeast was a shady place at the roadside where young people would bathe in the thermal springs and old people would recline under the olive trees looking at the young people. The trade routes from Oxiana and the Gulf of Persia converged nearby as did the main road from Herat, and it was a lively spot. It was pleasant to sit under the trees out of the sun away from the dusty highway, and watch the young people, and talk. Hamid would invariably pause there when returning home from his ambles about the Empire. There was a fruit seller who sold watermelons and he always saved one of his biggest and juiciest for Hamid, so the fruit seller had told Hamid anyhow, although Hamid was not to know if he gave out bigger and juicier watermelons to others whilst he was elsewhere. Anyway, Hamid would sit there guzzling on his watermelon, truly believing his was the biggest and juiciest, and would count out the profits from his latest scent-selling trip. Yes, yes, it was a place for reflection on pasts and for contemplation on futures. The place perhaps served a similar purpose for other beasts too. Dogs and feral cats lolled close by in the scrub positioning themselves for the chance to pounce on scraps and birds, red-bellied frigatebirds and golden-billed pelicans and parakeets and lovebirds, chattered in the trees. They were all beasts together, taking refuge from the heat. In time Hamid became quite a regular there, just like Samir the rug seller and Zand the turquoise trader. He looked forward to the transitory companionability of the olive groves by the hot springs. Here they were, old and aging men watching the young ones splashing in the water. '*How fares the turquoise business, Zand?*' '*Well enough Hamid, and what scent is your best seller this year?*' '*Might we barter together Samir, one of those fine rugs you sit upon in exchange for a bottle of this delicious fragrance?*' And there they were, gone again, off on their respective journeys, the best of friends, but not to meet each other again for months or years. There was no responsibility in that, Hamid thought happily. Which left one free for the unfettered pursuit of cognition.

The summer before last, Hamid recalled, the locusts had been particularly pestilent. Sharing the hot springs with mangy dogs or cats was one thing, but locusts were quite another! He had been on his way home from the northern mountains where, despite his best efforts, the people had seen little point in smelling beautiful. Proceeds had been scanter than on other trips and for inexplicable reasons the watermelon vendor was absent. He was not in his most benign frame of mind. And on top of this, the locusts! There were hundreds. Hamid caught one of those that crashed against him in his cupped hands, pulling the legs off one by one and the head last so that it suffered as much as was possible. Discarding the corpse, he began the process again. And again. Again again.

"A perfumer and a poet. Two of the nobler professions. And, so I had formerly thought, two of the gentler ones."

"I love the birds. My love does not extend to insects," Hamid glanced up from the task in hand. A man with an abnormally large head and a correspondingly underdeveloped body was leaning against the tree adjacent to Hamid's. The man's appearance was abhorrent enough that a lot of people would have quailed in disgust at it, but Hamid did not do this. Acceptance of others was an essential step on the way to improving one's soul and he smiled mildly back at the man as if he had been anyone else. This, he later reflected, might have been what swayed the man's decision.

"The Sultan has taken Herat for his capital," the man said. "I imagine you knew this?"

"I knew that."

"He is looking for men."

"Men for his court?"

"Perhaps. But for other kinds of men too."

That familiar fluttering behind the eyes. Hamid's old worst friend the tick was back. It returned unfailingly whenever he became unnerved. What other kinds of men were there that the Sultan could want? Those he wanted to feed to his lions?

"I already have my trades."

"And you should maintain them. None of the Sultan's men are officially the Sultan's men."

"It is, er, kind of you to consider me, really it is," Hamid rose hastily, sensing now would be a ripe time to rid himself of this aberration and carry on home.

"The consideration has already taken place, Farid Un-Din Attar. It began some time ago. Various factors were considered and you were chosen."

"What?" Hamid was flustered. He spilt his water skin in the dirt. His tick ate up his face.

"You are the Sultan's man now," the bighead with the puny body said flatly. "Try and look pleased. Plenty would kill for this honour."

"Why?" Hamid shrugged helplessly. "Because I killed a locust?"

"You did not kill a locust. You killed many locusts. And you made them suffer. And all that time the smile did not once leave your face."

The bighead nodded, or rather he inclined his hideous huge head once. Doing even this was a lot of effort for him.

"The wretched pate! In hot weather like this it is worse. Physicians tell me it does not necessarily follow that my brain is any bigger, regrettably. Nevertheless I have used the brain Allah did give me as well as I might, and for as noble a purpose as I could hope to on this Earth, which is to serve the Supreme Ruler of the World. You should feel proud to be doing the same."

Supreme Ruler of the World. Is that what the Sultan was calling himself now?

"The Sultan will send for you. You will know when. For what it is worth I should add that we are both great admirers of your work. What you say about those birds! It is as if you put a piece of paradise upon a parchment."

But such a mighty man as the Sultan could surely not be moved by the ramblings of a perfumer from the provinces! Little by little in this life, Hamid argued in his treatise on the betterment of the human soul, one could get increasingly close to Allah. Not so near as His hall, unless it was an unprecedentedly large one, but perhaps in His realm, perhaps setting a tentative foot within His borders. Bit by bit. The Supreme Ruler of the World! Hamid had to admit that to have such an admirer seemed like a very agreeable thing.

Hamid smiled.

The Jew did not smile.

The Jew never had, not since Hamid picked the man up in Constantinople.

Through their common Latin, the Jew had taught Hamid a reasonable amount of French and English in the many months since then.

But the Jew had never smiled once.

Hamid had seen a child die in Baghdad. She had simply fallen down dead in the street. On the vast plains of the Byzantine Empire a wild band of horsemen had very near trampled him and the Jew to death.

He had not expected the Jew to smile at these moments, but at least a token upturning of the lips every so often when they were taking dinner together! The food was rarely as good as in Herat, but Hamid had still gone to pains to ensure what they were served throughout their journey had been decent. And if not for the food, if not for the joy of serving the Supreme Ruler of the World and through him Allah, then at least for the gold! The Jew was being well paid by Hamid. At least smile because of the gold! The Jew's mirthlessness had made a long journey much longer.

And now they were arrived. In a land daubed in disagreeable layers of cold white that even had his camel complaining. In a dingy hall so chilly his teeth chattered. He had to wonder if he was at the correct address, for could this really be a festival such as the known world had never witnessed? With such drably clad revellers and—he took sidelong looks at their plates—such unappetising food? Furthermore, he could not help but feel the people here gathered were staring at him. Yes, yes, staring at him, and sniffing him like dogs! Anyone would think extract of cloves had never graced their nostrils before. As he began his waddle past these lower tables towards the upper table and the man who had welcomed him, Hamid entertained hopes that this room might be an antechamber and that an unseen door at its end might open to reveal the real hall, decorated with marble or turquoise and furnished with a few exotic fruit platters. But no, they were shifting along the bench at the top to make room for him. This was all there was.

They gave Hamid wine to warm him up, and he refused, and mead, and he refused this, and ale, and he refused, and hot honey and herb water, which he accepted. They gave him beef hearts, and he refused, and cheese, and he refused, and mussels, which he seemed to love more than anybody else.

"We are honoured you have come such a distance to attend this festival," Rhys said to Hamid. Hamid beamed radiantly. "You find us already begun," Rhys said. Hamid beamed and slurped a couple of mussels appreciatively. "I look forward to us being able to converse further after this evening's final performances," Rhys said. Hamid beamed radiantly. "Does he understand a word I am saying?" Rhys asked the Jew. The Jew frowned, although this was not so very drastic a change for his facial muscles from their normal way of being. "I believe so," the Jew said, "for we spent six months together on the road here and our only proper conversation each night was when I was teaching him the English and French tongues. I would consider it an affront to my tutoring methods were he not to understand any one word. My personal opinion is that once adapted to the cold he will be more receptive, although I can from my own experience confirm it is often challenging to ascertain the true mood of Farid Un-Din Attar, for he is forever wearing the same smile whether he is happy or angry or merely going about his daily business. Again, personally speaking, I find this deeply alarming."

"Merciful Heaven, my good man, what manner of beast was that you rode in on?" Gerald broke off from the list of the more palatable writings of Virgil he was relaying to Meilyr and Gwalchmai to turn to Hamid, who had squeezed in alongside him.

Hamid beamed radiantly.

From a fold of his cassock Gerald produced a portable inkpot and quill and a miniature book, which he proudly introduced to anyone who was listening as his book of notations. He waited.

"A Bactrian camel," said the Jew tiredly. It had been a long day.

"A *camel*," Gerald exclaimed, scribbling away. It was as if he had known this all along, and was just testing the Jew.

Hamid beamed radiantly, taking in everything he saw.

Quite predictably, when one has indulged in pleasure for several hours one feels more relaxed, loosened, uninhibited. One recounts a dirtier story than one would whilst sober; one belches more freely or demands a refill of one's drinking horn more vociferously, or grabs a serving wench's bottom or pulls her off outside for a frolic without preamble. And on a night like this Christmas night, the afore-mentioned consequences of indulgence are a little more exaggerated than in a standard merrymaking. Still, this is the first day of revelry here. There is no excess to it yet. One sees it has the potential to become like the legendary Roman or Viking debauches of old, but it is still early days. And because this is Wales, where there is a reverent respect for song in all forms and particularly for the vocal songs as performed by the bards, a modicum of sobriety is reserved by most for the performances still to be performed. At a standard merrymaking, true, the merrymakers would have let themselves go by now. At a standard merrymaking, there would only have been a few songs sung before things collapsed into bawdiness. But at a merrymaking like this, set to run all Christmastide and enter the pantheon of all-time debauches, at which songs will certainly be sung all day every day until the last songster alone remains standing, some discipline is required. And particularly now. Right now. The audience, it should be remembered, can determine everything during a performance. When they make sound this means that it can go very well for the performer or that it can go very badly. When they make no sound, of course, the same is true: it can go very well or it can go very badly. Oh, the subtleties of sound. But when an audience, like right now, drops from din to hush all of a sudden, this means anticipation. The Welsh and the Normans here understand this. The Irishmen understand this. The Norsemen understand this. There are those from Castile and Sicily present and they understand this too. And the newly-arrived fat man with the gaudy robes from Persia, he understands this, even if his knowledge of the cumbersome tongues these infidels in western Christendom speak is not absolute.

Anticipation is universally understood.

Chrétien read the audience and bounded onto the stage.

Next up, as everyone already knew, was the first of the starred entrants.

Mercy!

News about the rift between the Prince of Deheubarth and Cynddelw Bryddyd Mawr had even crossed the Channel to France. It was up there with the feud between Henry Plantagenet and Thomas à Becket in terms of fame. Rhys, like the King, did not normally allow any of his enemies to survive long enough for a rift to become too chasmic. That Cynddelw was still alive after so insulting the foremost Welsh ruler was interesting in itself. Most people thought it must be something to do with soul. Rhys wanted to embellish and embolden the soul of Wales, and to kill Cynddelw Bryddyd Mawr would be to kill that soul. But everyone assembled in that room was waiting tensely to see what the bard would have to say for himself, and how Rhys would react to what he said.

Mercy, mercy!

Chrétien uttered three words, because no more than three were necessary for this introduction.

"The Great One?"

The Great One Returns

(DECEMBER, 1176)

"WITH CHILD?"

"That is so, my roguish rascal. Say those words as many ways as you might and it will not alter the truth of them."

"How can you be so sure?"

"A woman knows. And a woman who heals for her trade knows it twofold."

Rough and unmannerly Avery had known Dog to be in their week-long acquaintance, but to resort to quite such a stream of muttered expletives as he now proceeded to do was excessive even for him.

"But it was a matter of mere days!" Dog said.

Avery grasped what Dog was getting at, but the Healer stared blankly at him.

"Since we were… since the night we spent together in the barton," he finished in a whisper.

The Healer's confusion vanished. With a blast of laughter she slapped her immense thighs once, twice, many times, and clutched Avery's shoulder for support.

"Bless you, my big-gut! You think the child is yours! Oh my!"

Her indelicate cackles hit the room just as the room was starting to quieten in anticipation of the next performance.

"Oh my! Oh my!" It was a full deep burst of a sound, like jolting out of a peaceful dream to churchbells being struck an inch from your eardrum. The entrance of the hazelnut-brown man with the eye-catching robes and the splendid scent of spices might have captivated the room's attention, but the Healer could not help but turn heads with her largeness and loudness.

"The child is not *yours*, my dastard!"

Like a boar on the run come to a large forest clearing, Dog did not know where to go to hide.

"You bewitched the churl, witch!"

"What spell did you place upon that dog-ugly chub to make him fair-looking enough to frolic with?"

"Get back to your backstreets, giantess, we don't want your filth in this hall!"

At the lower end of a lower banquet table, one has to be prepared for these low sorts of comments.

The haranguing was stemmed somewhat by Dog levelling venomous looks at the chief hecklers, but the musician was lacking his normal fire for retaliation.

"If not mine, then whose?" he asked hoarsely.

The Healer stopped laughing.

"Never you fret about *that*, my brawny ox."

"Madog, Madog!" Avery said teasingly, although he too wondered why the Healer was being so unforthcoming about unmasking whoever it was that had got her with child. "You are not a father. Your harp is still the only thing you need fret about!"

"I wouldn't have minded," Dog said. It was not a statement or a reply or a sharp retort. It was more utterance really. An utterance so uncharacteristically subdued it got lost amongst the many other sounds of the hall.

So flowed the conversation at the lower end of the lower banquet tables.

"Oui!" Niall Ó Maolconaire confided suggestively to Azelais the beautiful trobairitz the only French in his vocabulary. "Everyone in Connemara knows the word, so they do. We say it whenever we are about to slide down waterfalls, lady, or jump off cliffs or the like. Wheeeee!" "In fact I loathe Ovid and everything he represents," opined Luciano, a song-singer from the Kingdom of Sicily, to Navarro the wandering cantor of Castile. "Raids?" exclaimed Olaf of Bergen to a couple of other Norsemen, and then, misty-eyed with fond remembrance: "Not since I was a boy."

So the flows of conversations at the lower end of the lower banquet tables became trickles then drips then next to nothing at all as the hall grew in anticipation, quieter and more quietly yet anticipating the performance that would come next.

And perhaps it had been planned in this way, masterminded by the exceptional planning of the man from Champagne, Chrétien the most celebrated courtier of modern times, Chrétien who knew the best halls and courts in Christendom intimately, and the undercurrents circulating therein.

But it so happened that this *next* performance should come at the very end of Christmas Day, and that consequently the conjecture surrounding this *next* performer and his controversial doings should have had the entire evening to mount up to the greatest extent possible. To become as fraught as could be.

One voice carried on a little beyond the other babblings and burblings. "The way *I* heard the story," murmured Meurig Full-Voice, who was so-called because of a disorder of the larynx that prevented him speaking in anything more than a murmur, and thus had to load his tone with extraordinary inflection to appear interesting, "it was not *one* thing the Great One did to Lord Rhys!

It was many! Two times Lord Rhys invited the Great One to his court. Two times the Great One declined, giving extremely tame excuses, only to have been sighted at some wine house or other on the nights of both invitations. One slap about the chops, two slaps about the chops. Around the same time the Great One made some scandalous remarks about the Strata Florida monks, too: quite shocking by all accounts and when Lord Rhys had only recently taken over patronage of the abbey. Three slaps about the chops. Then there were the spate of verses the Great One wrote whilst acting as *pencerrd* to Prince Madog of Powys and Prince Owain of Gwynedd, which praised these two rulers at Lord Rhys' expense so it seemed, as if the Prince of Deheubarth was not and could never be of nearly the same eminence. Now I concede, we are bards, things get exaggerated so much from one telling of a story to another that a farmyard becomes a fortress and a peasant a prince, but whatever way you look at it, that is a minimum of four slaps, and you simply cannot slap a man like Rhys twice on each cheek and expect to wander off into the hills without there being repercussions!" He was a fairly interesting fellow, Meurig Full-Voice. But to be blunt, and in spite of his name which would suggest otherwise, his voice was just another voice in a room full of those who used their voices for their livelihoods and used them however they must, taking solid fact and amply embellishing and embellishing again: for want of a subtler term what Meurig Full-Voice was saying was tattle.

A stirring at the lower end of the lower banquet tables.

A craning of heads, not towards the dais for once but towards the opposite end of the hall where the draught was coldest and the ale pitcher was taking the longest time to circulate.

A scrabbling as several young men, students of bardism to judge from their gowns and fresh faces, hastened to get out of the way.

And so my children part before me, and they bare the path ahead;
just the path through the crowds before me: 'the Great One is come,'
they said; through crowds to the dais before me, the dais and Pilate
seated there; to Golgotha: for Pilate and his crowds to crucify me
there[1].

Cynddelw was in flow as usual.

"*True* greatness, dear child," he patted his youngest *cerrdorion* on the back in a grandfather-like fashion, "only comes when you relinquish your greatness. Remember what you witness this evening and on the evenings that follow in its wake, and learn by the many errors I myself have made. I acknowledge these errors, but when I walk up to that dais I will nevertheless use the crowd to my own advantage, because that crowd are not error-free. They all piss and shit and disappoint people too, and they are your clay, dear child, to mould as you choose. Grow up into bardism knowing how to hold a room! Observe how they on that dais expect me to prance to the stage at a finger click to perform for them, and how I do not. Observe how our fellow revellers on these lowly tables expect me to straightaway breach the subject of my rift with Lord Rhys, and how I will not. Toss the dog the bone it craves, and then the dog has no interest in you anymore!"

So saying the Great One lumbered down the aisle, two long tables of merrymakers either side of him and the dais ahead. Benches scraped back so that he might pass more easily. Cutlery clattered to plates as even the hungriest put aside, for the time being, matters of mere food.

The Great One was still a big man. His shoulders sagged more than they had, but they were still big enough that a bear's cloak made from the hide of a large northern bear was well filled by

---

1 No record of Cynddelw Bryddyd Mawr using these lines professionally exists. Song really did burst from him. He dashed off within moments lines others spent weeks polishing.

them. The bear's head flopped off his left shoulder; its tongue hung out. His walk as he approached the dais did look a little rheumatic, but he had been spending the night on the move or in hovels or houses of ill repute of late, and the winter in Wales had been vicious.

The Great One passed everyone in that hall as a traveller passes a stick or a stone or a stump at the wayside. The lower tables and the upper he treated the same way, and so he came to the stage. He played the audience's game against them, silently regarding them as they regarded him. Oh, how he held them! Had he twitched they would have felt the tickle.

"I would like to say some words," he bellowed. He did not mean to bellow; this was just how his voice naturally rode out of his throat and into a room. "Some thanks. Thank you, at the back of the hall but at the forefront of my mind now and for all time, to my dear children, my *cerrdorion* who…" he broke off and breathed deeply, evidently emotional, "…who have been the best pupils a tutor could wish to teach, and each of whom I am happy to announce is from this moment forth a fully-fledged *cerrdor cyweithas*… they are now bards! They have borne me… too long. Borne my moods, borne my love of large quantities of good wine, borne the fact that I could not bear to let them out into this world because of my fear of being left alone! I welcome them onto the stage of this noble profession. May they rise to the pinnacle of it as they deserve," his voice shook.

The dais and lower tables alike were dumbfounded. Every other performance that evening had been just that, a song sung, not some speech of dithering dedications! As for the *cerrdorion*, or the new bards as they should now correctly be called, they were experiencing an odd mix of elation and embarrassment. They had just got the dub from the Great One, but the Great One was up there muddying his prodigious reputation, making that dub more a burden than a blessing by his jabber.

"My dear, dear children! You are beautiful birds and you have flown from the nest. I may be up here but henceforth… it is I who look up to you," he raised both arms high above him and his head too, momentarily resembling a mage or a mad preacher. Then his arms dropped. His head drooped. "Thank you for your time," he said.

There was not a single clap, although there were one or two strangled laughs. The Great One was getting back down from the stage without performing a song of any sort! This was an outrage, an ignominy, an insult! Chrétien who knew the best courts in Christendom and had experience of all kinds of songsters singing at them glanced helplessly at Rhys and mouthed: *'what can we do?'* Three shambling paces back towards his seat at the lower end of the lower banquet tables paced the Great One, and the hall was agitated now. Everyone felt cheated somehow and soon enough, once the shock wore off, they would be venting their anger too. Three shambling paces. The Great One's head snapped up. He winked over at his newly-made bards. Then he loped back to the stage and *then*, in a mighty rumble:

> *Come you down the long way round –*
> *by mere and moor, to Cardigan,*
> *Traverse stark peaks, tramp forest floors –*
> *and come, at dark, to Cardigan,*
> *Trace the Teifi from source to mouth –*
> *where wends meet waves lies Cardigan,*
> *Pass the Preseli's to pasturelands –*
> *here at last is Cardigan.*

Here a light will be blazing brightly –
the castle, at Cardigan,
Their waters wondrous fish-replete –
their mead so sweet, at Cardigan,
Marvellous merriment is had –
within the walls of Cardigan,
The bards elsewhere cannot compare –
with those that sing at Cardigan[1].

"I thank you for your time," the Great One said again.

Nothing, nothing, nothing…

And then…

Uproarious applause.

The Great One's scheduled opponent for the bout withdrew immediately.

During the performance, several other things happened.

On the lower banquet tables, Niall Ó Maolconaire had asked Azelais the beautiful trobairitz if she might care to go for a walk in the castle gardens with him, and she had said yes. Meanwhile, Navarro the wandering cantor of Castile had admitted to Luciano the song-singer from the Kingdom of Sicily that Castile was not so very far from Toulouse. Navarro had travelled to Toulouse occasionally as part of various delegations, he said, and that whilst at that court he had seen that pallid pained-looking man in the scarlet cloak seated up there on the dais. Luciano held this was a reasonable coincidence, but not an exceptional one given that the troubadour Bernart de Ventadorn had been attached to the court of Toulouse for many years, ever since he fell out of favour with the Plantagenets in fact. Navarro granted this was true, yet that the exceptional thing in all this was not *that* he saw the troubadour

---

1   No record of Cynddelw Brydydd Mawr using these lines professionally exists.

but *where* he saw the troubadour. Navarro elaborated with a smile that because he was cursed with a sense of direction as poor as a woman's, he had become lost in the court's labyrinth of back corridors, and that he had wandered for some time, unwittingly getting further from the feasting hall. Such corridors distort noise, said Navarro, so when he had first heard the weeping it sounded nigh on demonic, and he had proceeded with trepidation. And there, deep in an inner room in the bowels of the court, Navarro had peered through a grill to behold this same Bernart de Ventadorn, similarly dressed to how he was tonight, alone and kneeling on the flagstones and weeping and repeating one word over and over: *unleash, unleash.* When Navarro had related this tale to others at Toulouse, and asked why this man should be weeping in a dark room rather than joining in the feasting, he had been told Bernart de Ventadorn never left his quarters, and had not in many months. The man took meals in his room, said Navarro, and, a further odd thing, left the tray outside his door for collection with the food and drink often barely touched but with one item always without fail missing: the knife. It was the most detested duty in the kitchens, relayed Navarro, to deliver meals even to the threshold, and that rather than ask the troubadour to return the missing knives, the servants had preferred to purchase new ones. Furthermore, Navarro leant close to whisper in Luciano's ear, whilst other eyes were glued on the performance of the Great One just now, he had seen this same man purloin a knife again, and stash it into the folds of his ghastly scarlet cloak.

And up on the dais, Maelgwyn had glared at his younger brother sitting at the right hand of their father, and vowed both would be sorry for how they had humiliated him. Maybe not tonight or tomorrow night but they would be sorry. Gruffyd had found Maelgwyn earlier with Cadwaladr, Owain, Maredudd and the two tavern wenches, and he had wanted a turn with them too, Maelgwyn had seen that. But Gruffyd was too bloody good and not in a saintly way; good because he was afraid of being bad. Some of the *teulu* had arrived just after and Gruffyd had been able to blame Maelgwyn and play the innocent, but Maelgwyn knew that really he was the son Gruffyd did not dare to be. The one who had no qualms about being bad. A cuffing, brooded Maelgwyn, he might have borne as a punishment for his misdemeanours. But it had been him alone cuffed, and the clout had knocked him into a door and gashed his face eye to chin. He would have a scar there now. And for Maelgwyn to be impelled to sit at the merrymaking with his wound still smarting as Gruffyd took his rightful place by their father, this could by no means be borne. There would be consequences. The only advantage to the current seating arrangements for Maelgwyn was that he was next to Cadwaladr, the oldest, nastiest product of his father's innumerable indiscretions, and not at all averse to doing bad things himself. Cadwaladr was not immensely inventive. But Maelgwyn could always tell him what to do.

Maelgwyn cared about Maelgwyn. But he barely registered in the consciousness of anyone else in the hall that Christmas night. He had inherited his mother's dark looks, but where she handled her misery stoically, every drop of his showed in the twists of his face. He was what a roomful of people were only too glad to turn away from; his father and brother what they happily turned towards. Fair, fine men. Maelgwyn could have spent his whole life trying, but he would never have been like his father, whose jests people laughed at quite genuinely and whose company people enjoyed. Maelgwyn glared at those fair, fine men. He glared at his father magnanimously thanking all for a memorable first day of revelry and expressing his hope that they would return next day for more. He glared at Gruffyd the portrait-perfect son. Maelgwyn could never have been like them. He was not at all sorry to have invested his energies in going the other way.

And so the merrymakers dispersed, to sleep in their quarters or vomit out the good food or piss out the good drink or carry on sleeping or eating or drinking in other places.

And those that went quickly would forever afterwards rue having done so, and get vexed when those that had lingered that little bit longer would recount in later years what happened next.

Hamid waved his hand at the Jew.

"Farid Un-Din Attar," the Jew ventured. "Would like to take the opportunity of bestowing some gifts upon the greatest prince in Wales."

"Gifts!" exclaimed Rhys. "I love nothing more than a gift! Indeed," he added, "my advisors tell me a significant proportion of the economy of Deheubarth is supported by 'gifts' so it would be in the realm's interests as well as mine for me to accept!"

Anarawd sat taut with his hand on his weapon, suspecting a trick. Everyone else's eyes widened as the Jew produced from a pouch a blue-green stone of rare beauty, cut in a perfect sphere.

"Turquoise," said the Jew, "from Farid Un-Din Attar's homeland. "This jewel represents the distance and differences between his land and this, and the journey he has undergone to be here."

The Jew rummaged in his pouch and produced then a vial, and everyone gasped because the aroma of the liquid inside was so lavishly luxuriously intense that it had already diffused through the closed lid to delight their nostrils.

"Frankincense and infusion of fig leaf," said the Jew, "one of the countless fragrances Farid Un-Din Attar has created. This vial represents his life's work and life essence. It is a memento of him."

"I am deeply moved," said Rhys.

Hamid beamed radiantly.

"For the third and final gift, Farid Un-Din Attar wishes to bestow upon you, we must go outside."

"Then let us go!" cried Rhys. "I do love gifts!" And in a less evident tone, he said to Gruffyd: "can he wish to give us a star?"

The Jew bid them all stand around the edge of the bailey, the very edge he specified sternly, and those from the dais and many of those curious souls on the lower banquet tables fanned along the perimeter wall, blowing on their hands and stamping their feet with dragon-smoking breath, watching waiting. The Jew walked into the central space and placed in the snow a wooden box. The box was no bigger than one that women might put keepsakes in, and quite plain in appearance. The box had a rope attached to it. The Jew put the lamp he was carrying down on the snow too, laid the flame against the rope until that was alight then ran faster than it had been hitherto presumed he was capable of moving towards where the others were. The snow was thick though. The Jew did not get as far as he would have wished.

The firebolt shot up out of the snow, spraying fragments of wood everywhere, hot as a furnace, bright as lightening, only it was inverted lightening, lightening that had come from the cold, wet, otherwise unremarkable ground of the bailey. The firebolt scorched some of those spectating even at thirty paces. The screaming began. Everyone thought the world had come to an end. The Jew screamed loudest of all, sprawled on the ground where the blast had thrown him.

"My arm!" he shrieked, and no one knew where his arm was but it was not on his bleeding stump of a shoulder, and everyone was too frightened to go over and help him, they were in shock, it was as if they had been cast into Hell, the firebolt had battered their eardrums and they could not hear sounds properly at all, only a shrill incessant ringing. And so the Jew's blood and shrieks drained untended into the snow.

Blood. Screams. Rhys heeded these only distantly. The incessant ringing had for him become a roar, like a crackling wind in the desert, like that which he had heard just prior to Hamid entering his hall on the camel. A hot wind crackling. Sand flying about. He staggered on through. And now he could see it in the dunes ahead. The water clock! *It may be the most intricate thing any of us ever see*, Rhys heard the King saying in a voice that was nothing like the King's, but slowed-down, like a half-wit's. For all the sand flying about in that desert, not one grain fell on the water clock. It looked beautiful, standing there on the dunes, beautifully intricate. Rhys stretched out a hand towards it and the swirling sand and crackling wind and the water clock too vanished.

There was Hamid, standing at his side in his rainbow-hued robes.

Most of the rest of the crowd were still in shock, gaping at the blackened, blood-stained space in the snow from where the firebolt had been unleashed. Some were comforting others. There were shards of wood to unpick from flesh. There were burns to salve. Some mumbled prayers but God was nowhere. The Jew was still screaming, although he had people helping him now.

Not Hamid though.

Hamid was at Rhys' side, beaming.

"This was to have been your gift to me?" Rhys asked Hamid. "This… this devastation?"

Hamid beamed radiantly.

Interlude

(DECEMBER, 1176)

THE SEA. The wild, winter-roughened sea.

The river snaking towards the sea and widening, at Cardigan, into silt banks and seagulls wheeling and razor clam shells and lugworm castings and coracles rising falling on the tide.

The farmland the river wraps around, frog-green normally but snow-white now, the lush lowlands of Deheubarth where snow never normally settles, snowed well under.

The snow, come down further and thicker than it ever has during the great peace of Rhys' reign.

The little town of Cardigan, little at least by the standards of England or France but big by the standards of Wales, a thriving capital within Wales, peeping out of the arrow slits and guard towers of its outer walls at this newly, thickly whitened corner of the world.

The river flows on into the rest of the world. But the rest of the world will be immaterial for a good few days yet. None but fools would put a boat into a sea so wild. None but fools would embark on a journey for or from Cardigan overland either, not in snow so thick and with more on the way. No one else is coming in now. No one else is going out.

Cardigan does look very nice, there in the snow.

It is a decently sized town: by the standards of Wales. Its castle is not small. It has seven towers, it is not in the small category of castle: Rhys has ensured that. There is sufficient food and drink for one thousand people for one month: Rhys has ensured that. Banquet tables laden with food and drink, and a fire burning, and the hall prettily bedecked in the plants of Welsh winter, holly and ivy, and entertainment all day every day.

Cardigan looks very inviting indeed this Christmastide.

And the travellers who have made it here for the most part want to be here, and for the duration: they want to win the contest of vocal song or the contest of instrumental song or they want to see who does win, or they have another unapparent motive. Those whose hospitality has been imposed upon are for the most part content to suffer the town's inundation of visitors, too. They might not enjoy having songsters sleeping on their floors or shitting in their river or carousing after hours in their streets but they see the economic benefit to themselves and the town.

But although no one individual or group can be blamed, people being together in these quantities in this proximity, in a town only really designed to function with a tenth of its current population, it puts an unavoidably barbed edge on things.

It is hard to find a place to be by oneself, to practise a song or take a quiet drink or woo who one wishes to woo. Each of these activities get constantly interrupted by other individuals or groups that soon enough grate at one's patience because—especially with this thick snow—there is barely anywhere to go to escape them.

So returning to the hall for another day's revelry and then another is not quite what it was the day before.

The mead that put a fire in one's belly before is more insipid today. The performances that were a startling new thing yesterday today have to be that much more striking in order to rouse the crowd. And as Chrétien the Frenchmen makes marks against some names on his slates and erases others and compiles his list of which performers from these early heats would come back to compete a second time against each other, the questions on the lips of those who have performed are: *am I through?* And if not: *why am I not through when he or she is?*

These things gnaw in one's brain, and one looks at one's fellow merrymakers differently. Petty dislikes develop: at she who belched with uncommon loudness; at he who barged into me just now; against they who do not whatsoever deserve to be in the next round at my expense.

And something else. Songsters are as highly strung as fine-tuned harp strings, they are as fragile as coral, they are about as restrained as earthquakes. With their voices and instruments they sing of dramatic things; of love, of destruction, of death. So it is perhaps inevitable that they should eventually start to embody the subjects of their songs and to become dramatic.

To be sure, all this sharpens the edge on things.

Cardigan looks very pretty and the festival is very fine, so some of the pre-eminent poets here gathered are recording in their songs. Even the Romans, they record, hosted nothing better than this. But their focus is on the revelry and on this festival's wondrous performers and performances. They say nothing of what happens in-between the acts.

In-between acts, the edge on things is at its sharpest.

"I feel as if only *now* have I begun to live!" exclaimed the young Marcher lord whose name no one could remember. He tossed his stick in a moment after Owain Cyfeiliog tossed his but dashing to the other side of the bridge cried in delight. "You see?" he pointed at the twig marginally further ahead in the current. "It is a sign!"

"But that is my stick in front," said Owain Cyfeiliog. "If it is a sign, the sign favours me."

"No, mine had the knob! Mine is the winning stick!"

"As you wish. You are today's winner."

Owain Cyfeiliog folded his arms and looked pensively over the parapet into the grey-black water. He imagined what it would be like to be a witch looking into a cauldron and knowing that as she did so she possessed the power to make happen whatever she wished anywhere in the world.

"It has been such a marvellous few days!" the young Marcher lord said gaily. "Such revelry! It is quite something, is it not?"

"It is certainly something."

"Of course I had known revelry before," the Marcher lord clarified. "I do not wish you to think me 'green' in this respect. I simply meant…"

"I do not think you green in this respect," said Owain Cyfeilog.

"I must tell you…" began the Marcher lord in a tremulously excitable tone.

"Go on."

"Angharad, Lord Rhys' oldest unbetrothed daughter, which is not at all to imply she is a bad match…"

"I know who she is."

"I have asked Angharad for her hand in holy matrimony!"

Owain Cyfeiliog regarded the young Marcher lord enquiringly.

"And she said that she would think about it! That she wished to celebrate her twelfth birthday in January as a girl but that afterwards she would consider my proposition!"

"And the Lord Rhys approves this match, eh?"

"Whole-heartedly! He can hardly wait for the union of our families!"

"I thought as much," said Owain Cyfeiliog, dispiritedly thinking of Deheubarth stretching all the way south through the young Marcher lord's lands to the doorstep of St David's.

"And should all go according to plan next autumn when the salmon spawn Lord Rhys and I will travel upriver to his favourite fishing place—it has the fattest salmon of any river in Wales, you know—and there we will take the engagement forward to its next natural stage: nuptials! Angharad will be almost thirteen by then. The time will be ripe!"

"I am pleased for you."

"And I am pleased! I am decidedly pleased!"

"But you are wrong about the fishing place," said Owain Cyfeiliog. "Rivers in Powys have fatter fish. Up there we use our mouths to eat the things, not to boast about their size."

"Have either of you seen my father?"

Owain Cyfeiliog and the young Marcher lord turned towards this rather abrupt shout. Meilyr ap Gwalchmai marched through the snow towards them.

"There goes one who looks lost when not clutching someone else's coattails," murmured Owain Cyfeiliog. And, to Meilyr: "But a moment ago. In Rhys' bedchamber, rigorously engaged in kissing the Royal behind."

The young Marcher lord flushed almost purple. Meilyr flashed irritation and disdain in equal measure.

"What right have you to mock Gwalchmai ap Meilyr in this way?"

"The same right as you have to come storming over here shouting at us as though we were your servants," Owain Cyfeiliog observed mildly, looking back out over the river and giving further consideration to the spells he would cast on people were he a witch. "Powys Cyfeiliog may not be much, but it is still the third-largest realm in Wales and as far as I am aware I am the ruler of it."

"You mean in *Pura Wallia*," the young Marcher lord helpfully cut in. "I believe there are several of us Normans with larger holdings these days! Particularly since Powys got chopped into little…"

"Quite. The third-largest in *Pura Wallia*."

"I ask your pardon," said Meilyr, stiffly enough that it did not sound like an apology. "What title then would you care to be addressed by?"

"I do not care a lamb's bleat about titles," said Owain Cyfeiliog softly. "It is your tone I dislike."

"And again: I ask your pardon. And I pardon you for speaking of my father as you did."

"Your father is a bottom-kissing fraud, and everyone with a drop of wit in that hall knows it."

"You may be a prince in Powys! But my father…"

"Is *pencerrd* to Prince Rhodri of Gwynedd, I know."

"And I am…"

"The *pencerrd* in waiting. I know."

"And I have rights! I have the right to ask you to explain your comments about my father!" Meilyr spluttered.

"Come. Do not act as if you are surprised! From what Cynddelw told me, it was only when he decided to go off teaching bardism again that Prince Rhodri made your father *pencerrd*! In the absence of anyone better!"

"Foul and insubstantial allegations!" Meilyr quaked with rage.

"You know the Great One?" the Marcher lord chimed in, impressed.

"We composed ballads together once upon a time. Now, why be so offended?" Owain Cyfeiliog said appeasingly to Meilyr. "Everyone knows you feed your father most of his choicest lines! And on the dais these last nights we have seen how abominably he treats you! This in itself is of no consequence to me; most bards have a bad side. But when a bard with a bad heart is then bad on stage and wins the judges' vote despite the hall applauding the opponent and does so two bouts in succession, it is small wonder questions about the relationship between Lord Rhys of *Deheubarth* and Gwalchmai ap Meilyr of *Gwynedd* arise, eh?"

"Questions?"

"It is political," sighed Owain Cyfeiliog. "I know it in my heart. My heart always tells me what is right. I get this… sinking sensation, here," he slapped his chest. "That is how I know. I had it the morning before Thomas à Becket was murdered and I have it now: a sinking. Lord Rhys has done a deal. I am disappointed in him, what with his professing to care about culture. Culture? Bilge water! He has done a stink of a deal. Cordiality with Gwynedd is imperative to Deheubarth, so he has promised Gwynedd the prize in the song contest."

"My father has his pride. He would never enter into such a base pact even if Rhys ap Gruffyd demanded it!"

Owain Cyfeiliog looked witheringly at Meilyr ap Gwalchmai. Then he looked out across the seal-grey water. As he did so, a coracle fisherman struggling to haul in his net tugged too hard and tumbled into the river. He squealed and thrashed around awhile. His net with all the fish in it landed in the vessel, and both coracle and catch drifted slowly off with the current.

And Meilyr suddenly recalled the words he had overheard his father muttering, when on the long way here from Gwynedd they had paused to pray. His father prayed in a just audible mutter. Usually it was God this or God that. Conventional orison. But a few times irregularities disrupted the flow. One phrase was particularly repeated. *Gwalchmai deserves to win.*

Meilyr stared dumbly at the fisherman with Owain Cyfeiliog

and the young Marcher lord. He was having thoughts about his father he had never had before.

The fisherman's instinct had been to swim after his coracle, not strike for shore. Energy spent, the man was floundering now. The temperature in that river could not be much for there were flecks of ice in it. The fisherman's squeals sounded strangely like a gull's.

"I hope the fellow receives assistance," said Owain Cyfeiliog.

"What if everyone thought that?" asked the young Marcher lord. "Then… then no one would actually help him at all, would they?"

"My father crushes me!" said Meilyr in sudden realisation. "If he is not here I know where he must be. He is on one of his walks. Look!" he thrust a sheet of parchment before Owain Cyfeiliog and the young Marcher lord, who looked. "I was only searching for him to tell him about my ideas for his next performance tomorrow night! Do you know why he takes his walks?" The young Marcher lord was nearest to Meilyr and Meilyr clutched at his shoulder, asking louder: "do you know why?"

The young Marcher lord shook his head awkwardly.

"Because people disgust him. We all disgust him and no one disgusts him more than me. I do try," Meilyr assured the young Marcher lord with tears welling. "I spend hours devising my best lines for him to use in his songs until my temples ache and I do not ask for one syllable of thanks. I just ask for his love!" Now Meilyr crumpled and embraced the young Marcher lord fully, snivelling big snotty blubbers. "I love him! Yet I disgust him!

"I know what it takes to write a song," said Owain Cyfeiliog slowly. "They called me the Poet-Prince of Powys once because of that: because I wrote songs. And I perceive the guests at this festival have invested much effort in composing songs to perform here. Were they to find out about your father's violation of the rules of song-singing, they would be appalled. Revolted. Reviled.

Repelled. And rightly. There would be no telling what they might do," he shook Meilyr until the bard's blubbering subsided. "We must put this right. You must convince your father to withdraw from the contest."

Meilyr embarked on a fresh fit of blubbing.

"I disgust him! He does not even speak to me! How can I convince him? I disgust him!"

Owain Cyfeiliog shook him again.

"Heed me. You must try. My heart tells me this is the right course of action. And my heart has never been wrong. I am certain you have the potential to be both a bard and a *pencerrd* many times more honourable than your father. Time to stand up on your own, Meilyr ap Gwalchmai, and make your father stand down! Time to take to the stage yourself!"

"And if I should fail?" Meilyr asked through his snivels. "If my father refuses to stand down?"

"In the first instance mediation is always best," said Owain Cyfeiliog. "Let us not go out a-hunting until we have mounted our horses."

Owain Cyfeiliog and the young Marcher lord and Meilyr ap Gwalchmai looked out to see what had happened to the fisherman. He had drowned.

On flowed the river, a slick of darkness without answers. People had died in it and danced in it and fought in it and frolicked in it and set sail from it and come back to it again. And afterwards it always looked the same.

Bernart knew darkness. He derived satisfaction from the fact he must know darkness better than anyone. In Toulouse he had gone months at a time without daylight. There had been candles in his interior room, but a lot of the time he preferred the flames extinguished.

Windowless. Flameless. Lightless.

There was a state of half-sleep when one was emerging from a dream and still imbued in the trappings of it, but conscious already of the outlines of the real world. Bernart had grown to love this state. One's desires, warped by the delusions of slumber into preposterous and fantastical things, wrong things, lived on into actual life and laid beside you in the bed. Light made them fade. Toulouse might have been a dying court but Bernart had created a crypt for himself within it. At some point during the day, if 'day' were the word, a cold panic would seize him, whenever a servant brought food to the door or when he heard footfalls on a nearby corridor. They are coming for me, he would think, they are going to ask for the knives back or say that enough is enough, my staying here like this could not be supported anymore. But no one had come. He had told them all he was working on a masterwork and perhaps they believed that was what he had been doing. Really though, he was blocked. He was checked he was constipated he was curbed. Blast it all, the words and lines and cansos and songs that once poured onto the page and into the hall for him were trapped behind a dam. And until he could find a way forth he did not want to show his face. He could not bear to brave the light.

Darkness. It was not always black. It was the pale faraway day chinking in, it was the glow of the dimming wick, things could be brown, brown like soil after rain or like leaves as they decay, and underneath these things it could be murkier. But supreme blackness only came when he screwed his eyes tight shut and buried his face in the mattress and covered his head with a pillow.

And he had produced something: in his windowless lightless room.

Not what he had anticipated though. Definitely not what the courtiers of Toulouse had anticipated.

What he produced was a dirge on darkness. Vile, penetrating lines that praised shadow and probed it to its deepest crevice. He was not sure where they had come from, but out they had come. The expressions of those courtiers were only half-alive anyway but they had passed several steps closer to death as Bernart performed his work. '*It is to be the first of two parts,*' he had informed the silenced room. '*The second I will perform upon my return from Wales.*' Ramon, his patron, had asked hopefully: '*And will the second part be… on light, perhaps?*' Bernart had done his best not to seem contemptuous. '*Light? No, the second part will not be on light.*'

Bernart picked his way through the snow on the road out of town, which had been shovelled clear as far as the northern gate but was still vexingly slippery in court shoes that tapered and twirled at the ends. Someone threw swill through a doorway and laughed when it splashed him. Someone else hissed "maggot" but when he turned around no one was there. At the gate there was a spattering of different tracks as though people had come this far then decided they could not continue, and beyond in the thicker snow only a few prints of those who had ventured further. He knew whose those were.

"Where are you going, bard?" the guard wanted to know.

"The mill."

"That mill hasn't worked in years."

"I know."

"Why are you going there then?"

Bernart had not foreseen this setback.

"Listen to me. Do you like the sound of silver when it clinks together?"

"Depends how much silver, bard."

"Six pieces of it."

"I'd like the sound of twelve better."

"Yours upon my return, if you stop asking these blasted questions."

"You don't have the shoes for it, bard."

"I know."

Bernart tried treading in the steps of those few who had come this way before him, but they had walked with long strides and Bernart was a fairly small man. His feet were soon soaked but he knew the snow, together with the distance from town he was going, guaranteed privacy.

Bard. He was a bard. He looked like a bard and had in the past composed songs and this was enough for him to be known to this day as a bard. Well, he had come through those early bouts had he not? The professional songster must still be within him somewhere, for that part had done its duty when called and mechanically remixed *Can vei la lauzeta mover* and *Tan tai mo cor ple de joya* with tinkering that ensured not even the darling of the court of Champagne could tell they were old songs. And he had his place in the last sixteen.

His mind turned naturally to the bungled abduction in the woods. He thought he had planned that so well. But if all had gone to plan and Marie had been brought before him, he still did not know what he would have done. The Bernart of the half-dream state would have chained her up and licked her cheek to shoulder to belly to the sweetness beneath. But would the Bernart of the day-to-day have been capable of doing anything? He recalled the drovers and their hundreds of cows. How often did anyone pass along that lonely road, let alone drovers, let alone so many hundreds of cows, let alone white cows, let alone in that slither of time when the abduction was happening? What he was wondering was: were those cows a sign? Were they a sign the dark fantasies in his half-dreams about Marie were supposed to stay in the dark half-dream room and scuttle away when the light was turned on?

The old mill was in a dip below the road to the north. From there, one could not see much of it but an ivy-hung gable. When one descended and came around on the dank river path to the entrance, one wished one had not made the effort. It felt and smelt like something had died inside: some thing, or many things. The door was wedged ajar with an opening just big enough to squeeze through. Through Bernart squeezed.

The three men De Braose had given him use of were there, sitting on a heap of old grain sacks. Even sitting down, they were almost as tall as Bernart. One had an ear missing and a swollen eye that discharged pus. Each of the three looked like they could snap Bernart in two with thumb and forefinger.

"So what's it to be?" asked one.

"Do you want her dead?" asked the second.

"Or senseless?" asked the third. "Or just subdued a little?"

"We can arrange for any of the above," the first clarified. "She's spending a lot of time with a Saxon from York of late, who also happens to be doing rather well in the contest of song. In fact, should he prevail tomorrow night against Olaf of Bergen, and again against the fat foreigner with the rainbow-coloured robes who seems to save all his intelligible words for the stage, he would be due to meet you in the final four. You see what I'm saying?"

Bernart had not said a word since arriving. He felt nauseated. He kept noticing small details about the three men that were making him increasingly unwell. Not only the earlessness and eye pus. The way another scratched his groin like a creature burrowing in hay. The muscle and bone structure of he who was doing the talking, pulsing as if there were things under his skin waiting to hatch.

"What I'm *saying* is: we take them both out together," the man's mouth moved. "And all of a sudden you have a mighty easy route through to the final."

"It is too much…" Bernart murmured.

"Too much? Isn't this what you wanted? Isn't this what you went to great pains to arrange?"

The pus oozed. The scratching increased. The things under the skin would burst out any moment. Bernart remembered kissing Marguerite under a tree long ago: *I see you are a true poet, my lord.* The pus accumulated—why did the man not wipe it away?

"I want you to leave," Bernart whispered.

"What? It was you that summoned us all out here!"

"And now I want you all to go away again. You will subdue no one and you will knock no one senseless and you will kill no one. Go home."

"But De Braose…"

"My arrangement with De Braose is void," Bernart said softly. "Go home."

He drew his scarlet travelling cloak around him and squeezed out of the dank, dark mill into the light.

Marie rolled the ball of snow until it was hip high and too heavy to push further. The resting place was somehow appropriate: right by the riverbank. Avery staggered over with the head and it was a snow figure, crookedly looking out at the river.

"Come!" she urged. "You must!"

Avery abashedly produced the cassock he had worn at York. He had not wanted to wear it out in the secular world, but had not been prepared to discard it before, either. He draped the cassock on the snow figure, fastening it with the sash.

"Beware ye who dare to enter the fortress of Cardigan," said Marie. "For first ye must brave the fearsome snow-monk!"

"A fat white face and a foolish expression," laughed Avery. "Not a bit like any of the upstanding members of the Catholic church, of course!"

"Of course!" Marie smiled. "Look, it is snowing again."

"Someone told me it never normally snows here."

"Well. It is now. I love the feeling of the snow. In my hair especially."

"You will find it difficult to feel it on your hair through that wimple!"

"There is no one around… would you mind if I loosened it?"

The reply choked in his throat and she already had anyway. He had glimpsed a strand of her hair in the church. He had thought to himself: it is as if these tresses do not want to be contained. Loosened, they were not just honey-coloured but corn-yellow and barley-brown too in places. He was conscious of looking too long at them, and glanced away.

"I wore those clothes with pride, you know," he said after a while.

"And now you are ready to let go, Avery of York?" she moved a hand towards his shoulder. Then she snatched it back. "Hark, what is that?"

They listened. Someone was approaching, and with an inane hum as he did so.

"It is *Asperges*. A song sung at Mass during the sprinkling of the Holy water. Only a churchman would know it!"

Marie hurried to hide her hair under the wimple again but it was too late.

A churchman *was* coming around the bend in the path. Gerald. He carried a bundle of books with him and seemed pleased with himself.

Marie's attempt to cover her hair only made it look more like she had been doing something of which she was ashamed.

The humming ceased.

"What have we here?" Gerald said, lightly but darkly. Lord of our skies, he had seen it all now! The boy who had caused all those problems for Archbishop Roger up in York engaged in a flagrant act of fornication with a married lady! These artistic sorts might be allowed to live their lives to slacker moral standards than the rest of Mankind, but look at her with her hair all over the place like a harlot and her cloak askew, the insatiable youth must have already had his way with her, and in front of a blasphemous likeness of one of God's helpers! Even entertainers had to adhere to some of the rules the church had set down, and when violations were occurring multitudinously before him like this, Gerald knew he should be taking note of them for inclusion in his document on the state of the church in Wales. *'Most Reverend Gerald de Barri, known to his flock as Giraldus Cambrensis or Gerald of Wales depending on whether they can speak Latin or not,'* Gerald imagined all the cardinals asking him in unison at some point in the very near future. *'What do you suggest that we do?'* Gerald placed his books on a tree stump, felt for his portable inkpot and made a few choice scribblings in his book of notations. "Perhaps it is best if I start by explaining *my* purpose," he said between intermittent hums. "A little leg stretch before this evening's performances to go and book-swap with the St Dogmael's monks! They asked me, you know: what is it *like* to be a part of Lord Rhys' festivities? I replied to them that it was all very well, these verbal... *recitals* of songs, and actually quite absorbing, but that there would come a time, though most would mock me for saying so, when the things will become consigned to history and these," he stooped to pat his books like he was petting a much-loved pet, "will become the new form of repository for information of all kinds! They said to me that they could not really foresee books becoming popular outside of church, there was the matter of widespread illiteracy and ignorance amongst the common people for one thing, and I waggled my little finger at them like this," he waggled his little finger, "and made the incisive observation that the church has always throughout history led the way! Anyway they do not have a *bad* library, the St Dogmael's monks, my own volumes are on the whole superior—but I digress—what matters is that we all withdrew satisfied with our exchange of reading material! And what of you two?" Gerald observed them with a smirk tugging at his features. "I believe in the mad dash of merrymaking we have become aware of each other without having had the time for proper introductions. You do not speak Latin, of course, but…"

"*Sic*," Marie said. "*Una lingua numquam satis est.*"[1]

"*Satis,*"[2] Avery said.

"Re*mar*kable!" Gerald exclaimed. "In that case you can call me Giraldus!"

"Marie," Marie bowed politely.

"Married," Gerald said with extreme emphasis, "to a man with ample holdings in Buckinghamshire and Caerleon, I understand?"

Marie did not reply. She was not sure she could call what she had a marriage anymore. But she was starting to see why Avery had reservations about this man. He made something seem bad before it had become bad yet. And she had noted the surprise in Avery's face at Gerald needlessly bringing up her husband like that, and this pained her.

"And I believe you know me, my lord Bishop."

Gerald gave a tight-lipped smile at Avery's deference.[3]

"I made straight for York upon my return from Paris, my good

1 "Yes. One language is never enough."

2 "Sufficiently."

3 Gerald is at this point in our story only an archdeacon, and not Bishop of St David's although he would already have been more than happy to be so known. But there is many a slip 'twixt the cup and the lip. This adage applies as much to churchmen as to anyone else. Everyone has a fall from grace within them.

fellow. Archbishop Roger was most upset by your accusations. Mark my words: were you on English soil you would be on trial by now for what you said about His Grace. Do you know what he told me before my departure? *Bring him to me*, he urged. If you hear word of him on your travels upturn any rock you can to find whereabouts he has crawled. And low and behold, against all the odds..." he effected the action of upturning a rock. "Boo!"

"What I said was true!" whispered Avery hoarsely.

"My good fellow, we all of us have our own truth! And the higher up we stand, the greater that truth. Now when someone lowly like yourself—who the church had taken in out of kindness, it is not irrelevant to add—wheels around and fires off the accusations you did about someone that high up... well, without any proof it becomes a matter of your word against his. The only one who might have shed light on the incident... the other boy concerned, I forget his name..."

"Theo. His name was Theo."

"*Theo*," Gerald smiled. "Once *Theo* died after the blood loss, there really was no one else to support your far-fetched allegation, was there? But what to do with you now? Benevolent Lord, aside from accusing Henry Plantagenet of wrongdoing I do not for the life of me see how you could have picked a worse person to make claims against. Archbishop Roger has a reputation to protect! How do any of us know you will forget the foul story you dredged up? How can any of us trust that you will keep your mouth sealed shut?"

"Forget!" Avery trembled.

"If you cannot countenance the deviances that take place within the upper levels of the church, Venerable Giraldus," Marie said, "maybe you are not best placed to find fault with others outside of church walls. Oh yes," she added icily. "Avery has not kept his mouth *sealed shut*. He has told me what occurred in the cathedral that night."

Gerald stared at Marie, stunned. Did this harlot have no limits to her audacity?

"We are not long in each other's acquaintance, my good lady. But I counsel you to carefully consider what you say to me from this moment onward! At the very least, I am witness to the fact the two of you have created this vile likeness of a cleric in choir dress!" He went over to the snow figure and struck it. The head lolled idiotically. "It is blasphemy! Blasphemy carries a punishment."

"Desist," Marie said.

As Gerald dealt the blows to the snow-monk, she crossed to the tree stump where the churchman's books were piled.

"I do not like to," she held two of the volumes warningly over the water's edge. "But I will."

Gerald gasped.

He stopped in mid-strike, just short of caving in the snow figure's head.

"I beg you! The brethren of St Dogmael's would never forgive me!"

Marie handed the books back gravely.

"With respect, I ask that you leave us alone now."

Gerald nodded. He clutched his books protectively. He was thunderstruck. But because he was Gerald of Wales, Giraldus Cambrensis the soon-to-be sure-to-be Archbishop, he did not remain thunderstruck long.

"A privilege to make your acquaintances," he managed. "Doubtless we will meet again."

He walked off rapidly, humming blithely to himself.

"I told you," said Avery. "He means devilry."

"Let us rebuild the snow-monk," Marie replied.

They rolled a second head-sized ball up and down in the riverbank snow, heaved it onto the monk's shoulders and rearranged his cassock accordingly. This time Avery did not carve a grin for the expression. He made the snow-monk's face a scream.

"My husband…" Marie began.

"I do not need to know about your husband."

"I wanted to tell you, but to tell you without telling you. I wanted to tell you in the song that I will perform tomorrow night. It is not so easy to say in everyday words. It is our great privilege as bards, Avery of York. If we find a thing too difficult to deal with we can take it to the hall and deal with it there."

"I am not sure I can call myself a bard!"

"For someone unsure if he deserves to be deemed a bard, you have then done outstandingly to outsing twice in succession men who were very happy to brag of their bardic abilities."

"Fortune favoured me," Avery said humbly. "I am honoured to be able to stand in the same room as these grand names of the literary world! Cynddelw Bryddyd Mawr the Great One, who turns even everyday actions into poignant poems! Hamid the Persian who quills the most beautiful words ever quilled by mortal man! Marie de France who forms new forms of verse and forms them for all!"

"Marie de France? She who you may meet in the final four should you come through your next two bouts? How would you feel about meeting her on the stage?"

"I would be delighted to meet her. But I feel that will not happen for my next opponent is a formidable singer of sagas, and has stirring experiences of sea voyages and battles and Norse beauties he can call upon whereas I…"

"…Have less experiences?" Marie asked gently. "But you have the most singular singing voice I ever did hear. And your compositions do not conform; they flow freely and surprise and enthral. Whilst Olaf of Bergen sings in the way all Norsemen do, lustily but with little originality. If I were him I would be glancing anxiously over my shoulder."

"But even were we to triumph tomorrow there would still be another bout for us both, and not straightforward ones. For I could face Hamid the writer of human history's most beautiful words and you could come up against Bernart de Ventadorn the master of the art of love songs. So our meeting," he blushed, "is far from assured. Regrettably far. Lamentably…" he trailed off because Marie's gaze could delve so deeply into you it went through you, could nail you to whatever was behind so that you became as good as immobilised. At least, Avery thought this. And from what he had observed at Lord Rhys' festival thus far, he was not the only one who did.

Their faces clouded over and although they did not know it then it was for exactly the same reason. The names 'Hamid' and 'Bernart' hung heavy in the air and this was partly why, for above and beyond the normal eccentricities to be expected in the entertaining profession there was something unquantifiably disquieting about those men. But Avery and Marie had been set thinking too about the darkness. Firmly and against their wills it pressed. In their young lives they had seen their share of terrible things, but these things had never engendered anything like this darkness. Clouded-over their faces stayed. Both *wanted* to confront it. Both wanted to meet the darkness head-on and deal with it on their own terms. But where does one turn? Where does one turn to stare darkness in the face so that one can say: 'come on then?'

"There is a moor far to the northeast of here," Avery murmured. "A Godforsaken place. I came across it on my way to Cardigan with Dog. We took shelter from a storm with a hermit, who lived in a cave there with his wife and daughter. He was the foulest-mouthed man I ever encountered and he was the holiest too. He spent a lot of time in trances. *Ascending onto the greater plain:* that is what he called it, and there he collected great unknowns to bring back down to the plain the rest of us are stuck on. Some of these he passed on to others. One of these he passed on to me."

"He told your fortune?"

"I suppose you could say that," Avery apprehensively glanced at Marie. "He could not be sure whether what he had seen applied to me or to Dog—we spent our time there together and perhaps our futures were intertwined in his eyes. What he told me is that one of us would soon die. One of us, he told me, or the ones that were closest to us in all the world."

He had thought Marie might laugh at him but she nodded, pensive.

"I kept trying to dismiss his words, for if we survived everything Wales pelted us with on the way here it hardly seems likely that the warm hearths and revelry at our journey's end should be what kills us, and neither Dog nor I are people one could care enough about to want dead!"

"And I suppose I would only need to be concerned were I the closest person to you in all the world."

"My parents are dead," Avery said hesitantly. "My siblings are not close to me and the others I held dear in York turned against me. There is Dog, of course, and the Healer—my travelling companions—but one is an uncivil churl, the other more than halfway to madness, and both are more or less jointly responsible for the six charges of murder I am wanted for across the border in the March. That is why I had to tell you," he felt as if he had stepped out over a cliff edge. "There is no one closer to me than you."

Marie gave a little frown then smiled, not happily but not sadly either, just with acceptance. Their hands were both at their sides, very cold and very close to each other. The vapour of their breath mixed.

"Now I am concerned."

It was the end of the year. The very end. Only one more day's light would fade in it and then it would be gone for good. There was a heartrending melancholy in such afternoons, as though the land needed to be let alone awhile, as though the fields and woods and hills would burst out weeping if looked at any longer. And on the other side of the river, by the dock where a skein of ice was forming between the cogs and knarrs and longships, threatening to block off the Teifi that was now the last means of escape from Cardigan, an ice which drove people within their walls, which pleaded '*let this land alone awhile*'—from this place stemmed a sound which seemed to the ears that heard it to be the only sound worth hearing because it summed up ends of years, it raised the listener up into a bubble or onto the wing of a goose and had them floating unseen through the deadly tired countryside on a solemn farewell. It was the twang of a bow on a string. A bow that did a dance through every note conceivable as Marie thought of the crashing Brittany coast and the gentle meadows of Caerleon and the dead-of-night room in Cilgerran where Pierrot had died and Avery thought of the soaring ceiling of York cathedral and the tree with the harp in it at Oswestry and the blasted bog of Berwyn. And the year emptied out here in this snow-laden grey-white valley, it came down to this, down to this song, this crwth playing by the dock on the other side of the river.

"Let us go and find who it is that plays so exquisitely," breathed Marie.

"Let us do so."

The ink was smudging slightly on the most recently used page in Gerald's book of notations, right where he had made his scribblings about Avery and Marie. No words. A picture. A picture of a gallows with an extended crossbeam allowing room to draw two bodies—a young man's and a young lady's—hanging from it side by side.

The Jew was in a bad way. He had lost a lot of blood.

He was lying on a makeshift bed in a chilly closet that smelt of mould and snow had heaped against the one window giving him a view only of white. It was as if he were already dead, with his burial shroud wrapped around him.

It was a long way from Constantinople. Six months of way.

He was bleeding into rank bedclothes in a chilly closet with no view, six months' journey from his homeland.

All he had to show for his last half-year's endeavours was a bag of gold that he clutched under the covers. He clutched this with his left hand, not very much more firmly than a baby clutches a parent's finger, because he was not accustomed to using his left hand for anything. He had done everything with that right hand. His arm was propped in the corner of the closet. It was in tact. It had been blown off in a complete piece fingertips to shoulder blade; not that this was remotely consoling to the Jew. Afterwards, no one had known what to do with it. It was enough for someone to endure losing an arm, let alone having it unceremoniously thrown away without their permission. A servant had sneaked into the closet whilst the Jew was still unconscious and placed the arm in its current position.

The Jew grew angry, weakened from blood loss and seeing his right arm like this.

"All this is your fault," he snarled at Hamid, who stood by the door, observing him. He spoke in English because he knew

Hamid's English was not perfect, although neither was it nearly so bad as everyone else at the festival believed, which irked the Jew too. Still, the Jew gained some petty victory, the only victory he was currently able to gain, by carrying on in English and using in his rage some words with which Hamid was not familiar.

Hamid beamed radiantly, arms folded across his belly.

"I know about you!" the Jew raged. "Do not think I do not know what you plan to do! I lead you across Christendom and teach you English and at your own insistence set off the gunpowder, and look at me! I cannot even pray properly now! And you stand there with that smile on your face, even now when I am wounded, and do not even bring me some wine to wet my lips! Will you not bring me some wine?" the Jew asked.

"Don't... drink... wine," Hamid said, smiling.

"Please," the Jew said. "What with all the revelry I think they have forgotten about tending me!"

"No wine," Hamid said.

"You are a monster!" the Jew exclaimed, although in his weakened state his voice did not have that much effect. "What is wrong with you? Six months I spent teaching you the English tongue and I know you comprehend it well enough but with everyone else you pretend to speak scarcely a word, which makes a mockery of my teaching methods!"

"Can't... slip... now."

"You are a monster! I know what you plan to do! I know what you already did! I know what you did to that whore! I will tell everyone!"

A shadow flitted over Hamid's face.

Once, on the road to the Gulf, where they appreciated fragrance and where business was very good, Hamid passed a man in the process of digging a deep hole. Intrigued, Hamid had enquired what the purpose of the hole would be. '*Why, to shout into,*' replied the man. '*Surely you do not need to go to such trouble if all you wish to do is shout? Why not pick a quiet stretch of road and shout there?*' The man had looked at Hamid as though this was a silly question. '*The road is not mine to shout on. This hole is mine. I will line this hole with slabs of marble and return with silk cushions on which to kneel as I shout into its depths. And I will know this is the best hole I ever could have shouted my torment into. And after I have shouted I will cover the hole up again.*'

The Jew did not understand. You applied fine scents to your salient parts even if you were going out riding over dusty plains. You ate finely when you took repast whether you felt hungry or not, because you could not predict what would happen on tomorrow's road. And if you carried a terrible burden and felt the need to set it down awhile and confess, you should do this with ceremony too. That was all he had done with the whore: ceremoniously unburdened himself, and then covered it up again.

As the Jew snarled threats at him, Hamid came over to the bed and sat on the edge, right on top of the Jew's one remaining arm. Hamid was heavy. The Jew howled for Hamid to shift his posterior elsewhere. Hamid took the rank pillow, placed it over the Jew's face and pressed down with the strength of a fat two-armed man.

"Can't… slip… now," he said as he pressed.

The Jew's protests took some time to cease.

Hamid's tick was bothering him. It was a very stressful thing, working for the Supreme Ruler of the World.

He thought wistfully of the frigatebirds and pelicans and parakeets and lovebirds flocking around those olive groves by the thermal pools on the road to Nishapur. He wondered if he would ever see the place again.

Quite often, musicians find there is no onomatopoeia to fairly describe the sound that is issuing from their instruments. A good musician is insulted if their drum-playing is represented by a 'bang' or their harp-playing by a 'twang.' This, after all, is why music exists: because it does something that nothing else can come close to doing.

So it was that Owain Cyfeiliog and the young Marcher Lord nobody could remember the name of and Avery and Marie and the Healer could do little else at the dock but relish the moment as Dog's bow glided over the crwth, creating sounds too hauntingly beautiful to be conveyed in words. There were no words that sufficed. But their movements did begin to show their appreciation in the tapping of their feet and the swaying of their bodies.

Owain Cyfeiliog chuckled the chuckle of an old man who suddenly feels the years stripped from him, and began a little jig. The young Marcher lord clapped his hands delightedly and joined in.

Marie and Avery moved together.

"My parents live faraway across the sea," she whispered. "They married me to a very old man when I was very young, a man who treated me as his possession and never showed me a single true kindness. The only one for whom I ever felt any affection was my attendant Pierrot, and he was murdered on the journey here. Those at this festival either resent me or want a piece of me. There is no one closer to me than you. This much space," she moved thumb and forefinger a small distance apart. "That is what is between us."

And Dog played. Like otters into water his fingers slid across the strings of his instrument and he played.

Niall Ó Maolconaire, who could smell a good time a mile off, and Azelais the beautiful trobairitz came down to the dock, and they started dancing too. Azelais looked tenderly up at the Irishman. He was one of a kind, and she did not mind the hard drinking or the heavy fighting. Niall Ó Maolconaire did not look at Azelais tenderly. He looked over her shoulder at Marie and Avery dancing together and his face did something abrupt and very strange. He broke away from the dance and picked up a stone from the dockside and hurled it at a duck, and missed, and hurled another and almost hit it, and the duck flew off squawking in pure terror.

And Dog played. And he sang a song that was popular that winter in Wales, one of those that was known and loved by all.

> *You're halfway to milk and honey land,*
> *when you turn that boat around,*
> *You're at the King's court carousing,*
> *then grow misty-eyed like a fool,*
> *You've chance to bring the reigning champion*
> *down forever to the ground,*
> *But as you raise your sword to swing,*
> *you pause and begin to recall:*
>
> *There's a reason you can't proceed,*
> *a reason you need to return,*
> *A wild country far across the sea,*
> *that you have to see once more,*
> *A place of blighted moors and bloody wars,*
> *for which you strangely yearn,*
> *You might die of course on the journey,*
> *but for Wales you'll set your course.*

And everyone wondered: if Dog played like this when only in practise between bouts, what might he be capable of later, when he took to the stage to perform for the next round of the contest of instrumental song?

And Dog played.

His eyes dragged away from his instrument for one reason and that was to watch the Healer.

And the Healer danced most wildly of all.

She seemed madder when she danced than she did normally. Her giant limbs thrashed everywhere. She danced like she had nothing to lose.

She danced heeding nothing but the song.

The Healer

(DECEMBER, 1176)

OF ALL THE HAWKERS and pedlars and touts and troublemakers gathered at the bridge outside Gloucester for the arrival of the boat from France, the Healer stood out. Physically she stood out, much to the chagrin of the others who at a foot or two less than her in height would go so far as accusing her of getting the devil's help with extending the length of her limbs to attract the attention of disembarking passengers. In her flaming curls and twinkling eyes and incredibly resonant voice she also stood out. But the Healer knew it was her wares that got her custom. If you had been on a pitching bed on a rough passage from Brittany or Normandy two days straight you could not always stomach honey-glazed ham haunch, but you would invariably welcome something to settle the constitution.

It was early November. Soon there would not be so many captains willing to undertake the crossing from the continent and the vendors—and to be sure, the pickpockets and tricksters and whores too—were out in force to make the most of the good business. She had her autumn specials lined up, her conker tonic for inflammations and her restorative of rosehip, which could eradicate seasickness even if the patient was out at sea in a storm.

He had bounded off the boat athletically before all the other passengers, given the other stalls the briefest of glances and come over to hers.

"What can I do you for, my dashing young highborn?"

He was a highborn, too. She could tell by his nose. He was a well-boned man.

"I require a cure for a rather sensitive..." his eyes had circled around as if afraid of being overheard, "...*chafing*. You know how it is, when lambs wool rubs repeatedly against damp skin..." he upturned his lips at her. "Does the remedy take long to prepare?"

"The best are mixed fresh, my highborn. And they are more effective as a result."

"I imagined so. I have pressing business in town. Might you bring it to my lodgings later? The Dean's house... you know it?"

The Dean's house. Oh my. He really was a fancy one.

He opened the door to her later himself.

She had handed him the salve.

He had fetched payment.

"I wonder. Might you apply it for me? You have the Healer's touch."

There were only moments between him asking that and him clasping her face in both hands and kissing it greedily.

'The Dean!" She had protested when she was able to get her mouth free.

"The Dean is out tonight."

Not many moments more and his ramrod was inside her, before she was quite recovered from the surprise of being kissed. It was not an unpleasant experience for its brief, desperate duration. It did not take him long to get it done.

She had lain dazed on the flagstones.

Still rampant, he had looked from the ripped-off garments to her to the garments again, aghast.

"Go!" he had cried. "Go!"

She had gone. And now she was back again.

She approached the outbuilding on the Norman side of the river, used by the monks of St Dogmael's for grain storage but deserted now because monks did not go abroad at this late hour.

This was why he had suggested meeting there.

She was thankful for the moon. There was enough of it to see by. The snow was freezing. The trees strained under the weight of it. The ground crunched.

The moonlight and the sound of snow underfoot let them espy each other when they were still a distance apart.

He pulled her into the lee of the wall out of sight of the track. He had the same urgency about him as before. Just as it had that evening in Gloucester, the urgency had ruffled his oiled hair back into its natural frizziness, and it bristled out around his tonsure like a bramble bush.

"How goes the night for you, my buck?"

"Tensely," Gerald muttered. "Pray tell me what it is, my good woman, and let us be done with it. My absence will be noted on the dais before long."

"You never were a man to waste time, were you my buck? Well. You have a little one on the way. I thought you would like to know."

"You are with child?" Gerald blanched. "And you believe I am the father?"

"It has slipped your mind what I do for a living. I make money telling everyone from silly chits to cheating wives how far along they are and believe me my buck, I know when a baby has sat two months in my belly! Which takes us all the way back to the day you docked from France."

"You must have met many boats around that time," Gerald laughed uneasily. "It could have been any sailor."

"How many have a big mole on the tip of their pecker?"

"What is it you want, exactly?" he smiled his apple peel smile.

"It is like this my highborn," said the Healer sweetly. "I will have another mouth to feed as a consequence of you planting your seed inside me. I was hoping you might have some suggestions."

Gerald, who had not rued any of his actions ever and absolutely not what had happened in Gloucester with the Healer, suddenly felt remorse. At least, he cursed his own bad luck and regretted doing it in the Dean's house, for it was in the centre of town and there could have been witnesses. He could not think what had come over him that night. He had been bewitched, perhaps. But what were the chances of his sole deviation from the one true path coming back to thwack him in the face?

"You wish for money for the termination?"

"I wish for you to be this baby's father."

"Do you live in a dream world, my good woman? I am poised to become the Bishop of St David's! Now take these coins," he scooped a handful of silver from his cassock pocket, "and get you gone. Plenty there to buy the little one food and clothes, if you will insist on persisting with the pregnancy—which I counsel strongly against. Come, do not dither, there are those who will be wondering what can have detained me out here at this hour of the night! Come!" he jangled the silver in front of her impatiently.

The Healer's arms stayed at her sides.

"Lord of our skies, I have made you a generous offer! I am an ordained cleric. You could surely not have been expecting a marriage proposal!"

"Not marriage. Just some support when he starts teething and takes his first steps, when he has an education such as you have had, when he buys his first sword or horse, when one day he starts a family of his own."

"He?" cried Gerald. "It is not a 'he' but a thing not yet come into being and it will never come, do you understand? It cannot come: not with me for its father. Ordained clerics do not beget children! Now for the merciful Lord's sake, take this silver. I want you to have it," he said with glib encouragement.

"It is not nearly enough. Not for a life. I shall have to keep coming back for more, my highborn, again and again and again. It is going to get very difficult for you when you are preaching from your pulpit at St David's and I come calling."

"Out of the question! This money is in full and final severance. This ends tonight! I counsel you my good woman: do not push me! One word from me, and the provincials here would be baying for you to be burnt at the stake as a witch!"

The Healer sighed loudly. Oh my, he was a tricky one!

There were odd noises coming from close by that could no longer be dismissed as a natural part of the night.

"What is that?" Gerald seemed the more perturbed by the sounds, somewhere between grasshopper's chirrups and a beaver gnawing a tree and some altogether heavier beast prowling around.

The Healer laughed.

"We've frozen our balls here long enough, wouldn't you say Angor?"

Dog scuffled out from behind a holly bush, then, and Anarawd emerged after him. Dog puffed his cheeks in and out, channelling spittle through the gaps in his teeth. Anarawd ground his molars on a chunk of tree bark. Other than that there was little to tell them apart.

"We can't have you making threats like that, churchman," said Dog.

"My good men…" Gerald began lightly, eyeing Dog's knife and Anarawd's sword and cudgel and gradually becoming paler. "I thank you for your intervention, but it is unnecessary. I shall be fine."

"Oh, I know you'll be *fine* churchman. We'll all be fine. By my faith, she's a big girl, she could perchance have dealt with you by herself and been *fine* but me, I like to be sure things are fine and Angor here gets paid for making downright certain that things are fine."

Dog smiled. The smile looked wrong. Anarawd smiled too, but a face like his just was not supposed to smile.

"I'll agree she's a bit of a witch and I'm not what most would call savoury but Angor's Lord Rhys' *penteulu* and the three of us together telling the same story with the rather damning evidence of your spotted pecker tossed into the middle of it, well!"

Dog and Anarawd and the Healer now stood between Gerald and the track that offered his only feasible escape. Anyhow, escape where? Brutes you could run from. But truths once out would catch you before you could run very far.

"I am a churchman. I cannot become a father!" Gerald said, half to himself.

"Do not sing yourself hoarse, my thrusting buck. You are a man of letters too. And such a well-prepared one, to carry an inkpot and a book of notations around with you all the time!"

Dog and Anarawd had taken one of Gerald's arms apiece and escorted the cleric to a fallen tree trunk nearby. Here he was invited to sit. Dog roughly fished in his cassock for the inkpot, Anarawd retrieved the quill with less ceremony and the Healer snatched out the book of notations. She flicked through. It was filled with mocking drawings of every guest of significance at the festival, sketched with uncanny accuracy. Gerald hoped she did not see the unflattering ones he had done of Dog and Anarawd, and fortuitously she did not. The Healer presented Gerald with a clean page and Anarawd helped him close his hand around the quill.

"I just want some guarantees set down in writing nice and official," the Healer said merrily. "Include something about annual payments to be made by a fixed date each year if you would. I will leave the wording to you, my highborn."

"And what of the guarantee that my being the father will remain secret?"

"You will have my word," shrugged the Healer. "Not quite enough for you to stop glancing up all uneasy at who might be knocking at your church door every so often, but I am an honest woman."

Gerald woodenly wrote out the letter. His hands shook. He recalled a horserace he had taken part in on the sands at Llansteffan when he was a youth. All the way to the cliff at the end they had gone. He had won. He remembered that. He had won.

"Let's get back," growled Dog, when the letter was finished and handed over.

"What of me?" Gerald ventured to ask.

Anarawd seized him, dragged him to his feet and then, as Gerald closed his eyes anticipating some horrible ugly act of violence, dusted off his cassock for him.

"You can come back too."

"Really, my good men?"

"Of course. And of course, with us stone sober and anywhere else other than in a hall full of gossiping songsters, you could be reasonably sure not one word of your horseplay would get out to stain your good name. Alas, the ale will be flowing and bards do detest secrets: they'll badger you and berate you if they sense you know something they don't. The most closely guarded secrets get leaked in a situation like that.

But then again gossip about someone else *in* the hall is of course that much more delicious than that about someone who has simply gone and slipped away. You could do that, churchman. The ale will keep flowing just the same, and soon enough they'll forget. Slip out into the snow and don't come back."

Gerald's mouth formed the thinnest, slightest curve.

"The advice is appreciated, my good men."

"And in case you chose the slipping away option, we already took the liberty of saddling your horse and packing your belongings. You're all set."

"And my books?"

"Every one of the bloody things is packed. Now what's it to be?"

"Forgive me," said Gerald softly. "I am just working it out in my head, my good men. There are really very few places I can go. Particularly in this snow…"

You're a big lad, churchman. You'll survive."

Gerald nodded, but he seemed a little vague—a little unsteady. His document on the state of the church in Wales, which he had organised with such loving exactingness into chapters on each of the pervading degeneracies, suddenly appeared unimportant. As did the cardinals to whom he would present his findings; as did the archbishopric he wanted to wrest from them. Damn the church, he thought. Had he entered into any other profession, become a sailor, say, then whether or not he impregnated a potion pedlar would be of no consequence. He was aware of walking—of one of the three of them shouting at him to move and him moving through the snow and away— but it was as if he were walking through something very viscous, as if the air were syrup or swamp, and each step was an effort.

He *had* won the horserace, had he not? He could remember the galloping, the beach opening up before him, the soaring in his chest. But he could not remember afterwards. He could not remember any of the other youths coming up and saying: '*well done Gerald*'.

"I've told you before to pay close attention as to who you drink with," Anarawd clapped Dog on the back. "Satan's sister, if you're going to marry the witch, pay it closer." He prodded Gerald with his cudgel. The cleric was tottering through the snow with the aimlessness of an old, old man. "Come on churchman, for the love of God…"

The Healer looked enquiringly at Dog as Gerald and Anarawd receded from view, the former with the odd good-natured jab from the latter.

"Well?"

"Well what?"

"Are you going to explain how a brute like you can casually call upon the services of Lord Rhys' *penteulu* just like that?"

"I told you before Cibon the fiddler was my father," said Dog. "But old Angor there slept with my mother on multiple occasions."

The Healer pealed with laughter.

"What's so funny?"

The Healer pulled him towards her by his frayed tunic and kissed him, biting his tongue naughtily.

"You *are* going to make an honest woman of me, are you not my brute?"

"What are you expecting? A bloody marriage proposal?"

The Healer laughed, loud as a jaybird, grabbing Dog's hand and placing it under her tunic on her swelling belly. Dog could not resist kissing her again. For the first time in a long time he did not care two hoots where he put down his harp and he kissed her and bit her back, easing his other hand around to that inviting white colossus of a bottom. Then he pulled away, as sheepish as on that morning in Oswestry when she had challenged him about the intensity of the potion he had wished to purchase.

"You don't always have to call me 'brute.'"

"Do I not, my burly rascal? Do you have another name in mind?"

Dog considered this.

"Just not bloody Madog," he said. "Now let's get back. I've got a song to perform."

Sixteen Songs

(DECEMBER, 1176)

"AS YOU ALL KNOW," cried Chrétien, when he sensed the excitement in the hall had simmered up to the brink of boiling over, "the last night of the old year only ends when the first dawn of the new one begins. Thus is the custom in Wales. Come, revellers, let us revel away this night! Such is the prestige of the Lord Rhys' festival that every manner of entertainer on God's great Earth has come to it and *this* is the night of the bard, the minstrel, the troubadour, the trobairitz, this is the night of anyone who has composed great songs and performed them well enough to survive three bouts of song-singing already! Sixteen remain in the contest of vocal song and by dawn sixteen must become eight, so each of these sixteen you shall hear tonight! Godly songs! Love songs! Lust songs! Odysseys of songs! Let us sing!"

Gwalchmai stepped up.

The furrows in his forehead were deep as cartwheel ruts; deeper still because of what Meilyr had said to him. Stand down? *He* was not one to stand down, *he* was one to stand up, *he* was a bard! He was *pencerdd* to Prince Rhodri of Gwynedd, uppermost poet of a realm on the rise! Meilyr had told him of what the word in the hall was: that he must only be in the last sixteen because of having struck some deal with the judges or the Prince of Deheubarth himself. What impudence! Impudent boy! He had long despaired of Meilyr but had never thought his son capable of rebellion. And Meilyr did not know about the arrangement he had made with Gerald of Wales and Rhys ap Gruffyd; Meilyr was challenging him without anything more than the word of a prince from a has-been realm as evidence. Who *was* Owain Cyfeiliog anyway? What *was* Powys? He called himself a poet-prince because he was not good enough as a prince or as a poet. Everyone knew the saying: *in his halls there is drinking without want, without refusal.* But it was only a saying because Cynddelw Bryddyd Mawr had said it, and everything the Great One said got immediately enshrined in legend. Thinking of the Great One made Gwalchmai doubly furious. The Great One had unseated Gwalchmai once before. But try as hard as he might and perform as brilliantly as he may, he would not unseat Gwalchmai again. Gwalchmai's name was as good as on the chair at Rhys ap Gruffyd's table already. *Gwalchmai deserves to win.* What an apt and well-formed sentence that was, and with a towering 'G' and an unmoveable rock of a full stop at the end of it. Still, he was furious. He stepped up with fury inside of him. To Hell with the lot of them and to the rankest recess of Hell with his son!

"Hell."

It was the title of his song but the word rang like rapped knuckles and as it hit the room even the judges wondered nervously if they had done anything bad enough in their lives to be sent *there* in their deaths.

Hell was not bad or hot to Gwalchmai, it was evil and bubbling with brimstone. There was no chance at redemption, but a certainty of readying for everlasting torment. He did not have use of Meilyr's vivid allegories because for the first time Meilyr had refused to supply him with any, but fury forced words from him like volcanoes spewed magma, and the words were striking. The room cringed. Gwalchmai's performance did seem everlasting. And when it was done, the hall hurriedly clapped for fear of experiencing such a place as that which the man from Gwynedd had just created in their heads.

The Monk of Blank Habit stepped up against Gwalchmai.

He had wished to come as a representative of his abbey, but his abbot had forbidden it. So he had journeyed in disguise, wearing a habit he had sewn himself with no similarity to any other known order. He had come because for him song *was* God. There was no way of coming closer to God than by singing beautifully. The Monk of Blank Habit was no stranger to singing. In his abbey he had sung with all his heart. At singing he was accomplished but at composition he was a novice. He really did just want to celebrate God, and come closer to him, but his song tinkled out like a docile cradle carol compared to what had come before. The Monk of Blank Habit, like the rest of the hall, was startled by Gwalchmai's ferocious drive, and perhaps this influenced his performance and the outcome.

Chrétien looked over at Rhys questioningly and gestured at Gerald the churchman's still-empty seat. Rhys shrugged and moved his index fingers around each other in circles, which meant: carry on as before. Chrétien made a show of conferring with the judges. One name on the slate was firmly deleted.

Azelais the beautiful trobairitz stepped up.

She was downcast, for Niall Ó Maolconaire the Irishman had been looking at Marie de France during the dancing yesterday, and it was worse when he tried to make light of it and say it was nothing but a look, because that proved beyond all doubt it had been much more. And that fit of temper when he almost hit the duck with the stone: that had not been nothing either. Was it her beauty? Everyone told her she was beautiful so frequently it was no more meaningful than saying the weather was nice but when the man she had chosen was looking lustfully at another she had to question either her beauty or his fidelity. This idea occurred to her as she stepped onto stage that she would upstage Marie to make Niall Ó Maolconaire see she was the better lady, although she knew this to be a dangerous course, as Marie was formidable opposition and everyone agreed on the fact. But Azelais was not done with this hall. She would have an impact on it yet, even if that only meant making one man in it feel significantly more remorseful than he currently did. And Azelais possessed the power of song to inflict whoever she wanted with whatever feeling she wished.

She stepped up with the innate confidence in her singing all singers raised in Occitania enjoy, with the calming knowledge that she was from the homeland of performed song. She sang of loves long gone, mostly men but women also. The majority of the lovers she sang of were fictional, but the portrayals were so convincing the hall and especially Niall Ó Maolconaire could never have guessed. The moral, sang Azelais, looking out with her beautiful eyes at every other man in the room bar Niall Ó Maolconaire, was that human beings always disappointed you and it was better to give your love to a donkey.

Ceridwen the fair stepped up against Azelais.

She had given herself her bardic name out of a love of justice: to illustrate that she was an honest competitor, that she would adopt none of the dirty tricks some bards will when trying to outsing rivals, that it would be purity of verse alone that carried her through. But perhaps because Azelais, who was a very beautiful trobairitz, had preceded her upon the stage, the hall assumed Ceridwen was talking about 'fair' as in attractive and here everyone noticed a discordance or, as some saw it, a hypocrisy. Ceridwen was not attractive. She was plain and neckless and she was singing about love too, as Azelais had been. Did physical appearances factor into a song contest judge's decision? They should not, but they did. Most of the venerable old judges on the dais had not slept with their wives in many a long year. If a beautiful lady and an ugly one sung of love the beautiful one would invariably be adjudged to have sung better; it was as disgusting to those judges to think of an ugly woman in love as it was for them to think of an old woman in love.

Chrétien and the other judges needed only a token exchange of glances. The necessary adjustments to the slate were made.

Niall Ó Maolconaire stepped up.

He had been drinking steadily. That cleared his head. Others called it 'hard drinking' but Niall Ó Maolconaire called it 'steady.' The tragic thing was that him and his brother Rhys might have been the best of friends, if they had been drinking partners at his favourite tavern in Connemara say, where buxom Sorcha would come and pleasure them all of a Saturday, Rhys would have loved that. Rhys liked the ladies, Niall Ó Maolconaire could tell. Unfortunately, Rhys had fashioned a rather nice, neat clean realm for himself over here whilst at the same time emptying every last bit of shit from his privy over Ireland. Now he was not about to hold *that* against Rhys, heads of countries came to bloody disgusting agreements these days that spattered their citizens in thicker shit and often had them drowning in muck. But that little chat he had been wanting the two of them have brother to brother? That had not happened. Niall Ó Maolconaire had been trying, but ever since Christmas morning when they had met at the dock, Rhys had been decidedly more distant toward him: as if he were one insignificant irritation too many. But others were being heard,

Niall Ó Maolconaire noticed, others but not him. And it was a little thing he wanted. Just for Rhys to use that influence he held with King Henry when he attended the next King's Council and ask him in the nicest possible way to call off his Norman dogs from Ireland. Niall Ó Maolconaire felt his brother Rhys should have already sat down with him to have that chat, all things considered. Particularly after he had let Marie alone when he saw Rhys had wanted a piece of her himself, and settled for that Occitan slut Azelais instead. He was convinced he had made the wrong choice there: the more so since Azelais' song about her string of sweethearts. Azelais said 'yes' too easily. Niall Ó Maolconaire liked a challenge; coyness was a virtue in his eyes; women obviously had to assent to his advances eventually but they should not go down on the haystack without playing a bit of a game first. He supposed he was the shaft in his own arsehole sometimes but that was how it was. He liked a bit of a game first. Like the one Marie was playing with him now. He liked that very much.

He stepped up onto the stage with a fair few winks and waves and stopped in front of the dais to do an Irish jig that went down well. The hall was probably thinking he had got carried away but he was not carried away. He had been drinking steadily, not excessively. He made a mental note not to sing an angry answer back at Azelais. Affairs of the heart had their place, but he was conscious of the copious covering of shit daubing his beloved Ireland at the present, and of how someone really needed to start clearing it up soon before the stink spread into Connemara. Now the Irish knew some things about song just like the Welsh, they had all been Celts together once upon a time as his brother Rhys had pointed out the other day. And now Niall Ó Maolconaire constructed a clever little epic. *The Young Lady's Dream*, he called it. He took for his protagonist an immediately likable young girl, as opposed to a prince or a king which would render the poem overtly political, and subtly placed her on the shore of a stinking, war-torn yet unnamed land looking wistfully across the sea to Wales. This, her father had told her, was what a fine country *should* look like. Niall Ó Maolconaire was blessed with foxing wordplay. The hall laughed because on one level he was funny, but on the deeper darker level the majority of the audience were unwittingly laughing at themselves. The Norman merrymakers, for example, denounced the warmongering sour-faced foreigners Niall Ó Maolconaire described as taking over the unnamed land in his song and violating his protagonist. Like dogs amongst a flock Niall Ó Maolconaire's words ran rings around his audience. They were left grinning. But in actual fact many should have been smarting at the deftly laid layers of insults.

Wace of Northumbria stepped up against Niall Ó Maolconaire.

Wace hailed from a border town continually being bickered over between England and Scotland, and had not in any of his three bouts so far quite been able to shake off the impression that he was beset by an unsettled man's hatred of outsiders. He was attached to the Plantagenet Court and had evidently accrued some experience of performing, sufficient to have narrowly beaten Luciano the song-singer from the Kingdom of Sicily in his previous bout. But the room had hardly relished his harangue about the Scots then—for in some vague way Wales imagined Scotland as an ally in a battle against generation upon generation of oppressors unfailingly issuing from England—and whilst Wace had tempered his song this time, revellers were soon trembling at the bard's flagrant bigotry, which now seemed to turn on the Welsh: on his own hosts!

Chrétien conferred with the judges, who were by this stage plied with mead and vocal in their disparagement of this last act.

Wace's song breached the rule set down before the contest began that every performance should in some sense embody the spirit of Wales. And one name was swiftly removed from the slate.

Prydydd Y Moch stepped up.

He was a bard from Gwynydd beloved for his personifications of various animals, usually of the farmyard variety. He had quilled verses about a homeless dog that longed to please her master, but made mistakes at key moments and was thus outcast from every household she tried winning a place at. He had sung about a horse sick of being ridden places he did not wish to go and he had sung about a bunch of disgusting pigs, based in England strangely enough, which continually invaded other animals' farmyards. This was the reason he started to be known as Pydydd Y Moch, which meant 'Poet of the Pigs' in the English tongue. But Pydydd Y Moch *knew* whom he was stepping up against. He *knew* what name was after his on the slate and so did the room and this knowledge hampered his delivery. It was unfortunate because otherwise Pydydd Y Moch might have gone far. Normally when he sung about dogs or horses, his audiences were transported, trotting along in the moment and seeing the world through beast's eyes. This time though, his verses about the wolf asleep in the woods seemed insincere.

Cynddelw Bryddyd Mawr stepped up against Pydydd Y Moch.

Cynddelw was thinking of the first room he ever sang in, the kitchen of one of the chief henchmen of Prince Madog of Powys. He had come with his father, who travelled around that district selling rags. The servants had been about to slam the door in their faces. But his father had given him the last-hope nudge, and Cynddelw had sung out a variation of a folk song popular back in those days, only with many of his own more meaningful lines substituting the originals. Mouths gaped. '*We will buy your rags if the boy sings for us during supper.*' He opened his mouth and out came words ready sculpted into stanzas sparkling with startling consonance. He was born poor, but in knowledge that he had great talent. He could sing the dullest thing into singularity.

"Many of you assembled here know what it is to travel," Cynddelw boomed to the room. "We travel around and sometimes on the road, perhaps, your eyes like mine glaze over and temporarily we cease to feel the drizzle slavering, or the wind as it bites. What do we do then, beloved bacchanals? We philosophise. I have been philosophising of late about greatness. What makes us great? I had always believed our greatest act in life should be to do the thing we love best in all the world and do it often: whether that be making sweet love to a woman," he paused and the hall chuckled, "or speaking out against wrongdoing even if that wrong is committed by the highest authority in the land," he paused and the hall did not dare now to give any reaction whatsoever. Cynddelw shook his head at his audience and the bear's head on his cloak shook too. "The greatest act we can make in life is to give to others! Allow me to say this in another way." The crowd would allow it, although sweet Jesus, other performers had got up and come down again in the time the Great One was taking over his introduction. "You bards get your gift from God, am I correct?" there were murmurings of agreement across the banquet tables: yes they did, yes they did. "Horseshit! Hog swill!" Cynddelw looked dreamily into the near distance as the room gawped in amazement. "To those of you in this room with true talent I tell you this. Your gift comes from *love*!" his voice saturated with emotion. He was starting to sound like a romantic fool. "Do not fight love! It is the greatest weakness of every last one of us and it is our weakness because we fight it. Give in to it! Give in to love!"

The Great One was toying with them, the room sensed. Yet again he had not made a single direct reference to his rift with the

Lord Rhys, despite knowing that this was expected of him, despite knowing that this was why the hall hung on his every word like this. But those there who had seen him perform before detected a wistfulness in his delivery that had never previously been present. Those there who had seen him perform before thought that the Great One was building up to something. And after that all-meaning word 'love', the Great One finally threw himself into his song. He sung of a place that could only be Powys, and of a certain wine house there that stood alone on the track up into the hills, and of its owner who had captured his heart like Calliope captured song on her lyre and taught him the real meaning of life. And the room thought: how harrowing. Even the mites in the dust of the wine house floor in the song were consequential.

Chrétien imitated his bosom being pierced by a dart. The applause, led by Owain Cyfeiliog, who was ecstatic over the powerful evocation of Powys in the Great One's song, lasted so long the conference between the judges as to which performer should progress only needed to be the briefest formality. And another name was removed from the slate.

Navarro the wandering cantor of Castile stepped up.

He had sailed through his first three bouts jauntily, imbuing his songs with a flavour of his carefree Mediterranean lifestyle, and seeming exotic in comparison to the opposition. But Navarro found himself caring about this bout much more than any of the others, because he had discovered just prior to strolling up to stage that his next opponent was Bernart de Ventadorn. To outsing the master of the art of love songs was still a fine string to one's bow, a magnificent feather in one's cap. Few could claim to have done it. But Navarro had further motivation. Navarro had seen Bernart hiding away in the bowels of the court at Toulouse, ranting. And then Navarro had retold the story; spreading throughout the hall word that Bernart was mortal, vulnerable, beatable. Now he came to the stage aiming to flush Bernart away for good. Navarro's good name demanded that he do so, for one cannot very well ridicule a rival songster and then fail to beat them in a bout of song. Combining the green-grey beauty of Wales and the gold-red beauty of Castile in his verses, he sang about meeting his truelove in the Welsh valleys and whisking her away to Spain to lie with him there under a stand of orange trees. It was a great performance. And it had to be great, because of what would come after it.

Bernart de Ventadorn stepped up against Navarro.

He had stared into the abyss down there at the mill. He was reeling from sighting the awful drop and inhaling the updraft from its stagnant depths. But he had pulled back. He felt lightheaded but he was on firm ground. There was one last song from his old body of songs he could get away with singing. One more, and then the only thing he would have left would be the dreadful dirge on darkness that had so repulsed the courtiers of Toulouse. That, or his flow would be unblocked. His eyes kept involuntarily slipping to Marie on the dais just below him and to prevent this he had to hold his gaze straight ahead, rigid as a madman's. The cansos he now performed had always been favourites of his, and had retained their truth down the decades. He sung of love, of course, prettily sketching it out to begin with through images of the budding spring then introducing the melancholy: of how his love could never be fully returned, of how he knew this yet still lived in hope of it, of how he retired to his quarters to reflect on his longing and reaffirm his devotion even if that should prove futile[1]. Were those making merry on this last night of the old year witnessing a master or a has-been? They were none too sure. Here was a man who could rouse a room, but who, in his manner, chilled still more than he thrilled.

---

1   Such is the theme of *Can par la flors josta.l vert folh* by Bernart de Ventadorn

And Chrétien had to hand over to Cibon to provide entertainment in the interlude whilst he and the other judges hotly debated which of these two performers should progress. After an age, a name was wiped from the slate.

Unwin Honey-Tongue stepped up.

Sometimes every thing can go right in a young man's life. He can have doting parents, and siblings prepared to take on punishing menial work in order to further his own prospects. He can have a handsome education, an allowance so generous he can afford to employ his own maid from a young age, looks that cause women's hearts to flutter and influential friends that make him numerous offers of employment and will sometimes plead with him to take up posts. Things can go so well for him that he does not need to come into contact with any unsavoury aspect of life. He is not out after dark much, because he has countless merry gatherings at castles to attend. He has people to look after his debts and his health. His whores never, ever have venereal diseases. Such a young man was Unwin Honey-Tongue. To be fair to him, he could have done very decently doing nothing at all, but he did have aspirations. He spent a lot of time languishing on silk cushions reading books, some of which had been bound and illustrated especially for him, and one day he came out with it: '*I simply must write*,' he announced. His friends and acquaintances rolled their eyes and asked whether he might reconsider and become a knight, which would be infinitely more interesting and give him access aplenty to eligible young ladies. '*I must write,*' he replied. Mere weeks later, Unwin Honey-Tongue had composed Occitan cansos, Welsh awdls and couplets in English, French and Latin: each so pleasing that listeners were known to rub their hands together in glee afterwards. Even those who did not want to could not help humming the verses. They were words that made people feel pleasant. A lot of the time, a song-singer's performances got judged on nothing more than how pleasant the words were upon the ear, and the judges appointed to judge in Rhys' hall were like most judges. As Unwin Honey-Tongue sung in his satin-soft voice of the beautiful, wealthy ladies that frequented a certain fortress in a beautiful wealthy part of the March, only Chrétien could find any fault in the performance. There was not a single shocking adjective. There was not one out-of-the-ordinary noun. The words were absolutely unsurprising.

Marie de France stepped up against Unwin.

The hall to her was a fresh just-turned page, unlike life, which was complicated by the scribble and scrawl of centuries of thought and consequence. Her eyes searched for Avery along the rows of revellers on the lower tables, but gave up when the thought struck her that to look at him as she sang might not be appropriate. But she wanted to look at him. She supposed that really he was her newly-turned page. Almost. Half-turned. She held the corner of the leaf, but was wary of fully turning it over for some reason. Wary even though she wished to turn it and put those old chapters behind her; wary, maybe, because she had turned pages like this before. Not finding Avery, her face assumed its public expression. Calmness. Composure. Slight amusement. The expression a face gives in front of a mirror before it goes out into the world. The audience thought long and deep, but none of them had ever beheld a woman who seemed so at home upon the stage.

"No one knows much about her," Chrétien murmured to one of the judges. "She appeared at Windsor one day, with a fat bumbling man it could scarce be believed was her husband, poor lady! Her husband had been known at court before: known but never noticed. Everyone noticed him once he had his new wife. He bumbled about with a simpleton's smile plastered over his face as usual, repugnant but redeemed by the graceful lady at his side. The smile twisted into a scowl whenever another man stole a lustful look at her, and *that* happened more and more. It was not because she invited the attention. She was quite reserved. But mercy, when you give beauty a voice! No one could have prepared themselves for how captivatingly she told a story. Soon enough they were not requiring nearly so many other entertainers at Windsor. Not on the days she came."

Marie sang the song she had been perfecting of late. The song she had begun as she listlessly paced the grounds of her husband's big, bland, neatly hedged Buckinghamshire estate; that she had enhanced as she endured his ream of remarks about this or that man he had observed looking at her lasciviously, about how hard done by he was to give her so much yet get nothing back but unfaithfulness, about how he knew of men that locked their wives up for much less. The song she finished at Caerleon, where the meadows were the colour of emeralds and ships from faraway lands came up the Usk trading sun-swollen fruits from the south and fine fabrics from the east, King Arthur's land. Marie sang a story in rhyme, the history of one of the bravest knights at King Arthur's court. Marie sang of a jealous lord who imprisoned his comely young wife in a tower so no other man could get at her, a lord who pretended to love her but had seldom lain with her or shown her a single true kindness. Many a long year this comely young wife was imprisoned. She pined for a real knight, like those in fables of old. If one pines plaintively enough one can get one's wants miraculously granted, and so it was with her: a knight did come. He came in through the one place not guarded: her window. He arrived in the guise of a bird then metamorphosed into a human, henceforth showering her with the affection she had been deprived of and becoming her lover. The tale ended in tragedy. The jealous husband mortally wounded his comely young wife's lover. But the affair bore her a son and he grew up to be a renowned knight who avenged his parents[1]. The pace of the performance caused the mouths of all in the hall to gape like silly fish on hooks. The lines stuck in them. There was so much intense detail many wondered where Marie could possibly have gleaned inspiration for such a strange, sad tale. But only one amongst the many merrymakers knew the truth.

Rhys glowed with pride, as if he had personally trained Marie to this lofty level of song singing. He thought of how much mightier a host a performance like this rendered him, thought of Cardigan like a beacon, like a flaming fire on one side of a vast darkness that even those on the other side of the darkness could look across at and marvel at and say: *there* burns a blaze!

Chrétien had beheld magnificent acts in magnificent halls, but now he was a silly fish on a hook like everyone else. When he finally regained his senses, one name was deleted from the slate.

Avery of York stepped up.

'Avery' alone would have sufficed for him, and thus did he begin to introduce himself, meekly adding 'of York' only after a pause during which he recalled how Marie addressed him, how Marie's hand touched his shoulder, how Marie's thumb and forefinger were but a fraction of an inch apart as she whispered: '*This much space. That is what is between us.*' He felt as he had when on errands into the secular world of York very early on spring or summer mornings, when few people were up and about but after the dawn had already brightened the archways and alleyways and cobbles with its beauty. He had taken ownership of whole streets then. Whole streets that resonated with day's doings yet to be done, with marketplace banter and street performers' singsong, with the rustle of ladies' robes and the clank of merchants' coins; whole

---

1 Such is the theme of *Lanval* by Marie de France.

streets lit up just for him. He felt as he had after he first sung his songs out to an audience in the hermit's cave in the middle of the moor, and when they had toiled on across the bog next day to crest the rise and behold the road to Cardigan stretching away below them. He felt serene. He felt certain of his purpose. Vocalise a bad thing and you can vanquish that thing. It ceases to be a guttering shadow that swallows you. It was as Marie had said: taking your troubles to the hall and shouting them out into the open there unburdened you. You became lighter. In his previous bouts he had sung of his disillusionment with the church and of the hypocrisy of some aspects of church life. And he had garnered a small following through his words. Followers that liked this hitherto unknown vying with the most renowned practitioners of vocal song; followers torn between the love they were forced to feel for the church and their hatred towards its hierarchy, for prospering on their hard-earned tithes whilst their poverty deepened and their prayers remained unanswered; followers that would not dare speak out themselves, but quietly admired anyone with the spirit to do so. But in his previous bouts, his scathing of the church had been tempered. Now it became intense.

"I sing again of the church, friends," Avery said. "I know of little outside its walls, but of what goes on within I know more than enough. I do not wish to offend the devout amongst you. This is not an offensive song. It is a defensive one. It is a defence of the innocents harmed by the very people who should have protected them!" His voice trembled indignantly and the hall sharply drew in breath: this could not be a fabricated tale, for indignation like that could not be feigned. "A tale in two parts! To tell of its full reprehensibility in one song could not be done, so I give you now the first part. Should I make it through to the next bout, you shall have the conclusion. Theo!" Avery's voice shook with unprecedented resonance, with the full force of his slender frame that so belied the bellows-like lungs inside it. It stabbed through the hall walls, into the snow-laden castle bailey, out to the gates to where Gerald was readying his horse and baggage for departure. The churchman heard it and froze. "Theo! This song is for you!"

Avery sang of the exquisiteness of voice when it reaches its greatest reach, when it touches notes so low it conjures up dread and so high it sets you shivering with the shrillness. There were few on Earth whose voices could attain such extremes, Avery's song reflected, when you heard a voice like that you were privileged, he or she who possessed a voice like that should be cared for, cherished, kept safe. He sang of a boy in one of Britain's mightiest cathedrals who could claim to have such a voice. He sang of a boy who sought the protection of the church, but who found horror instead: horror that stemmed from within. And then he brought the song to a close, just shy of describing the horror itself.

The hall thought it a clever tactic indeed, to leave a question hanging as to what this horror was. They needed to know! This bard *must* get a chance to sing again or they would be forever in suspense! In absence of an answer came chaos. The song divided everyone. The pious were incensed but so were the non-believers. The former accused the latter of devising hideous stories for effect, and then of heresy. The latter accused the former of hypocrisy, and then of heresy. Food and drinks were thrown. Fistfights broke out, fuelled no doubt by this being thirteen songs into the last night of the old year, and drunkenness being advanced as a result. Chrétien could not quieten things and it took Anarawd to threaten repercussions for calm to gradually descend.

In the tumult, Rhys smiled. To think he had only let that youth into the contest at the last hour! That was the thing with waves: they rose and broke and fell. It was not easy to ride the crest, but stay on the crest a leader must. Dip under and you were done. He loved the instinctive momentariness of rule. Sometimes there were mere moments to judge what was best and jump to the next wave before the one you were on broke beneath you. And these last few performances had set the room alight, memorably so. He knew for fact that the pre-eminent poets in attendance were scrawling verses about what had happened here on their parchments, and that this would ensure his own enshrinement in songs yet to be sung, halls yet to be built, towns yet to be populated. He had done this. All this was because of him. He thought back to the early days: him and his brothers, God rest their souls, scaling some fortress in their threadbare tunics in desperation. Back then he could not have imagined surviving so long, much less achieving all this.

In the tumult, Malegwyn sneered. Look at his father, merry damnably merry, and Gruffyd grinning away alongside like his father's puppet. There was only one place to go after tasting greatness, Maelgwyn snickered: down.

In the tumult, Avery's smile found Marie. She could not hold it long. But it was long enough for someone to notice. The difference between Niall Ó Maolconaire and other merrymakers was that he did not drink intermittently to excess, but constantly in moderation. Whilst others were sleeping it off he carried right on. His body had built up an ox-like tolerance to alcohol and it took a lot more to floor him than it did your average festivalgoer. Now as other drinkers' vision blurred, his became lucent. He saw that smile between Avery and Marie and smiled to himself at it. He did like a game and Marie had played along well. But enough was enough. He was smitten. "Time to stop playing, honeyhead," he murmured.

Olaf of Bergen stepped up against Avery.

Olaf had been a song-singer his whole life long. In Bergen, an

'Olaf' was already a much-used substitute term for a really rousing ballad. But Olaf had the lusty Viking blood of his forebears pumping through him and when he sang, he defaulted to the dastardly daring exploits of Norsemen for subject matter, for what could be more riveting? A hazard-fraught sea voyage, a battle or three and a ravishing Norsewoman featuring somewhere near the conclusion: this was the recipe for each of Olaf of Bergen's songs. It was possible to predict almost to the line when the first sea monster would appear, when the first sight of land and when the first taste of love, which was rarely anything more profound than a burst of passionate frolicking in-between battles. There was a great deal of comfort to be gleaned from his ballads. An audience experienced a total adventure from embarkation through to heroic death, with lust and liquor in liberal doses along the way, without ever leaving their seats. And Olaf's performance had a similar effect on everybody this time too. But it was a fantasy. Exploits like those he sang of had not occurred in decades, whilst the performance before had told of a real scandal unfolding right at this very moment. The Norseman did not doubt that he would progress any more than his ancestors had doubted their ship would reach shore through the throes of a storm. But the judges reached their own conclusion without much ado. Chrétien struck a name from the slate.

Bran the Bard stepped up.

Bran's employment of all twenty of the Welsh poetic metres had impressed during the earlier heats. He used them by the book. His songs could have come straight from a set of instructions on how to compose songs. In this same correct, clipped manner he launched into an elegy he entitled: *The Wondrous Light of Angelsey*. It was about a bard, on Angelsey, who observed the wondrous light and imagined it was God speaking to him. Perhaps against lesser opposition in earlier heats, Bran's performances had sounded better. But from the judges' reaction to his tame allegory, it seemed this songster had gone as far as his talent could take him. That, or the judges were subdued for another reason. Subdued, perhaps, because they knew what was coming.

And Farid Un-Din Attar, whom the room had been told to call Hamid, stepped up against Bran.

This fat foreigner unnerved almost everybody. It was not just his fatness or his foreignness; it was not even his delicious smell or his robes, which were gaudier than those most kings wore, although admittedly a combination of these things did arouse suspicion. The continual radiant beaming they could have dealt with too, were it an isolated oddity. What no one could fathom was how someone who sung songs in such rich English and French could, when he was approached in normal conversation, do nothing *but* flash that radiant beam in reply as though he were incapable of understanding one word. This made people feel Hamid was concealing many things from them. This they did not like.

No, people could not like Hamid.

Yet people were in awe of Hamid too.

The general view was that he was probably a sorcerer, to be treated with extreme caution. Even the judges, who should really have known better, thought this; that it was advisable not to eliminate such a person too soon so as not to invoke his anger. And another thing: a thing nobody wanted to admit was a thing. Hamid's verses were laced with terrible loveliness. They were superior to most verses performed thus far. His lines must *be* bad. They issued from a character that was wholly unlikeable, after all. But they sounded so good.

Hamid himself was unconcerned by the room's opinion. His thoughts were far away. They were with Zand the turquoise trader and Samir the rug seller, they were under the olive trees of Nishapur gobbling watermelons. Recently though, an unpleasant thing had been happening when he let his mind drift to these happy thoughts. That repulsive bighead, the Sultan's agent, had been sticking his bulging pate into Hamid's memories. He could not think of those thermal springs anymore without them being tarnished by the bighead saying: *'you are the Sultan's man now.'*

Yes, yes, there was nothing like taking one's sandals off after a successful spell of scent-selling, letting the hot air circulate around the toes, passing the time of day with the other merchants and gorging on good fruit, nothing to better it if one did not have some bighead loitering in the shade making demands on one.

But Hamid had heard the stories about the Sultan in the days before he became the Sultan, stories about the fates that befell his enemies. That they had been killed was not the noteworthy thing; one could expect death if one lost in battle. Those that opposed the Supreme Ruler of the World, though, had never simply been killed. Some got dismembered or deprived of their eyes so they could not run away in the afterlife to raise an army in response; some had their families sought out and butchered down to the youngest child so no one remained in the bloodline to wreak vengeance. Plenty met far more elaborate ends too, for the Sovereign of Mankind was a creative man. Hamid did not care to die. But he would do absolutely anything he might to avoid death at the hands of the Supreme Ruler of the World. *'Go forth with your verses, perfumer. Win Islam glory and make these damned infidels in Christendom believe in us. Do not fail me.'* Hamid's radiant beam did conceal many things. And utmost among them was fear. He knew that if he did not exactingly complete the task the Sovereign of Mankind had charged him with then he would never return to his former life. He would not have any life at all.

Turning to face the merrymakers he adjusted his robes. The room gagged on the cloying sweetness of his fragrance. Hamid had taken in all fifteen of his rivals in the contest of vocal song. Beaming radiantly, he had observed which of these posed the greatest threat. He knew what he must do now: on the stage and off it. He heard the Sultan in his head even now. *'Do not fail me, perfumer.'*

Oh, the terrible, terrible loveliness! Out Hamid's verses floated like pollen: another passage from his *Conference of the Birds* about the birds who journey to find a new king, words no one from Christendom had heard the like of before. In his mind's eye, all the birds he sang into being had assembled to embark on their odyssey at his beloved olive grove on the road to Nishapur: a place where the world's most exotic trade routes met, a place where fabulous journeys began and ended. And in spite of themselves, every one of the revellers wanted to go on the journey Hamid described. The words opened up untold possibilities for them. Hamid was a terrible person, they all knew it in their guts, but his words were so lovely. One merrymaker imagined herself flying on the backs of the birds depicted, and being worshipped by them. Another imagined himself being painted in gold, then floating on his back across a sea of nectar, to a land where he was plied with strange sweet fruits and seduced by angels. Oh the loveliness oh the terror oh the loveliness!

And somehow, although even Chrétien could not say precisely how for he swore it was not him that did it, a name got removed from the slate.

And the dawn of the new year stole under the door.

The Last Eight

(JANUARY, 1177)

CHRÉTIEN took the last of his slates and wrote:

*The last eight in the contest of vocal song at the castle of
the Lord Rhys ap Gruffyd in Cardigan are as follows:*

Azelais the beautiful trobairitz versus Gwalchmai ap Meilyr
Niall Ó Maolconaire versus Cynddelw Bryddyd Mawr
Marie de France versus Bernart de Ventadorn
Avery of York versus Hamid

Touching The Sea

(JANUARY, 1177)

MARIE STOOD on the battlements. Her hands clasped a horn of hot honey and herb water too foul to drink but welcome for its warmth. The snow, still knee-deep, had part-frozen in the night. The revellers that had retired to the encampment below the castle for some sleep were up again already, brushing ice from their tents, stamping feet to keep warm, crouching close to whatever fire they could. Tracks had been beaten through the snow, but none too far: just along the main street of the town, just down to the river.

White the snow, black the river, opaque the sky. As if the colour had drained away from the world.

"I beg your pardon."

She swung round, startled. Her brow cleared. Avery.

"And I give it to you," she smiled.

"It… it is a new year."

"A time for burying old grudges. Even the warlike Welsh would put aside their differences before New Year arrived. Everyone deserves the chance to start again."

"Indeed. In fact I wondered if I might impose upon you… I thought of taking a walk. Would you join me?"

"Walk? In this snow I would struggle to get very many steps. It would near enough come up to my waist."

"Of course. It is just that… forgive me. It was a foolish notion."

"What?"

"I want to… I must go and touch the sea. It perhaps sounds strange. I saw it before of course, from a distance. But I never touched it. You know. I want to feel it on my skin."

"Touch the sea?" Marie looked intently at him. "As in fingertips? Or as in taking off your clothes and swimming far out?"

And she was someone who, when she mentioned fingertips, you could not help but stare at the fingertips of. And she was someone who, when she mentioned taking off clothes, you could not help but imagine naked. And this for Avery was a stretch of the imagination, for he had come no closer to seeing a naked woman than a likeness of the Virgin Mary.

"I will know when I am there."

Was she laughing at him? He could not be sure.

"Something to do with starting again," he added. "I cannot explain exactly."

"You do not have to explain. I was thinking of an idea."

She bid Avery wait awhile and went to look for Olaf of Bergen.

She found him in the hall with five Norse companions, continuing last night's revelry even though it was late morning and everyone else had long since withdrawn for a rest. Serving wenches were attempting to clean around them but did not dare ask them to move. For a man who had drunk as much as he had, and whom an unknown had beaten in a bout of bardism, Olaf was in reasonable humour. His ancestors had been reared on those legendary Viking debauches of bygone decades and had instilled over generations extraordinary powers of endurance. Olaf was seasoned for lasting month after month of perpetual darkness during which time there was nothing to do but make merry in a hall or perish outside of one, and a dusk to dawn debauch every night for a week was not so very exceptional an undertaking for him. He was singing in a mournful tone about a battle with a sea serpent, and his companions stamped beat with strange boots that had binding up to the thighs. Marie sat down and listened and tapped her feet in time too, and none of them seemed to mind.

"You could not have understood one word of that, my lady," Olaf said dryly when he was done.

"I understood the cadence. And I admired it."

"We Norse bards live for cadence. We find it in all places. In the roll of the sea. In the clash of battle-axe on battle-axe. In the writhing of our women as we make love to them."

His companions chuckled, but not dirtily.

"That comes across."

"Not enough to the judges of last night's singing. Scuttled I was by your youth from York. Sung off stage by a novice!"

Marie blushed a little at Avery being described as her 'youth', but did not correct the Norseman.

"If it is a consolation, I believe Avery of York's song was outstanding, and that against others your ballad would have seen you through."

Olaf shrugged.

"If you are beaten you are beaten. A bunch of old battlers like us have had their share of beatings! I am surprised you are seeking our company though, my lady, and not out with your youth celebrating. Odin knows I would be, had my ballad been better loved. I would be carousing away with the wench of my choice," he looked levelly at her.

"It is not like that between us," Marie dropped her gaze to the floor.

"No? Then it should be. Life ends suddenly enough. If there is a mead cup to your liking, drink it whilst you may!" his companions chuckled again—not dirtily—and he thumped the flagstones to stress his point. "To the dregs! Now spare me the flattery for my songs and tell us the real reason you sought out some half-drunk Norsemen to squat with."

Marie looked from one to the next.

"I would like to borrow your boat."

Olaf and his companions laughed heartily.

"I suppose you know how to sail, my lady?"

"No. I would need you for that."

"And why would we leave this warm hall to go out on a gusty sea on a woman's whim?"

"Not a whim. My…" she hesitated, because she was not sure any more what she could or should call Avery. "Avery of York wishes to touch the sea."

"Touch the sea," Olaf repeated the words slowly. But he did not mock Marie de France. It was inconceivable to him that one could reach adulthood without having touched the sea, but one should not be mocked for wanting to do so. The sea was the most profound thing on this Earth. No man woman or beast should die without having touched it. "It is but a matter of following the riverbank west a few miles. Can he not walk, and save our old bones the trouble?"

"He could walk. He could walk to it and dabble his feet in it and maybe brave swimming in it for a moment. But you and I have been out in many a boat, Olaf of Bergen. And you and I both know a paddle on the shoreline cannot compare with a voyage on open sea."

"This sea is a wild sea. One does not sail a wild sea without good reason."

"Really?" said Marie. "Why? Because you are frightened?"

Olaf thumped the flagstone. The flagstone came off worse.

"No Norseman fears the sea! The sea is our lifeblood and our death blood! But some things one must concede cannot be conquered, and the sea is such a thing. When it flattens one sails forth. When it swells one seeks harbour. Go against it and…"

"Yes?"

"You awaken something," Olaf said, a little ashamed. It sounded silly when a big Norseman confessed to superstitiousness, but now he ploughed on. "Something dark. Something you will wish you never awoke."

"I understand if you are afraid. It is one thing to sing of sailing storm-tossed seas, and another to sail them yourself. I do not blame you. No one has a right to assume Norsemen are as courageous as the characters from their songs."

"Our songs ring true," Olaf avowed in a voice that was not loud but that people listened to. "In every song I ever sang, I sang of my ancestors' voyages and by Odin each voyage took place with all of the exploits I described! We Norse are no cowards!"

"Your ancestors must have been very brave. Now please excuse me. I must find someone in this town today brave enough to grant me what I wish."

"You will do no such thing! In all my days I never had my bravery questioned, and New Year will not start with it being brought into doubt either! In Odin's name!" sighed Olaf with an exasperated glance at his companions. "Make love to a woman but do not ever debate with her!" He hauled himself up and screwed his eyes shut. The room did not completely stop spinning. He still felt the churning of a great deal of ale inside of him. But the sea cured all, he thought. It took one to death's door. And it showed one what life was, too. "Ready *Olafssud* for the water! The ship is not named after me," he thought it necessary to clarify, "but after the saint. And in a sea like this we will need his blessing."

Olafssud was a karvi, the smallest size of longship, with a malevolent-looking dragon for a figurehead and six rowing berths that the Norsemen quickly took up, hauling on huge oars to slip the vessel into the current. Olaf took the rear pair of oars, and Marie and Avery sat on a bench just behind.

Already in the widening river it felt different. A strong salt wind. An increased smell of brine. Pitching as the first effects of the tide unsettled the water.

"Touching the sea!" roared Olaf, purposely letting go of the oars a moment to alarm them and stretching his huge calloused hands over the sides to feel the spray. "What did you have in mind, my lad? A splash? Or a soaking? Do you want to peck the sea on the cheek or give it a big wet embrace?"

The Norsemen were elated now. They told jests that were actually quite amusing and chanted sea chants and chuckled good-to-be-alive chuckles. The hall was behind them. They had been beaten in song but at seamanship they could not be beaten. Their knowledge and language for the sea ran as deep as its depths, and they taught Marie and Avery some of its secrets. "*Unblakkr*" they pointed to their ship, and this meant: wave-horse. "*Rás*" they pointed to the water, which meant this was a strong current. "*Grunn*" they pointed under the water, towards the slime and rocks and strange creatures that dwelt there in the deeps without ever seeing daylight, and this meant the part of the seabed that was seldom or never exposed.

Marie clapped her hands in delight, for she loved it when her ideas worked out. Because Avery's eyes were shining, shining with more wonder than she had ever beheld in another human being. And this was how to look at the world, like new-borns do. His eyes marvelled at the jests of the Norsemen, which were not at all dirty, at the gulls and gannets and guillemots and great auks that perched on the rigging, at a dolphin that leapt from the water at one point and danced through the waves in front of them. They passed the abbey of St Dogmael's and Avery shouted "God bless you!" at a couple of the monks gathering seaweed on the shore. They passed the wide tawny beaches of the rivermouth, where a family were writing in big shell-studded letters the words 'PAX ET AMOR' on the sand, and Avery shouted back at them: "peace and love to you too."

Then the wind snatched his words away and whipped up white horses. He toppled back into the boat and had to clutch Marie to steady himself and even after he had, his arm stayed around her shoulders longer until it became almost awkward.

"Do you ever pray?" he asked her breathlessly. "I prayed and prayed at York and God never granted me what I wanted. And afterwards, you know, I stopped actually asking God for anything, but the act of wishing for things several times daily I continued, for it was engrained in my habits. And now. Since we met. Everything I ask for I seem to get! I hope for my songs to be well received, and they are. I harbour a wish to touch the sea and here I am in the middle of it on a real Viking longship, and here you are with me, and…"

Avery got no further. Olaf instructed his companions to man the boat and turned to grab him by his midriff, hauling him upside-down over the side so the waves washed right over his head and shoulders. He struggled, but Olaf's grip was as strong as the grip of a man who hauls in huge and obstinate fish from deep, deep down, and Olaf held him there for a numbing, terrifying age. When he was let up again he needed a while to fight for his breath and was shaking from the ice-coldness.

Olaf was chuckling.

Marie was laughing.

Avery was indignant but too cold to speak.

"*Now* you have touched the sea, my lad. Now you are baptised!"

"I never saw you with such colour in your face, Avery of York!"

"Do you feel it yet?" they all wanted to know. And Avery did not understand what they were talking about. He just felt numbness. But as his skin dried, he did begin to feel something: a beautiful, burning, trembling tingling.

"By Odin, I can see you feel it now!" cried Olaf. "Does it feel like angels dancing on your skin, my lad? Only the waters of the west of Britain do that! Does it feel like lions purring inside of you? Does it feel like lyre strings the instant they stop playing and there is that gentle throb to them you feel compelled to touch, because somehow the touching brings you closer to the song?"

"Yes!" Avery said. "Like all those things! Like… like…"

"Like starting again?" Marie suggested.

Avery's eyes sparkled. That was how it felt. Good. That was how it felt.

"Thank you," he whispered and, when the Norsemen's backs were turned back to the handling of the vessel: "Thank you, Marie."

It was the first time he had called her that and they both smiled in recognition of this.

Now she could hold her smile. Now there was no hall to watch her. But even though she could have she did not; her face flickered like the warm hall fire flickers in a sudden draught.

"What is wrong?" Avery asked her softly.

Marie rarely prayed, but she thought maybe it had been a mistake not to have done so more frequently. Normally, she had wished for things only after those things had gone. She pined for Brittany when she was married, and separated from it by a sea. She yearned for a happy marriage after she had arrived at the conclusion hers was finished. She longed for Pierrot once Pierrot was dead. '*Something dark,*' she heard the Norseman saying. '*Something you will wish you never awoke.*'

"Nothing," her smile returned. "Did you know this river has fatter fish than any other in Wales?"

"Fish!" exclaimed Olaf. "Why did you not say?"

His companions produced hooks, lines and a net. With the guts of the first catch they smeared the hooks and then they were biting at will and on whim—eel, herring, haddock, horse mackerel—and Olaf ran a net alongside awhile and caught more. With big silly grins on their faces they took turns to land them and a pile of fish several score deep built up on the boat bottom.

And for a moment they all forgot about the castle of the Lord Rhys and everything therein.

For a moment it was about the moment, the happy moment, the happiness of being at sea catching fish.

Bottle the moment, eight happy humans and a load of goggle-eyed fish.

Catching the fish has made the humans happy. They hold the slippery creatures up like trophies, like representations of their happiness.

Happiness.

Flapping. Flopping. Floundering.

Closer.

The ash greys of the flapping haddock, the tarnished metal hue of the flopping herring and horse mackerel, the slate-after-rain black of the floundering eel.

Closer.

Their pectoral and pelvic and dorsal and adipose and anal and tail fins, like brittle stands of dwarf trees bent in wind. Their stares. Their bafflement, their innocence, their unconsciousness. Their scales like useless little gemstones with the lustre fading.

Closer now.

And under the fins, behind the eyes, between the scales, the oncoming stink of putrefaction. Death.

This then is happiness.

As they came back to the dock in the last of the light, they saw someone standing in the brown trampled-down snow of the path back to town.

"A word if you would, lady," said Niall Ó Maolconaire to Marie with a wink.

"If you wish."

"Without the boy."

"Anything for my ears I am content for Avery of York to hear too."

Marie had observed Niall Ó Maolconaire looking at her on a few occasions but had assumed that was just his playful way: until the dancing the other night. He had acted oddly then, staring at Avery and her and straight afterwards almost hitting the duck with the stone. What if the duck had been hit? It did not bear thinking about. Since then she had been trying to avoid the Irishman.

"I cannot think, friend, what you could possibly need to say to this lady in private," Avery said hotly.

"You'd be surprised, brother."

"I am no brother of yours, friend."

"When you put it like that," said Niall Ó Maolconaire in an easy lilt, "I suppose I'm not necessarily your friend… brother."

"Hush!" Marie cried. "Wait for me," she said softly to Avery.

"I will be in the hall."

Not knowing what to do, for the Irishman could have floored him with one thump if he so chose, Avery retreated. He glanced back anxiously over his shoulder several times. Marie's head was bowed gravely. Niall Ó Maolconaire stood extremely close to her. He laughed a playful tinkling laugh and waved mockingly at Avery. Then Avery did not glance back anymore.

He approached the castle the long way: around the back to the servants' entrance. He smiled ruefully. He would never learn. Had he not entered the cathedral at York by the side door that night, he would never have seen the Archbishop in the midst of that terrible act and he would still be there, sing-singing away in the choir oblivious. Perhaps some things should stay buried. Or, at least, be unearthed by someone who could do something about it.

The guards lazily waved him in. They were thoroughly sick of songsters by now, strutting about with their pretensions, mood swings, whims and crafty wordplay. They did not know where they were with such types. They would rather have dealt with an actual invasion.

A vast part of the rear of Lord Rhys' castle had actually been relatively calm this past week. The stables were here, full to bursting, and some stable hands were tending the horses and the camel, but the beasts themselves had not been ridden, for this was not riding weather. The garden was here, and had supplied many of the vegetables for the feasting, but everything that could be retrieved before the snow got too thick had been retrieved, and so there was a hiatus of activity. Chancing minstrels had pitched up the odd tent or lean-to, but as darkness fell everyone had made their way to the hall for the performances of the last eight in the contest of instrumental song. And Avery would do the same, he decided, for Dog would be performing and could surely use his support. He would listen awhile to the music, by which time Marie would have concluded her conversation with that roguish Irishman.

Despite being close enough to the revelry to hear faint strains of crwth and harp and pibgorn music, it was quiet here. In the quiet Avery noticed more. He seized on certain things he might otherwise have overlooked.

In the stables, tucked into an edge behind the champing animals as if someone had wanted to hide it from view but done so hurriedly, was a chest. The lock kept clanking in the wind. It was open. Inside were books. A dozen or two intricately bound volumes illustrated with monastic illuminations. He had never beheld so many beautiful books together. Most abbeys could not boast a library as extensive. Strange, though: he knew of only one festivalgoer with a collection of books. The churchman. And the churchman had not been seen since the night before last. Why would he abandon the books he professed to prefer to most people out here in the snow?

Avery refastened the chest and walked up into the garden, colliding with Hamid who was waddling as fast as his plump frame could carry him through this snow in the opposite direction. Hamid always walked as if he was protecting something of immense value under his brightly-hued robes, and on this occasion he was. Out into the snow tumbled several wooden boxes, about the size of those a woman might put keepsakes in.

"Forgive me!" said Avery, and knelt to help Hamid pick them up.

The boxes had small lengths of rope hanging from them but were otherwise quite plain in appearance; what made Avery realise they were of immense value was Hamid's reaction. He glared at Avery in undisguised contempt.

"I beg your pardon, friend. Nothing broken I hope?"

Hamid shook his head and his face relaxed back into a big, empty beam.

"Can't… slip… now," he said. And he hurried off towards the stables.

The man understood everything, thought Avery, how strange that he should choose to pretend that he did not.

Cold now, Avery made his way hastily towards the warmth of tonight's feast, where revellers stuffed from seven days' worth of over-indulgence were steeling themselves for more. Against the outer back wall of the hall squatted a woman he had espied loitering around the castle since the festival began. Not aristocracy but well-dressed; not an entertainer of any sort but remarkably acquainted it seemed with every single entertainer. She was deep in discussion with Bernart de Ventadorn. That much Avery could determine even from behind because of the bard's scarlet travelling cloak. Neither had yet noticed Avery. He slowed his pace and hung back behind the apple trees, watching them.

Presently, Bernart pressed some coins into the woman's palm and the woman deposited them in a bulging sack at her side. In return the woman pointed towards the far end of the garden, towards an ivy-trailed wall with a little old gate in the middle. Bernart nodded as if this was perfectly obvious and took his leave.

Avery left it a few moments, then approached.

"Who are you, lady?"

"Me? I am the odds-maker. And you are Avery of York."

"How do you know that?"

"We've got the odds on every songster, you know. It's our business to know as much about each as we can."

"And what do you know about me?"

The woman gave a knowing smile.

"The odds have just changed."

"From what? To what?" Avery asked helplessly.

"There are two clear favourites now. Hamid, the Persian Perfumer whose words are like musk and—come from nowhere, mind you—Niall Ó Maolconaire the Merrymaking Irishman. Bernart de Ventadorn, Veteran of Versification is just behind them. And Gwalchmai ap Meilyr the man from Gwynedd: he's in with a sniff too or should I say a snort," she impersonated Gwalchmai snorting.

"But there are four more names besides left in the contest! Azelais the beautiful trobairitz, who will bout next with Gwalchmai, Cynddelw Bryddyd Mawr the Great One, who will bout with Niall Ó Maolconaire, Marie de France who will bout with Bernart and I, who will bout with Hamid. I do not understand how you can dismiss all four of us!"

"Odds are not like your romantic songs," the woman sighed, abstractedly running her hands through the coins in her sack. "They are based on science."

"The science of what?"

Avery was nettled. The Great One could sing a song about a dormouse and make it astounding, he would be more than a match for that Irish rascal. Marie was talented, as well as stunningly beautiful, and the judges would surely choose her over the pale, ailing and frankly alarming Bernart, who was a has-been relying on lines composed long ago in his youth if the whisperings in the hall were to be believed. The way Azelais evoked past love affairs would stand a chance of outdoing the God-fearing railings of Gwalchmai, whose continued progress was beginning to look suspicious. And him? He would not have much hope against Hamid, the writer of the most beautiful words ever written, true, but sometimes the stage threw up surprises.

"Favourites are calculated upon many factors. History, talent, standing with Lord Rhys, but more and more in these later bouts sheer determination is most important of all. Romance doesn't come into it. We're running a business."

"So your four favourites are more *determined*? Is that what you are saying?"

"Do I question how you bards compose verses?" the woman retorted. "Gwalchmai ap Meilyr believes God will grant him victory no matter what and Azelais is flighty. Niall Ó Maolconaire delights audiences and has a real resolve about him of late, whilst the Great One is refusing to redress his rift with Lord Rhys and sing a reconciliation song, which the hall is most disappointed at. As for Bernart de Ventadorn, who has a reputation to rescue, and Hamid, who has travelled eight months just to be here, we have to favour those two over Marie de France and yourself," she explained matter-of-factly, adding in a softer tone: "it's like this. We're confident our four favourites will be prepared to do more to win. Now. Want to place a bet?"

"Which way did he who was here before me bet?"

Something flickered within the woman's face but she looked back at Avery blankly.

"I don't know what you mean. No one else was here."

"He in the scarlet cloak," Avery whispered hoarsely. "He gave you money, and then you pointed towards that wall with the little old gate in it over there. I saw him with you just now."

"No one else was here."

"You are not being truthful, lady. I saw you with him!"

"No one else was here," the woman repeated. She looked at Avery with a touch of sympathy. "I am so, so sorry it has to be like this."

Avery stared at her a moment longer, then shook his head.

"You… you are a liar, lady!"

"No," her voice floated after him as he strode off into the hall. "I am the odds-maker."

Dog was performing. He had set his harp up on a stand in front of him but was playing a pibgorn too, trilling a haunting introduction to the melody he would soon pluck from his strings that had already reduced the room to awed silence. Most musicians had taken to the stage performing just one instrument but Dog made handling two seem straightforward, and he was singing as well. The song they had all danced to down at the dock the other day. And with the added poignancy that the pibgorn brought, the sound made the travellers in that hall think of braving a terrible journey then finally after many a desperate day sighting the destination; it made the warriors there think about wandering a battlefield as the sole survivor, horrified but happy to be alive.

"You're halfway to milk and honey land, when you turn that boat around," Dog sang.

Dog glanced at the door and caught sight of Avery and had time between notes to give him a wry nod. And Avery was happy for his travelling companion, because no one was coming close to him and he was sailing towards victory like a ship with strong wind in its sails. The Healer wheeled around at Avery's entrance and flashed him a wink, and Avery was happy for her too, because he knew her baby would have a good father in Dog. And Marie came into the hall, clearly upset, touching Avery lightly on the shoulder because he was at the very back and no one else could see and still managing to smile through her sorrow at him. And Avery was happy because she was safe. Avery was happy. And he had a sudden soaring thought, a flash of a future in which Dog and the Healer and the baby and Marie and him were seated on a grassy bank beneath a tree on a fine day in summer, Dog playing his harp and the rest of them singing because what else was there, what else was better than that?

"You're at the King's court carousing, then grow misty-eyed like a fool," Dog sang. *"You've chance to bring the reigning champion down forever to the ground, but as you raise your sword to swing, you pause and begin to recall."*

Marie pulled Avery outside.

"What did that rogue say to you?" Avery asked urgently. "Are you quite well, Marie?"

"Let us not speak of it," she smiled, although she had been crying and her wimple was askew.

"Did he? Did he…?"

"I wanted to show you something," she said, evading an answer and in a voice that intimated she did not want to discuss it, whatever it had been.

Numbly, he followed her.

Back into the garden they went.

The odds-maker was still there, squatting against the wall counting her coins. She inclined her head at them as they passed, and pointed to the far end of the garden at the ivy-trailed wall with the little old gate set in it.

On into the garden they went.

On into the snow-bowed shoots of leek and skeletal fruit trees. One apple still hung from a branch, against all likelihood one rosy apple, what were the chances of that?

On through the garden they went.

And at the end of the garden was the ivy-trailed wall set with the little old gate. The gate only yielded with an effort. Through the gate was another smaller walled yard and at the end of that was a rough little stone cottage. She led him inside.

Inside was stacked with spades and shears and saws, watering cans and wheelbarrows, mattocks and pots and trowels and trug baskets, the redundant tools of a garden buried by snow. But amidst the implements was a table, a workbench of sorts, sturdy and smelling of soil and sawdust.

"It will not be used again until the snow goes," Marie said. "Now it is ours."

"Ours?" Avery whispered.

"To practise our songs. The contest is far from over. There is at least one more bout for us both, and maybe two or three. Does it not beat stumping about in the snow for a place where you might ready your lines in peace without some songster heckling you? None will find this place. Look. Here is parchment and ink and quills. Here is your stage," she patted the table. "Here is your audience," she pointed to herself.

"Why do you do these things?" he dared to ask. He was trembling. "I surely do not deserve such kindness, so why...?"

"*There's a reason you can't proceed, a reason you need to return,*" Dog sang. "*A wild country far across the sea, that you have to see once more.*"

"Because," she stood on tiptoe and her mouth found his and he did not know what to do. He was petrified, so did what she did, for that could not be wrong. Their lips sunk together. It was like eating honey, like bathing in warm water, like... it was like nothing else he had ever experienced before and, he felt, like nothing he would experience again. Marie opened her mouth further so he did. Marie let her tongue slowly search for his, then deeper, then frenziedly. And so he did the same to her. He pulled back in disbelief and kissed her forehead and her eyes, her beautiful sad clouds of eyes. Then he kissed her long neck and her surprisingly powerful shoulders. She helped him. She loosened her indigo travelling cloak and exposed enough of her that he knew it was right to expose more. Then her cloak and his, her tunic and his and her chemise too were on the floor of the gardener's cottage, covered in sawdust and soil. People said Marie was calm and composed but she was not, it was part of the performance she gave to a hall, she was not normally calm at all but now there was a calmness to her, she had swum a long long time through a sea without ever sighting land and suddenly she felt as if she had reached the shore.

She guided his hands to her breasts and belly and bottom, and he was not doing what she did anymore, he did his thing and she did hers, he cried and she cried. And they made love, an elegy of love, there in the gardener's cottage. They were safe there. None would find that place: so Marie had said. But someone had found them. Someone was outside in the walled yard. That someone placed boxes about the size of those a woman might place keepsakes in, all around the door of the cottage, then trailed ropes, two to be precise, across the snowy ground leading away from it.

"We should get back," Marie murmured.

Avery watched her, fascinated.

"I do not wish to."

"Yet we must, for now."

"Thank you!" he blurted out.

She laughed.

"You do not need to say that."

She slipped back into her clothes, fluidly as a spirit, like a wild spirit one might never quite tame.

"Wait!" Avery fumbled for his clothes clumsily. "I am not leaving you alone, not now!"

"We should return separately," Marie said, and touched his cheek once with an outstretched finger. Her finger was cold. Like dew. She smiled reassuringly. "I will see you in the hall, Avery of York."

"*A place of blighted moors and bloody wars, for which you strangely yearn,*" Dog sang. "*You might die of course on the journey, but for Wales you'll set your course.*"

Back towards the hall Marie went. She stepped into the snow; started across the walled yard towards the little old gate that yielded only with an effort. The two flames danced passed her from two different directions, each moving towards the same point, the cottage doorway. She watched the flames in confusion. How could flames do that? But she had seen flames do something similar before, she remembered, recently.

"Avery!" she screamed.

The flames danced on and came together by the carefully positioned boxes. And Marie flew. She flew like a fledgling learning to fly and crashed against the little old gate with considerable force. She felt heat. She felt pain. Then she felt nothing for a while.

She opened her eyes. She was in the arms of someone she did not know.

The odds-maker.

The odds-maker grimly held Marie's face to her chest so that she could not turn round. But she wanted to turn round. Why should she not?

She wrenched herself free. Sharp pain seared along her sides for her trouble. But she was free. She turned back towards the gardener's cottage.

There was no gardener's cottage left.

Just a heap of rubble: smouldering rubble.

"Avery," Marie said again. It seemed a small word, sighed out into the night like that. "Avery."

Touching the Sea—by Avery of York

When you do not know what it is to live—why, then go to the sea!
Sense the spray surge upon your skin—
sense the tide come in then go out.
Feel the icy thrill as under you plunge—to death, to get set free,
This is the time to shout from the brine: "I know what life is about!"

Feel For The Hall

(JANUARY, 1177)

FEEL FOR THE HALL. It is not a book.

The hall does not have fingers fondly running along its spine or thumbs eagerly, expectantly flicking its pages. The hall cannot be passed as a gift between friends or travel in a chest from one house to another. The hall remains in one place for the entirety of its existence, taken for granted and for the most part utterly unappreciated. The book gets preserved in an abbey or a castle in the autumn of its years; the hall gets abandoned for a better hall somewhere else, its stone appropriated for marking field boundaries or paving a highway.

The book tells a tale in neat well-considered words selected by the masters, and in some instances the mistresses, of word selection.

A book is a polished gem of recorded information.

The hall tells a tale too but it is not a neat polished one.

It is a rough tale, an unhingedly happy, miserably sad, depraved, debauched and sometimes tedious tale: a raggedly raw tale. And it is a tale much closer to the truth than that which the book records.

The book, for example, tells of a Christmastide of merrymaking.

The hall, meanwhile, tells of mutton bones strewn across the floor and drink spillages seeped into the floor, and if the eating and drinking have been excessive the tidemarks of vomit and piss too.

The book tells of nigh-on one thousand merrymakers making merry.

The hall has the scrawl in a corner where one of the Great One's former *cerrdorion* wrote of his fear that the Great One might be going soft. The hall has the broken bench leg, where Hamid sat down too heavily with his big sagging hindquarters and caused the bench to collapse. The hall has Azelais' gossamer-fine golden tresses, where Niall Ó Maolconaire pulled her to him perhaps too roughly in one of his fits of temper. And by its entranceway, the hall has the traces of dung where a camel released its bowels in sheer fright at what it saw. A particular puzzle for the archaeologists that would come to the site in centuries to come, the dung was: Bactrian camels had not been thought to arrive in western Wales until much later.

The hall resounds with echoes, the roar of Rhys and the sneer of his firstborn son at his expense, the titter of Chrétien and the cackle of the Healer and the disdainful snort of Gwalchmai at all his rivals and actually at every other person attending the festival.

Right now, it resounds predominantly with tears. Tears and mutters and stunned silence, which has its own sound too as any performer will confirm.

Because Avery of York was well liked, not only by Marie but by many. Everyone opined just how much they had liked him now that he was dead. They liked him because he had always had a sunny word for everyone, he had been an innocent but through that innocence had shone a truth against the world, bright indeed in this age of falsehoods and injustices. Those on the dais liked him because he had enriched the festival, he had come to sing his songs with no greater or lesser a motive and that was how song-singing should be. Pure. The other performers liked him because he had reminded many of them of how they were when they started out in this tricky, tragic business of bardism. He had been unafraid to sing on any subject and he had been accomplished and oh, his voice: they would always remember that voice. But he was dead. Now they could never hear the eagerly awaited second part of his song that promised to reveal the horrific practices entrenched within the church hierarchy.

Avery was dead, and at the time of his death he might have been well liked, but he was not well known and not deemed influential enough to mention in the history of things. He fell alone in the forest.

And therefore the book will not record him. Not even a footnote.

But the hall will record him. In the weeping wept into the cracks between the flagstones and wept most of all by Marie, who normally seemed so calm and composed. In the thousand shards of fine pottery from a plate hurled by Dog at the wall when he heard what had happened. In the discord rumbling through the ranks of revellers, who no longer wanted simply to perform, or to see performances, but wanted answers.

Answers. This is where a book does come in useful. Most of the time there are answers in a book or, at least, most of the answers. The book is written by a writer; it is overseen by an all-seeing eye that claims to have knowledge of everything taking place in the book, and stage-manages the material therein, and provides answers.

The hall just is.

No answers are in evidence there.

Chrétien had maintained for days that something was afoot: that foul play had been sizzling away like lava under the surface of this festival since the moment it begun. He had understood that in such a large group of performers, some would have that cog in the brain that does not turn as cogs in brains should. He had understood that amidst all those overly sensitive highly-strung desperate-to-succeed natures, something would sooner or later snap. Perhaps it was true what he had overheard Owain Cyfeiliog say: that the Welsh were so conditioned to war there was never more tension amongst them than during a peace like this. But Chrétien also believed in spectacle. He believed in the show going on until all had been shown.

"It *has* been a largely successful festival, seigneur," he pacified Rhys who was pacing around the *ystafell* in agitation. "Unprecedented revelry, the best bards in the Christendom in attendance, some sublime performances. Word of its magnificence *will* get out," he approached Rhys and stood at his shoulder, adding softly: "I will tell of it in the foremost courts on the continent."

"I have been blackmailed and threatened with a war on three fronts! One of the contestants has been murdered! Anarawd told me there would be trouble. And I did not listen to him."

"Anarawd is a brave warrior," said Chrétien gently. "But he is not like us. He does not understand culture. Mercy! Is my court, Champagne, renowned across Europe for its warfare? No seigneur! Anyone can wage war. And everyone has. Culture is what separates the great from the good. You have come this far with your contests of song. Do not abandon them with your name so close to an eminent place in the chronicles."

"So how do I handle this? What do I say to the hall?"

"You let me do it, seigneur, as I have been honoured to do thus far. I am not good at much, but I do know how to say the right words to a roomful of revellers."

Rhys had been staring out of the window but he glanced out of the corners of his eyes at the Frenchman, who was far closer than he had thought, inches away, peeping at Rhys through long lashes with his cherubic eyes.

"And what to do about my cousin?" Rhys looked away again hurriedly. "He seems to have left us. Does this release me from the deal he forced on me?"

"It is your choice, seigneur, whether you continue to let your cousin's choice progress. In my opinion Gwalchmai ap Meilyr is an embittered, puritanical old bore whose pious outpourings would be better suited to a second-rate church service. By right he should have been ousted three bouts ago at least."

In spite of his agitation Rhys had to smile at this.

"You were right. You do know how to say the right words. I dislike him myself."

"Yet you must decide what you dislike most, seigneur, that pious old bore or the possibility of war on three fronts."

"I dislike him! And Hamid the Persian, however many months he spent travelling here! And that Irishman, Ó Maolconaire! And that locust De Ventadorn! The trobairitz Azelais has an aggravating voice. As for Cynddelw…"

"I understand, seigneur," soothed Chrétien. "His audacity, not singing you a reconciliation song!"

Rhys was glad Chrétien appreciated this fact.

"I liked Avery of York," he reflected. "I like for the small man to have his chance against the big man. I was a small man once, you see."

"I cannot imagine you as a small man, seigneur."

Chrétien blinked his long lashes. His nose hung too far down and not far enough out from his face but Rhys had been harsh, he now thought, to adjudge the Frenchman unhandsome as a result.

"Very well then," Rhys said, breaking away from Chrétien's intense gaze. "You will join me in a horn, perhaps, before we go back in? There is the last of the claret, and I would rather drink it with someone who appreciates good wine."

"You *are* a generous man, seigneur."

The host of the festival and his judge brought their horns together.

"To a successful festival, then."

"To you, seigneur. To us."

Rhys drained his claret uncomfortably and left the room.

Chrétien allowed the wine to circulate his palate a little longer. He was right. He did know how to say the right words to a hall.

"Avery of York was a performer like many of us," he was shouting from the stage a moment later. "His death will not go unpunished! The guards have been doubled on the town gates and beyond them the snow is thick: rest assured the perpetrator will not escape. They will be rooted out. But if you or I were to die, we would not want to bring about the death of the greatest festival of song these shores ever saw! The contestants that are left have come from as far as Persia and Ireland and France to perform at *this* castle. Should I say to them that their journeys and performances have been in vain?" he paused, it was a rhetorical question and he knew no one would challenge him, but he offered them the opportunity all the same. No one did. "So be it. So let us sing! By the time tonight is done there can only be four remaining in the contest of vocal song!

And to sing this first bout off to a sensual start, all the way from the sultry south of France, the belle of Occitania, the beautiful trobairitz… Azelais!"

Azelais did approach the stage, but not with anything like the allure she had exuded in previous bouts. She had swollen eyes. Her hair had been hastily arranged. This time she derived no reassurance from her Occitan homeland being suffused as it was with the legacy of performed song. She had overseen Niall Ó Maolconaire with Marie de France yesterday evening, not long before that fateful blast, and had overheard them too. She had picked bad men in her time, but none were bad like Niall Ó Maolconaire. He was bad by comparison to other hard-drinking hard-fighting Irishmen; he was abominable, perilously attractive and abominably wicked.

Azelais faced the hall, although she faced it through a haze of anguish, and sang:

> *And there we are, I've come this far, I'll go no more.*
> *Rather than see you stay with me, I'll seek succour*
> *Up in the hills, far from your ills, I'll start anew:*
> *More preferable, pleasurable, than seeing you.*
> *Crueller weather is still better than your temper.*
> *Give me the worst: Snowdonia's stark December.*
> *Give me worse still, its steepest hill, its sharpest peak,*
> *Its murderous cold, wild and vile wolds, bleakest of bleak,*
> *Over one day of your saying sweet nothings,*
> *Which have become to me loathsome abhorrent things.*
> *Your looks so fine I'll leave behind for blasted rock.*
> *You are so false that death's of course a finer shock.*
> *Yes, death, you beast, you foul disease, you pestilence,*
> *You blight, you strife, I'll take my life, my existence,*
> *I'll strip naked, sever my head, and sacrifice*
> *Myself—I'll die! Rather than lie with you I'll die.*

Chrétien applauded Azelais loudly. In the circumstances, she had been good. Over a week into a stint of merrymaking all song-singers began to flag, they had over-drunk and over-eaten and overcome these excesses to still dig deep into the reserves of their talent and produce something wonderful, regardless of rowdy crowds and precious little sleep. Chrétien had seen plenty of bards crumble under this immense pressure. Those that pulled through and performed distinguished themselves as true professionals. And Azelais evidently had external issues as well. This was common too in Chrétien's experience: linger long enough in any hall, and a songster would latch onto another songster for a passionate, transient time that invariably ended in tragedy. But Azelais had pulled through even so, and her performance had got the tap on the table from the Great One, which he only gave ever when he heard songs sung in flawless Welsh metre.

Chrétien clapped as hard as his delicate hands would let him, and besides his appreciation for Azelais he was rousing the room so the next performer that would step up against her might seem as flat as possible. He looked over at Rhys, as he had before each of Gwalchmai's appearances upon the stage as if to say: surely *now* we can dispense with pretence and expel this sullen sermoniser from the song contest! But Rhys shook his head. And deflated, for he hated to see the integrity of song-singing stained and to see staid, preachy performers advance whilst talented ones bowed out, Chrétien announced the next act to the hall: "Gwalchmai ap Meilyr, the man from Gwynedd."

Gwalchmai strode to the stage in his usual whirlwind of fury, as fast as if he were on one of his walks in Snowdonia, striding up some cwm. He glared out at the banquet tables like an eagle sighting prey far below its perch. He imagined holding each member of the audience under the cold grey Welsh sea until they started to choke, scrubbing the blasphemy off them. By God, they would be clean then. Owain Cyfeiliog had taken him to one side just before this evening's performances, and said again to him what Meilyr had said: that he should stand down from the contest of song, for the sake of fair and honest song-singing stand down or at least call off whatever stink of a deal he had done and perform on the same terms as everyone else. Gwalchmai had not even dignified this with a reply, but had heard Owain Cyfeiliog say as he turned away: "you might live to regret your decision." Regret, was it, and how was a once-was prince of a drab part of Powys that had long been grovelling at the feet of Gwynedd going to make him feel regret? And the voice inside his head urged: *Gwalchmai deserves to win, Gwalchmai's singing deserves to win.*

If singing were the right term for it, rather than rasping the words out or thundering the words out, Gwalchmai sang:

Before I become a corpse, may I have the exhaustion of penance.
May my purpose be successful in true belief,
In devotion, in faith, in illustrious company,
To be borne by my God to my deserts
From the tumult of this life with its very great oppression,
Helpless is the beginning of life even for one with
abundance of splendour
And its certain end as painful as death,
And there is no avoiding the bitter lodging
Of a cold bed in the covering of earth.
Alas for us the fate that has been given to us
In excessive habit of sin leading to failure.[1]

Chrétien need not have worried about the atmosphere flattening. It was dead. The crowds were too aghast to applaud, they were already prostrate in their pits, in their cold beds in the covering of earth, choking on the soil, each line another shovelful in the mouth. They applauded only as a painfully delayed afterthought,

1   From *Mea Culpa* by Gwalchmai ap Meilyr

as a fruitless attempt to stave off the fate so brutally sketched out for them. Surely now, thought Chrétien. Surely this was too dreadful a dirge for Gwalchmai to feasibly be allowed to progress! But Rhys was looking at Chrétien and shaking his head and, downcast, Chrétien knew whom he must let through.

Serving wenches circulated with more food and drink, and with sides splitting and heads swimming the merrymakers consented. They were on a journey now as intense as the journeys they had made to be here, the sinking, sagging journey of the over-indulged. When drowning in the wine vat, save yourself by drinking the wine: this was their way of thinking, now that they had been at this surfeiting nine days straight.

Anarawd came over in the lull to say in Rhys' ear that he needed a word. Rhys instructed Gruffyd to keep an eye on things, and in particular on Maelgwyn.

Maelgwyn had been acting strangely even by his low standards. He had been whispering to others amongst Rhys' brood continually through the last performances. He was trying to garner support for his latest scheme, perhaps. He was one who wore a look like he was forever hatching schemes, targeting the bastard offspring of course for they had the weakest links to Rhys and were easiest to prise away.

Rhys adjourned with Anarawd to the *ystafell*. As they closed the door on the hall, to the surprise of both Chrétien slipped in after them.

"This doesn't concern you, parrot-feather," growled Anarawd. "This is a matter of the realm, not of bloody poetry."

"Mercy!" said Chrétien brightly. "Tensions are running high! I beg to differ. I am managing the stage out there. If something untoward is occurring, I need to know what to say to the hall."

"Tensions!" Anarawd spat. "I'll teach you some things about tension, parrot-feather! Tension's when you're crouching in bushes hiding and an enemy outnumbering you by hundreds is on the hunt for you close by baying for your flesh. Tension's when your men start defecating with fear and you are squatting there wondering if the stink will reach the enemy's nostrils and give you away. That's tension parrot-feather!"

Chrétien looked wide-eyed.

"Fascinating!" He emitted a little titter to Rhys. "How fortunate you are, seigneur, to have a stout Celt like this one watching your back!"

"Simmer down the pair of you," said Rhys sternly. He was aware that since Chrétien's arrival he had been spending much more time with the Frenchman than with his trusty *penteulu*, and that Anarawd probably felt undervalued as a result. But he needed them both on side now. "You first," he said to Chrétien.

"Your son, seigneur, Maelgwyn..."

"I do not have the time to deal with my son at this moment."

"But seigneur..." Chrétien persisted. He needed to tell Rhys what he had overheard Maelgwyn planning.

"Enough," said Rhys. "Watch him and when this festival is done I will deal with him. Anarawd?"

"He who's next up. The Irishman. He's been asking again for a private audience with you. Says he doesn't see why he alone shouldn't get granted one."

Rhys' face clouded. Anarawd clamped his hands on his hips and champed on his wedge of tree bark and waited. Chrétien batted his eyelashes and readjusted the parakeet feather in his cap and waited.

"I have a history with Ireland," Rhys said shortly. "Not one I am ashamed of. But one certain factions resent. Niall Ó Maolconaire represents one of these factions. I have long feared reprisals for my part in their troubles. It should come as no shock I suppose that this should return to haunt me now. Everyone uses these occasions to make demands, and the Irish make more demands than any other race. They believe it their right because of how rigorously the Normans have shafted them from behind these many years."

"In a reign as long and far-reaching as yours, seigneur, you cannot hope to satisfy all parties all of the time," started Chrétien gushingly.

Anarawd was about to suggest to Chrétien in no uncertain terms that he put a stopper in it, but Rhys held up a hand.

"I cannot grant the Irishman an audience. Not now, not ever, do you see?"

"You fear he'll make an attempt on your life?" Anarawd asked. "Satan's sister! He might have fought some backwater brawls and knocked a few women about. And you might be past your best. But I've seen you in hand-to-hand combat, I'd like to see him try!"

Rhys shook his head.

"I fear for his demands. He will have a list of them and use my part in his country's problems for leverage. He will be asking me to back Ireland against Henry Plantagenet at the least. If I hear the man's demands, Anarawd, I am duty bound to accept or reject them. I cannot be favouring one side or the other when I am the pivot. You know how fragile the great peace is."

"As you wish," Anarawd nodded. "But you know the old saying as well as me. Take to the hall what you can't otherwise remedy. What if the Irish bastard tries that?"

"We should return, seigneur," urged Chrétien. "What should I say to the hall?"

Rhys pulled at his moustache in thought. Why did the Irish always put one in these awkward positions? '*I am come to avenge my countrymen*,' an exaggerated version of Niall Ó Maolconaire's voice echoed in his head, '*for the disgraceful bloody mess you put*

our nation in, so I am.' The Irishman was not a problem that disappeared when one closed one's eyes any more than Ireland was. Niall Ó Maolconaire was from the same stubborn bloody stock as the rest of them were. Certainly, this was a matter to pull up at the root. He had it. It was a risk, but rule was risk.

"There is another old saying," he said. "Let a performance run its course." He looked at Chrétien. "Rouse the hall and give Niall Ó Maolconaire a nice introduction." He looked at Anarawd. "He will step up next against Cynddelw Bryddyd Mawr, will he not? After he loses, offer the Irishman an apology for my having no time for him and one of my herds of Dinefwr whites as a goodwill gesture."

"A generous gift!" exclaimed Anarawd. "King Henry would be pleased with that! But he'll be hard pushed to fit fifty cattle on that tiny boat of his back to Ireland!"

"I doubt a single Dinefwr white would fit on his boat," smiled Rhys. "But that is not our problem, is it?"

"And now, revellers, I give you a great gift!" trilled Chrétien. "The chieftain of epics, the crooner from Connemara, a man who empowers his poetic performances with politics and poignancy. Yes, he is wild! He likes a drink and a fight, but who minds that when he delights us on stage, when he foxes us with his wordplay, lures us in with his lines and spins webs around us with his stanzas... Niall Ó Maolconaire!"

Niall Ó Maolconaire's eyes sparkled. He had woven a length of red ribbon into his sleek locks and looked as fresh as he had on the first day of the festival. He was an argument for turning to alcohol excess, sound reasoning for embracing revelry in every form, he lived life out to its outermost edge and thrived from it.

He skipped up to the stage. How similar he was to Marie de France, he thought. Rotten luck they'd both had in love, but that was a base for forging something rather lovely between the two of them. They shared a certain playfulness too, although it had gone a little beyond playing yesterday. He hummed the strains of a ribald tavern song as he went, replacing the chorus with: "*Common ground, honeyhead, I'll make love to you on common ground!*"

He got close enough to smell her hair last night. It had smelt like blossom, so it had. He developed the image, and held it at him and Marie running naked together through a meadow on the first day of spring. Ah. If only the Normans weren't sucking the life out of every other part of Ireland apart from the alehouses and brothels, he would have been a much better person.

"This is called *Return to Connemara*," he proclaimed with a wink, and sang:

And I return to Connemara clean, for Wales and England too,
Have come and granted what I want:
freedom from Norman tyranny,
My country saved, my drinking staved,
my temperament tempered anew,
Now Normans came, saw, conquered,
went, our fields feel green with liberty!

And the crowds could not help delighting in Niall Ó Maolconaire's performances, what with his merry expression, tinkling voice and ability to make drinking and other depravities seem meaningful and even admirable.

Chrétien, now: he knew all about undercurrents in crowds. And he understood as clapping shook the banquet tables and plates and cutlery that this was the time to feed the room with more.

"We have heard him big-heartedly tapping the table in support of other songsters," he leapt to his feet. "We have seen him dazzle with his own lightening-quick lines. He outdoes the colourful reputation that precedes him every time he steps up to perform. No one knows what is next with him and we quiver in suspense now… the Great One!"

Cynddelw shambled up from the very back of the hall. On the way up, his gaze fixed fancifully at some imaginary spot above the heads of those on the dais. And once he was on the stage and turning to face the revellers, everyone felt he was looking out over their heads too, far away to some place they would never ever see. Had the Great One lost it, with that sentimental talk about love in his last bout? Did he comprehend that they expected a reconciliation song out of him, like they would expect a priest to give a sermon in church or a commander to make some speech before a battle? Did he comprehend what was at stake here? *It was a chair!* Not just any old bench but a chair at the table of Lord Rhys, a share in his proceeds from pillaging and taxation, a say in the doings of the realm! The Great One should keep his eye on the prize, the room thought. He should stop getting distracted because great ones could take tumbles too, they could fall fast and fall hard like anyone else.

The Great One opened his mouth and the room readied for anything, further philosophising, more ramblings about love, after all his unorthodox performances thus far they really were ready for anything at all. And the Great One sang:

I that they call 'The Supplicant', call down and supplicate
True constant protection
On your doors, swayer of battle!
On your doorman, dawn of the land!

I call down your protection, hide not your help,
Repentance befits me.

Court-silencers, cry Silence!
Silence, bards – a poet speaks!

I invoke protection, Deheubarth's quick bounty,
That true stay of minstrels,
Your tumult of shield-bearers,
Your hosts, and your royal sons.

I invoke protection, quick bounty and bastion,
No king withstands you,
On your hosts, pillar of battle,
On your war-band, worth their mead.

King falcons of Britain, your chief song I fashion,
Your chief praises I bear;
I'll act as your bard, your judge,
Your support, it befits me.

That my song may answer, lord, I sing –
Since I've come, O hear me!
Lord of lleision[1], lion of war,
Ease your wrath – I am your poet.[2]

Gasps. Sharp gulps of breath. Undisguised stupefaction. He had done it! Just when they had despaired of the Great One, he had gone and given them the greatest reconciliation song they could have dreamed of! What striking words to sing himself back into favour! Ecstasy seized the hall as revellers imagined rifts in their own lives—distanced siblings, jilted lovers—and breaching them

1 The Welsh word is likely related to 'vocalization' but let us not detract from Cynddelw Bryddyd Mawr's alliterative genius.

2 From *To the Lord Rhys ap Gruffyd, Prince of Deheubarth* by Cynddelw Bryddyd Mawr

as the Great One had just breached his. But those who had seen the Great One perform before in Mid Wales, North Wales, the March, wherever the seminal man had wandered to sing out his heart: they detected a certain sadness in his voice tonight, underneath the outer layers polished for the stage. And somehow instinctively these festivalgoers knew in their guts that Cynddelw Bryddyd Mawr was bidding them and the hall and every other hall farewell; that they would not see him perform again. So the ecstasy of the merrymakers became part laughter, part tears.

Marie ate nothing. Marie drank nothing. Marie gave only the vaguest indication she was still in the hall to those on the dais that tried engaging her in conversation.

She heard Chrétien introducing her and mechanically made her way to the stage.

She was thinking of the last days of her life.

She tried to focus just on Avery, on the river, in the castle gardens, in the gardener's cottage, in the hall. This castle was full of memories of him.

But when she looked to the lower banquet tables her eyes kept catching Niall Ó Maolconaire without at all wanting to, which set off other less pleasant memories. He had abused her down by the dock. He had let it all out in hot, spirit-heavy breaths. Obscenities. How she aroused him and how he could bear no more. Things he wanted to do to her. Things he had done to women in Ireland that had initially disgusted them, but that they had then enjoyed and begged for more of. He humiliated her and then he horrified her and he made it sound like a game. It seemed like his hands had been all over her, because he had described in explicit detail how he would put his hands over her if she would abandon that callow youth from York, and come to a man that knew what women wanted deep down. She had felt sordid and used afterwards; had wanted to run to Avery and wrap herself in his innocence.

And when she tried to find another place on the dais to look at she sensed Bernart de Ventadorn, reeling her in like a fly into his web. She should have known. Since the very beginning of their journey here he had acted oddly towards her. At Striguil, she remembered with a shudder, she had come out of the river dripping wet and he had stared at her, not as if he was attracted to her, she could maybe have understood that, but like he wanted to consume her very life essence. That had not been the only time either. She recalled him during the attack by those brutes in the woods too, crouching against the bank and watching as she got dragged off and Pierrot died trying to defend her. Watching like he had known it would happen. What was wrong with him?

What was wrong with men?

She thought angrily: was this what it was to be a woman, to be tossed about like a boat on a storm of men's lust?

No, she thought. Pierrot, she thought. Avery, she thought. This is for you.

"*From the Flames I Rise,*" she intoned. And coldly, contemptuously, unflinchingly, she sang:

> *My road's rough but I – derive some relief:*
> *My Lord rides with me, right alongside,*
> *He's a bright brave one, a brilliant bard: everyone's favourite,*
> *he who'll save me,*
> *The road holds robbers, rogues and ravishers –*
> *of ladies like me: but it's in hand,*
> *My Lord's shining bright, a brilliant star:*
> *guiding us bravely, on through the hills.*
> *I thank you My Lord: I believe you charm –*
> *myriad ladies, yet you help me,*

This reassurance – lends me much solace:
out on that rough road – of rogues and such,
My Lord tells witty tales, would take on ten men:
what a wondrous man – I chanced upon,
My brave bard from France: garbed in bright scarlet,
master of love songs, my Lord, my knight!

And now Marie adopted a new stratagem, staring straight at he who had wronged her in case he or the room were in any doubt she would be unmasking him, then continuing:

As we reached the woods, I felt his look burn –
at my back but thought: he still meant well,
We came to the shade, I saw his arm raise:
was still not afraid – I'd come to harm,
His order was heard: he could not do it;
mercenaries instead – came to those woods,
First they brought me down, bereft me of clothes:
my servant and horse – killed brutally,
And my Lord watched on, with slobbering lips:
waiting for me to – be brought to him,
My Lord watched waited, waited to rape me:
what did I my Lord, to rouse your hate?
Could you see in me – youth, perhaps a soul,
some talent for songs – that you so lack?
The cows came, my Lord, you'd no care for cows,
you and your men fled – and I was spared,
And my soul remains, could not be stolen:
and your well stays dry, your lust on hold...

"It is a lie!" Bernart cried.

He was paler than pale; corpse pale.

The hall was astonished, then indignant. Interrupting a song when it was plainly still unsung: this was unprecedented.

"How dare you impede the singing of a song at my festival?" Rhys demanded. He did not need to shout to make Bernart squirm.

"I am sorry, my lord, but she misrepresents me."

"Misrepresents you? She has not mentioned your name!"

"But she looks at me, my lord, she looks at me and accuses me: the room has seen her do it!" Bernart appealed to the revellers with a smile as he might have done in the past at the Plantagenet Court. But that was a long time ago. His smile was ghastly. "Maggot!" someone heckled from one of the lower tables. There were snickers. A well-aimed mutton bone hit him in the face.

"You will be silent until the song is sung," Rhys said. He would have said more, but knew the audience were damning Bernart more utterly than he ever could have. "Carry on," he told Marie.

She nodded, mercilessly.

"And my soul remains," she repeated her last line. Each word now was a nail in Bernart's coffin, and she hammered them in hard. "And my soul remains, could not be stolen: and your well stays dry, your lust on hold."

> *But you plotted, my Lord, with monstrous resolve:*
> *to pluck me once more and pinch my soul,*
> *And you seized your chance, in the gardener's house:*
> *tried to take from me my soul again,*
> *An innocent died at your hands again:*
> *but this does not end in smoke and flames,*
> *Yet again I rise, from the flames I rise, to shout of your sins,*
> *and shout your name:*
> *Bernart de Ventadorn!*

"He that you burned saw me naked… my *lord*. He that you burned had me in a way you shall never have me, and my pleasure my *lord* was immense. I want you to know that."

So saying Marie strode from the room.

Another mutton bone hit Bernart, followed by a blancmange.

"Maggot!" the hall cried. "Locust!" Then someone bawled: "let's string the maggot up where he belongs," and in the way that quite often happens in halls because people are sheep, they really are, the crowd was soon baying for Bernart to be hanged.

The rules of performed song-singing were in some ways quite similar to those of Confession: whatever was said was supposed to stay in that room and could not be used against anybody else afterwards. But Confession was conducted with no one else but priest and confessor around; performed song-singing affected a whole hall full of intoxicated and therefore opinionated merrymakers.

"Hang the maggot, hang the maggot!"

"Come! Are we barbarians?" Chrétien appealed, not because he felt sorry for Bernart but because he wanted to avoid chaos. "Are we simpletons? We are gathered here to celebrate song! And by song should he be allowed to answer these accusations! He is after all due to step up next, having sung his way through to the last eight, and deserves this chance… Bernart de Ventadorn!"

"Trial by song, trial by song!" the crowd chanted.

Bernart was shoved forward, his scarlet cloak splattered by blancmange. The worst of the derision had dwindled. Like a fretful little insect when its rock is upturned Bernart writhed in the cruel expectant light of the stage.

"Seigneur?" Chrétien prompted.

But nothing would come. He had nothing. Nothing except…

"Seigneur?"

"D… darkness," Bernart began to croak. "Darkness…"

"Maggot!" the jeers chimed out, "Cockroach! If that's his trial, he's guilty! Murderous maggot! Defiler of decency!"

"Silence!" Rhys stood up. "I oversaw many trials and must say I never saw such evidence of guilt in a man! The crimes that took place away from this castle I may not judge at this time but that which occurred within it, and during this festival..." His voice went quiet with outrage. "You, Bernart de Ventadorn, will answer to the charge Marie de France makes here and now! Did you or did you not last night carry out the murder of Avery of York by... what is that thing called?"

"Box of fire," Hamid said, beaming radiantly. They were the first words anyone could recall him having uttered all evening. It was an odd thing, but the most noticeable man in the hall had slipped through to the final four without anybody really noticing. Avery of York was no longer there to meet him in the bout so by default he had progressed. And with Marie, whom he would now certainly meet for a place in the final, so out of sorts, Hamid might well beam. Because he was within touching distance of fulfilling the Sultan's wishes: of triumphing in the contest of song, and of beating these infidels at their own game.

"Exactly. Did you or did you not?" Rhys demanded of Bernart.

Oh, the cruel, cruel light of the stage.

"I... I pulled back," whispered Bernart almost inaudibly. "I pulled back from the darkness."

"What is he blathering about?" Rhys appealed to Chrétien, as had become his habit when coming up against some quirk of a bard he simply could not fathom.

"He appears to have a bad case of stage fright, seigneur. I have seen it render bards insensible for months."

"Stage fright!" Rhys scoffed. "Either he is innocent or he is guilty as charged, and if he cannot speak up in his defence I must assume the latter and deal with it accordingly!"

Bernart turned this way and that, pale and petrified. He could not see one friendly face. It was an entertainer's worst nightmare: to be in a hall where there was not one friendly face.

"If I may, my lord?" From one of the lower banquet tables, Navarro the wandering cantor of Castile got to his feet.

Rhys and the rest of the room turned in surprise.

"I am no friend of this man," Navarro said with a quiet smile. "He knocked me out of the contest of song, after all. But I am also acquainted with him a bit better than most of you. I knew him at Toulouse. The hall already knows of my encounter with him there. What they do not know of is my encounter with him last night, to which Luciano the song-singer from the Kingdom of Sicily can attest, as we were there together, partaking of a flagon of Sicilian Muscat[1] to wash away the disappoint of our losses. He was out by one of the seven towers of your castle, my lord, letting his own blood with a knife from your banquet table. He was there all the time that we were. Before we all came in for the first of the evening's performances, he left our sight only for the interval it takes a full-bladdered man to piss. A strange bard he may be, my lord, but I can tell you from my observations at Toulouse that this is no murderer and I can tell you the same from my observations last night. These boxes of fire, as we saw when the Jew set one alight, require time to position. Much longer than a man takes to piss."

"Is this true?" Rhys inquired of Hamid.

Hamid beamed radiantly and said nothing. Nor was it in his interests to.

"I know you understand me," Rhys said exasperatedly.

Hamid beamed radiantly.

"Right. Call in that Jew!"

---

1 Apollo was purportedly seduced with the same wine.

But no one had seen the Jew in quite a few days.

On the dais, the young Marcher lord no one could remember the name of was gaily accepting a refill of mead when the serving wench, who had poured drinks smoothly the entire festival long, spilt the entire contents of her pitcher in his lap.

"Ooh!" exclaimed the young Marcher lord. But that was neither here nor there. No one cared what the young Marcher lord did or did not do. No one could even remember his name.

"My lord, I pray you'll forgive me!" the serving wench sobbed. "It's just when you mentioned the Jew. I was supposed to be looking in on him now and again, but what with all the serving I clear forgot about him!"

"Compose yourself," Rhys said gently. "Now. Can you remember *where* you were supposed to be looking in on him?"

Still quite distressed, the serving wench nodded.

"Anarawd!" Rhys said.

Angharad scarcely had time to mop the spilt mead from the young Marcher lord's lap before Anarawd was back.

He carried the stiffened one-armed body of the Jew.

The serving wench sheepishly brought in the other arm.

"I did dress his wounds, honest to God! He was getting better!"

"There's a letter," Anarawd growled, setting the Jew down. "But it's in bloody Latin!"

Chrétien held out his hand.

"Pass it to me, seigneur."

"If you read this," Chrétien read to the dumbstruck room, "then I am dead. As I write this I am in exquisite health. I never debauch. I have use of all my limbs. I have just journeyed across Christendom from Constantinople to Cardigan by foot." Chrétien opened his eyes wide and put some histrionics into it. "Yet I do fear for my life! I fear for it, because there is one who sits among you today who wishes to take it! I know about him! I know about what he has done! So Hell-bent is he on getting what he wants and winning the contest of song that he has killed already, and by everything I hold dear I know he will kill again! He knows I know it! I fear my usefulness to him is finished and therefore I fear for my life! And the name of him I fear is Farid Un-Din Attar! Hamid!"

The hall was silent.

Rhys looked from his family to the officers of his household to his guests and then to Hamid, as baffled as the rest of them.

The roaring again. The parched desert wind again. He had struggled through the dunes, and he was finally there, and there it was. The water clock. A beautiful elaborate unequalled thing, standing out of the ochre sand. It was the most intricate thing he had ever seen or would ever see, and there it miraculously was in the middle of the desert. Just the water clock, and him: he could take it! He *would* take it! He reached out to its face, its hands, its tubes that channelled water along them at exactly the rate the hours and the days of the world elapsed. What a thing!

And it was gone. It was buried under the sand, or perhaps it had never been there at all. The sand trickled through his fingers, back into the desert.

"It's pissing it down!" Anarawd growled. He glanced over at Rhys, who was holding a lump of melting snow at arm's length, letting it trickle through his fingers, back into the sodden ground. "I said it's pissing it down!" The *penteulu* glanced at his lord shrewdly. "The snow will be gone soon at this rate."

Rhys was still far away. He was in a desert he had never set foot in, trying to touch a water clock he never would touch.

"The prisoner's ready when you are," said Anarawd. He nodded tersely and left Rhys with his thoughts.

As he stumped off through the slush of the snowmelt he very near bumped into Chrétien.

"Well, parrot-feather. There's just one more bout of bardism remaining and I can't say I'm sorry. Trouble I said this festival would be and trouble it has been. I hope you've not forgotten our little pact? Until the last song is sung, remember? Then you fly on back to France."

"I have not forgotten our arrangement, seigneur."

Chrétien waited until Anarawd was out of earshot.

He glanced over at the Lord of Deheubarth, standing on the battlements looking out at the valley of the Teifi, at the river that flowed from the heart of the realm to the edge of it and bit his lip. He could not determine what the man was looking at: whether at something that was really there in the snow, or at something that had once been, or at something that one day might be.

Only one more bout of bardism there was indeed. For Gwalchmai ap Meilyr and Cynddelw Bryddyd Mawr had both reached the final four, and Cynddelw had made the emotional announcement that he had sung all the songs he cared to sing in his life, and conceded his place in the final to Gwalchmai. And Marie de France and Hamid, who had been due to contest the other place, could not because Hamid was chained up in the dungeon at the base of the keep, and that left Marie as the only other contestant remaining.

"I must leave at first light tomorrow, seigneur."

Slowly Rhys turned his head.

"The last song will have been sung. I will have played the part I was asked to play. And I wanted to say…" Chrétien chose his words with care. "You have surpassed yourself with this festival, seigneur. I say that from my heart having seen my share of revelry. No hall in Christendom can have witnessed the like."

"Chrétien of Troyes," smiled Rhys. "You came to Cardigan as a criminal and you leave it as…" How did the man from Champagne leave it, exactly? Not as his friend. They would hardly see each other again. But nor could Rhys claim that he had found the Frenchman's presence at his castle unpleasant. As what then? As someone who had come together with him for a time to create something truly remarkable, Rhys thought, it was best to leave it at that. "Is there anything at all you would like?" he asked instead. "Name it and it shall be yours."

"I leave it with a story, seigneur. I could not hope for more. And I will tell it," he added softly. "As we agreed I will tell it in every court I attend."

"And what will it be?"

"Seigneur?"

"Your story."

"Mercy, seigneur! The words will tumble out and then we will know! Some courtly epic I daresay, with comedy and tragedy and love of course thrown in somewhere. They are quite the thing these days."

"Well then. I must go and deal with our prisoner," Rhys said, more abruptly than he intended. Then he said: "Thank you."

Two little, brittle words: their vapour rose into the damp Welsh morning and they vanished.

"I will see you in the hall, seigneur."

The dungeon smelt of sweat and faeces and fragrance.

It appeared crowded at first glance, but this was because the other prisoners, five pickpockets and a poultry pincher, were bunched on one side of the dank room in order to avoid Hamid, who squatted by himself on the other and was not beaming anywhere near so radiantly as he had been.

Rhys had the guard convey Hamid out through another door,

to an anteroom that made the main dungeon seem fairly bright and airy. Here, they were forced to squat, for the roof was low. Things scuttled in the shadows. The only light here came from Rhys' torch.

"It is dark in here," observed Rhys. "That must be particularly hard to bear for someone like you, accustomed to the sun. The more optimistic perspective is that thus far you have only endured a day of it, not a lifetime. Now let us dispense with the horseshit. I know you understand what I am saying. I have a proposal for you. Substantial evidence points to your having committed two murders. Equally substantial evidence points to the fact that were the King of England to decide on a whim—and he does have his whims—that he wanted to bring an end to the great peace we currently have, my realm would fall to the Normans and I would lose everything.

But our destinies could be different. You could be leaving here at dusk tonight, with your two-humped beast and some of my best men to help you on your way as far as the border with England. And I could be annihilating whatever force the Normans or anyone else choose to throw at me for the remainder of my days." Rhys rocked back on his haunches and held up the torch to Hamid's face. "Yes. I see you comprehend what I seek from you."

Hamid nodded.

"The box of fire."

Rhys nodded.

"The box of fire, yes. You will write down for me in great detail the recipe. I want to know exactly how to make those blasts you made, and how to make them bigger."

The guard brought parchment and ink and a quill, and thoughtfully a slab to lean on too. Hamid wrote, slowly at first because he was accustomed to writing right to left.

"There it is in the English tongue," Hamid said. "With, er, every instruction save the very last."

"Why is the very last instruction not written?"

"I travelled eight months across Persia, the Byzantine and Holy Roman and Empires, the Low Countries, England and Wales to be here," Hamid said. "I came here with one purpose, and that was to perform my words at your tournament of vocal song. I promised one in the land from which I come that I would endeavour to win it…" he tailed off, perspiring suddenly and recalling what he had seen on the other side of the partition in the bathhouse at the palace in Herat. He recalled the shadow cast onto the screen as the Sultan had moved closer to it: the abominable likeness of an enormous curled-up baby. "I beg you. Let me at least try to honour that promise. Let me bout with Marie de France for my chance to win, and if I lose it will at least be a proper loss."

Rhys examined the plump hazelnut-brown man before him, this man with the gaudy robes and exotic scent. Hamid came from further away from Deheubarth than any other person Rhys had ever met. Yet some things transcended borders of land and sea. One of these things was fear. Rhys saw Hamid was afraid of something far greater than rotting away in a dungeon for the rest of his days. This was part of the reason Rhys was letting Hamid go. Hamid's real punishment was out there somewhere.

"I was at Gloucester not so long ago," Rhys said reflectively. "I saw something there of such beauty… a water clock. It was so intricate. I knew when I beheld it that I would never again behold an embodiment of what beauty truly was. It had all these tubes, as elaborate as the veins and arteries of the human body, and water channelled along them at exactly the rate that time passes. Can you imagine? I have dreamed ever since about possessing that water clock…" he chuckled, like one chuckles at a child when they say something incredibly far-fetched. "But I am not ever going to possess it, am I?

Write the last instruction. If you do, you will have your life and your liberty. And that is more than many of us have."

Liberty! Hamid's tick was back. It was worse than ever, actually. This Rhys ap Gruffyd seemed a reasonable man but he could not know what he was saying! There was a cord no one else could see tied to him at one end and to the Sultan at the other. The next greatest leader in the world could grant him a city or a country of his own but if the Sultan tugged the cord then to Herat Hamid would be pulled. And so to Herat he might as well go: go and face the Sultan and tell him that he had failed. Liberty! Liberty did not exist for him. Not since that day at the olive grove on the road to Nishapur when that hideous bighead had loomed into his life and delivered him his damning sentence: *'you are the Sultan's man now.'*

The Sultan's man now, Hamid thought wretchedly, and the Sultan's man forever more.

It was tidy, thought Rhys, as settled as could be. He would face no attack from the north now. He may yet have a firm ally in Gwynedd, when Gwalchmai returned with the greatest prize a man from Gwynedd could win in Deheubarth: a chair at the table of its prince. And if perchance the Normans did come from the east, he would be more prepared for them than he had been: he would have a fire to fight their fire. As for Ireland...

"Rhys brother! A bloody gloomy old day, so it is!"

The one person he had been taking such pains to avoid. Rhys froze, caught in the open so near yet so far from the doorway of his hall.

"Good day to you, Niall Ó Maolconaire," he said as pleasantly as he could.

But Niall Ó Maolconaire could do pleasantness too, he could do pleasantness very well indeed.

"Not so good on the crossing back to Ireland, Rhys. Rough at the best of times, that crossing, but the weather looks to be getting an awful lot worse so off we'll go."

"You are leaving us then?" Rhys managed to conceal his relief.

"That's right, brother. Now. Your man did send your apologies for lacking the time for a private audience with me, which I respect, but seeing as I've caught you like this…"

"I am very busy it is true," Rhys said hastily. "This moment, in fact, I have an engagement."

Annoyance flashed in Niall Ó Maolconaire's face.

"I see how it is, brother. It's just that with me off back to Ireland…"

"Regrettable," Rhys said. "Now really, I must be on my way."

How he cursed the day he ever got involved in the Irish issue.

"Well it's been some festival Rhys. Not at all the outcome I wanted, what with you not having time to hear me despite finding time to hear everyone else that cared for an audience. But I thank you for the cows," the Irishman's voice burbled out all pretty and treacherous. "Although as I know you know, brother, even that's something of a slap about the chops as far as gifts go, for I've only the one boat."

"You could always come back," Rhys said, having banked on the fact that he never would, not all the way from Connemara.

"Yes, never you fret brother," Niall Ó Maolconaire gave a sinister little tinkle of a laugh. "I'll be back very soon with a much bigger boat. We can have that chat then, perhaps."

'And I'll be coming to avenge my countrymen for the disgraceful bloody mess you put our nation in, so I will be brother, and only taking your life will satisfy me,' Rhys imagined the Irishman's words coming after him.

But as he hastened to the hall to avoid anything else that Niall Ó Maolconaire might say, all Rhys actually heard was that little tinkle of a laugh.

Niall Ó Maolconaire laughed all the way down to the dock.

He had a mind that could cut and paste at will. It could remember every single one of the unspeakable acts the Normans had committed in Ireland, but overlooked quite a few of the unspeakable acts he had committed in his fits of temper.

At the dock as he unhitched his boat's mooring ropes and took a last look back at the castle his mind did turn to Marie, but not in a remorseful or even a sympathetic sense. It did that thing those who commit unspeakable acts will often do, which is to turn the events as they really unfolded on the night of Avery of York's death around somewhat.

Yes, he had made a few suggestive remarks to Marie that night, but she had invited them, teased them out of him, she had provoked him and excited him, until despite being a playful fellow he had just not wanted to play anymore. Feeling spurned, he had thrown stones at some ducks and kicked the bow of the nearest boat until his foot hurt, and when neither of these things worked because of course white-hot temper like his took a lot longer to cool, he had pursued her. He had known where his little honeyhead had gone, and whom she had gone there with. He had stamped towards the castle gatehouse. Around the front of the main hall. Behind.

"Tss, crooner from Connemara! Chieftain of epics!"

"What is it?" He had whirled impatiently towards the double-chinned woman squatting in the shadows.

"You're joint favourite, you know. Want to place a bet?"

"Joint? Along with who?"

The odds-maker had pointed towards the end of the garden at

the ivy-trailed wall with the little old gate in the middle, in the exact same direction he had been heading anyway.

"It's all explained down there."

Through the garden with its snow-bowed shoots of leek and the skeletal fruit trees and against all likelihood one rosy apple, still hanging from a branch. Down to the ivy-trailed wall. Through that little old gate.

Inside was a walled yard with a gardener's cottage at the far end, a light burning within. He had known that they were inside, his honeyhead and that callow youth from York, rutting like rabbits.

Bernart de Ventadorn had been shrunk against the gate, quivering. He had clutched at Niall Ó Maolconaire's hand.

"I cannot do it," Bernart had whimpered.

"Do what?" Niall Ó Maolconaire had asked.

Bernart had pointed.

Hamid had been knelt in the snow, laying two long ropes carefully across the yard. The ropes led to some boxes, stacked around the door of the gardener's cottage.

Hamid had lit a second torch and passed one to Niall Ó Maolconaire.

"Can't… slip… now," Hamid had said.

Hamid had lit one rope. Niall Ó Maolconaire had lit the other. Bernart had covered his face with his hands, but still watched through a crack in his fingers.

They had all watched a moment.

The ropes had caught well. The two flames had begun a steady dance towards the doorway of the gardener's cottage.

All three had withdrawn to a safe distance, and watched a little longer.

Bang.

Bang went the drumroll.

The hall held their breath.

Tonight on the dais, tonight, the end of Christmastide, the two chairs on either side of the Lord Rhys were symbolically empty.

At the end of the night, the winner of the contest of instrumental song and the winner of the contest of vocal song would take their seats there.

The drumroll announced a group of young maidens clad all in white with wreathes wrought of flowers and grasses and corn adorning their hair. They danced up either side of the hall like fairies around a fairy ring. Up to the dais they danced and placed two sheaves, made of the same materials, on each of the vacant chairs. These would be presented to each of the victors.

Then an immense sword, large as a very tall man, was borne in by two sword-bearers, and placed on the stage in its scabbard. Chrétien explained that this sword would be used to tap the victors in each contest on each shoulder. He unsheathed the sword partway, and proclaimed that this sword could only ever be drawn to this point, because no one should draw a sword against a bard. To do so would be to kill song.

Then lavish birds, peacocks and quails and swans, were placed on each banquet table. The birds were cleaved open and out tumbled many wondrous treats, honeyed almonds and mead cakes, cinnamon scented venison, capons and crayfish tails, lamprey and loach, fritters and frumenty, all good things.

The merrymakers were ready. They had done it every night eleven nights straight so they could do it for a twelfth. Their bellies were bloated, and their heads dizzy with drink and with dance and with debauch, but they could manage a twelfth night.

And Marie stepped up.

She had lost. Even if she won, she had lost in more ways than anyone else would ever understand.

She stepped up.
And she sang.

Part Three:

THE WINE HOUSE ON THE TRACK UP
INTO THE HILLS

Cardigan Castle Battlements

(JANUARY, 1177)

DAWN.

Maelgwyn and Cadwaladr went around, surveying their handiwork and snickering.

In Rhys' chapel they had daubed, in big tarry letters on the wall above the altar: 'THE WRITING IS ON THE WALL FOR YOU.'

On the door of Rhys' *ystafell*, the same: 'THE WRITING IS ON THE WALL FOR YOU.'

Now they had come to the place on the battlements Rhys liked to come sometimes to contemplatively gaze out over the river.

And above the far riverbank in vast stone-lined letters in the melting snow was their greatest triumph, because this they had had to do in the dead of night whilst ensuring the result would be visible from the place on the battlements where Rhys liked to stand:

'THE WRITING IS ON THE WALL FOR YOU'

"You idiot!" Maelgwyn thumped Cadwaladr.

"What?" Cadwaladr was hurt.

"You have spelt it wrong!"

The Cleric's Quarters in the Île De La Cité

(JANUARY, 1177)

"A LETTER FOR YOU, GIRALDUS."

Gerald came to the door with the snivels he had not properly shaken off since that unlovely tramp through the snow in Deheubarth during Christmastide.

"It is from Wales," the young novice observed, quite unnecessarily because the seal on the back did clearly state: 'St David's, Wales'.

Gerald's heart soared. It was from the canons. It would be word of his appointment as Bishop!

Gerald bid the novice wait for his instructions and tore open the letter. More than joy, the sensation he was experiencing was relief. Because this meant that nothing could have got out about that night at the Dean's house in Gloucester.

The canons regret to inform you that on this occasion your application to become the new Bishop of St David's has been unsuccessful. However, should this position become available at a later date, the canons would welcome you applying again.

Gerald's eyebrows wove together in incredulity, then in wrath.

"You!" he thundered to the novice who was quite beside himself with fright. "Ready my horse for Rome! We will see what His Holiness has to say about this outrage!"

Outside the Lodging House in Llanddewi Brefi

(JANUARY, 1177)

IT WAS RAINING.

The priest stood in the doorway of the lodging house, peering out into the rain-swathed darkness.

Good God. Them again. Those two grim pilgrims from the north that had visited just before Chirstmas. His heart sank.

"The men from Gwynedd!" the priest feigned a warm welcome. "What an honour to see you pass by again."

"Good evening," smiled Meilyr ap Gwalchmai with more friendliness than the priest remembered, so much more that it made him guarded.

The priest squinted beyond Meilyr. Through the murk he could just make out two horses tethered down by the gate, one bearing quite a lot of baggage, but no sign of anyone else.

"Your father wants to commence with the devotions, I suppose? I seem to recall you both wanted to get straight on with it before without so much as a bowl of my rabbit soup."

"Actually," said Meilyr, "my father is in rather a bad way."

"What ails him?"

"Actually," said Meilyr, "he is dead."

"Dead?" cried the priest. "My poor man!" he patted Meilyr consolingly on the shoulder. "Why, how did it happen?"

"Robbers," said Meilyr flatly.

He did not see the need to tell the priest that it had actually been bards. It was as Owain Cyfeiliog had said. No one should be allowed to violate the rules of song-singing as his father had done. They had urged him to stand down. But his father had not listened. He had not stood down. So they had told the hall. They had told the hall about the stink of a deal Gwalchmai ap Meilyr had done to secure his victory in the contest of song. The hall had been every bit as appalled, as revolted, as reviled and as repelled as had been predicted. And from thereon in only one outcome had been likely.

"Why, let us get him inside!" the priest exclaimed.

"There is no need," said Meilyr. "He is dead after all." He clapped the priest heartily on the back. "Come. Let us go and get some of your rabbit soup! And perhaps afterwards some wine and dice-playing?"

The Welsh Side of the Severn

(JANUARY, 1177)

THE WORDS OF BERNART'S bard warbled through the frigid morning.

> *"He is the great De Ventadorn, the master of romance,*
> *Ruler elect of rhymes of love across the vasts of France!"*

The bard had been attempting to enliven his master every morning since they had left the castle, but to no avail.

The forlorn tunnel of trees down which they were making their way muffled Bernart's bard's verses.

Bernart was like the walking dead. And versions of the same dead thought circled around his head: *how could it have come to this?*

The tunnel of trees yielded to open ground and sloped to the grumbling grey waters of the Severn. They were almost out of Wales.

Bernart's bard tried again:

> *"De Ventadorn ventures back to France to return to Toulouse,*
> *There they long to hear his songs of love that delight and amuse!"*

"Go and ring the bell to rouse that blasted ferryman, lad," Bernart said gloomily. "Blast him! One task to do and he cannot even do that! I want to leave this blasted country!"

Bernart's bard obediently hurried off to the water's edge.

The bell rang.

Bernart shrieked.

"Master!" Bernart's bard was at his side in an instant.

Bernart was on his back in the mud with a madman's smile transfixing his face. At first Bernart's bard feared the worst, but Bernart's eyes flickered open.

"My inspiration," he gasped. "It has returned."

The Port Close to Caerleon

(JANUARY, 1177)

MOST OF THE SHIPS at this time of year would be here until the start of spring, having sails patched or hulls caulked, but some of the more intrepid crews were already bringing boats in and out. Boats bound for great places: for Waterford, for St Malo.

Marie stood, half in a trance, huddled into her warmest wool cloak, loving this clatter and clank of activity despite the biting wind.

"My lady?"

A wizened old sailor: addressing her with a worried expression.

"Are you quite well, my lady? I've seen you here several days now, watching the boats. This is no place for a lady like yourself. Do you live around here? Can I perhaps escort you home?"

"I did," she said.

Her voice was as clear and detached as the wind, but it did not make any sense.

"My lady?"

"I did live around here. Not now."

"Where *do* you live now, my lady?"

She did not answer straightaway.

There was a moment of silence, with the old sailor watching Marie and Marie watching the water, imagining it becoming briny and tides unsettling it and a strong salt wind blowing out to open sea.

"You are with the boat bound for Brittany on the morrow, are you not?"

"Yes, my lady."

"Secure me a passage," she said. "I am coming with you. I am going home."

The Hall of the Court of Champagne

(February, 1177)

THE HALL DID seem very ornate, that was Chrétien's first thought, almost farcically ornate. But his eyes, after over two months away, gradually reacquainted themselves with the finery.

At the end of the hall, the countess was seated on her throne surrounded by her attending ladies, watching the sword-swallower and the blind boy who could play the lyre with his toes performing simultaneously.

"Mercy!" cried the countess when she beheld Chrétien. And then, to the attending ladies and the sword-swallower and the blind lyre-playing boy: "leave us please!"

"My patroness," smiled Chrétien, spreading his arms out wide.

"*Ma petite cerise!* Back from the land of King Arthur! Oh, do tell me," she entreated, allowing him to kiss her hand and sit at her feet. "You must have collected such fascinating stories there!"

"As it happens," said Chrétien mischievously. "I do have something rather wonderful for you."

An Eating-House in Constantinople

(MAY, 1177)

THE BENCH CREAKED as Hamid sat down upon it and a rich puff of his fragrance impacted on the nostrils of the other diners. Some of them complimented him on his scent and an intelligent debate on perfume ensued. Hamid relaxed, and felt the sun warm his skin, and ordered a platter of stuffed prunes.

He did love this city. It was a sophisticated city, a true marriage of east and west. You could go and sit at any eating-house and order stuffed prunes or pomegranates or baked aubergines flavoured with every spice conceivable. No one gawped at your camel here.

Since Rhys ap Gruffyd had freed him, and the days and weeks and months on the road had passed, Hamid had started to become more relaxed. He still had the nightmares about what the Sultan would do to him sometimes, but not so often. Anyway, he believed he *would* have won the contest of song if he had been allowed to compete, and surely no one all the way over here would know if he distorted the truth slightly and made it known that in fact he *had* won.

Someone slid onto the bench alongside him. Someone very deformed.

A monstrous, bulbous shadow fell across Hamid.

"Farid Un-Din Attar," said the bighead, with a sinister smirk. "I have been looking for you..

The King's Council at Oxford

(MAY, 1177)

"**SILENCE!**" roared Henry Plantagenet, and all the way down the long table of nobles there was silence. "I wish to know what our ally in Wales, Rhys ap Gruffyd, has to say about all this!"

At the word 'Wales' the room would have fallen silent anyway. Most of the nobles were Norman and had no great love of talking about Wales.

Warily, the nobles turned down to the end of the table to where Rhys was sitting.

Rhys looked back at them all with faint amusement. The last time he held their attention like this, they were on opposing sides of a battlefield.

"The Welsh invariably raise multifarious objections at my councils," Henry said. "Can it really be, for once, that they have none? What does Wales think about appointing my son Lord of Ireland and bringing all these quarrelsome Irish kings into line under him?"

"On the subject of Ireland, my King," said Rhys, "you have my complete support. But from a recent experience of my own, I can advise of one course of action which will help you achieve your aim."

"Pray tell us!" Henry exclaimed. "What is that?"

Rhys smiled.

"Come down particularly hard on Connemara."

Somewhere on a Fine Summer's Day on a Grassy Bank beneath a Tree

(JUNE, 1177)

DOG FINISHED THE SONG. It had been outstanding, as befitted the victor in Lord Rhys' contest of instrumental song. He placed his harp down with exacting care against the tree trunk and turned to squeeze the great white bottom of the Healer, who was even greater than she was normally, being so heavy with child.

"*Now* you show me some attention, my stocky songster! Now, once you have taken pretty care of your precious harp!"

"Don't start!" protested Dog. He found the extremely pregnant Healer even more attractive than usual and on such a fine summer's day as this one he just wanted to take advantage of the heat and his desire and the pleasant location and frolic with the big witch for a while.

"What would happen if something was to happen to your precious harp?" the Healer said naughtily. "What would you do then my dastard?" And with a laugh and before Dog could react she grabbed his harp and placed it high in the cleft of the tree, far above Dog's reach.

Dog looked up at the harp in the tree.

Suddenly, he was not enjoying the day any more. The sun was too hot and the Healer was annoying.

A gloom enveloped him. Half a year ago it was since that

morning in Oswestry and he remembered it like it were yesterday.

"What's wrong with you?" he snapped at the Healer gruffly. Then he felt bad. She couldn't have known. He tried to explain, but he could not really ever explain. "I'd be lost," he admitted softly. "I'd be lost without that bloody thing."

The Wine House on the Track up into the Hills

(MARCH, 1194)

THE MOORS looked glorious up there, all bursting with colour. They had never looked better than they did today.

Not much good that was when you had an ailing wine house to run, Millie thought as she cleared away the mess from last night's merriment. Times had been tougher of late: less passing trade because of a spate of attacks by brigands. Folk in the valley were tense. The girls she employed were tense. They did not know if the next man through the door would seek to be pleasured by them or to kill them. These were tense times.

Tense enough that when her newest girl, a real client-pleaser but with air between her ears, rushed in bawling that a big horrible man dressed as some sort of wild animal was marching down the track towards the wine house, Mille treated the news with less scepticism than normal.

She went outside, shielding her eyes against the sun. One man, sure enough, was approaching. The man waved, and bellowed.

"My Calliope!"

Some wild animal!

The bear's hide cloak around his broad shoulders had passed its best. The head of the beast drooped and the tongue hung out idiotically. His beard was almost a year bushier, and flecked with white.

"Millie, my Calliope!"

"Cynddelw Bryddyd Mawr," she said, hands on hips.

Not a day had gone by when he had not dreamed of those hands. Big, red-raw hands. Hams of hands.

"And without any of your students of bardism to buy you your drinks or laugh at your jests and make you look good."

"And I am ecstatic at their absence, my Calliope who feeds the fire of a man's muse like wood fuels a furnace."

"I've told you before. I'm not wooed by your fancy words."

"I am done with the lot of them, Millie. I told you before that when I returned here it would be for one reason and one reason alone. Can you have forgotten it?"

Millie had not forgotten it but it had hardly played on her mind either. He had surely said such pretty things to a dozen different girls in a dozen different towns, and she had a business to run. She had no time for foolish talk.

But he was throwing that blasted bear cloak onto the ground. He was kneeling down on one knee.

"Be mine, fair Millicent, loveliest wine house owner of all the lovely wine house owners in Wales."

"Cynddelw!"

"Be mine, be mine, be mine!" he bellowed, lifting her up. "I am done, Millie. I shall perform in halls no more. I have sung my last song."

"Cynddelw!" she was shrieking as he tossed her up onto those broad shoulders of his. "Cynddelw!"

"Be mine, Millie!"

She clung on. She clung on as bellowing with laughter he ran with her away, away from the wine house, away away, away on the track up into the hills.

'Y Gwir yn erbyn y Byd, A oes Heddwch?

Heddwch!

Calon wrth Galon, A oes Heddwch?

Heddwch!

Gwaedd uwch Adwaedd, A oes Heddwch?

Heddwch!

The Truth against the World, Is there Peace?

Peace!

Heart to Heart, Is there Peace?

Peace!

Shout above responding Shout, Is there

Peace?

Peace!

Author's Note

I believe researchers into any aspect of history have their 'moment'—that is to say, the point when they unearth that document containing the most relevant and resonant information relating to their period of interest. In months of research, of trawling through piles of extraneous books and pamphlets, it is the equivalent of discovering the diamond in the coalmine.

Your heart skips a beat.

Well, mine did.

My 'moment' with the research for Song Castle was reading the passage from the Brut y Tywysogion (Chronicles of the Princes) where, under the year 1176, there appears a paragraph devoted to the 'grand festival' of vocal and instrumental song hosted by Rhys ap Gruffyd in his castle in Cardigan. But the real skipping was being done by the Brut y Tywysogion: why, when this was evidently a festival of exceptional pomp by the standards of the times, was there only one scant paragraph on it?

But I was captivated enough by the idea of this wondrous celebration of culture, in a time renowned for its rampant barbarity, to want to write the account the Brut y Tywysogion did not.

And whilst there are no direct references anywhere else to Rhys ap Gruffyd's festival, which of course would cement itself in history as the first Eisteddfod, I found plenty of other clues to assist me in embellish that lone paragraph into a 100,000-word novel.

There was the poetry of the bards, in Wales, but also in France. These bards left a trail of words in their wake that the history books did not: a trail that enticed me to develop some into characters.

Amongst the Welsh contingent, Cynddelw Brydydd Mawr really did exist, and really does seem to have been regarded as the foremost bard of his day: he was an outspoken figure to judge from his verses, sufficiently so to be excommunicated! Gwalchmai ap Meilyr also existed, and evidence from his poetry suggests he was increasingly bitter and pious in his later years. Neither can be proven to have attended the festival, but the occasion is recorded as attracting entrants from across Wales, England and other countries further afield, and why would the best (as Cynddelw and Gwalchmai were) not have participated?

And as for the French? Marie de France, regarded as one of the 12th century's best writers, and especially fascinating because she was a woman excelling in a man's profession, did live in Wales, and demonstrates detailed knowledge of the country in her work. Chrétien de Troyes based one of his famous Arthurian tales in and around Cardigan, and if he was familiar with the town, why not with Rhys ap Gruffyd and his contest of song?

Gerald of Wales, another of the book's central figures, was a well-known scribe himself in the late 12th century. He documented his own life vigorously, and I owe a lot to his 'Journey Through Wales' (1191) for its evocative contemporary depictions of the country. He was known to have been on Welsh soil in 1176, being the bishop-in-waiting of St David's, with a talent for sniffing out the big occasions and indeed with Rhys ap Gruffyd as his cousin.

History has made far stranger leaps of faith than to tie such people to one place at one time. And if there were an occasion to have linked such figures, this would have been it. If there were an occasion where the colourful poetic traditions of Persia,

Occitania, Brittany, Scandinavia, England, Ireland and Wales came together—this would have been it.

But tougher yet than researching the people and places of 12th century Wales was researching and writing songs for the bardic characters to sing that remained faithful to the exacting poetic metres used in the country at the time. Tough, particularly, as I did not, do not and may never fully speak Welsh, and the metres were designed to fit the language. Contained within the book are a Rhupunt, as sung by Azelais after being spurned by Niall Ó Maolconaire, and a Toddaid, with which Marie shames Bernart, as well as a Toddaid Byr and a Traenog. These are written in English—a concession to non-Welsh readers—but hopefully give some insight into the form. In those days there were 20 recognised Welsh metres. Today there are 24, although outside of the Eisteddfod festivities most are seldom used.

And what of the Eisteddfod, still today Europe's greatest competitive festival of song and poetry? A richly celebrated event within Wales, and ablaze with ritual and tradition, it still makes little of its early history, and away from Welsh soil is even less known-about. I whole-heartedly believe a festival like this would have begun with a bang. For me, the mix of personalities likely to have been involved with the 1176 festivities—a proud and strong-willed prince, and a cast of controversial, boastful and brilliantly talented bards—could not have produced any outcome other than a memorable one.

Rhys ap Gruffyd's festival was held in a town newly taken from the Normans and thriving like it never had before, and it was held on a scale impressive even by the highest Norman standards of the age. It was Wales announcing its rise from the Dark Ages onto the world stage of poetry, and music, and song.

I certainly think that deserves to be remembered.

Author Thanks

The further back into the past you delve with historic fiction, the more help you need with authentically and convincingly recreating the past. Nigh-on nine centuries back, reliable resources are scant indeed and that help becomes all the more cherished.

In the research of Song Castle I could thank the authors of the 50-odd texts and reference books, written at various points over the preceding millennium, that I read to get a better understanding of life in Wales in the 1170s, but there is not the space here, and the majority are in fact already dead. Amongst the land of the living, however, there are several people I need to specifically thank.

First and foremost: Kerry Christiani (its-a-small-world.com), for her help and support throughout, and particularly with the photo shoot for the cover, as well as the illustrations within. Amongst the Welsh history buffs and experts I spoke to, Paula Ellis at the Retreats Group of hotels based in St Davids, Dr Chris Caple at Durham University and Sue Lewis and Glen Johnson at Cardigan Castle stand out. I would also like to thank Meurig Williams (www.meucymru.co.uk) for supplying the harp used on the cover, and giving me some valuable insights into medieval harps.

And this goes almost without saying (and yet not quite), thank you to the team at Urbane Publications for their patience and support in bringing Song Castle into the world...

Song Castle is the second novel by **Luke Waterson**. His debut, *Roebuck*, set in the 16th-century Brazilian Amazon, was published in 2015 by Urbane Publications. As a travel writer he has also written for publications including the BBC, the Independent, the Telepgraph and the Guardian, and written or contributed to over 50 non-fiction titles. Several of these are about Wales. **lukeandhiswords.com**

Urbane Publications is dedicated to
developing new author voices, and publishing
fiction and non-fiction that challenges, thrills and
fascinates.

From page-turning novels to innovative
reference books, our goal is to publish what
YOU want to read.

Find out more at
urbanepublications.com